HALFHEROES

HALFHERO TRILOGY BOOK TWO

IAN W. SAINSBURY

For Auntie Hazel, who always said I should be a writer

PREVIOUSLY IN CHILDREN OF THE DETERRENT: A CATCH UP ON HALFHERO BOOK ONE (WITH SPOILERS)

...

The Deterrent is the world's first superhero, found in 1969 as an amorphous blob of slime (Abos) inside a strange cylinder buried in London. Years after the discovery, a chance spillage of blood on the cylinder starts a process ending in his transformation into a seven-foot-tall being who can fly, is incredibly strong and can move objects with his mind. Despite Britain's attempts to exploit him by drugging and brainwashing him into acting as a national hero, he disappears in 1981 and is presumed dead.

Abos doesn't return until 2015, when one of his children (the halfheroes) tracks him down to ask for his help in destroying Station, the military department that drugged him, and which is now developing an army of hybrid super-soldiers. Abos is no longer male, having used female blood to grow his new body.

Daniel Harbin is the eldest child of The Deterrent, and has as much, if not more, cause to hate Station, as they lied to him, used him, and kept him in a semi-catatonic state for a decade and a half. Together with Abos and George (Georgina) Kuku, another halfhero, they destroy Station.

George dies, but Abos uses George's blood to grow her third body.

Daniel and Abos start new lives, free of the past, unsure of what the future might hold.

Peace and quiet, perhaps?

Yeah, right.

1

Daniel spat out a tooth and looked at the concrete floor. It was smeared not only with fresh blood from that night's fighters but discoloured a dull brown by the thousands preceding them. The frenzied shouts of the crowd had taken on an almost hysterical quality. Cash was still changing hands as new odds were given, but many inveterate gamblers had forgotten all about the money at stake. This was the most ferocious fight they had ever seen, and the spectators jostled for space around the steel cage containing the combatants.

Many watching felt their hands dart involuntarily to the pockets that would usually contain their phones. Not tonight. Filming was banned, and considering the place was run by Mr Cole, no one had refused to leave their phones at the door. The alternative was leaving their severed heads in a skip.

Looking up from the floor, Daniel raised an eyebrow at Gabe and Sara, who were on the less dangerous side of the padlocked gate. They looked worried. As they should.

Daniel saw Sara's eyes widen, and he rolled to one side

just before his opponent body-slammed the concrete patch he had vacated. He backed away to the far edge of the cage and eyed the man picking himself up from the floor. *Man* wasn't really the word for the thing facing him, though.

"Go on, Spot," called one of the handlers from the front row. Spot. Cute name for a cockerpoo, perhaps. Not so cute for this guy. His head twitched a little when he heard his name. As he stood and shuffled forwards, he focussed on an imaginary mark in the centre of Daniel's chest. He hadn't once attempted to make eye contact. Spot was a few inches short of six feet tall, so the top of his head was at the level of Daniel's chin. His dark hair was shaved. His forehead was large, coming down in a ridge of bone above his eyes that made him look like he was concentrating. Or angry. Or both.

Daniel swallowed, tasting his own blood for the first time he could remember. *He looks like a toddler trying to get close enough to a fly to swat it,* he thought, as Spot lumbered towards him. The way the man moved reminded Daniel uncomfortably of the two hybrids he had fought in Station. That time, he'd lost three toes, when one of them had chewed his foot.

Not that his limp was giving him a disadvantage now. Spot moved with all the grace and speed of an irritable sloth. Daniel watched him lumber closer and thought of the boxing matches he'd seen on TV as a kid. This guy was no Muhammed Ali.

Float like a butter dish, sting like a twat.

He laughed at the thought as he backed away, and Spot growled. People didn't laugh when they faced Spot. They screamed. They whimpered. They begged. Eventually, everyone who faced him made no sound at all.

Daniel let Spot get close enough for the mouth breather to take a swing at him. He was ready for the speed this time.

He'd been caught off guard before. Too relaxed. Maybe a little bit cocky. After all, Daniel had never lost a fight in his life. At six-foot-four, and broader than any steroid-pumped poser, all but the stupidest hard-cases gave him a wide berth, even when he was trying to be anonymous, hunching over and keeping his head down to make his bulk less noticeable. Now, rather than wearing his usual loose clothing, he was stripped to the waist, his body covered in a sheen of sweat. Slabs of muscle moved across his chest and upper back like tectonic plates. Any normal opponent would be looking for the door.

Spot wasn't a normal opponent. He didn't so much throw a punch as detonate one. His fist, held loosely in front of his shoulder, moved faster than the human eye could track. It was all the more difficult to avoid because of the contrast between the speed and accuracy of the punch, and the slowly shuffling creature behind the attack. That first punch had been so unexpected, Daniel had felt his head snapped to the side before he'd tripped over his own feet and fallen.

This time he was as ready as anyone could be when confronted with Spot the wonder psycho. He twisted backwards as soon as the punch was unleashed. Anyone attacking at normal speed would have missed the target as Daniel rolled his head away, but Spot's right hook landed. It just didn't land hard enough to do any real damage. It still hurt, though.

Daniel jabbed back with his left hand, hard. Daniel's jab was capable of breaking solid wooden doors off their hinges, and often had. Used against a human body, it should have been enough to produce massive trauma, requiring a lengthy stay in hospital.

Only, this time, it didn't. Spot howled, and his eyes took

on an expression previously unseen by anyone other than his handlers. Spot was injured. Daniel's punch had been carefully aimed, hitting him, as Gabe would have put it, "directly in the intercostals." In layman's terms, Daniel had planted his fist just under Spot's armpit, towards the ribs. Gabe had made a careful study of anatomy, and he knew every area of weakness he could exploit in a fight. Daniel had picked up some tips and was trying this one for the first time.

While Spot came to terms with the new concept of receiving, as well as inflicting, damage, Daniel jogged over to his corner. It was a corner only in name, as the cage was no more than a steel fence around a circular area with a diameter of thirty feet. Outside the cage was a gap of five feet, then the barriers holding back the crowd. Each fighter's team watched from these gaps, as did Mr Cole's representatives.

Sara held out a towel, and Daniel quickly wiped his face and handed it back.

"What did I tell ya?" said Gabe. "The intercostals. Hurts like a motherfucker."

Sara was looking at Daniel's bloodied face and frowning. "Are you going to be okay, Daniel?"

They had been prepared for this mission, briefed at length. It wasn't simple—no IGLU mission ever was—but it had seemed more straightforward than most. Penetrate the Birmingham underground fighting scene, win enough fights to get an invite to the big one, which was *literally* underground, as it was held underneath one of Mr Cole's money-laundering restaurants in the city. Win against his best fighter, get an audience with the man himself, and take him into custody. Mr Cole, whose criminal empire was rapidly expanding, had discovered a new sideline in weapons and was acting as the middleman in deals arming certain terrorist groups. The government had asked for help, the UN had been made aware, and a phone call had been made. Three weeks later, Daniel, Sara, and Gabe had found themselves in Birmingham. Ten days after that, they had received the invitation to tonight's fight.

The plan had unfolded just as Sara had said it would. Until now.

"Is he—?" said Sara.

Daniel nodded. "Yep. Must be. But there's something really, really wrong with him."

"Shit," said Sara. "Can you handle it?"

"I think so. I hope so."

"Incoming," said Gabe, and Daniel turned to see Spot moving in his direction, his eyes pinpricks of rage. The noise of the crowd swelled again, but Daniel could still hear Spot's howl. It was the sound of a creature who wished to inflict a great deal of violence on the man who had dared hurt him.

"See you in a minute," said Daniel.

"Wait," said Gabe, coming forward. "I have a plan."

Daniel looked at him, then jerked his head towards Sara. "She's the one who has plans," he said, "not you. She got the brains, and you got the - nope, hang on, you didn't even get that. She got both. Hardly seems fair."

He glanced over his shoulder. Spot was getting too close.

"Look, I'll take him on a circuit of the cage. Tell me when I get back."

"If you get back," said Gabe.

"Funny guy," said Daniel, and set off, jogging backwards, keeping Spot at a safe distance.

Sara watched him go, chewing her bottom lip. This wasn't in the briefing. No one had said anything about another halfhero being on the bill. Especially a psychotic halfhero with brain damage.

THE INTER-GOVERNMENTAL LOGISTICS UNIT was a small, deniable branch of the United Nations.

Daniel's involvement with IGLU (everyone pronounced it *igloo*, naturally) had started when, a few weeks after he and his superhuman parent, Abos, had moved to a farmhouse in rural Cornwall, his local post office had handed him a blank envelope with a smudged, foreign postmark.

"Bit weird," admitted the post office manager. "It arrived last week with a note describing you, explaining they'd forgotten your name, and where you live, but that you'd be popping into the post office within the next week. So here you go."

The letter inside intrigued Daniel enough to call the number underneath the signature. The main reason he took the risk was the first two lines:

I am writing because my best friend told me how to contact you and insisted that I did. Her father was The Deterrent. She says you are her half-brother.

Daniel had purchased a cheap mobile phone and ridden two-hundred miles before calling. One lesson he'd learned during his first thirty-eight years of life was not to trust anyone.

Saffi, the woman who had picked up the call, had understood his paranoia and answered all his questions. Over a series of phone calls (which he made using new mobile phones bought from multiple locations), she had filled Daniel in on the background leading to her letter.

Saffi's best friend was a halfhero with gifts which had

come at a significant price. She was hospitalised, requiring round-the-clock care. Many of her major organs could not function without medical intervention. The private hospital's fees had exceeded the means of her family, but when Saffi had alerted her UN employers about her friend's abilities, they had picked up the tab.

Saffi's friend may have lost the use of her body, but the power of her mind had grown exponentially as her physical capabilities had weakened. She sensed patterns where no-one else could, warning of political upheavals and humanitarian crises. Saffi passed on her predictions, which proved to be unnervingly accurate. The only problem was timescale. Saffi's nameless friend predicted events days or, sometimes, hours before they occurred. On very rare occasions, she could look weeks ahead. She'd known a day in advance that a certain building would collapse near Liverpool Street station in London. She had known how to find Daniel, but not accurately enough to provide an address.

After weeks of talking, Daniel had agreed to meet the IGLU team. Both of them. Not much of a team, but—as Saffi had pointed out—it wasn't exactly as if there was a big queue of halfheroes asking for work. Meeting Sara and Gabe wasn't a massive risk, since Abos was shadowing Daniel, ready to step in if necessary. Abos and Daniel had discussed whether he should reveal that The Deterrent was still alive, albeit now as a woman, but both had been reluctant. Station was gone, any remaining children were in their late thirties, and Abos's years as The Deterrent had been a convincing enough warning about the pitfalls of being a public figure.

In the event, Abos was able to preserve her anonymity. The meeting—at a roadside cafe in Yorkshire—went well. As he'd said to Abos afterwards, "It's weird. I made it to my mid-thirties with a mother I haven't seen for twenty years and no other family. Now I have you, a sister, and a brother."

"A family," said Abos.

"Well, kind of. Don't hold your breath for the sitcom."

Since the meeting, he had joined the IGLU team on missions all over the world. They cleared the way for disaster relief agencies to access areas hit by earthquakes, hurricanes, and floods. They rescued hostages from armed groups of all political persuasions. They disarmed and incapacitated terrorist cells with plans for mass destruction.

All of which was fine, but it wasn't the best part. Daniel had friends. Real friends. He needed them, and they needed him. *That* was the best part.

OF COURSE, having friends was all very well, and most of the IGLU missions had been...well...fun. Better than staying at home. But when his friends were on one side of a steel cage, while Daniel was locked inside with a crazed super-strong opponent who wanted to rip him in half before, probably, eating the pieces, having a cup of tea while watching Loose Women actually seemed pretty appealing.

2

S *hit.*

Daniel was on the concrete floor again. This wasn't part of the plan. He wasn't sure how to finish this. He was banking on the element of surprise being a decisive factor. What he hadn't banked on was Spot having any surprises of his own.

The slow, shuffling, lumbering style of his opponent wasn't the whole story. Not by a long shot. It was certainly Spot's favoured technique, following his opponents around the concrete ring with all the speed of an injured tortoise, waiting for them to come close enough to be on the receiving end of one of his blindingly fast punches. But it wasn't the only trick in his arsenal. Daniel was amazed that Spot had an arsenal at all. Or he would have been amazed if he hadn't been lying half-stunned on the floor again.

The last time he'd looked, Spot had been on the far side of the ring. He had covered the distance in a blur of speed. Daniel, whose reactions were keener than most, had only just begun to react, pivoting to the side, before a huge fist caught his shoulder and lifted it cleanly out of its socket, tearing muscles as it went, spinning him away. He'd hit the cage, hard. Then he'd hit the floor, slightly less hard, but still painfully.

Shit.

He blinked sweat away and got to his knees. The volume of the crowd's response was incredible. They'd never seen anyone get up after one of Spot's punches. This guy had taken two of them and was still breathing. More money changed hands. No one had bet on Daniel to win, just on how long he would survive. Now there were a few takers for a Daniel victory. But not many. Most of them had seen Spot fight before.

Daniel got up, holding his shoulder and wincing. It would heal in a few days, but he didn't have a few days.

"Hey, buddy." Why was it only Americans could say *buddy* without sounding like a tit? He looked through the bars. Gabe was even shorter than Spot, medium build, average looking. Enemies underestimated him. He enjoyed showing them the error of doing so.

"Hang on." Daniel grabbed his dislocated shoulder and, before he had time to think about it, pushed it back into his socket. He roared with pain as he did so, and specks of bloodied spit hit Gabe's face.

"Jeez," said Gabe, wiping his face with the back of his sleeve. "You coulda warned me. All better, big guy?"

Daniel moved his left arm slightly and roared again as the torn muscles protested.

Gabe wiped his face with his other sleeve. "I guess not. Here's Plan A."

He talked fast, and Daniel nodded. "For a short-arse Yank, you're okay."

Gabe looked as if he was about to respond, but Spot chose that moment to point at his injured opponent, beat his chest and roar to the cheering crowd before turning to face Daniel again.

"Quick," said Daniel. "What's Plan B?"

"Oh. There isn't one. I just said that to make you feel better. Make Plan A work, that's my advice."

"Great advice, just...great."

Daniel started jogging backwards again, his shoulder sending fresh jabs of pain to his brain with every step.

Spot was confident now, his glittering eyes following Daniel's progress as the crowd settled into a no doubt familiar chant of, "Fuck him up! Fuck him up! Fuck him up!"

Daniel admitted to himself that Gabe's idea had merit. He could beat Spot on his own, but not without sustaining more injuries. He'd already effectively lost the use of his left arm. If he was going to be of any use when the IGLU team met Mr Cole, he could do with keeping all of his other limbs in working order.

He hated fighting other halfheroes. It wasn't the fact that they were harder to beat, it was the fact that they had chosen badly, become the bad guys. It was rarely as straight-forward as that, but, however they had got there, they had ended up on the wrong side. Criminals, mercenaries, assassins even. It was depressing.

Looking at Spot, he doubted any real choice had been involved. The halfhero facing him was well named since he displayed no more intelligence than a canine. There was a studded dog collar around his neck, but it wasn't there as part of his outfit. His handlers had led him to the fight at the end of a chain. Both of them carried cattle prods. Daniel's adversary looked like he'd been trained to fight in the same way dogs are prepared for the fighting pits.

Daniel got to the position Gabe had indicated and

stopped, looking at those rage-filled eyes on the far side of the concrete ring. Spot prepared to charge.

Yeah. Perhaps I'll save feeling sorry for him until this is over.

Daniel came up onto his toes and bent his knees, bobbing like a tennis player waiting to receive a serve. His knees creaked as if to remind him he was far closer to forty than thirty. He tried not to blink as he watched Spot, readying himself, knowing he could move quickly for a big man, and hoping it would be enough. He was waiting opposite his corner. Thirty feet away, Sara was standing directly behind Spot. Gabe was off to one side, his body tense.

Daniel had been caught napping the first time Spot had charged him. This time he was looking for the signs. No one can go from a standing start to top speed without a moment's tension and a period of acceleration, however brief. Daniel saw it just as it began, a dipping of Spot's shoulders, the top half of Sara's body becoming visible as he crouched, his back leg bending to propel him forwards.

Daniel moved immediately, but as the halfhero opposite threw himself across the distance between them, he wasn't sure he had been fast enough. The speed of the thing was incredible. Daniel shifted right and pivoted onto his left foot, bringing both his fists together as if swinging an invisible hammer. His shoulder screamed, but he ignored the fresh agony and swung both arms anti-clockwise as he continued to pivot, his right foot leaving the ground while he turned through forty-five degrees. Daniel liked to think the move was balletic, but he didn't know of any giant ballerinas with only two toes on their pirouetting foot.

He made it out of the path of the oncoming maniac. Just. Spot brushed past with the lightest of touches. At this speed, there was no way he could stop. Daniel was supposed to act as a braking mechanism. Instead, Spot continued towards the padlocked door leading to his corner and his handlers, who were already throwing themselves out of the way.

As Daniel's hands swung round, he felt the massive ripple of force along his arms that meant Gabe's plan had worked. He didn't need to see Sara to know that she had stepped up to the cage and pushed her hands forwards, a subtle gesture that would go unnoticed as everyone focussed on the action at the far side. The top of the ball of energy that she had summoned hit Daniel's arms, spinning him faster. He lost his balance and fell, mercifully onto his right side. As he hit the concrete, he heard a sound like a freight train derailing at speed.

Daniel looked up. Spot's back had taken most of the impact of Sara's intervention, and it had added significantly to his already impressive momentum. He had hit the cage at the edge of the padlocked door, his head and shoulder bending the steel as he went through. Rivets had popped, and welds had given way under the sudden, unprecedented, pressure. He hung there now, like the ugliest doll in history, unconscious, half his body out of the cage, blood running down his face.

Daniel took a few breaths. Gabe winked at him from the other side. Sara smiled. A couple of suits were approaching and, as Daniel watched, one of them bent and whispered something in Sara's ear. She nodded and replied, pointing at Daniel. It looked as if the rest of the night's fun was on, then.

Daniel put his elbow on the concrete and pushed himself onto his knees. Another few breaths, then he stood up.

And the crowd went mental.

Mr Cole's office was somewhat of a contrast to the fighting pit underneath his favourite sushi restaurant. Instead of concrete floors and bloodstains, there were parquet floors and the biggest rugs Daniel had ever seen. Rather than the smell of cigarettes, beer, and piss, a faint hint of lotus blossom pervaded the space. This wasn't due to a plugin air freshener. As eight bodyguards directed the IGLU team across a small bridge in the centre of the room, Daniel glanced down at the artificial stream that divided the upper and lower levels. It led into a pool containing a dozen koi carp. And real lotus flowers.

"I'm impressed. I thought Spot would retire undefeated. He was quite a find." The man speaking was walking down a staircase that followed the wall to their right before curving into the room. He was small, a little overweight, and was wearing olive chinos with a black silk shirt.

Casual wear for the villain in your *life,* thought Daniel, and covered his laugh with a cough.

Cole paused at the foot of the stairs and regarded Daniel with distaste, before turning to Sara. "There was really no need to bring your pet with you, Ms Gray. You've made your point. And he smells."

Daniel bristled and almost spoke before remembering to leave the talking to Sara, as agreed. Besides, Cole did have a bit of a point about the smell. He'd just spent the night brawling, dispatching four progressively tougher opponents before they'd brought out Spot. Still, he'd had a quick spray with a deodorant. How bad could it be?

He noticed Sara and Gabe were standing a few paces away. Oh. Pretty bad, then.

"Mr Cole, Daniel is my colleague, as is Gabe. We work as a team."

"Hmm." Cole stepped away from the staircase and showed them to a vast sitting area. Daniel chose a pure white armchair and flopped into it, enjoying the tiny wince on Cole's face.

A lackey glided to Cole's side. "My usual," said Cole, before turning back to his guests. "What would you like to drink?"

"Oh, a glass of champagne for me," said Sara, and Cole tilted his head approvingly.

"I'm cool," said Gabe. Cole continued to look at him. "I'm good." Still nothing. "I don't need a drink, man."

As Cole still seemed intent on ignoring him, Daniel shouted after the lackey as he walked away: "Oi! Garçon. Lager. And make sure it's cold."

Daniel hadn't expected to like Cole, but this was worse than he had thought. He was one of those crime bosses who didn't like to get their hands dirty, who relied on others to perform all the unsavoury acts that allowed him to live in a place like this.

"How much did this pile set you back?" said Daniel. "I mean, I know it's only Birmingham, but, still."

Cole didn't rise to the bait, and Sara gave Daniel the briefest of glances. *Oh yeah. I'm not supposed to talk so much.*

Daniel shut up, but when the drinks arrived, he slurped loudly and managed a particular fine belch halfway through the bottle.

"Cheers, Cole."

That one earned him a glare, and he decided to lay off. This was Sara's party now. It was just that fact that the man insisted on being called *Mister,* and was known for having people beaten when they forgot.

Tosser.

"Mr Cole," began Sara, sipping her champagne. "You said you had a business proposition. Why don't you tell us what you have in mind."

Cole's eyes flicked from her eyes to her lips as she drank. Gabe and Daniel exchanged a brief glance. It wasn't the first time they'd felt invisible when Sara negotiated with a heterosexual male.

Sara looked like a pin-up model. Not the kind you see in a car mechanic's office when you go to pay your bill, feel awkward about, almost say something, then don't. More like a Hollywood star of the nineteen-fifties. She was beautiful, she knew it, and she wasn't a dick about it. A rare combination.

Not long after they had met, Daniel had asked how she dealt with unwanted male attention. Sara had laughed.

"I hardly get any." Seeing Daniel's unbelieving look, she had patted his hand mock-condescendingly. "Listen, poppet, men don't approach women they think are out of their league. It's a natural law."

Daniel had persisted. "But some of them must pluck up the courage. Or think they're good-looking enough to have a go."

"Yeah," she had admitted. "A few. I tell them I'm gay."

Daniel laughed. "Does that work?"

"Yes. It does, Daniel. Because I'm gay."

"Ah. Oh, great. Now I feel like a cock."

"Well, if you're desperate, I can ask around...?"

Since then, Daniel had been trying very hard not to assume all beautiful women were straight. His excuse to Sara had been that attitudes had changed in society during the fourteen years he'd spent in a semi-catatonic state.

Until recently, he'd thought LGBTQ was a sandwich.

Now Cole was succumbing to her magic. Well, that wasn't the whole story. There was Sara's other talent, too, one she'd grown into during adolescence as a child of The Deterrent. She was nudging him, mentally. She was being subtle about it, just reinforcing ideas Cole might already have about her, amplifying some, discouraging others. She'd demonstrated her power on Daniel early on when he'd questioned its usefulness, and he'd eaten three raw onions thinking they were apples before he knew what she was doing.

"What I want," Cole was saying, "is to make you an offer for your creature here."

He pointed at Daniel. "I know *what* he is. I know who his father was. No, don't waste time trying to deny it. Halfheroes are a rare find indeed, but they are not an urban myth, as you and I both know, Ms Gray."

Sara was silent. Cole smiled.

"Don't be surprised. My business is built on information. You have been in town for less than two weeks, but your boy here has made quite an impression. Even so, no one thought he stood a chance against Spot. No human would. So, shall we start the negotiations, Ms Gray?"

"Well," said Sara, "if we're going to be open about this, I think you'd better call me Sara."

Cole smiled at that. Daniel wondered how he would react if he knew he was in a room with not one, but three, halfheroes. Well, he'd know soon enough.

"Very well," said Cole. "Sara. And," he lowered his voice, "you must call me Crispin."

"Crispin!" repeated Daniel, loudly, spraying beer on the rug. One of the bodyguards made a noise that may have been a snigger.

Cole's face coloured, and he started to stand up.

"I'll tell you what," said Sara, smiling. "Why don't we discuss this in private, Crispin."

Cole recovered his composure aided, Daniel was sure, by another mental nudge from Sara.

"Yes," said Cole, "why not?"

He stood, walked to the foot of the stairs, and waited for Sara. A nod to his guards, and they turned their attention to Daniel and Gabe, who stayed in the seating area.

"Make sure our guests are comfortable," he said, "and don't hesitate to shoot them if they try to leave."

Daniel raised his bottle in mock salute, but made sure he caught Sara's eye. She would have to be careful. Cole was a violent, volatile man who'd risen to the top of the underworld by going further than anyone else; having someone beaten up for a careless remark, killing any serious rivals. Sara would do well not to underestimate him.

"Let's talk on the roof," he said. "It's a beautiful night."

"Perfect," she said.

The biggest bodyguard went to walk with them, and Sara turned to Cole in mock surprise.

"Really?" she said, with a flirtatious smile.

"Really," he returned, smiling back.

Daniel felt a moment of unease as he watched the three of them follow the curve of the staircase up the wall and out of sight.

Daniel winked at the guards, who had now removed their guns from hidden holsters and were projecting an air of professional menace.

"All right, boys? Any danger of another beer?"

No one moved.

"Well, the service here is bloody awful. Don't expect a tip."

The seven men were stony-faced.

Daniel checked his watch. Not long before midnight. The next few minutes were crucial. He knew Sara had hooked Cole, but the fact that he insisted on bringing the bodyguard suggested he might be capable of resisting some of her mental nudges. Even so, he was talking to her alone, which meant he had taken the bait. He wanted to buy Daniel, break him psychologically the way he'd done to that poor bastard in the cage, and use him as his new fighting dog.

He knew Sara could handle the bodyguard, and as soon as she was on the roof, she'd send the text calling the helicopter.

It was all fine.

So why did he have a bad feeling?

He heard rotor blades. They were getting closer. He signalled to Gabe, positioning his fingers on the beer bottle and tilting his head slightly. He'd take the four on one side, Gabe could deal with the three behind him.

Gabe nodded. The approaching helicopter got louder. One of the guards frowned, brought his jacket cuff up to his mouth and spoke into it.

"Carver?"

It was the first moment there had been any kind of distraction. Gabe responded immediately, saying, "indigestion."

As soon as he heard the code word, Daniel counted silently to five, knowing Gabe was doing the same.

One...two...three...

The guard spoke into his cuff again. One of the others looked over.

"Carver? You there?"

...Four...

"Carver!"

...Five.

Daniel moved at precisely the same moment as Gabe, throwing himself forward from his chair, but before he was on his feet, Gabe had passed him, and the first guard was on his way to the floor, a jab behind his ear inducing a blackout. As Daniel picked up the five-seater couch, wincing at the strain it put on his shoulder, Gabe's second target received a precisely positioned punch to his solar plexus that would leave him struggling for breath for an hour. At the same moment as the first bullet pinged painfully off Daniel's chest, Gabe dived to the floor. The third guard was still raising his weapon when the smaller man slid into his feet, and he fell. Before he could react, Gabe pinched a spot near the top of his nose. The guard twitched and passed out.

Meanwhile, Daniel had been hit by another two bullets, but the sofa was finally on its way, collecting three of the four guards and sending them crashing into the far wall. The last man turned and ran for the stairs. Gabe was still on the floor when the guard started his ten-yard sprint. When the man reached the foot of the stairs, Gabe was waiting for him.

The surprised look on the guard's face was still there when his legs crumpled beneath him.

"You really must teach me more of that stuff," said Daniel as they ran upstairs.

The noise of the rotors was very loud now.

Neither of them said what both of them were thinking.

Why hasn't it landed?

THE HELICOPTER WAS HOVERING a short distance away from the roof, its searchlight trained on the figures beneath. As Daniel and Gabe reached the top of the stairs and the open glass door, they were just in time to hear a gun shot. The chopper's light went out, and it took a few seconds for their eyes to adjust.

When they did, they could see that the situation they found themselves in wasn't quite what they had anticipated at the planning stage.

Cole had not been mentally, or physically, subdued by Sara, and was not meekly on his way to the waiting helicopter. Instead, he had a gun in his hand and was looking towards the door where Daniel and Gabe waited. The helicopter hovered about fifty feet behind him.

Sara was standing at the very edge of the roof, to their right. She was standing very still. Six feet in front of her was Spot, his misshapen head bandaged, but otherwise in fine, psychotically dangerous, condition. Daniel could vouch that Spot was one tough bastard, but he'd never have suspected he was quite this resilient.

Daniel could see the problem. Sara couldn't risk using her power. She might manipulate the air around her, or cause one of the big terracotta pot plants nearby to fly towards Spot, but she'd only get one chance. They'd all seen how fast he could move. And a fifty-one-storey fall would be long enough for her to thoroughly regret trying her luck.

The guard who'd come up with them was lying on his side halfway between them and Sara. Part of his head was missing.

"Spot tends to be a little excitable when I first let him out," called Cole. "He'd never attack me, of course, but anyone else is fair game, aren't they, boy?"

A guttural growl was Spot's response.

"Come on, Daniel. May as well come out. Welcome to the team. I might even let you share a kennel with Spot once you've been through my training programme."

Another growl. Sara eyed the creature warily.

"Cole hasn't seen you," Daniel whispered to Gabe, trying to keep his mouth perfectly still. Gabe was behind him, and about a third of his width. "Follow me out, closely."

"Gollow nee out glosely? Got it."

Daniel made a mental note to slap Gabe later, then walked out. He could hear Gabe breathing behind him. If he could get close enough for his fellow halfhero to use his speed, they might still salvage the situation.

Cole held up a hand.

"That's far enough."

Shit. Not close enough.

"Daniel, this is a one-time offer. Agree to join me, and I'll let Ms Gray go. You've already lost one of your friends tonight downstairs,"—

"Wrong, bozo!" whispered Gabe.

—"but that's what you get for bringing knives to a gunfight. Now call off the helicopter, or I'll let Spot have her."

Daniel waved a hand at the chopper, and it banked away.

Gabe nudged his back. "Charge him. I'll go left, you draw his fire."

Daniel didn't move. "And Sara?" he whispered, looking at Spot, who was drooling.

"If that thing is trained as well as this jerk claims, he won't move unless she does. And I know she won't move. You have a better idea?"

Daniel closed his eyes. He couldn't see another way, but he hated the unknowns. He reminded himself, not for the first time, that Sara was the best one at making plans.

"You don't have time to think about it, boy," called Cole. "I am not a patient man. Yes or no?"

Daniel opened his eyes.

"You ready?" whispered Gabe.

"Well?" said Cole.

"Yes," said Daniel, and charged.

The first few seconds in any fight normally determine the final outcome. Those crucial seconds didn't go at all well for the IGLU team on the Birmingham rooftop.

Caught by surprise, Cole still managed to squeeze off two shots as Daniel approached. The first went harmlessly past his right ear, but the second hit his injured shoulder, ricocheted away and hit Gabe in the neck. He fell to the floor and clasped a hand to the wound. Cole aimed at Gabe's head and held up his hand at Daniel, who skidded to a stop five feet short of him.

Daniel could understand how Cole had got to the top. His decision-making under pressure was rapid and efficient. Sara was pinned against the edge of the roof, Gabe was down, and Cole was still in charge.

"Back off, boy," said Cole. This whole *boy* thing was getting old fast.

Daniel did as he was told.

"That's far enough. Now stay."

Wanker.

Daniel heard rotor blades. The helicopter was back, approaching the rooftop cautiously. The pilot had interpreted his gesture as an order to circle and return.

"Nice try," said Cole, shooting a glance at Gabe. Daniel looked. Gabe was keeping pressure on his neck, but it looked like the bullet may have nicked the jugular, in which case he'd need to keep pushing until they could get him to a hospital. He'd heal fast, but heavy blood loss would have much the same result on a halfhero as a human. He was out of the fight.

"Two halfheroes," said Cole, looking at Sara. "Sneaky."

Yeah, well, thought Daniel, *you're not quite as clever as you think you are, mate.*

"Shame I only need one," said Cole, and raised the gun towards Gabe.

Daniel moved immediately, but he knew he was too late. The gun came up, Cole's finger tightening on the trigger. Daniel put everything he had into reaching him, and threw himself forwards in a rugby tackle. As he did so, he saw Cole's feet leave the rooftop, his shot going wide.

Daniel hit the deck hard and looked up. Cole was travelling backwards at speed, his arms flailing. He was heading over the edge of the roof. Luckily, there was a solid object between him and the ground, fifty-one storeys below. Unluckily, the solid object was a helicopter, held aloft by five rotor blades.

They were called blades for a reason.

Daniel looked away, but couldn't prevent himself

hearing the series of *thunks*, the brief stutter of the chopper's engine, and a sound like a heavy shower of rain with particularly big drops.

At that moment, his brain, after seeing the *effect*, deduced the *cause*, and Daniel knew Sara must have sent the burst of energy that killed Cole. He looked across the roof in time to see her fall, choosing to jump rather than be caught by the charging Spot. The creature had no way of stopping himself and followed her over the edge with a howl.

Daniel scrambled to his feet, ran and, before he could think about it, threw himself over the edge.

4

Daniel saw Spot first. He'd stopped howling and was dropping silently towards the distant street. Maybe dying was a relief. Whatever they'd done to him, whatever it was Cole had meant by his *training programme*, perhaps Spot was better off dead.

Sara hadn't screamed. She was falling skydiver-style, limbs spread. Daniel knew she'd be thinking fast, but even Sara couldn't think herself out of this one. Gravity couldn't be argued into looking the other way.

Daniel fell head first, arms by his sides until he reached her, then flung himself into the spread-eagled position. His brain seemed to have shut off completely. He'd gone after her because he was the toughest, he'd recovered from every injury. If he could get underneath her, he could break her fall.

Maybe he should have thought it through a bit more thoroughly, but it was too late now.

He grabbed Sara and twisted round so that she was above him. As soon as she saw him, she turned her back to his chest.

A second and a half later, he felt a push like a strong gust of wind blow them away from the building. Then, still a good thirty storeys from the street, he crashed into something. The something he'd crashed into exploded around them, and the world went dark blue. He couldn't breathe. He felt something solid at his back and pushed up.

His head broke the surface of the water a second before Sara's. They swam to the side and pulled themselves out, then lay there gasping. Daniel flexed his muscles experimentally. The pain in his shoulder had been joined by some spectacular aches in his back. Other than that, he seemed remarkably not dead. Which was good.

"Quick thinking," said Sara, rolling off his chest. "I mean it. Bloody quick thinking."

Daniel sat up. They were on the roof of an exclusive apartment complex. The bar by the pool was still open, and a middle-aged couple in bathrobes stared in disbelief at the new arrivals.

Daniel looked up at the taller building they'd fallen from. Sara had pushed them across a four-lane street to hit the pool.

"Hell of a shot," he said.

"Wasn't bad, was it? Did Cole, er...?"

"He went to pieces," said Daniel. She looked blank. "That was, you know, a Bond line. Witty. He went to pieces? Because he hit the helicopter and... oh, never mind."

As the chopper came closer, he went to the bar.

"Any chance of a lager to go?"

Daniel got three lagers. The open-mouthed barman hadn't even charged him. Back in the helicopter, Gabe couldn't manage his, so Daniel drank it for him. They headed to the nearest hospital. He was going to be okay.

They didn't speak much. Their mission had been to get Cole off the street, but they would have preferred to have arrested him. It had all been a bit messy.

"We did our best," said Daniel, clinking his bottle against Sara's. "And the guy was a total scumbag."

"True," she said. They both took a swig.

"So," said Sara, brightly. "Got plans for next week?"

"Yes," said Daniel.

"Anything nice?"

"No," he said. "Not nice. Not exactly."

5

The scalpel was less than an inch from Daniel's right testicle when Abos burst through the door.

"I've found one!"

Doctor Pollock (who had long since become inured to remarks about his name and his chosen profession), raised an eyebrow, withdrew the razor-sharp implement to a safe distance, and looked over his shoulder.

"Sorry," said Abos. "Didn't mean to disturb you. I want to speak to Daniel. Do you mind?"

Pollock didn't move. He looked back at his patient, from between his open legs.

"Friend of yours?"

Daniel shifted his weight, mindful of the ominous groans the hospital bed was making under his considerable bulk. He looked at Abos, then back at the doctor. He wondered what Pollock's reaction would be if he answered the question truthfully, and told him that the young woman currently eying his shaved testicles was, in fact, his father. On reflection, he decided it not to shock the man with a razor-sharp instrument poised over his knackers.

"Yes," he said.

"Could you ask her to return to the waiting room, please."

Abos looked like she might protest. Daniel cleared his throat.

"Abo- um, Amy?"

Abos was too strange a name to use in front of others. It would only lead to awkward questions, and the real answer —that it stood for Amorphous Blob Of Slime—would lead to even more awkward questions.

"Yes, Daniel?"

Abos looked calm and, as always when standing still, did so with a preternatural lack of movement which unnerved anyone not used to it. But Daniel noticed a slight widening of her eyes and a tiny hint of muscular tension around her lips. Doctor Pollock edged away from her, sensing something he would never have been able to put into words.

Daniel held up a hand.

"I know you've been looking for a long time."

"Thirteen months and twenty-three days."

Daniel nodded.

"Would another ten minutes more make much difference?"

Abos considered the question before answering.

"Oh. Do you want to finish here first?"

Daniel took a deep breath, tasting the metallic tang of the antiseptic splashed over his genitals.

"Yes, please."

She didn't move. After a few seconds, Doctor Pollock straightened up and looked at her, the scalpel still in his hand.

Abos had grown her current body from George Kuku's blood. At first, it had been strange for Daniel to see that face every day. Now, it was hard to remember Abos as anything other than this striking black woman with an open smile and, behind her brown contact lenses, golden eyes.

"I'll wait outside, shall I?" said Abos. The doctor said nothing. Abos turned at the door, looking under the sheet covering Daniel's open legs.

"Are they supposed to look like that?" she said. "I'm sure mine didn't."

The doctor twitched. Daniel glad the scalpel was still a few feet away from his boys.

Abos left, shutting the door quietly behind her.

Doctor Pollock turned back to his patient.

"Expecting any other friends to drop in?"

"No. Sorry about that."

Daniel closed his eyes and tried to relax, knowing there was little chance of the vasectomy being a success if he didn't do so. He had briefed Pollock on his unusual physical attributes, overcoming the man's scepticism by stabbing himself in the thigh with a scalpel and bending the blade back on itself. The doctor had agreed to make his incisions as slowly as possible, as instructed.

It was hard to think of anything other than what was occurring between his legs, but Daniel gave it his best shot. He felt the stitches go in as if Pollock was pulling an invisible string attached to his navel. It was a bizarre sensation.

A few minutes later and it was done. He swung his legs round and sat on the edge of the bed.

Daniel suspected Pollock was already mentally composing his account of the first vasectomy on a halfhero. The name and address he had used to book the private procedure were fake, but he still treasured his anonymity.

"Thank you, doctor. I'm afraid I won't be able to attend any follow-up appointments. I heal fast."

"Yes, yes, that's fine. Just change the dressing after two days. The stitches are dissolvable, a few hot baths with plenty of salt in the water will take care of them."

Daniel carefully put on his trousers. There was a tightening sensation in his groin as his body began to heal the incision.

"Doctor Pollock, I appreciate you fitting me in at such short notice." Both men knew the amount paid for the op had guaranteed a swift climb to the top of the waiting list, but they observed the social convention of not mentioning it.

"Not at all, not at all. It was fascinating to meet you. I'd always considered halfhe—" His voice tailed off for a moment as if he was worried about causing offence. "Half, um, that is, well, *enhanced*, er..."

Daniel sighed.

"Halfhero is fine. It's not a bad nickname for us."

"Yes, well, I suppose. I'm afraid I thought halfheroes were an urban myth. I mean, if The Deterrent had fathered children, one might have thought they would follow in his footsteps, perhaps, righting wrongs, protecting the country, and suchlike, er..."

He stopped speaking again, spotting the corner he was neatly painting himself into.

"Not that I'm implying you should do that. Not at all. Of course not. No, no, no. I, ah, respect your right to a private existence. Couldn't have been easy growing up as a child of a superhero. Especially when he disappeared. Probably dead. Terrible shame, that. I wonder how on earth it happened? He was remarkable."

Daniel wondered how Doctor Pollock would respond if he told him The Deterrent was not only alive but had been standing in the same room ten minutes ago.

"He was. Doctor?"

"Umm?" Doctor Pollock had drifted into somewhat of a reverie. Daniel suspected he was wondering how to title the piece he planned submitting to The Lancet.

Daniel picked up the scalpel he had bent on his thigh.

"I'm so glad you respect my right to a private existence." He began bending the scalpel between finger and thumb, forming a rough circle of metal. "I'd be upset if I thought you didn't."

He put the scalpel on the tray. Doctor Pollock swallowed.

Daniel eased himself off the bed, wincing. It wasn't pain, just the disconcerting sensation that his genitalia had taken a leave of absence, replaced by what seemed to be an egg box stuffed with cotton wool. He reached into his back pocket and placed a thick envelope next to the scalpel.

"A bonus to show my appreciation for your discretion. And to cover the damage to your security camera outside."

What dama—? Oh." The envelope disappeared into Pollock's pocket as he bravely overcame his distaste for the sordid business of finance. A few hours later, he would feign surprise as his practice manager showed him the unrecognisable lump of metal hanging where the security camera had been.

"Is there a back entrance leading out to the carpark?"

Pollock opened the door to a corridor and pointed at the fire exit.

He watched Daniel leave with mixed feelings. He was a few thousand pounds richer, but he couldn't help but regret not being able to write that article. A real shame, just when he'd thought of a title for it: *Slicing Open A Super-Scrotum*.

Ah, well.

ABOS WAS WAITING in the carpark, next to Daniel's Yamaha. She wore leathers and a helmet as if she was prepared to ride pillion, but Daniel knew she was unlikely to be doing that.

Some time alone on the bike would give him time to think about what she'd said in the clinic. Abos had been searching for so long, Daniel had begun to suspect her quest would never yield results.

Had she really found one?

"Where?" he said as he got closer, resisting the almost overwhelming urge to scratch his crotch.

"Cromer."

Daniel stared. The only word he associated with Cromer was crabs.

The irony wasn't lost on him.

6

A bos rode on the back of the bike until they were out of the carpark. The spring foliage in the lane was taking on the greener hue that signalled the start of summer and, although Daniel couldn't hear anything over the sound of the engine, he knew the late afternoon birdsong would be loud and joyous. Often, he and Abos would have stopped to listen, but when she squeezed his shoulder to stop him, he knew she wasn't after another lesson in British birds and their habitats.

He stopped the bike. Abos slid off and, keeping her helmet on, jogged into the forest.

Daniel eased himself from the seat and followed, aware of sensation returning to his bruised testicles. He loved the speed and the freedom of the motorbike; the instant feedback of the tyres on the tarmac as he leaned into a corner. The only aspect of biking he wasn't able to share with fellow enthusiasts was the element of danger. If he fell off, the damage to the bike, other vehicles and their occupants were the only real dangers. An impact that would break normal human bones might only leave a small bruise or two on him. Even they would fade within a few hours.

What Daniel had failed to consider was how bad a choice a motorbike was for a man who had just undergone a vasectomy.

"You're an idiot, Harbin," he muttered as he limped along the path, adopting a more wide-legged gait than normal.

Abos met him at the edge of a clearing.

"Not worried you'll be seen?" said Daniel.

Abos shook her head, her voice muffled by the black helmet.

"It's getting darker, and there's cloud cover. "

Abos pushed up her visor, reached in and squeezed out her contact lenses, putting them in a small case before zipping them into a rucksack pocket. Her golden eyes scanned the clearing before settling back on Daniel. He would never get used to those eyes.

"Meet you at the pier," she said. "How long will you be?"

Daniel had chosen a private clinic in leafy Surrey for his procedure. The Yamaha could cruise at double the national speed limit, and easily elude the police. On the couple of occasions they had given chase, he had dived down the nearest country lane, grabbed his bike and jumped over the hedge with it. When the sirens had faded, he'd jumped back over, faced the other way, and roared off.

He reckoned on being able to make the run in well under four hours, but his nether regions were now itching as the anaesthetic wore off, and Daniel suspected he would need a few, as the apt American expression has it, comfort breaks.

"Five hours, give or take."

"Give or take what?"

Daniel waited. After a few seconds, Abos spoke again.

"Oh. It's an *expression*, a *turn of phrase*. Right?"

"Right." Abos's command of the English language was excellent - she had spent decades teaching the subject in a Welsh school. But there were blank spots, and they included slang or local expressions. Not every piece of knowledge accumulated during the time in her last body had transferred to this new one. Sometimes, the way she spoke was very much like George, and George's vocabulary was different to Cressida's.

Daniel tried to clarify his meaning. "It means I'll get there when I get there."

Abos looked confused again. Daniel often forgot that he wasn't talking to a human being. Moments like this reminded him. Whatever Abos was, despite sharing human DNA with George, Cressida, and Station scientist Roger Sullivan, she definitely wasn't the tall, athletic-looking black woman she appeared to be. He spoke again before she could say anything.

"As soon as I can, okay?"

Abos stepped into the forest. Seconds later, Daniel saw her helmet appear just above the trees. It was early evening —Daniel had made sure his appointment at the clinic was their last of the day—but still hours before sunset. He tried not to blink, determined not to miss the moment she left. Her head dropped into the foliage below. He kept his eyes fixed on the spot he had last seen her and was rewarded by a glimpse of Abos heading upwards at just under the speed of sound. A sonic boom would draw attention. Her progress was still stunningly fast. It registered in Daniel's brain as a grey smudge between the tops of the trees and the base of the clouds, like a scratch on the lens of his eye that faded in seconds.

Certain she had gone, he undid his belt, popped his

trouser button, and put his hand inside his pants, groaning
with relief as he gently scratched his throbbing groin.

IT WAS a long ride with a sore crotch.

Daniel picked his way through the M25 rush hour traffic.
He was travelling clockwise, despite knowing it would add a
few minutes to the trip. If he had turned east instead of west
when getting on to the motorway, he would have had to take
Dartford Tunnel. Daniel didn't like being underground
these days. Not if he had a choice.

At least he could make progress even when cars, vans,
and lorries had slowed to a crawl. Within forty-five
minutes of leaving the Surrey lay-by, he had flicked on his
indicator and swung the Yamaha's nose north onto
the M11.

He thought about his early days at Station when he
found out he wasn't the only child of his superhero father,
The Deterrent. Abos had been a busy boy. The number of
pregnancies he had left behind during his two-year spree in
the limelight was still unknown, but it may have been
hundreds. Most of Abos's children hadn't survived puberty.
Daniel's own offspring had fared even worse. His DNA had
been used to create monsters.

Hence the vasectomy. He wanted no more of fatherhood.
The decision had been an easy one. Maybe, just maybe, he
would have a normal relationship one day. This operation
made things simpler.

Daniel had bought a farmhouse in Cornwall, only a few
miles away from the cottage he'd stayed in after destroying
Station. George had left him enough money for many life-
times. She'd also left instructions on how to contact her

criminal connections, allowing him to create multiple false identities for himself and Abos.

No one but the conspiracy theorists believed The Deterrent was alive anymore, and information concerning Daniel's continuing existence was buried along with the rest of Station's secrets. They were off the grid, invisible.

Daniel made his first stop near Stansted Airport, watching the planes come and go as he sipped coffee and surreptitiously scratched his balls. He felt a strange distance between himself and the other travellers. He knew he should feel closer to his fellow-humans than he did to Abos. But he didn't. If he hadn't developed powers, he might have been one of these weary travellers. That tired-looking dad with baby sick on his shoulder. That businessman scribbling figures on a notepad for his bored colleague. What about the teacher in charge of those teenagers, having a sneaky cigarette himself? Any of those lives might have been Daniel's.

He wondered what they made of him. He looked forbidding, unapproachable. Daniel carried himself in a way designed to discourage curiosity, walking with a bodybuilder's froggish gait, keeping his head don, avoiding eye contact unless it was necessary, keeping conversations to a minimum. His bulk was intimidating enough to put people off. As he looked around, he saw people look hastily away.

Good luck finding a girlfriend if everyone is scared of you.

Just as the thought entered his mind, he glanced at a group of nuns at one of the tables. One of them was looking at him. A pretty face, younger than he'd expected. Blue eyes. She smiled at him, an open, unfeigned, happy smile from one human being to another. He smiled back, the chasm between himself and everyone else closing a little.

Yeah. You've still got it, Daniel. You could pull a nun.

He laughed at the thought. The pretty nun chuckled to herself before nodding at him and turning back to her companions.

He didn't wonder at the sense of kinship. The nun had decided not to have children, too. There were differences, of course. Daniel doubted the nun had previous children who were murderous, genetically modified half-breeds. Also, the nun's childlessness was due to celibacy. Daniel, once the bruising had faded, hoped to be as un-celibate as possible.

He got back on the road, heading north-east.

The traffic thinned the further he went. He stopped once more, in Norwich, grabbing a sandwich and eating it standing by his bike. By the time he set out on the final leg of the journey, the sun was down, the roads were twisting, and his bollocks were healing nicely.

7

A brief summer shower came and went as he reached Cromer, fat droplets sizzling on the Yamaha's exhaust. Daniel pushed up his visor. As he negotiated the cars in the town centre, he caught the first salt-tang smell of the sea. He slowed to walking speed to let a group of giggling women cross drunkenly in front of him.

Daniel left the bike on the Esplanade and walked towards the pier. There was no need to call Abos. He could see her from a few hundred yards away, staring out at the black, rumbling sea. As if aware of him, she turned and waved. He waved back and quickened his pace.

Abos met him halfway, and they walked along the cliff path, heading south-east.

"Ever heard of Black Shuck?"

Daniel shook his head, dropping his customary bodybuilder's walk to keep up with Abos.

"It's a local legend, hundreds of years old. A huge dog, with eyes like flaming coals. It appeared in churches, along roadsides, and in fields, terrorising people."

"A dog?"

Daniel had stopped walking. Abos turned and beckoned him on without slowing. Daniel broke into a jog to catch up.

"Seriously? We're here for a dog?"

"You have accepted me as both male and female."

"Yeah, true, but... human. You're human. Well, not human, but, um..."

Daniel was quick to see the flaws in his own reasoning. Finding out Abos was not confined to a single gender should have warned him off lazy reasoning.

"Any species?" he said. "You could be any species at all?"

Abos turned onto a narrow path leading down to the beach. It was fully dark now, the moon obscured by clouds.

"Yes, any species. In theory. As long as the requisite amount of genetic material is provided."

Abos's voice was faint. Daniel realised he had slowed down, and couldn't even see the path, let alone his companion.

"Shit."

Daniel stepped forward and missed the path completely. He fell about fifteen feet, landing on his side in the sand with a *wumph,* which sent half a dozen of Cromer's famous residents scuttling sideways for cover as fast as their claws could take them.

He stood up and brushed sand from his clothes. "Should have just done that in the first place. Quicker."

Abos loomed out of the darkness. "Are you all right? It's this way."

Daniel followed, the sea a constant murmur on his left.

"How much genetic material do you need?" When Abos had first taken on human form, the catalyst had been the blood from a broken nose. Which was how much, exactly? Daniel had never thought about it. Half a cup? A tablespoon? When he had brought Abos back, he had used ten millilitres of George's blood to start the process.

"I don't know. When I'm dormant, I have no awareness."

"Tell me about this dog, then - Black Shack?"

"Shuck. The first recorded sighting was in the sixteenth century when it appeared in two Suffolk churches during a storm. They thought it had come from hell. There are dozens of other sightings from every other generation, right up to the present day."

"And it's supposed to be knocking about around here somewhere? In Cromer?"

"Well, the legend confines it to East Anglia. But dogs don't live for hundreds of years."

"Even giant dogs from hell?"

Abos considered the question, falling into one of her familiar silences.

"I was being facetious," said Daniel.

"Oh. Okay."

She had come to a stop in front of a crumbling piece of land, which looked like every other crumbing piece of land. Rocky, sandy, grassed over in places. She turned back to Daniel.

"In my first body, I was over a foot taller than Roger Sullivan, the scientist whose DNA started my awakening. When I came back using Cressida's blood, I was much taller than her, which is also the case with my current form."

Daniel had only ever seen George in a wheelchair, or—after her death—in bed, but he knew she hadn't been close to six feet, unlike the woman standing beside him.

"The process that forms my bodies also improves on the original. So I searched for accounts of humans, or any other creatures, that were bigger than average. Black Shuck was just one of many possibilities."

Abos was staring at one spot on the beach. Daniel could see nothing unusual about it.

"The sightings were far more regular during one period in the late nineteenth century. During that time, a few differences to earlier accounts drew my attention. The Black Shuck they described only appeared in a small geographical area. And one detail, mentioned in five separate accounts, was the most telling of all."

Alongside an improvement in vocabulary, Abos seemed to have developed a propensity to build dramatic tension. At least, that was Daniel's thought until Abos turned away, leaving her story unfinished. He stepped forward and tapped her on the arm.

"What detail?"

Abos didn't respond. Although he was inured to her long silences, they could still be frustrating.

"You said one detail was the most telling. What was it?"

Abos brought her attention away from the rocks and back to Daniel.

"Oh. The eyes. All accounts say they glowed. But between eighteen eighty-four and eighteen ninety-seven, they didn't glow like coals. They were described as being more like lanterns, or candles, or even, in one case, stars. But they all agreed on one thing: the colour."

"Gold?"

"Gold."

With impeccable timing, a gap appeared between clouds, and moonlight illuminated the scene. Among the pebbles on the beach, Daniel noticed at least a dozen, small, perfectly round, white stones. He supposed it was some natural phenomenon.

Abos held a hand towards the rock face and, with a loud crack that sent a few dozing gulls wheeling upwards, a fissure appeared, widening quickly. It opened to a gap about two feet wide and four feet high. Inside was thick, impenetrable blackness.

"Here," said Abos, shrugging off her rucksack and placing it on the sand. Reaching inside, she took out a thick plastic sheet. Each side was dotted with metal eyelets threaded through with a cord.

"How can you be so sure?"

Abos smoothed the plastic sheet flat onto the beach. A light gust of wind threatened to lift the corners, so she weighed them down with stones.

"The Cromer Black Shuck was shot by a retired Colonel called Alfred Smythe. His account was in the local paper. He claimed he had shot the animal, and it had fallen from the cliffs. As he couldn't produce a body, he was dismissed as delusional. His insistence that the tide must have taken the body was laughed at, judging by the letters page the following week."

"You think the body didn't disappear."

"I came here yesterday afternoon. I know it didn't."

"How?"

"I could sense it when I got close. Like being tickled by a blade of grass. So soft, so easy to miss. But once I got within about half a mile, it was unmistakable."

Abos took off her jacket. She reached into the hole, stretching into the gap she had created.

"Why didn't you do this yesterday? Why now?"

"I wanted you to be here."

A movement caught his eye, and Daniel looked at Abos's arm. As he stared, a dark, headless snake crept along her skin, followed by another, then a third. The snakes stopped moving when they reached the material of her T-shirt, but others joined them, sliding over the bodies of their fellows.

Abos's arm was soon thick with a slowly moving mass of slime.

She stood up. Her arm was covered, her hand now concealed behind a shapeless, writhing mitten. All colours were rendered in the blues, greys, and blacks of night, but Daniel didn't need light to know the slime was the colour of mushy peas.

Abos place her hand on the plastic sheet and the slime moved down her flesh, becoming a pool. When her arm was completely revealed, she folded the corners of the sheet together and pulled the cord tight to form a sack.

Daniel said the first thing that came into his head.

"Wow. Much better than using a tea urn."

He followed Abos back up the cliff path, still talking.

"I mean, the urn wasn't a bad idea. It did the job, right? But this is great. Watertight, well, slime-tight, portable... I mean, you can fold it up when you're not using it. Brilliant! I should have thought of it. Lugging that tea urn halfway across London with a broken wrist. I'm babbling, aren't I?"

They were at the top of the cliffs. Now that the moon was out, Daniel could see a golf course, the nearest hole about twenty yards from the cliff edge.

He remembered the strange round white stones on the beach.

"Golf balls," he said.

Abos looked concerned. "Are they still hurting?"

It took Daniel a few seconds to work out what she was referring to.

"Actually, they feel fine." They did, too. He hadn't scratched for at least thirty minutes.

Abos put her helmet back on.

"I'll see you back at the house," she said.

Daniel did a quick mental calculation.

"I'll stay at a hotel tonight. It's a fair ride to Cornwall. Might not get back until tomorrow evening. Woah!"

He looked down at the golf course. They were hovering about a hundred feet above it.

"You're supposed to ask first."

"Sorry. I want to get it back home. Fast."

Her excitement was easy to understand. Daniel supposed that, if he were the only human being alive, finding a companion of his own species might be a pretty big moment.

"Okay," he said. "Don't forget the Yammy."

They started to drift over the town, back towards the pier.

"We'll need to make a stop, anyway," said Abos.

"A stop? Why?"

"We need blood."

8

A bos set Daniel and the bike down on top of the Shard, a striking glass tower dominating the London skyline. There was a good practical reason for this - if a man, a woman, and a motorbike needed to descend from the sky without being spotted, choosing the highest point in the city as a landing site gave them decent odds of getting away with it.

Abos dropped from the top of the Shard and headed for the Thames, landing in deep shadows under one of the city's more anonymous bridges. The streetlamp nearby had been smashed, and there were discarded syringes on the concrete. Drug pushers waited in doorways and in cars with darkened windows, while thin, tired-looking girls in short skirts and heels waited for customers.

Abos kept her helmet on and walked briskly out of the darkness, crossing the street and heading towards the lights of a nearby hospital. Someone hissed an invitation from one of the darkened cars, but didn't pursue it when she ignored them.

The hospital was as well-lit as the riverside had been

dark, and cars and ambulances kept up a steady stream of traffic at the entrance. Dockfields was a training hospital with a blood storage facility. George's contacts had provided a list of institutions across the country with blueprints showing the location of stored blood in each. Dockfields was one of the busiest.

Abos kept her helmet on, flicking up the visor to show half her face. She held her rucksack in front of her as if she were getting ready to hand it to someone. She walked into the main entrance, looked up at the signs, then turned left past the desk towards Pathology.

The nearest receptionist called after Abos.

"Hey! Can I help you?"

"Blood," said Abos without slowing, holding up the rucksack. The receptionist took in the leathers, helmet and sense of urgency projected by the tall woman, assumed she was a courier, and waved her on before returning to her call.

Because Abos struggled with deception, she had spoken the truth. She was there for blood.

The fridges were full in the Blood Issue Room, and Abos went straight to the door bearing that day's date. She took the first pack she found, then grabbed another two, hoping the next trips she made would be as successful as the search for Black Shuck. She put them in the rucksack, turned around, and saw a shocked older woman in a white coat standing in the open doorway.

"What on earth do you think you're doing?"

Abos spoke without guile.

"I need blood."

The woman went straight for the walkie-talkie on her belt.

"I need Security at the Blood Issue room now. And call the police."

There was only one door, and the woman was blocking it. Abos ran straight towards her. For a moment, it looked like she would stand her ground, but once it was clear the leather-clad female wasn't stopping, the woman flattened herself against the wall and let Abos pass.

At the end of a long corridor was a fire escape. Abos headed towards it, keeping her speed down to a human level while she knew she was being watched by cameras. She heard running steps from around the corner at the end of the corridor and knew she wouldn't make it without a confrontation.

She changed course and ducked into another corridor, which had doors leading off either side. There was no exit at the end of it.

From behind, Abos heard the woman's voice directing the security guards. "She's in Eden Wing."

Abos opened the first door she came to and stepped inside. It was a dark locker room with one window, big enough to get through but set high up in one corner.

The running footsteps stopped outside the door, and the handle turned.

Two men entered, flicking on the lights. They scanned the room, one of them staying in the doorway while the other quickly checked any open lockers. Satisfied, they withdrew and ran to the next room.

Abos watched them go, her back flat on the ceiling five feet above their heads. She floated across to the window, pulled it open and dropped down to the carpark.

Five minutes later, she was back at the river - the area where she'd landed was near a no-go zone in a rough neighbourhood, which was a perfect place to take off unobserved. Wary of running into the dealers or the pimps, she took a different route back, approaching the bridge from the north along a path covered in litter.

With perfect timing, a BMW cruised to a stop parallel to the riverside path.

The men inside wound down the darkened windows and shouted something incomprehensible. Abos didn't need to understand the slang they used to know the kind of thing they were saying. The tone was universal. She sighed and turned to face them.

Doors clicked open. Three men walked towards her. The fourth remained in the car, the engine still idling.

Abos let them approach. It was possible they wanted to help her, fearing she was lost. It was possible. Just not likely.

They split up as they got closer, the biggest—a gold tooth flashing in the starlight—grinning and murmuring constantly. Whatever he was saying caused the other two men, now closing off her other possible escape routes, to snigger. When they were within a few feet of her, they stopped. She had one on each side, and Big Boy directly in front of her.

Hooking his thumbs into his belt, Big Boy stopped smiling. He nodded at his friends. They came at her quickly, one aiming to restrain her while the other produced a knife.

Abos took a step forward as the first man reached for her. He stumbled as his hands found air where she had just been standing. Before the second man had time to react, Abos turned, grabbed them by their jacket collars and brought their heads together. Not hard enough to cause any permanent damage, but hard enough to hurt.

The man with the knife dropped face first onto the path. The other joined him, clutching at his head and moaning.

Big Boy went with his first instinct, which was to reach around to the small of his back and grasp his handgun.

By the time he'd raised the weapon, the woman had gone. The dumbstruck expression on his face was only there for as long as it took him to realise she was behind him. Abos made her location clearer by reaching into his trousers, taking hold of his underwear, and pulling upwards until the waistband reached his shoulder blades. He squealed and dropped the gun.

Abos hoisted him over her head, took a glance down-river, then threw the man over half a mile back towards the London Eye.

As she turned, she heard a distant splash.

The BMW's driver had his earbuds in. He sang along, missing the sight of the woman with the helmet sprinting fifty yards before soaring upwards and out of sight.

THE SHARD SWAYED, like a ship at anchor. Daniel wondered if a fall from this height would kill him. He was pretty sure it would. That night in Birmingham had been painful enough, and they'd only fallen about twenty storeys before landing in water. A car might break his fall, he supposed, the metal crumpling as it slowed his progress. If that happened, he might snap some bones, but he fancied he'd survive. It would bloody hurt, though.

He was so lost in speculation, that when Abos spoke quietly into his ear twelve-and-a-half minutes after leaving, he yelped in surprise.

"Can you carry this?"

Abos was holding out three gel bags full of purple-red blood. Daniel tucked them into one of the bike's panniers.

"Any problems?" he said.

"Not really."

Daniel sat on the bike and waited. Thirty seconds later, a businessman stumbling back to his hotel after a wallet-draining evening in Soho stood in front of a poster featuring the unlikely automotive flying star of Chitty Chitty Bang Bang. The poster exhorted families to come and see the impossible become real. The man, remembering how much he loved the film as a child, tried to make a drunken note in his phone to take his family as, three hundred metres above him, a woman flew south, accompanied by a halfhero on a motorcycle.

Daniel's phone rang. He pressed a button on the bike's handlebars.

"Hi, Saffi," he said. "You realise you're the only person who ever calls?"

Her voice was husky, with an accent Daniel had never placed. Saffi sounded amused.

"I hear there are apps for this kind of thing, no? You can find yourself a nice girlfriend. Anyway, you lie. I know Sara calls you sometimes."

"She's my half-sister. I only have eyes for you, Saff. You know that."

She laughed dutifully. It was a sexy laugh. As he had never seen her, Daniel imagined Saffi to be tall, brown-eyed, and drop-dead gorgeous. Nothing else could match that voice. UN protocols and a secret iron-clad international agreement between the countries funding Saffi's activities meant the two of them were unlikely to meet. Daniel had just enough nerve to flirt under those circumstances.

"Perhaps you can buy me dinner one day. In the mean-time, could IGLU borrow you this weekend?"

"What do you have in mind, Saff?"

"I'm afraid it's one of yours again."

Another halfhero gone bad.

"Oh. Shit. At least tell me it's somewhere warm this time. Exotic. Five-star hotels?"

"Newcastle."

"Oh. Glamorous, Saffi. Cheers."

"My pleasure, Daniel. It's your turf. I'll send you the details. Gabe and Sara will be there tomorrow."

Daniel estimated it would take him at least three-and-a-half hours to get to Newcastle, even with light traffic and the bike's speed. He could get some sleep till lunchtime, read through the briefing, and be prepared by the time the others arrived.

"I hope you're serious about that dinner." He knew Saffi was smiling on the other end of the line.

"Completely."

"I'd be upset if you were just pulling my chain."

"Oh. Is this some sort of sexual reference, Daniel?"

He felt himself reddening and started babbling.

"No - no! It's a, you know, an expression, it's like, are you stringing me along, are you pulling my—no, that's worse. It's just a turn of phrase, you see, it doesn't mean...hang on."

Saffi was giggling.

"You bloody wind-up merchant."

"I've sent the link. Shall we debrief afterwards?" She delivered the line without a hint of flirtatiousness but left a long pause.

Now it was Daniel's turn to laugh. "You're outrageous."

"I don't know what you mean."

She rang off before he could respond. Daniel turned to Abos, grinning.

"Change of plan. Can you drop me near a motorway?" Then, quickly, remembering the way Abos struggled with colloquialisms, "But don't, you know, literally drop me. Just set me down, Gently. Please."

9

Abos reached Cornwall before dawn, taking the blood samples and going straight to the lab. She flicked a switch by the door and the two long fluorescent tubes fizzed into life. The lab didn't live up to its name. There were no gleaming aluminium surfaces, no rows of test tubes, no bands of computer monitors. Nothing beeped. Originally an animal feed store, the smell of straw and grain still rose from the rough stone floor. The walls were unpainted. Low wooden beams studded with iron nails crossed the space, a radio dangling from one of them.

Two gleaming bathtubs and two very large tables dominated the centre of the lab. Abos opened the door of the large fridge in the corner, placing the blood packs inside. From the other shelves, she removed handfuls of fresh fruit and vegetables, taking them over to the nearest bath and, after putting the plug in place, dropped the food inside. After a few trips back and forth, the tub was half-full. She eased the tied plastic sheeting from her back and poured in its contents before fetching a pack of blood from the fridge.

Abos poured the blood on top of the slime and food,

then reached behind her and turned on the radio. It was tuned to the BBC World Service. Abos had learned the English language in Station's laboratory while growing her first human body. She must have achieved it by being aware of the surrounding conversations. Her future brother, or sister would have the radio on twenty-four hours a day.

ABOS DIDN'T SLEEP. She spread out her pages of research and fired up Daniel's laptop, bringing up tabs full of websites she had been studying for months. Twice, she checked on the bath in the lab.

Early afternoon, her phone rang.

"Hello Daniel."

"Hi Abos. Great all-day breakfasts here. I've had three plates of egg, bacon, and potatoes. Tell me you've eaten."

"Not yet. I may have some cereal."

"It's just not fair," said Daniel. "I mean, not only are you stronger than me, but you can fly and move stuff around with your mind, like Yoda on steroids. And you do all that on two pieces of toast and a glass of orange juice? How is that right? If I don't shove food down my face every few hours, I pass out."

The fact that Abos could not explain her abilities, was frustrating, but not surprising. Daniel had a liver that carried out over five hundred roles within his body, but he could no more have explained how it did it than he could have recited all of Hamlet.

Abos put the phone on speaker and washed up the dishes from a takeaway two nights earlier. She enjoyed doing domestic tasks. The setup in the farmhouse with Daniel had soon begun to feel normal. After the first few weeks, they'd stopped treating each other like mysterious, exotic creatures and had relaxed. As the months had gone by, the initial strangeness had worn off, replaced by undramatic happiness, which seeped into their consciousness unnoticed.

"There's an update from Palindrome," said Daniel from the phone on the windowsill.

Palindrome was one of George's contacts, a hacker who treasured his or her anonymity. Anna, or Ada. Otto, perhaps. Daniel had an email address and a phone number for Palindrome which always went straight to voicemail. The voicemail message was female, so they both referred to her as a woman.

"She says there's only one loose end from Hopkins and Station, but it's—in her words—a doozy."

"Doozy?"

"Something big. She's traced financial transactions from the turn of the century amounting to a few million pounds. But it's all hidden behind shell companies and red herrings."

Abos frowned, not sure she understood the expression. Daniel, as if he could see her, explained more straightforwardly. "Hopkins, or Station, was paying someone a lot of money in nineteen-ninety-nine and two-thousand, but he did everything he could to make sure no one knew who, or why."

"So you cannot find out what he was doing?"

"Palindrome thinks she can. But this was back before the internet had its fingers in everything. She says many of the records are on paper, and it will involve old-fashioned legwork. It'll take time and money. She wants a hundred thousand for the job. I think we should go ahead. It's Hopkins' last surprise. We're done with him forever once we find out what he was spending money on. It was a long time ago, it's very unlikely it can affect us now. But I want to be sure. Agreed?"

"Yes, Daniel. Let's be sure."

"Okay. Good. What's your plan for the next few weeks?"

"I have two strong leads to pursue. One in Russia, the other in Egypt."

"What about Boudicca? She still a candidate?"

"Yes. There are enough independent descriptions of her physical prowess, including one where a large tree uprooted itself and fell on her enemies. I have a historian in Cambridge working on it for me. It's proven difficult to find evidence of her burial place, but she's narrowed it down to three likely sites."

"And how's our guest? Everything go okay?"

Abos looked out towards the outbuilding where another member of her species—the *only* other member, as far as she knew—was undergoing the changes necessary to become a living, breathing person.

"Yes. The process is underway."

"Great. I should be back on Monday. I'll call if that changes. See you soon."

Since Abos had stepped out of that bath in the cottage in her new body, she and Daniel had spent many hours discussing who, and what, she was. An alien? A man-made experimental being? Even a spontaneous evolutionary leap by some subterranean species? Nothing seemed to fit, but Abos was clear on one point: it was unlikely she was unique. Surely somewhere out there, there were others like her. But where was the evidence? Where were the historical documents describing beings with superhuman power?

For a while, Abos had concluded that she was exploring a dead end. It had been a casual remark from Daniel that had changed everything.

~

"WHAT ABOUT GOLIATH?" Daniel had said one night, over a year ago.

"Old Testament, King David's Goliath?" Abos had taught at a primary school and her knowledge of human history was better than Daniel's, which he couldn't help but find somewhat galling. Her ability to retain learned knowledge from her previous existences gave her an unfair advantage. She would have been great in a pub quiz.

"That's the bloke, yeah," said Daniel. "He was a giant, right? He might have been one of your mob."

A quick internet search had revealed that Goliath's height was put at somewhere between six foot nine inches and nine feet.

"Even at six-nine, he was a big bastard. Everyone was smaller then, weren't they? He might be another Abos, Abos."

A brief flurry of excitement had faded when Abos had reminded Daniel that Goliath's severed head had been presented to King Saul.

"I don't know what would happen if my body was incomplete when I returned to my dormant state," she said. "It seems unlikely that, if enough of my corpse were missing, I'd be able to grow a new body. I don't know."

"Kind of hard to test. Want me to fetch an axe?"

"Joke?"

"Joke."

Deadpan humour was usually wasted on Abos. She had raised another problem with Goliath. "There's no mention of the head becoming slime, so either Goliath was human, or severing the head and removing the blood flow to the brain prevents my kind from returning to the dormant state."

"Yeah, well, never mind," he said. "It was just a thought."

Daniel had forgotten about it the next morning when he came downstairs to find Abos sitting at the computer, writing in a notepad. The table was full of scribbled pages, sorted into piles.

"Have you been doing that all night?"

"Yes."

"What are you looking for?"

"It was what you said about Goliath. It made me stop thinking about history, and start looking at stories, myths, and legends. If a being with unexplainable powers appeared now, it would be reported by social media in minutes. But go back a few generations, and you didn't even have cameras. More generations still, and the printed word was a novelty. Historians piece together a version of the truth from the stories they uncover. But the stories describing inexplicable supernatural events are labelled myths or folklore and are not included in the history books."

"So some myths and legends might not be myths and legends at all? They're reports of other Aboses?" Daniel frowned. "If you're right, we're going to need a better name. Aboses is a bloody mouthful."

Abos indicated the piles of notes.

"Each of these describes a legend featuring a creature that was larger than average. I filtered likely candidates by focussing on those who with some kind of power. Strength, speed, flight, any mental manipulation of matter."

"There's a name for that," said Daniel. "Telly Savalas or something."

"Telekinesis. I have found candidates from the past few

hundred years. I will start with them as the geographical locations are easier to pinpoint in more recent accounts."

"Great. How long before you find one?"

"I don't know. A few weeks, I hope."

That had been nearly thirteen months ago.

Now, the research had paid off. There was another Abos beginning its transformation in a cheap bath in the shed outside.

10

Newcastle

12:40 am

Daniel raised the night-vision binoculars and swore. These were his least favourite jobs. The man the IGLU team had targeted was, on one level, just another petty criminal and drug dealer who was expanding his patch. The problem was, this dealer was a halfhero.

"Half-twat," he muttered. Saffi had warned him it was 'one of yours,' but that didn't make it any less depressing. Every child of The Deterrent was a member of Daniel's extended family.

"You're an embarrassment, bro."

As there were so few halfheroes out there, Daniel took every bad apple personally. Since joining IGLU, he, Sara, and Gabe had broken up the criminal operations of four rogue halfheroes, alongside their regular missions. A new prison with enhanced security measures had been secretly built near Gravesend, holding those four halfheroes, and no one else. Two were British, one Spanish, the other American. All were multiple murderers. Daniel hoped the prison would welcome another inmate shortly.

The man in question was drinking with some of his cronies. Dave Davie Davison—or TripleDee as he insisted on being called—was celebrating adding another housing estate to his portfolio of weed, crack and crystal meth clients. According to the online file, he'd achieved this by breaking the arms of every other dealer on the turf. When retribution arrived, Davison had put himself front and centre in the fire-fight. The bullets had bounced off him, and he'd only lost three members of his crew, which he'd considered an acceptable price to pay.

Daniel tried to find some sympathy for his half-sibling. Davison had grown up in a rough area, with, according to the file, an alcoholic mother and—of course—an absent father.

"You and me both, pal," said Daniel, as he tucked the binoculars into his rucksack. "No excuse for being a scumbag. Even if your mother named you Dave Davie Davison. And Triple Dee just makes you sound like a giant tit."

He could hear the men's voices carrying across the street as he walked away. He grunted.

"See you tomorrow, boys."

DANIEL DECIDED a nightcap at the hotel bar wouldn't hurt. There was something about hotel rooms he found unnerving. The carefully made beds, the hard-wearing carpets, the desk and lamp, the television. The colours. In mid-price hotels, which were IGLU's preferred choice, he would wake up, flick on the light, and have no idea which continent he was in.

Anything uniform, or institutional, reminded him of Station. Hotels, hospitals, offices, they all gave Daniel the creeps. At least, that was the excuse for the state of his bedroom at home.

Home, he thought. *That's the first time I've thought of the farmhouse as home.*

He was still smiling when he rounded the corner of the bar.

"What you smiling at, Harbin? You get lucky or something?"

Daniel looked up to see Sara and Gabe at the far end of the bar, with four ludicrous-looking cocktails, all pink umbrellas and twisted straws, lined up in front of them. Daniel, still smiling, hugged them both, then put his hand on Gabe's head. He towered above the other man. He took a look at Gabe's neck. There was a tiny mark where Cole's bullet had hit him. It looked like he'd cut himself shaving.

"Luck is not necessary when you're a looker, like me," he said, winking at Sara over Gabe's bald skull. "It must be terrible to have to shave your head so no one knows you're ginger."

"Oh," said Gabe, "oh...I'm hurt. Or was that supposed to be funny? You're gonna have to use a codeword or something when you're trying to crack a joke, Harbin. So we know when to laugh. How about *lame-ass*?"

"I think you'll find that's lame-*arse*. How about short-arse instead?"

"Lay off it, love-birds," said Sara. She blew them a kiss, and the half-dozen businessmen who had been studiously pretending not to check her out felt their mouths go dry.

Sara pointed to the cocktails.

"It's happy hour. Two for one."

"Half a lager, please."

"Pussy," said Gabe.

When the beer arrived, Sara dropped a pink umbrella into it and raised her own glass.

"Here's to taking another scumbag off the streets tomorrow morning. Salut!"

11

_____

Yusupov Palace,
St Petersburg, Russia

Abos waited for a few minutes outside the yellow-painted palace on the bank of the Moika river until a party of French tourists arrived. They bustled up the steps, overheating in their fur hats, far too hot for the time of year. She tagged onto the back of the group, following them through the polished, carved wooden door. As she'd hoped, once inside, the staff assumed she was with their party, even addressing her in broken French.

The interior of Yusupov Palace was breathtaking, and Abos stood in the main lobby gazing up at the massive chandelier. The red-carpeted staircase was wide enough to take a coach party, even if they were still in the coach.

Abos found a young woman selling audio guides.

"Rasputin?"

The young woman led her back to the main desk, and a few more hundred roubles bought her a different coloured ticket, a pointed finger downstairs and the words, "La, madame."

She didn't need the audio guide because she had re-read her research notes before leaving that morning. The life and death of Grigori Rasputin, despite taking place only a century ago, still inspired pages and pages of commentary. It was difficult to separate fact, speculation, and plain fiction. The notorious Siberian mystic had undoubtedly existed, gaining the trust of Tsar Nicholas II, and the enmity of many of the Tsar's advisers. Photographs of the charismatic monk showed a long-haired, bearded figure in a simple robe, with a disturbing Charles Manson-gleam in his eyes, and a set of teeth that would keep an orthodontist busy for a decade. The teeth and his unwashed animal stench seemed not to deter the thousands of women he seduced.

When Abos had read about Rasputin's seduction technique (he attempted to undress every woman he met, surprisingly few of whom tried to stop him), she shuddered with the recollection of her own behaviour as The Deterrent. The fact that she had been manipulated chemically and psychologically were mitigating factors, but she still saw the shadow of her own shame in the predatory sexual behaviour of others. Rasputin had risen in status and power in the Russia of the Romanovs, and he had abused that power, taking sexual advantage of others. Abos, born as a man once, and a woman twice, while belonging to neither gender, had a unique perspective. She had long ago concluded that whatever did, or didn't, dangle between your legs gave you no licence or excuse to act like evolution had passed you by.

She reached the basement room where Rasputin was reputed to have died. Waxwork figures of the monk and Prince Yusupov—one of the conspirators—dominated the tableau. Rasputin was seated at one end of a table laden with food and wine while Yusupov stood staring at him. Well, not quite. When Abos followed the sightline of the figure, she found his attention was focussed on a pepper pot. It diminished the drama somewhat, as it looked like Yusupov had been driven into a murderous fury by a condiment.

Abos allowed her mind to drift out of focus, like someone trying to see the 3D image in a magic eye picture. There were parts of her internal landscape that were unreachable, half-glimpsed vistas and edifices that loomed in the distance before vanishing again. This method she was exploring of untethering her mind brought her within touching distance of those hidden parts of her consciousness.

She closed her eyes.

Nothing. Nothing at all, for a while. Perhaps Rasputin had been human after all.

The anecdotal evidence suggested otherwise. After consuming enough poisoned wine to kill four men, Rasputin had reportedly asked for another bottle. Yusupov had shot him in the back, twice. When he'd survived that, Yusupov and his fellow conspirators rolled him in a carpet and threw him into the river.

Abos felt the feather-like touch she had been waiting for. It was as if a starving woman had just caught the smell of fresh bread from a hot oven half a mile away. It was faint, but it was there. Not in the building, but nearby.

She felt fingers tightening on her forearm. Disoriented, she took a half-step back in surprise, her mind snapping away from its interior landscape and re-engaging with the world outside.

A small, wrinkled woman was saying something in

halting French with a strong Russian accent. Abos smiled down at her, confused. The woman was tiny. She looked as if you'd need to open at least three other wrinkled old women before you got to her.

"Madame," the woman repeated. "Votre amies. Ils sont departée."

"My friends have gone? Oh. Yes. Thank you, merci."

The old woman still had her fingers locked on Abos's arm. It took a hundred-rouble note to loosen them.

The sensation had gone—for now—but Abos had been sure of the direction. She hurried out of the palace and, keeping the river on her left, followed it for nearly a mile to a spot about a hundred yards short of the Krasniy Most - the Red Bridge. She slowed her pace, letting her mind drift again.

This time, the sensation was there immediately, stronger. She stopped walking and looked out into the brown water of the Moika.

There.

ABOS RETURNED after dark and found the same spot. A quick scan of the quiet street revealed no security cameras. She took out her contact lenses and removed her clothes.

Abos slipped into the cold water at the edge before diving, letting her mind guide her to the right spot. She found a place where the sensation was at its strongest, then broke for the surface, taking several long, deep breaths. When she dived again, she built up speed as she descended, her legs blurring, hands clenched above her head.

She ploughed through a century of weeds, silt, and assorted detritus as if it wasn't there. When the sensation she was looking for was as clear as if a heavy curtain separating them had been drawn aside, she stopped and waited.

As the seconds went by, her held breath beginning to burn her lungs, she wondered if she could have been mistaken. But then, suddenly, there it was: a sliding of muscle-like slime, purposeful, covering her fists and moving onto her arms, settling there.

She swam upwards, broke the surface of the Moika and took a few quick breaths, her heart beating like a drum'n'bass track.

Sirens, not an uncommon sound in St Petersburg in the early hours, were getting louder. She glanced to the northeast as two police cars crossed the Red Bridge.

Abos scrambled up the bank and retrieved her clothes, bundling them up and holding them close to her chest, the slime now covering her upper arm. Hearing a shout as one of the police cars came closer, she abandoned all hope of a subtle exit and shot into the air, climbed above the clouds, and headed back to Britain.

12

There's a school of thought, made popular by the police raids shown on rolling news stations, TV shows and movies that pre-dawn—raids are the best way to catch criminals unawares.

The argument has flaws. The main one is the assumption that the person on the receiving end of these raids will be blissfully asleep and completely unprepared for a police visit. Along with the rest of us, career criminals have heard that five am is considered to be a good time to shove a battering ram through a door, run in carrying truncheons, tasers, or even guns, then stamp about, shouting and being unpleasant. Which is why these criminals, if they are planning to be asleep at five am, make sure that they have a bunch of highly motivated henchpeople who are very much awake. Dogs, too.

The latest innovative alarm systems with infra-red triggers and concealed night-vision cameras are snapped up by thieves, drug-dealers, assassins, and extortioners. Secret rooms and hidden exits are also popular.

No. The best time to catch a criminal is in broad

daylight, when they've had a good breakfast, seen the kids off to school, and are dealing with the mid-morning dip by brewing coffee and cracking open the custard creams.

That was what TripleDee was doing when Daniel, Sara, and Gabe took care of the two men at his gates, tying them up and dragging them into the bushes.

His coffee cup was halfway to his lips when the alarm sounded. He flicked a switch on the TV remote, and the screen in the corner of the kitchen changed from a game show to a view of his wrought-iron gates. Which weren't there. There was a gap twelve feet wide instead. It looked like they'd been ripped off the walls and thrown away. Which was exactly what had happened.

The triggering of the alarm sealed the house. The front door could withstand a standard police battering ram for at least twenty minutes, but, now he'd seen what had happened to his gates, TripleDee headed straight for the secret passage in the basement. He lied to his girlfriend about the identity of his visitors. No point scaring her.

"Hinny, coppers are here."

A female voice came from the floor above.

"Oh, shite."

"Dinna worry, pet. I'll give 'em the runaround. Just stay hyem and stall 'em. Plead ignorance, you're good at that."

"Fuck you, Triple."

He laughed. "Mind, they're plain-clothes. Just keep the busies busy, pet."

The door swung shut behind him with a solid clunk as he hurried down the steps to the basement.

Five seconds later, there was a knock at the front door. After a short pause, there was another knock—louder this time—and a male voice.

"Open up."

Tammy, the longest suffering of TripleDee's many mistresses, shuffled down the stairs, belting up a silk robe as she did so.

"Hold up, there," she said, "I'm on me way."

She made a big performance of sliding back four bolts and a chain before opening the door and admitting three people. The woman looked like a supermodel, the little one looked like that bloke off the Crystal Maze, and the other one was huge. Even bigger than TripleDee.

She smiled at that one.

"If you're looking for ma gadgie, he's not here. He'll be back later. How about a brew while we wait, eh?"

She put a hand on the massive one's arm and smiled at him encouragingly. Then the supermodel looked at her, Tammy's mouth opened of its own accord and she heard herself say,

"He's down there. There's a tunnel." She looked at her hand. It was pointing at the door leading to the basement.

"How did you make me do that, you witch?"

Daniel kicked the door off its hinges. It flew ten feet forwards and ended up at the bottom of the stairs. The three of them followed it.

Tammy, her wits restored, shouted after them.

"It's only wor netty down there, ye daft bastards. I was kidding about the tunnel."

She stared after them, wondering what the hell had just happened.

GABE WAS LOOKING PUZZLED as they followed the tunnel.

"Which country was that woman upstairs from? What's a netty? I couldn't place the accent."

"I think it was Wightish," said Sara, with a straight face. "You know, from the Isle of Wight."

Daniel chuckled at Gabe's confusion as they jogged down the tunnel. It was lit by bare lightbulbs, hanging above them.

"They have their own language there? Man, what the hell's wrong with just having the one language, like we do in America."

"What, Spanish?" called Daniel over his shoulder. "Or Chinese?"

"Funny guy!"

"Or do you mean English?" said Sara. "Because, like Chinese and Spanish, English isn't your native language. The clue's in the name."

"Like I keep telling you, we improved it."

"Example?"

"Right...yep, okay. Sidewalk."

Daniel had stopped in front of another door, at the end of the tunnel. This one was massive, iron, flush to the wall and had no handle. It could only be opened from the other side. A small buzzer and a grille showed the preferred method of requesting entrance.

"Sidewalk?" Sara looked incredulous. "Where's the poetry? To avoid being run over and squashed on a road, we walk on the side. Side...walk."

"Better than pavement. What does that even mean? I get *pave,* that makes sense. But *ment?* What the hell? To avoid getting squashed, we ment on the pave? Oh, now I say it like that, I see the beautiful poetry to which you refer."

Gabe pointed at Daniel.

"You gonna press that buzzer?"

"I don't think so. Ready?"

They nodded. Sara stepped up.

"Don't I get a turn?"

She stared at the door. Her face didn't change, there was no obvious moment when she released the energy she had gathered, but the door buckled inwards, masonry crumbling on either side. It held. Just barely, but it held.

Sara smiled.

"I think we may have lost the element of surprise."

Gabe smiled back at her.

"Maybe we should make up for it with extra violence."

"Sounds like a plan."

Daniel raised a foot and leaned back, ready to deliver a kick that had once sent a parked transit van, loaded with carpets, over a road and into a field. Its owner had parked it in a disabled spot while he went to get his lottery ticket. That kind of thing really wound Daniel up.

Just before he unleashed the kick, a small creaking sound came from the door. All three of them watched as it fell backwards and landed in the room beyond with an echoing crash and a large cloud of dust.

Daniel shrugged, stepping onto the door and into the room. The others followed.

It was a basement not unlike the one they had just left. They had only travelled about a quarter of a mile. As they climbed the stairs back up to ground level, and he put his hand on the door handle, Daniel surmised they would emerge into a house very much like the one at the far end of the tunnel.

He was wrong.

He pushed the handle down. The unlocked door swung open. That was the first surprise.

The second was the fact that the ground floor of the house the three of them stepped into had been altered. All the interior rooms had been knocked through into one large space. Concrete floor, bare walls. Heavy nets at the windows to keep up the appearance of a family home from the outside. The space looked like it was used for storage. There were lighter patches on the floor where pallets or boxes must have stood. It was probably where the drugs were kept. More discreet than the traditional warehouse in the docks, he supposed. The nets meant they were in semi-darkness.

The third surprise was the number of people in the room. Daniel looked from left to right. Besides TripleDee, there were six men, and two women, vague shapes in the gloom. All looking relaxed, confident, and grim. All spoiling for a fight.

TripleDee stepped forward. He was a big man, only just short of Daniel's six feet, four inches. His shaved head was tattooed with some kind of Celtic script. Daniel hoped the tattooist had written something that translated as twat.

"Daniel," he said, nodding as he spoke. "Gabe. Sara - shit, they never mentioned your looks. Seems a shame just to beat the crap out of you."

Daniel caught Sara's glance at him. How the hell did this guy know their names?

One of the other men spoke from behind him. Another big guy, bearded and grinning. Some people who deal drugs can't resist sampling the product. This beefcake looked to be one of them.

"Well, what's the rush?"

"The man said one o'clock, ya gobshite. You know what traffic's like at lunchtime."

One of the women joined in.

"Yeah, and there are roadworks on the A167. Bloody nightmare."

Gabe felt they had lost the upper hand.

"Can we just punch them already?"

TripleDee laughed.

"Do your worst, ya tiny bag of shite."

TripleDee cracked his knuckles and ostentatiously rolled his shoulders as if warming up.

"But before ya get all cocky like, ask yourself this: what do ya know about any of us?"

Daniel got a bad feeling.

"Ah mean, man, you were happy with your odds, right? Three against one? Overkill, normally, but since I'm like you, you canna rely on taking me down one on one. Ah'm a halfhero, you know, I'll put up a fight. But, man, did you think you're the only ones who ever thought of teaming up?"

Sara, Gabe, and Daniel looked at each other.

"Nah," said Sara. "I've read your file, Davey. You were near the back of the queue when brains were being dished out, and I think you tripped and spilt most of yours. Someone else organised this little reception party."

"Enough talking," said Davey and stepped forward, fists raised.

Sara and Gabe were trained fighters. Daniel knew he didn't have to worry about them. He was the amateur, the one with the fewest fancy moves. His sheer size, power, and tenacity made up for it. He was the only person ever to have faced, and defeated, two hybrids. He had needed a little help in Birmingham with Spot, but that was only because they had been on the clock. He had a reservoir of rage to draw upon. He only had to remember the fourteen years of his life that were taken from him by Hopkins and Station.

Daniel thought of that as he ran to meet TripleDee. As two more figures in his peripheral vision moved towards him, he was very glad he'd had three full English breakfasts that morning.

TripleDee was making a mistake. He was leading with a

haymaker, a blow which would be devastating if it landed. Against anyone who could fight, a haymaker was a bad choice. It was too well signposted. But TripleDee was fast. Faster than any human, anyway. And an adversary with human reactions could never avoid the bone-shattering disaster heading his way.

But Daniel Harbin was only half-human.

As his opponent's arm whipped towards the side of his head, Daniel dropped to his knees and delivered an uppercut directly between the man's legs. The haymaker passed harmlessly overhead, and TripleDee made a strange wheezing sound. Daniel grabbed a fistful of crotch and, still kneeling, swung the man in a circle as the other assailants— one male, one female—approached. They were both knocked off their feet.

Daniel slammed the drug dealer onto the concrete floor, stood up, still holding the semi-conscious man by his crotch, and ran forwards until skull met wall. TripleDee slumped, unconscious. He wouldn't be getting up for a minute.

The man and woman were back on their feet, more wary now. Daniel turned to face them.

On the far side of the room, Gabe was inflicting pain. He was strong, tough, like all halfheroes, but his forte was his speed. Not just the pace at which he could cover ground, but the speed of his reflexes. He could react to a blow that had already landed, moving his head away so fast that the impact had no more effect than someone kissing him. He was almost impossible to put down.

Gabe was dancing between three adversaries. Their blows were coming at him in a blur of speed, but he was avoiding them, parrying and coming back with shots of his own. Gabe wasn't much stronger than a human, but his knowledge of pressure points compensated for this disadvantage. As kicks and punches came his way, he found a gap in the onslaught and jabbed his fingers into a spot less than half an inch in diameter, just under the chin of the nearest man. The result was unconsciousness and paralysis. The man fell backwards. He would wake up within thirty seconds to a minute, but the paralysis could last up to fifteen minutes.

Gabe realised he had dispatched the weaker of the three. The two remaining opponents were fast. Maybe as fast as he was. He was being driven backwards by the ferocity of their attack.

As he blocked them, something unprecedented happened. Gabe inexplicably decided to drop his guard.

It was only for a split second, but it was long enough for four or five blows to land, and Gabe fell. He rolled and got back to his feet, but he was shaken. Someone had planted an idea in his head.

The man smirked.

"Asshole," said Gabe, wiping blood from his mouth.

Sara had worked out what was going on within the first five seconds of the fight. She saw three distinct groups form amongst their opponents, each heading for one of the IGLU halfheroes. The ambush was well planned. There was more at play here than a small fry drug dealer flexing his muscles. She could see the speed of Gabe's opponents, and the strength of Daniel's. She had no doubt that everyone had been briefed about what they were about to face.

Which meant she would need to be careful.

Now she knew why they had cleared the space. Not only did it give them clear lines of attack, it removed objects that might be used as weapons by someone who could manipulate matter. Someone like Sara.

What she was hoping they *didn't* know, was the technique she had taught herself after meeting Daniel. The one she's used that night in Birmingham. One long afternoon, Daniel had told them about Station, about the years when he was drugged and manipulated into killing other halfheroes. He'd described the only mission he could remember in cathartic detail. Days later, Sara had asked him to elaborate on the abilities of one particular adversary that night in Shoreditch. Daniel had described the way his assailant had manipulated the air itself, moulding it into a weapon, using it to send significant blows from some distance.

Sarah had spent months learning how to do the same. Now was another opportunity to put it into practice.

She was facing three men. She focussed.

All three were swept off their feet. Before they could get up, she hit the nearest with a blow of energy the equivalent of having a bowling ball thrown into his stomach by an enraged silverback gorilla.

The man ended up in the corner. He was still moving, rolling onto his hands and knees and coughing.

She turned to face the other two. One of them ran straight through the door to the basement. She smiled at her remaining opponent.

"Probably just remembered he'd left the gas on."

The man smiled back. Sara was about to attack when he moved—fast—and pushed her backwards. She hit the wall hard.

"Now I'm just pissed off," she said, taking a step forwards.

There was a noise and a blur of motion behind her, where, a fraction of a second before, there had been nothing.

Gabe had found himself, for the first time in his life, outmatched. They weren't as fast as him, but there were two of them, and as quickly as he tried to plant ideas in their heads, one of them was doing the same to him. He jabbed at throats that weren't there, moved the wrong way to avoid a kick. Before he knew what was happening, too many punches had landed, and he was on the floor, curling up to avoid more punishment.

Daniel, meanwhile, was trying to adjust his normal fighting style of hit hard, take punishment, and hit some more. One of his opponents was planting ideas in his head, and he was sweating trying to resist them, while simultaneously blocking the attacks coming his way. He found a tiny gap in the confusion and put a fist in someone's face, his mind clearing as the woman hit the floor hard.

"So it was *you* doing that," he said, and he turned his attention to the man. Fit and wiry, but no match for Daniel's strength. He could see Gabe was in real trouble, and Sara had just shouted in surprise. He needed to finish this guy.

Daniel punched him in his solar plexus hard enough to wind a rhino.

Only, he didn't. The punch didn't land. The guy was moving out of the way before Daniel knew what was happening. It wasn't that he was fast. Gabe was fast, faster than anyone Daniel had ever met, and he could respond to an attack with reflexes almost beyond belief. This was different.

Daniel tried again, a feint with his left this time, intended to move the man into the path of the right hook he was unleashing.

He missed. Again.

What the hell?

To his left, Sara had failed to anticipate an attack, because the attack itself was impossible. She had the wall at her back, which closed off one approach. Or should have closed it off. She was facing down her single remaining opponent, intending to nudge him into thinking he was being attacked from behind. Before she could do it, the man who had run away came back. He walked through the solid wall at her back and pinned her arms.

The man in front of her reached into his pockets and pulled out handfuls of something. From where Daniel was standing, it looked like a cloud of grey dust surrounded both his fists. Sara pulled her face to one side, but it was too late. The man's pockets were full of ball bearings. He shared her ability to manipulate the physical world around him with his mind, and—before Sara could mount a defence—he sent the tiny balls streaking towards her. They hit her legs, her midriff, her ribs, and her neck, neatly missing the arms of the man holding her.

The unmistakable sound of snapping bones was followed by a merciful descent into unconsciousness, and Sara slumped.

Daniel screamed with rage and redoubled his efforts, tiring quickly as every blow missed its mark. He failed to notice TripleDee get to his feet behind him, or Gabe's opponents leave his crumpled body and turn their attention to Daniel.

As his energy ebbed to a dangerously low level, TripleDee pushed him, hard.

Daniel's view of the room tilted as he fell. He tried to get up, but three of them sat on his chest and legs.

TripleDee was gesturing to someone, asking them to bring something. Daniel struggled, but something was pushed over his nose and mouth.

"Yep, Ray is a complete bastard to fight, isn't he?"

TripleDee's voice seemed to come from further and

further away. Daniel felt as if he were being pulled along a tunnel, the light dimming.

"He can see into the future. Only a few seconds, so don't ask him for the lottery numbers. Canny in a scrap though."

Panic and despair were replaced by nothingness as Daniel finally slumped. He didn't hear TripleDee's final words.

"Champion. Tough fuckers, mind. Let's get masks on the other two and toss them in the van. They're about to make us all rich."

13

The guide was waiting at the agreed place, north of Saqqarah, just outside Cairo. A few pyramids could be found nearby. The area didn't quite have the same appeal for visitors as the Great Pyramid and Sphinx at Giza, but enough tourists added Saqqarah to their list of excursions to bring a little affluence to the neighbourhood.

Mahmoud was in the bar at the Pyramid Country Club when Abos texted him. He met her outside, in the shadows. A single woman in Egypt wandering about alone after midnight, he warned, was a terrible idea. The couple of hours spent in the bar waiting for her text had boosted his sense of chivalry. He insisted on chaperoning her. This extra service would, naturally, necessitate an extra charge.

"We have agreed your fee, and I do not need protection, thank you." Abos—or Abi, as she had introduced herself to Mahmoud—would rather he'd emailed a map, but her contact had insisted on a face-to-face meeting. Probably to get more money out of her.

"I cannot allow it." Mahmoud was adamant.

"You will allow it. The map, please. I have your money."

Abos took out an envelope stuffed with Egyptian pounds.

Mahmoud put his hand in his jacket pocket. Rather than the map, he pulled out a knife and waved it around himself.

"You need a guide. For protection. The fee will be double. I will keep the map."

"This map?"

Mahmoud's eyes widened. The map had been in his other jacket pocket. He frowned and raised the knife, only to find his hand was empty. He felt a sharp sensation in his stomach and looked down. The tip of his knife was pressing against his shirt. The woman was shaking her head.

"I do not need protection. I'm disappointed at your attitude. Goodbye."

She walked away, disappearing into the darkness.

Mahmoud said, "Abi! Wait!" and took a step forward. His trousers fell down, and he tripped into a ditch. As he stood up, he grabbed his belt. She had cut right through it. He peered into the darkness and shouted after her.

"Perhaps we go for a drink sometime?"

ABOUT FIVE MILES FURTHER NORTH-WEST, out of sight of the Djoser pyramid car park, a working quarry plied a trade it could trace back for thousands of years. Silica sand was exported all over the world for glass production, water filtration, even golf courses.

At two in the morning, the site was silent. Abos flew over it, looking for a location four hundred yards away from the south entrance. She found it within minutes; a deep shadow on the side of a rocky dune.

She alighted a few feet away but didn't let her feet touch the ground. No point leaving any physical evidence. The only person other than Daniel who knew she was here was Mahmoud, and she doubted he would tell anyone about their encounter. Why didn't he take the agreed fee? Why try to cheat her? She sometimes thought she would never understand humans.

For a moment, she wondered if she had the right spot. It looked unpromising, a cave entrance four feet high. Had Mahmoud been selling false information? For his sake, she hoped not. He would be shocked to discover she had his address.

She flew to the entrance and let her feet touch the sand so she could crouch and move into the blackness beyond.

Scorpions and beetles scurried away as she shuffled inside. After a few feet, she came up against a stone wall. Her eyesight was keener than a human's, but she still had to feel her way around the rough surface. After only a few seconds, she found what she was looking for on the left side of the wall. A narrow gap, wide enough to squeeze through. After a few, sliding sideways steps, she found she was descending. The incline became more acute, leading her deeper underground.

This was it. Bastet's tomb.

She flicked on the torch, confident now that its light couldn't be seen from outside. The path widened as it descended, and Abos was able to walk upright. It doubled back on itself three times before reaching the chamber. Abos guessed she was at least two hundred feet below the desert surface.

The chamber was a large, open room with four pillars. The pillars featured the only decorations: they were covered in carvings of cats.

At the centre, there was a stone sarcophagus, large enough to contain three people. Next to it was a stone shelf, designed to hold the huge lid when the occupant of the tomb was ready to reemerge. This was the tomb of a goddess. She was expected to come back to her people.

But Abos wasn't looking for a goddess. She hoped her studies, phone calls, emails, and bribes over the last year may have uncovered another member of her species to join Shuck and Arthur in the lab. Well, in the third bath she'd ordered for the old outbuilding. She had named both her guests during their weeks growing new bodies. Black Shuck had become Shuck, Rasputin was Arthur. His Russian name had been Grigori, but—even if only a quarter of the rumours about him were half-true—she thought a clean break from the past was in order. And Arthur had been the main character's name in one of her favourite books.

What did one call a cat goddess? Bastet was unusual and sounded too much like an insult. She'd have to think about it.

Abos put her hand on top of the huge slab. The whole sarcophagus was plain, but its sheer size made it impressive. She wondered how an ancient civilisation could accomplish such feats of engineering. Daniel had bought a wardrobe just after they'd moved into the farm, and after three days, the doors had fallen off.

Bastet had drawn Abos's attention because of an unusual change in the way she was portrayed. For decades, she had been depicted as a warrior goddess of the sun, with a human body and the head of a lioness. Over the course of a few years, the pictures had changed to that of an enormous cat, worshipped so avidly that cats, even now, were treated with guarded respect. In ancient Egypt, cats were often mummified along with their rich owners. When the temple of Bastet was discovered under the streets of Alexandria, six hundred stone felines were found standing guard over the mummified bodies of three hundred thousand cats.

The evidence suggested a real being at the heart of the myth.

Abos shut her eyes. When she had found the tomb, flying above it, there had been no telltale sensation of proximity. She wondered if it was due to the depth at which it was buried. But now, with her prize so close, she still felt nothing. Was it possible that a certain type of stone blunted her perceptions?

Abos put both hands on the side of the sarcophagus. She hesitated. Something wasn't right. She put her hands on her hips, took a step back and looked more closely at the shelf next to the tomb. There were scratches that lined up with the lid of the sarcophagus. And something else was strange. The dust. Or rather, the absence of dust.

She came round to the opposite side and placed both hands on the lid. She pushed, gradually adding more pressure. After some initial resistance, the massive stone slab slid smoothly away and onto the shelf beyond, the grinding rumble echoing around the walls of the tomb.

Abos looked inside.

It was empty.

MAHMOUD TURNED over in his bed, muttering. Despite the late hour, he was struggling to get to sleep. Every time he closed his eyes, he saw her. The beautiful black woman who had humiliated him. He had replayed the encounter over and over, wondering how he had been bested so easily, and so ignominiously.

Drinking at the club had been a mistake. He could rarely afford the *imported* whisky, and the promise of an excellent payday had led to over-indulgence. One drink was fine, to settle the nerves. Two was okay, but three, four, or five? Foolish. His cat-like reflexes had been compromised. It would be different if they met again. He would teach this Abi some manners.

He scratched his capacious stomach as he dozed. Perhaps he should lose a little weight? Mahmoud liked to think his bulk made him intimidating. When you are, perhaps, not as tall as you might be, a large girth provides gravitas. So he had read somewhere and did not doubt it. When his wife had moved out, she had called him fat. She had always been shallow. Many women found the larger man attractive. He had read this in an American woman's magazine at the dental surgery.

This Abi was probably one of those women. She was sexually attracted to larger men. Almost certainly.

His scratching had moved a little lower when a breeze lifted a few strands of hair from his scalp. Odd. Mahmoud always left the window open an inch, but now he could hear his curtains flapping, and the noise of the city was clear. He must have left it wide open. He was more drunk than he thought. No wonder that foreign wench had got the better of him. Well, if he ever saw her again...

Surrendering to the inevitable, Mahmoud shifted his legs over the edge of the bed, levered himself into an upright position, and lowered his feet into his waiting slippers.

Only then did he open his eyes.

"Hello, Mahmoud," said the black woman.

He threw himself backwards, slid over the satin sheets his wife had insisted on buying and fell off the bed. Scrabbling around in the semi-darkness, he found the bedside drawer and opened it, grabbing the weapon within before getting to his feet and brandishing it.

"You!" he said. "What do you mean by this? I warn you, I will not be fooled this time. You have made a big mistake."

The woman was sitting on the edge of the sofa. She looked at the frightened Mahmoud, his boxer shorts gaping, his vest riding half way up his hairy stomach. She patted the seat next to her.

"Come and sit down," she said. "I have some questions I'd like to ask you. And you should put that down."

Mahmoud stared at the vibrator in his hand with horror. He had opened the wrong drawer.

"Aaah!"

He dropped it onto the carpet.

"It isn't mine. I have never seen it before. It is my wife's. I am married. She is on holiday. You are sick, *sick*, thinking it is mine. How dare you?"

"Mahmoud?"

"What?"

"I will not hurt you. Come here. Sit on the bed if you like."

Slowly, never taking his eyes off her, Mahmoud moved to the end of the bed and sat down. He risked a glance at the open window. So that was how she got in. But he lived on the twelfth floor.

"How—?"

The woman shook her head. There was something different about her. His eyes flicked away from her face then back again. It was her eyes. They were gold.

"Now, Mahmoud, tell me, who else has been in that tomb? They must have taken specialist equipment down there to open the sarcophagus."

Mahmoud, with some difficulty, looked away from those

golden eyes and thought for a moment. The American had paid enough money to buy his wife's share of the apartment. With a bonus to guarantee his discretion. The man hadn't threatened him explicitly, but Mahmoud had been left with the clear impression that were he to speak of their business transaction, he would regret it.

He looked at the woman again. He knew how to handle a woman.

"I'm sorry," he began, "but I don't know what you're talking ab—"

His lips went dry, and his tongue flopped to the bottom of his mouth. Every piece of furniture in his apartment had risen from the floor and was floating. Looking through the double doors to the room beyond, he could see every pot and pan, plate, knife, and dish drift up to the ceiling. His table and chairs were already there. With a whimper, he scuttled backwards to the middle of the bed as it, too, rose from the floor.

Mahmoud stifled a scream. The woman's face appeared at the foot of the bed. She was flying now, her golden eyes blazing. She looked down at him, and he had an epiphany.

Her eyes, her features, her power... she is Bastet herself! The goddess!

He supplicated himself before her, muttering entreaties and prayers, assuring her he would tell her everything she wanted to know, begging her mercy for not recognising her godhood earlier, apologising for the whole vibrator thing, although that was really his wife's fault, she must have left it there.

"Mahmoud?"

"Y—, yes, Goddess?"

"Tell me who was in the tomb."

He told her everything.

14

TripleDee and his crew delivered the IGLU team to their contact at the far end of an airport carpark closed off to the public.

They arrived in a large panel van and two black Teslas. The Teslas were TripleDee's pride and joy. He was fond of pointing out that a silent car was the perfect choice for a criminal. He couldn't see what was so surprising about a drug dealer wanting to save the planet, either. If humanity screwed the ecosystem, there'd be no crack-heads to keep him in business.

The van and cars pulled up alongside what looked to be a motor home or RV, modified by a rich paranoid with no taste. It was dark grey, windowless, and as big as a council bungalow. There were a satellite dish and an array of aerials on the roof.

As the halfheroes emerged from their vehicles, a man stepped out of the front of the RV. A second man stayed behind the wheel.

The first man, dressed in a dark suit, white shirt, and no

tie, stepped forward to meet them. Average height, brown hair, a symmetrical face. Utterly forgettable.

"Mr Davison?" Even his voice was bland, with an anonymous American accent.

TripleDee, climbing carefully down from the passenger seat of the van, raised a hand.

"That'll be me. Robertson?"

The man nodded.

"Your boss here?"

Robertson shook his head, smiling.

"My employer is a busy man."

"I'm sure he is, but this is pretty bloody special."

The man shrugged. He looked at the assembled group, noting bruises and bloodied features. Some were limping.

"Did they give you any trouble?"

"Some. Nothing we couldn't handle, like."

"Hmm. Nine against three?"

"Listen, man, they are trained fighters. And that Daniel guy...it was like punching a tree. Made of iron."

"Show them to me."

TripleDee bristled at the tone of command in the man's voice, but he walked him round to the rear of the van without a word. Robertson was about to hand over more money than he'd made in the past two years, after all.

He opened the rear doors. Daniel, Gabe, and Sara were each lying on wheeled ambulance beds, with intravenous drips supplying the drugs to keep them unconscious.

Robertson climbed in, seeing broken bones and battered faces.

"You tried to kill them?"

"They're not so easy to kill. They—we—heal fast, too."

"Yeah. So I've heard. Okay, let's do business."

TripleDee smiled broadly at that and winked at the others. They all climbed the three steps to the RV door, which was already open. TripleDee gave it a look as he passed it. It was more like a door you'd find on a 747 than a motor home.

Inside, a polished boardroom table and chairs dominated the space, which was lit by LEDs flush to the ceiling. There were ten chairs, laptops open in front of nine of them.

TripleDee took a seat at the head of the table and waited. The last to file in was Ray, the least dangerous-looking of all, shabbily dressed, balding, his unkempt beard streaked with grey. But TripleDee knew not to underestimate him. A man who could see the immediate future was a great ally, but next to impossible to double-cross.

"All of us in a room together?" said Ray. "This has got to be the most halfheroes in one place ever, right?"

TripleDee glanced at Robertson, who had followed him in.

"This wouldn't be a trap, now, would it?"

Robertson chuckled without an iota of humour.

"You're the most powerful individuals in the world. How am I supposed to trap you? Howell here can walk through solid matter."

A grunt from the man in question was his only answer.

"Two of you can place ideas into my brain as if I thought of them myself. One can fly, all of you are strong, and a couple of you are pretty much bulletproof. Ray here has his own private window into the future. How's the view, Ray? You see me betraying anyone?"

Ray stood on the threshold a few seconds longer, then sat down with the others.

"Excellent. Now, if you would all enter your bank details, I will transfer the money. You can confirm the transfer online or by phone."

Robertson began to close the door. Everyone else stood up. He paused, putting both hands up, palms towards them.

"Sorry, folks, but we have to seal the environment. With the door open, electronic signals other than the ones routed through the array on the roof can still get in or out. With the door closed, we are un-hackable. Once you have confirmed the transfers, I will open the door. I'm staying in here with you. No foul play. Ray?"

Ray seemed relaxed about the idea and, knowing nothing unexpected was about to happen, the rest of them re-took their seats.

Robertson pulled a lever across the door to create a seal. Everyone typed bank details into the form on the screen. Robertson sat in the tenth chair, folded his hands on his lap, leaned backwards and closed his eyes.

For a few minutes, the tense silence was broken only by the sound of fingers tapping keyboards, accompanied by the occasional curse as the bigger specimens among them hit two, or even three, keys at once with hands more used to punching than typing.

Ray broke the silence, jerking his head up and pointing at Robertson.

"Not asleep!"

"What?" TripleDee pressed RETURN before looking up. Ray was trying to get up. He staggered a little, then sat down again, heavily.

"No," he said, "no, no..." He fell forward and was still.

TripleDee swung round to look at Robertson. The sudden movement made him dizzy. The American's hands had moved from his lap and now hung at his sides. His mouth was open, and a line of drool reflected the overhead lights.

"Shit," said TripleDee. Or, at least, that was what he tried to say. It came out as a long, "shhhhh," before his own head sagged. He was heavy, leaden, exhausted. His eyes wanted to shut, and there was nothing he could do to stop them. He was dimly aware of the others slumping to the side, or falling forwards onto the table as he watched the scene darken and become dreamlike, a smoky phantasm with no substance. Then he slept.

Three minutes later, the door hissed and opened outwards. The driver, a gas mask obscuring his features, stepped into the room and opened a sliding cupboard door inside the RV. Moving with practised speed, he removed small tanks with triangular black rubber masks. He attached the masks to the sleeping halfheroes in order of size, largest first, turning on the valve at the top of the tanks and making sure the gas was flowing before moving to the next.

Only when he was sure that everything was working as it should did the driver turn his attention to Robertson. He hooked his hands under the other man's armpits and dragged him outside, propping him against the wheel of the RV. He jumped back into the cab and flicked a switch to stop the flow of gas from the air vents in the room behind him.

Then he lit a cigarette and waited for Robertson to wake up.

15

Abos got back to Cornwall before dawn, as the sky in the east was taking on a pinkish glow.

She thought about what Mahmoud had told her. There were others of her species out there, but someone else was looking for them. How many had they found? Her mind hovered around questions she had no answers for, worrying at them, poking them, rolling them around to find a way in.

She stood still, breathing the air and watching the sky lighten.

Lately, once or twice a day, she had taken to stopping whatever she was doing and just *existing* for a moment. Her life was unusual, but her day-to-day, minute-to-minute experience of the world was surely similar to most humans. Self-awareness was as much a mystery to her as it was to humanity's greatest thinkers throughout history. Pausing now and then didn't give her any new insights, but she enjoyed it. No, *enjoyed* wasn't quite the right word. It made her feel grounded, as if she were *here*.

Her first life had been one of subservience. Manipulated

by Station, used as a figurehead for a political system she neither understood nor believed in.

Her second life, in a body grown from the blood of Cressida Lofthouse, was one of escape. Of denial. She feared falling into the hands of Station, or others with an equally ambiguous attitude to freedom and the rights of individuals. She hid her power, pretended to be what she appeared to be: a quiet, intelligent school teacher who enjoyed her privacy.

Her children had initiated the sequence of events leading to this, her third life.

George had contacted her by email. The existence of children had been a shock. That so many of them had died at puberty was horrifying. The abilities of those who had survived—in George's case, abilities that Abos did not possess—and the news that Station was now manipulating, or killing, them, was the turning point.

Abos had become angry.

Station had fallen, George had died, and Abos had used her blood to grow this, her third body. Memories threaded through each existence, but they faded. She could barely remember much from those early years. Many of the faces of the children she had taught in Wales had blurred, their names forgotten.

Her awareness of self was strong, but the nature of that *self* eluded her.

She had no history. Like a baby left on an orphanage doorstep, her origins were unknown. Unlike the baby, her species was also unknown.

As she watched the last stars disappear as the sky got lighter, she wondered if she came from another world. Perhaps the yearning she sometimes felt when she looked at the panoply of stars was something other than the awe and wonder humans experienced.

Abos remembered that she was supposed to be enjoying breathing, standing on the living earth, being alive.

Everything was beautifully uncomplicated when she surrendered to that.

This morning, she couldn't do it. With every breath, she became more aware that the next few weeks would considerably complicate her life. The man looking for members of her species may have come to the same conclusions about the provenance of certain mythical or legendary characters. And he had the money, power and connections to get in and out of Egypt, desecrate an ancient tomb, and leave with stolen material, unchallenged.

According to Mahmoud, this man was an American. He had overheard his name, but, as it was commonplace, Abos wasn't sure how much help it would be.

His name was Robertson.

TWO OF THE bathtubs now had occupants. In the first, Shuck was now fully grown. At least Abos hoped so. She and Daniel had bought the largest baths they could find, but the male body shifting, stretching limbs, and flexing newly grown muscles was close to seven feet tall. His enormous feet were dangling over the edge.

Abos spoke to him, but there was no response. She remembered reading Cressida's diary. It had taken two months for her (or, rather, him, as she was then) to become conscious after her first body had grown. Her second, and third bodies, had grown more quickly, but she didn't know how, or why. Shuck had been here for nearly six weeks. She or Daniel would have to stick around from now on. It would hardly be fair to let their guest wake up in a new body, and a new century, alone.

She took her phone out of her pocket. Daniel's bike hadn't been in the yard. It wasn't the first time he'd been late, but he'd always sent a message. Not this time. She tapped the screen, then put the phone away. He wouldn't thank her for waking him up at 6:30 am.

Rasputin—*Arthur,* she reminded herself—was also growing a body, although it was still a day or two away from being fully formed. Abos stared down at it.

"Oops," she said. "You're not an Arthur at all."

She thought for a moment before remembering the Asimov books Daniel had given her. "How would you feel about being a Susan?"

Radio 4 was playing the Today programme. As well as absorbing the language, Abos hoped her kin would begin their lives with a thorough understanding of current affairs.

An item on the news caught her attention.

"A recap of the headlines. The government is under pressure to reveal the exact nature of the Ministry of Defence facility near Gravesend, which was the scene of an explosion late last night. No one was believed to have been hurt in the incident, which took place just after midnight. Opposition parties are calling for an enquiry after rumours surfaced that the site was being used as a high-security prison. The Ministry of Justice will make a statement later today. Technology news: the world's richest man, Titus Gorman, is expected to make another of his surprise announcements later today at a..."

Abos stepped back out into the yard, closing the door behind her.

Gravesend was where the four rogue halfheroes

rounded up by Daniel and his IGLU colleagues were being held.

Where was Daniel?

CRUISING at an altitude of up to fifty-one thousand feet, the Gulfstream G650 was capable of a top speed of over eight hundred miles an hour, making it almost as fast as Abos.

A sixty-seven-million-dollar jet used by the richest individuals in the world, the Gulfstream was fitted out with large leather seats, sofas, even beds. Passengers travelled in absolute luxury, their every whim catered for by the discreet staff, arriving at their destinations refreshed and happy.

Not so the passengers who had flown on the G650's previous trip. It had made the flight from Newcastle fifteen hours earlier and, after refuelling and checks, plus a thorough valet, was now heading in the opposite direction. It wouldn't be landing in Britain this time, instead, taking its owner to a technology symposium in Geneva, where he would deliver the keynote address that evening.

The owner sipped a glass of mineral water and ate salted nuts. He would normally avoid salt, but his nutritionist had advised him to up his intake when flying long haul.

He tapped a button on his armrest.

"Sir?"

"Patch me through to Robertson at the Facility."

"Yes, sir."

He glanced around the cabin. There was no evidence at all of the twelve passengers Robertson had brought over. They had crossed the Atlantic in style but remained unaware of it. There had been no need to secure the individuals in question, as, once they were onboard, an intravenous anaesthetic drip had been inserted into each of them. They had been treated with care, the medical staff doing whatever was necessary to ensure their flight passed comfortably.

A convoy of SUVs had met them at Space Harbor before transferring the passengers to the Facility.

The Facility itself was new, purpose-built and awaiting its first guests.

"Sir, I have Robertson for you."

"Thank you."

Robertson's face appeared on the screen. He looked rested and unruffled. He must have slept on the flight. It takes a certain kind of person to fall asleep while surrounded by twelve of the most dangerous people on the planet.

"Any problems?"

He already knew the answer. He considered his vision for the future far too important to risk being derailed by unexpected obstacles. He had delayed beginning the project until every potential problem was anticipated, examined, and eliminated.

The existence of halfheroes had been the single greatest unknown, the one bug in the software that had the potential to undo all his work.

The risk they posed were too great to ignore. Action had proved necessary. Today, the final obstacle would be removed.

"No problems at all, sir. Everything went smoothly."

"Good. And are you okay? After-effects?"

Robertson smiled.

"I'm fine, sir. Felt a little groggy for a couple of hours. The medical staff gave me some pills. I slept for a while. Fit and healthy."

"I'm sorry you had to go through that."

"It was necessary, sir. I understood that. And I'm in good shape. No damage done."

"Thank you, Robertson. I won't forget what you did."

Robertson looked abashed at the compliment.

"Thank you, sir."

"Can you show me?"

"Yes, sir. All of the new arrivals?"

"No. Show me Daniel Harbin."

According to his information, Harbin was the oldest. The first halfhero to live through adolescence. But there were gaps in Harbin's personal history that even his resources couldn't uncover. A bit of a mystery, Mr Harbin. Now working for the UN's secret sideline, IGLU.

The video feed showed a huge man sleeping on a simple bed in a plain room. There were no windows. There was a desk with a tablet and a stylus on one side of the bed. On the other, there was a toilet, wash basin, and monsoon-style shower.

As prison cells went, it was well-equipped. Not a bad place to spend a night or two.

The man in the plane turned off the screen and sipped his water. He regretted the necessity of the action he had taken. Depriving someone of their liberty when they had committed no crime was unethical. But it was, by far, the lesser of two evils. His vision must be allowed to take shape without the threat the halfheroes might pose to it.

He could live with the guilt. He would have to.

The jet banked, and he pressed another button to darken the windows against the sun.

Every known halfhero alive was sleeping in individual cells inside the Facility, the most secure prison ever constructed. The new intake, which included the four thugs Robertson had collected earlier that day, would join the fourteen already captured. They were all as comfortable as he could make them without compromising security. He hoped they would adapt quickly to their new situation. They would be his guests there for—by his most conservative estimate—at least three years.

He turned and looked at the six figures sitting at the back of the plane, headphones on, eyes closed. The scientist he had met all those years ago moved between his charges, checking them as they slept.

Finally, the day had come. Ten years ago, it had been a dream.

In a few hours the world would know what he had spent the best part of a decade planning. And the world would change. For everyone. Forever.

ABOS SLEPT FOR THREE HOURS, then went downstairs to make a pot of tea and a bowl of porridge.

She called Daniel, but it went through to voicemail.

She texted him their agreed password if they needed an urgent response: *Lofthouse.*

Daniel was meant to reply with *Kuku.* He didn't.

Abos sat at the table and drank her tea. Daniel was probably fine, but he had always checked in before, let her know when he would be back.

His laptop was in his room. She brought it down to the kitchen table and opened the email program. She used the passwords Daniel had given her and opened the encrypted folder. There were two new messages. The first was from Palindrome.

· · ·

FROM: ten.palindrome@emordnilap.net
> Subject: update - it's getting interesting
> Abos ignored it and clicked on the next, from Saffi.

FROM: saffiiglu@globmail.com
> Subject: RED

Daniel, where are you? What happened? I can't reach anyone in the team. Gravesend has been compromised. Please respond as soon as you receive this.

ABOS CHECKED THE TIME. It had been sent fourteen hours ago.

Decision made, she went upstairs, changed into her leathers, grabbed her helmet and ran back to the yard. She would start looking in Newcastle. The cloud cover was almost non-existent, but if she flew, she could be there in twenty-five minutes.

She was just pushing the helmet onto her head when she heard the crash from the lab.

16

S ausages. *Roast chicken and potatoes with parsnips, carrots, and gravy. Pizza, the big ones, family size. Two of them. Fish and chips twice, no three times, with extra chips and five litres of curry sauce. King prawn madras with a chilli naan. Motor paneer, sag aloo, pilau rice.*

Hungry.

Daniel half-opened his eyes. The light was wrong. Should be coming from the window to his right. He closed his eyes again.

Freshly baked bread. Sourdough. Cut into slabs and buttered thick enough to see your teeth marks. Homemade marmalade. Sticky toffee pudding.

Groaning, he turned his head to one side and tried opening his eyes again, expecting to see the Cornish light bathing the fields outside. Instead, he saw a washbasin, mounted onto a stone wall.

Really hungry.

He closed his eyes a second time, giving his memory a chance to fill in the gaps. He had experienced the same disorientation before in hotel rooms. Sometimes, waking in the middle of the night in complete darkness, he had tried to picture the room in which he was sleeping. The position of the door, the window, the desk and chair, the bathroom. Only when he was sure he knew where everything was would he flick on the light. Half the time, his mental picture was totally wrong, and he would experience a moment's utter confusion while his brain tried to process the reality his memory had failed to provide.

Really, really *hungry.*

This was not quite the same. There was something he couldn't remember, a fuzzy, blurred sensation where his memory of where he was ought to be. It would come. He had to relax and... shit; he was so hungry. That wasn't helping. He wouldn't be able to think straight until he satisfied his craving for food. Daniel needed at least five thousand calories a day to keep his body and mind sharp and active. He needed food, now. He wasn't sure if it was time for breakfast, lunch, or dinner, and didn't care as long as he could eat immediately.

Daniel opened his eyes again and sat up, taking in his surroundings. Oh. This wasn't good. This wasn't good at all.

The room was about the size of his bedroom in Cornwall. That was all they had in common though. The lack of a window made him uncomfortable. Light came from above. The walls, floor, and ceiling were all stone, as if the room had been carved from solid rock. The bed was iron, the mattress thin but comfortable. A light duvet covered his body. The ambient temperature was on the warm side.

Daniel threw off the duvet. He was wearing white cotton trousers with a drawstring and a white T-shirt. Neither of which were clothes he owned. His body ached as if he had been in a fight. He *had* been in a fight, hadn't he? Yesterday?

The lack of bruises on his hands suggested it had been longer ago than that.

He looked at the desk. There was an A4 pad of lined yellow paper and a pencil. There was also a twelve-inch tablet. He recognised the distinctive design and the mottled white plastic casing. It was a state-of-the-art Globlet, the best-selling tablet in the world. Its boast that a minimum of forty percent of its components, and all of its casing, were constructed from recycled materials made it a desirable item among the ecologically concerned tech-savvy. Everyone else just bought it because anything with Glob branding was always the best in class.

A message was pulsing on the screen in retro green-on-black capitals: WELCOME. Daniel looked at the only door, opposite the foot of his bed. It was flush with the wall. At the bottom was a gap of about three inches. The door looked was metal; solid and heavy. There was no handle. Not on the inside, at least.

Pushing aside the urgent requests for casserole, fish pie, or steak his brain was receiving from his stomach—with only partial success—Daniel got up to investigate the door.

He stumbled and fell to his right, managing to get a hand on the toilet lid to stop him hitting the floor. After the dizziness passed, he heaved himself to his feet.

He checked around the edges of the door, running his fingers along the point where stone wall met cold metal. There was no discernible gap. Daniel pushed, but the door didn't move an inch.

Poached eggs. A dozen of them, on top of a mound of spinach, with loads of salt and black pepper.

Easing himself to the floor, he lay down on his side and looked out through the gap at the bottom of the door. The stone floor continued outside until it was interrupted by a stone wall about eight feet away. He couldn't see the ceiling, but he thought it would probably continue the all-stone theme. By moving his head as far to the right as possible, Daniel could see another door, further along the corridor, with the same three-inch gap at the bottom. He moved to the far left. Another door was visible.

Mashed potato. Piles of mashed potato with butter. And cheese. Not grated, just broken into chunks the size of a baby's fist.

He heard a click and a hiss. It came from somewhere further up the corridor to his right. The sound of footsteps and trundling rubber wheels on the stone floor. A trolley appeared, stopping at the first door.

"Hey," called Daniel. "What the hell's going on?"

No response. Daniel moved his face against the gap. He could see up to the knees of the figure standing by the trolley. Black trousers, black boots. But none of that mattered because the trolley was loaded with covered plates, and plates meant food, and food meant *trifle and waffles and pancakes and gammon and churros and spaghetti Bolognese and ribs and pan-fried sea bass.*

The figure took a plate and crouched about three feet away from the door. Daniel could see it was a man. Black T-shirt and a black baseball cap. Black seemed to be a theme. He'd already guessed he was a bad guy. It seemed like overkill to broadcast the information through his choice of clothing.

The man took the cover off the plate and picked up a broom from the side of the trolley, looking for all the world as if he was about to sweep up the plate on the floor. He moved, and Daniel saw it wasn't a broom. It was more like a snow shovel. The man—the guard, more accurately, because it was clear this wasn't a five-star resort and spa—used the shovel to push the plate through the gap in the door, a small flick of the wrist sending it on its way like a curling stone.

The guard pushed the trolley until it came to rest opposite Daniel's door. He repeated the procedure, uncovering the plate and getting the shovel. Then he stopped because Daniel's face was blocking the way.

Daniel said something he thought was only ever said in books, or on TV.

"Where am I?"

No reply. From this angle, all Daniel could see of the man were his boots. But he could see, and smell, the food. Pasta, with a tomato sauce. A sealed transparent plastic container with what looked like orange juice inside.

Daniel tried again.

"Who are you? How did I get here? What do you want? Answer me!"

The only response he got was a motion with the shovel indicating he should move out of the way. When he didn't, the man placed the cover back on the food, put it onto the trolley and walked away.

Daniel screamed after him, but he might as well have been shouting at a rock.

"I'm moving, I'm moving, okay!? Look, I'm not in the way. Bring it back. Bring me the food, please! Come on! What the hell's wrong with you? You utter nob. When I get hold of you, I'll push that shovel so far...oh, he's gone. Perfect."

During Daniel's rant, the man had delivered a plate to the next room before pushing the trolley away.

Daniel took a deep breath and tried to calm himself. It didn't work. He could feel his anger building, becoming rage. He let it happen, furious at being locked up like this. He gathered his strength, pushing aside the dizziness, ignoring the hunger. Three steps back, then he turned his shoulder to the door and charged.

Daniel hit hard, bounced backwards and fell. The dizziness was worse. He had to wait a few seconds before checking to see if he had broken through the door or just dented it. When his vision was clear again, he checked the damage. Or, rather, the lack of it.

The door was unmarked. He had hit it with everything he had, but he had made no impression on it. It was built to withstand more damage than he could inflict in his weakened state. He would have to get a significant amount of calories into his body if he wanted to break out.

How often was shovel boy going to come round with food? Daniel put his hands on his stomach and groaned. He moved his fingers under the T-shirt and felt his ribs. He had lost weight. When had he last eaten? He remembered breakfast at the hotel with Gabe and Sara. The waitress had asked him if he'd like his eggs poached, boiled, fried, or scrambled and he'd said *yes*. Yes, please, to all the above, and yes, he would be delighted to pay a supplement. Three eggs cooked in each way, please. Yes, twelve in total. The waitress had blinked a few times, then gone to the kitchen with a story to tell. Meanwhile, Daniel had eaten five croissants and loaded two plates with sausages, beans, black pudding, bacon, mushrooms, tomatoes, and hash browns.

His stomach groaned like an old man with toothache.

There was no mirror. Daniel put his fingers on his face, pushing at places where, he remembered being repeatedly punched. There was a tiny amount of tenderness. Given his rapid recovery rate, that meant at least two days, maybe three had passed. He'd been unconscious for that long?

The pain in his stomach was affecting Daniel's ability to think logically. He put all his energy into building a coherent picture of the events that had brought him here. He, Gabe, and Sara had fought rogue halfheroes in Newcastle. TripleDee and the others had been expecting the IGLU team. Tipped off, somehow. Daniel's last memory was of lying on the floor with three or four of them holding him down. After that, nothing.

I need food. I have to eat, I have to eat now.

Daniel sat on the bed and put his face in his hands. He was so weak he could barely think. He fell into a kind of trance, the pain of hunger synced with his pulse, sending waves of agonising need up to his brain.

Finally, he lifted his head. Something was flashing to his left. It was distracting. Good. Distraction was good.

He moved to the desk, pulled out the chair and sat down. He picked up the Globlet.

WELCOME

He stared at the flashing word for a few more seconds, then touched it with his forefinger. The word faded, and the screen went dark.

The video had been filmed in an office. An office that was a masterpiece of minimalism. A huge brushed-steel desk dominated the room, empty of everything but a sleek computer and a pad of yellow paper like the one next to Daniel's elbow. The walls were light green, but it was a green you rarely saw outside magazines read by interior designers. They wouldn't have called it *green*. It was sure to be *Printemps de pistachioed pot-pourri* or some such wank. There was a painting on the wall to the left of the desk. It looked as if the artist had bought a massive canvas and lined up all her tubes of paint, only to be interrupted by the doorbell. While she was away, a small child had wandered in, squirted a blob of every tube onto the blank space, smeared it about, rolled in it, thrown up in one corner, taken a shit in the middle, then left. Probably worth a million at least.

There was no carpet. The floor was polished concrete. It looked expensive. Daniel didn't know how he knew it was expensive concrete, but he was sure he was right. Anyone who owned an office that size wouldn't go for cheap flooring. The architect had probably claimed it was *concrêt,* a revolutionary new kind of surface.

Behind the desk, the floor to ceiling window opened on to a breathtaking view. It looked like a desert, but the sand was pure white, rising and falling in dunes. It was unlike anywhere Daniel had ever been. An other-worldly sight.

Then the man whose personal-trainer-toned buttocks had moulded the contours of the ten-thousand-dollar chair behind the desk stepped into shot. Daniel couldn't believe what he was seeing at first, until the man spoke, admitting he was Daniel's jailer and apologising for the rough treatment.

Daniel shook his head, wondering if starvation could produce hallucinations. He paused the video and looked at the face on the screen.

There was no mistake. He had seen that face hundreds of times, heard that voice. Daniel stared at the screen.

What the hell?

bos spoke quietly, trying to communicate the lack of threat to the terrified man crouching in the corner of the lab.

Shuck had woken up alone, opened his golden eyes to find he was lying in a strange, slippery container with little idea of where he was, who he was, or even *what* he was. He had scrabbled his way out onto the cold, hard floor. From there he had crawled into the furthest corner, which was where Abos found him.

"Shuck," she said. "Your name is Shuck. I am Abos. Can you understand me?"

The man nodded, his eyes never leaving hers.

"You must be confused. And hungry. Will you come with me? I can get you some food and drink."

She stood in the doorway, waiting. Shuck moved away from the safety of the corner. He used his hands and feet to cross the room.

"You're not a dog, now, Shuck," said Abos as he reached her. "Here, take my hand."

Shuck reached up, his fingers finding those of Abos and

gripping tightly. Slowly, shakily, he allowed himself to be helped to his feet. When he stood up fully, he was almost a foot taller than Abos. He had shoulder-length brown hair, which he brought one hand up to touch. He looked at the way Abos was standing and copied it. Then he looked at himself and back at her again, puzzled.

"And I'll get you some clothes," said Abos.

Half an hour later, Shuck was sitting at the kitchen table, his face a mask of concentration as he tried to master several new skills. One of these was the act of sitting. Abos could see he found it unnatural. Almost as unnatural as the clothes—Daniel's jogging bottoms and a T-shirt—which he kept pulling at in a desultory way.

The next challenge was eating soup with a spoon. The moment Abos put it down in front of him, Shuck lowered his face and took a long lick of hot liquid, burning his tongue and yelping. Abos fetched a glass of water and held it while he drank. Then she showed him how to use a spoon and watched, fascinated, as he copied her movements. It was like watching a baby; the fingers trying to grasp the spoon first missing it entirely, then pushing it away, finally grabbing it and holding it in his fist. Within a few seconds, though, he moved from infant clumsiness to a more adult grace, his fingers moving along the spoon until he held it the same way as Abos. He mimicked her movements until all the soup was gone.

"Good?" Abos buttered a piece of French bread and held it out.

"Good." Shuck bit into the bread. He tore it with his teeth with a slight canine shake of his head, but he was acting more human all the time.

Abos put the kettle on.

"Do you remember anything before being here?"

Abos herself remembered her lives in previous bodies, but her own experience had been consecutive, the end of one existence followed by the next in a matter of days, or weeks. Shuck's last body had been killed over a century ago. And it hadn't been human.

"Yes. A little. I was not—," he indicated himself and Abos,"—this. I was different."

"A dog. You were a dog."

"A dog," he repeated. "Yes. But not a dog. And I am not this."

"You're right," said Abos, pouring the hot water onto the teabags.

"And you, you are not this either."

Abos was impressed at how fast Shuck's mind was adapting. She knew she had taken far longer as The Deterrent.

"Right again. You and I, we are the same."

There was a pause this time as Shuck considered what he wanted to ask.

"Me. You. What are we?"

Abos waited until he looked up at her, two members of the same species meeting another of their kind for the first time.

"I don't know. I hope you and I, and Susan, and any others we find, can find the answer together."

"Susan?"

"Drink your tea and I'll show you."

Susan's body already filled three-quarters of the bath. She had a head of black hair. She was moving slowly, stretching, just as Shuck had done. He looked down at her, then over at the bath he had crawled out of.

"She will wake up as I did. She is with us."

"Yes. I found her in Russia."

"Putin, election, fake news."

Maybe Radio Four hadn't been the best choice.

"I found you in this country. In Norfolk. I don't know if that was the only body you've had. The dog, I mean. You haven't had one since."

She stopped talking. Shuck seemed to accept that he had once been a dog, was now a human, but actually was neither. He had calmed after his initial awakening and appeared relatively unperturbed. Abos thought back to her first few hours, and days, of life as a human. She, also, had accepted her condition without drama. Infant humans need support from adults for years before they become self-sufficient, and their remarkable brains still require well over a decade to be capable of sophisticated modes of thought. She, and now Shuck, had accomplished the same in hours. They were unlike the humans they resembled. For an instant, she felt a powerful sense of connection to the new being she had found.

They walked back to the kitchen. Abos picked up her mobile phone. Still no message from Daniel.

She stretched out a hand and a heavy pot lifted itself from the top of the stove and floated towards her before landing in front of Shuck.

"Can you do that?"

Shuck looked at the pot. It lifted into the air and made the return journey to the cooker, settling back onto the hob.

Abos knew now that Shuck was developing faster than she had. Whether this was because he had already experienced another life, she didn't know. But it made her feel a little better about what she had to do next.

"Shuck, I have to go."

He looked up, his expression neutral.

"I have a friend, a—" She hesitated for a moment. She

had planned having this discussion tomorrow. It was hardly the first thing Shuck needed to know. But any obfuscation now would only look like a lie later, and she wanted nothing but transparency between them. She had an odd feeling she couldn't lie to him anyway.

"Not a friend."

"Your son."

She looked at him, the same neutral expression on her features. Abos did not display her emotions through her face and body the way humans did. She had been surprised to learn that people could not read each other's unspoken language. To Abos, it was as if they were holding up a sign with their feelings and intentions written in big black letters. Her own blank features made her unreadable, and Shuck was the same.

"Yes. My son. I had many children. Most died between the ages of eleven and eighteen years."

There was a weight in her stomach at that, a surprising heaviness. She sometimes experienced spikes of emotions she struggled to name. As much as anything ever troubled her, these spikes did. They came unbidden and departed the same way. She could not control them.

"Why did they die?"

She needed a moment before replying, although she did not know why.

"The combination of our species and humans leads to a dangerous instability in adolescence. Human hormones change at that time, brain growth experiences a new spurt and the body develops. Puberty, the time when humans mature physically in preparation for reproduction, triggered unexpected changes in the children I fathered. Changes that caused tumours, or brain chemistry anomalies that killed them."

If Shuck was surprised by her use of the word 'fathered' in relation to her offspring, he didn't show it. Then again, he'd been a dog. A change of gender was unremarkable in comparison. She continued to speak, increasingly mindful that she needed to go to Daniel.

"Those who survived developed powers like our own," she said. "Some halfheroes—the name given to my offspring —can do what we did with the pot, but not with anything heavier. They are weaker, more vulnerable than us. And they cannot fly."

"I can fly?"

"I don't know. Did you, in your last body?"

Shuck considered the question for a second.

"Perhaps. I remember running so fast it seemed I was no longer touching the ground."

He floated off of his chair, stopping when his hair touched the beamed ceiling.

"Well," said Abos, "you can now."

bos left Shuck watching a news channel on TV. She had given him a quick lesson in how to use her tablet and asked him to work through a *Learning To Read* app. Once he'd got a grasp of the language, he could look at her notes on possible locations and previous identities of others of their kind. There was a cheap mobile phone on the table with two numbers programmed in, hers and Daniel's.

In the yard, Abos tightened the helmet and checked her leathers were zipped up and secure. Looking through the window, she could see Shuck studying, flicking through the pages of the reading app with increasing speed.

The sky was cloudless. No chance of any cover. The safest option was to make the trip at just under her top speed. If she pushed beyond that, she would break the sound barrier and make the midday news.

With one last glance at Shuck, Abos set her face to the left of the still-rising sun and flew.

She often listened to Daniel's music in the air, so she soared over the green, brown, and yellow patchwork of

England to the soundtrack of Cars, by Gary Numan. Daniel had insisted it was an important piece, and 'a catchy little bastard.' Abos frowned as she listened. Perhaps she lacked the cultural background to appreciate it.

In less than half an hour, she could see Newcastle and Gateshead below, the River Tyne curling as it reached the sea beyond. She overshot the city so she could approach from the coast, increasing her chances of not being seen.

She touched down on a small stretch of deserted sand at South Shields and climbed up to an open, grassy area with benches facing the sea. As Abos was removing her helmet, a small boy was tugging the sleeve of his mother.

"Mum! Mum! Can I fly too? Like the lady? Can I? Can I?"

"Maybe later, if you're good," said the woman, without looking.

"Yeah! Great!" The child grinned at Abos. She winked at him as she passed.

Coming in from the east meant that she was ten miles out of the city. In the interests of preserving her anonymity, she called a taxi.

The driver kept looking at her in the rearview mirror. Abos was used to being the centre of attention. She was six feet tall, wore her hair cropped close to her skull, and her skin was the colour of dark, cocoa-rich chocolate. Even so, people were usually a little more subtle than this driver, who was struggling to keep his eyes on the road.

When he looked for the seventeenth time, she remembered that she hadn't put her contact lenses in. Her face was striking enough as it was, but add eyes the colour of honey, and she was unforgettable.

"I'll get out here, please. Stop the car."

"Here, pet? You sure? Not the safest area, like. Scumbags round here will pinch yer hubcaps while your engine's still running. And they'll rob you as soon as look at you. I wuddna let my daughter walk round here on her own. Don't take it the wrong way, pet, but a pretty thing like you... that's all ah'm saying."

"I can look after myself, thank you."

He still didn't seem keen on leaving her there, even after she'd given him a decent tip. She tried to reassure him.

"I have friends on this street. They're expecting me."

"On *this* street?" He looked incredulous. He was still looking at her eyes. She pointed at them and smiled.

"Contact lenses. They're fashionable."

"Right. If you say so, pet."

As soon as the car was out of sight, she ducked behind a wall and put in the brown lenses. When she stepped back onto the pavement, a group of young men had appeared from a house opposite. They were all shirtless, smoking roll-ups, most clutching cans of strong beer. The leader had a large dog on a chain. Abos was not sure of the breed. Its head was like a lump of bone, its body muscular and scarred.

The gang crossed the road towards her with a kind of shuffling, swaying gait. They looked like a boy band that had fallen on hard times. Abos walked away, towards the city. When they altered their course and upped their pace to cut her off, she considered running, then realised they might be helpful. Daniel hadn't talked much about the IGLU mission, but he had said it was another halfhero. If so, and if that halfhero was a criminal, who better to ask about recent events than the local lowlife?

She stopped, then turned to face them. The leader smiled and came to a halt four feet away, taking a long pull at the joint he was smoking, before blowing the smoke towards her. His followers stood on either side, a pace behind, deferring to his authority. The dog looked up at her and gave a misanthropic rumble of warning.

"Dre don't like you."

As an opening gambit, it was as unoriginal as it was unfriendly.

"I don't like him, either. Now, you probably want my money. Or were you planning on attacking me? Is your motive in approaching me a sexual one? I don't understand the impulses behind rape, but psychologists claim it's usually about power, rather than sex, and you have no power."

"You what?"

"Disenfranchised young people like you have no power. I'm in a hurry. I have sixty-five pounds in cash and two credit cards, but I won't give you the PIN numbers, so please don't ask. As for my body, you're not my type. I'm happy for you to have the money, but I'd like information in return."

The leader's cigarette hung from his mouth and his eyes were flicking in all directions.

"She police, d'ya think?" This from—by the look of him —the youngest. He wasn't smoking but was carrying a can of beer. He had no marks on his arm. Yet.

"Shup, Tosh." Tosh shut up, but they all peered at Abos afresh, trying to work out if she was connected with the local constabulary. Tall, black, wearing leathers. Carrying a helmet, just got out of a taxi and with a southern accent. The leader gave his verdict.

"Nah. Let's do her."

They rushed her, pushing and shoving, bunching around her to stop her breaking away. Abos allowed herself to be jostled, the malnourished animal snarling around her ankles until they were all inside the house opposite.

They pushed her into the front room and followed her

in. Heavy curtains kept out the daylight. The fifty-inch flat screen showed a paused military POV game. There were three big sofas and, over in the corner, a single mattress, stained and surrounded by needles, pieces of foil, and other paraphernalia. It was towards this corner that they pushed Abos.

"Right," she said. "That's far enough." She said it with such authority that they stopped dead for a moment until the leader laughed and made a grab for the zip on top of her jacket.

Abos reached up and snapped his finger. He went very white and very quiet very quickly. Then he took two steps back. The others followed his lead, not knowing what had happened. Once a gap had opened between her and the young men, she glanced at the sofas. They moved.

Tosh was the first to notice, and he leapt to one side as the sofas peeled away from the wall. He watched, wide-eyed as the furniture reared up and pinned his friends against the curtains.

The dog had squeezed through the gap between the sofas and was straining forward. The leader, now gasping with the pain from his finger, dropped the chain.

"Dre! Have her!"

The dog, conditioned to obey his master's commands, ran. It was a tightly wound aggression machine, teeth bared, drooling jaws opening in preparation. But dogs are pack animals evolutionarily predisposed to submit to the alpha, so when Abos commanded him to sit, he did exactly that. He looked up and whimpered, before lying down, his head on his front paws.

"Dre..." whispered the injured leader. "You little twat."

"Right," said Abos. "Tosh here seems able to speak in complete sentences, so I will ask him some questions."

"You keep your mouth shut, Tosh," said the leader, then, "Oh, no. Come on. Please. Aaaagh!" as Abos approached, took hold of another finger and snapped it.

"I don't have time to be nice," she said as he sobbed. "If Tosh doesn't answer my questions, I will continue breaking your fingers. Then I'll start on your friends."

Every head swivelled towards the leader. Feeling the pain in his fingers more keenly than the loss of face, he hissed his response.

"Tell her what she wants to know."

TOSH'S INFORMATION led her to TripleDee's door. According to the boys in the house, TripleDee ran the city. There were rumours that he was a halfhero, impossible to kill. Whatever else he was, he was the boss.

TripleDee had gone quiet for the past few months. The business was ticking over, but he had become more hands-off than he had ever been before. The talk was that he was planning something big. There was plenty of speculation: a new source of heroin, an expansion of the prostitution business by buying a few hundred refugees and putting them on the streets. No one knew for sure.

Strangers started arriving a few weeks back, staying at TripleDee's place. All of them, according to Tosh, 'big fuckers.' It was obvious they were waiting for something.

Then, yesterday morning, whatever it was they had been waiting for, happened. According to what Tosh had overheard from Tammy, TripleDee's girlfriend, 'a bald fella, some tart, and a massive bloke even bigger than wor Triple' had turned up and she hadn't seen him since. It was over twenty-four hours now since he and the strangers had disappeared. Two of his cars were in a far corner of the long stay car park at the airport, but Tammy said his passport was still in the kitchen table drawer.

It was a mystery, and it left a gap at the top of the Newcastle criminal hierarchy. If he didn't show up in the next few days, things would get messy.

One thing was obvious. The disappearance wasn't part of his plan. Tosh said TripleDee had booked a private session with two of the new girls for the evening of the day he disappeared.

"No way in hell he was ganna miss that while he could walk and his nob was still working, see?"

She saw.

She followed the leads.

The airport car park contained the two Teslas Tosh had mentioned, plus a van. Abos looked through the windows. The second car was unlocked and still had the miniature car that served as a key sitting on the dashboard.

She forced the door at the back of the van. Inside were three wheeled beds and three drips, the unmarked bags hanging from them leading to needles designed to be inserted into a cannula on the back of a patient's hand.

Three beds. Three drips.

Abos stood back from the vehicles. The way they were parked was odd. They weren't right at the edge of the car park. They had drawn up in a row, facing the fence, but leaving a gap of fifty yards.

Almost as if something had been there yesterday, and they'd parked in front of it.

Abos looked at the tarmac. There had been no rain for over a week, so nothing as obvious as muddy tyre marks were visible. She crouched down at a spot twenty feet in front of the cars. There were five cigarette butts on the floor, within a few inches of each other. There were no others within sight. Someone had been here for a while, on this spot. Waiting for someone?

She walked the whole perimeter of the small airport, not knowing what she was looking for. The fence got close to the end of the runway to the west, and she was surprised to find a boy of about thirteen with a pair of binoculars standing in a gateway which afforded a good view of the planes.

"Hello," she said.

"All right?" He looked a little wary, bending down to pick up a plastic bag which contained sandwiches and a drink.

"Are you watching the planes?"

The boy looked at her with a mixture of pity and annoyance. Abos smiled.

"Stupid question. Right. I am here to look as well."

The boy said nothing for a few moments. There was a plane taxiing to the far end of the runway. The boy held his binoculars up to his face, put them down again, then scribbled something in a notebook he took out of the bag.

"Is that one interesting?"

The pitying look was back.

"737. Jet2."

It sounded like code. She fell silent again. Daniel was much better at talking to people.

The boy kept shooting sly, sidelong glances at her as if sizing her up. Abos kept looking ahead. They both watched the 737 roar overhead. When the noise had faded, the boy spoke.

"Saw a C17A Globemaster a couple of years back. That was amazing."

"A Globemaster? Is that unusual?"

"Massive, int it? Military. Kuwait Air Force. Should have heard the noise. Brilliant."

"That sounds exciting."

"Yeah."

"You here every day?"

"Most days. After school."

It was Sunday, Abos remembered.

"Were you here yesterday?"

"In the morning. Missed footie practice to come."

"Why?"

"Ma mate called me. Lives in the farm over there." He pointed across the road. "Said there was a private jet in. Fancy, like."

"Do you get many private jets?"

He laughed, not unkindly.

"In Newcastle?"

Not knowing how to respond, she said nothing. The boy produced a phone. He flicked through some images, then held it out to her.

"Had to look it up when I got home. Gulfstream G650. Took off just before lunch yesterday. Wasn't on the list of departures, either. I couldn't find out where it was going. If I hadn't taken this photo, no one would have believed me. Me dad was fuming when I showed him. Couldn't believe he'd missed it. Want a sandwich?"

Abos looked at him, scruffy, enthusiastic, out on his own on a Sunday morning because he loved planes. Hobbies. Another human trait she couldn't identify with.

"No, thank you. I have to go."

After a few steps, she turned.

"How far can it fly? The Gulfstream?"

"Oh, man, they're amazing. Especially the ER. Stands for

Extended Range. Eight thousand miles. You could get to Japan, or Indonesia without refuelling."

Abos walked away. If Daniel had been in one of those cars or—more likely, given the company—unconscious in the van, he could be eight thousand miles away by now. In any direction.

Her next visit would have to be to air traffic control, for a look at their schedule, although, she suspected the private jet's itinerary would be unlisted.

She took out her phone and checked the airport's departure schedule. No unusual flights listed yesterday. She could hardly walk up to the control tower and ask to see the logs. The last flight of the day departed at ten o'clock. She would come back at eleven.

As she was about to put the phone away, it vibrated. The name came up on the screen: *Shuck*.

"Are you okay?"

"Have you seen the news?"

"No. Why?"

"You need to come home now."

"I can't. I have to find Daniel."

"No. You must come back."

"Shuck. I will. Soon. But—"

"There are more."

"More what?"

"More of us. I can see them."

Abos didn't know what to say. She could fly back, see what was happening and still be back at the airport tonight. She regretted turning down the boy's offer of a sandwich.

Shuck had said something else, but she had missed it.

"Can you say that again?"

"Yes. There are six of them. And he says there are more."

19

Geneva

On that Sunday, one room, in one hotel, in one city, contained a group of men and women whose combined wealth exceeded that of the poorest five billion people on the planet.

Preparations for the event had been extensive. The wing of the Grand Palace Hotel housing the ballroom had been closed to guests for a month. During that time, it had been redecorated, every item of furniture replaced. A specialist security team, brought in to provide twenty-four-hour surveillance, spent two days sweeping the building for bugs.

Every pane in the ballroom's famous glass dome had been replaced. According to the manufacturer, the new toughened glass could withstand the impact of a short-range missile. Since the promotional video showed technical director standing behind the product while soldiers fired one such missile at him, it had become a best-seller.

When the day of the speech arrived, every member of every guest's bodyguard team wore an earpiece, ready to take directives from their host's head of security. All the bodyguards were courteous and professional. They were also suspicious, heavily armed, and ready for trouble. If any of them were unimpressed by the average-looking, unexceptional man in charge, they said nothing.

Robertson didn't care what they thought of him. He knew that by the end of the evening, their professional pride would be in tatters.

THE FOOD and wine were exquisite. As the afternoon wore on, the guests relaxed, enjoying a rare occasion when professional rivalries were, if not forgotten, at least put aside. The CEO of a telecoms company shared a bottle of All Saints Museum Muscadelle with the woman who had poached a third of his North American business. A games developer shook the hand of his most bitter business rival - the brother he hadn't spoken to for over a year.

Outside, chauffeurs polished the immaculate paintwork of a fleet of the most luxurious automobiles on the planet, before huddling together in groups of four or five, smoking and complaining about their employers.

Everybody in the ballroom had an opinion—leaning into each other to express it—about the man sitting alone at the far end.

At three-thirty, the subject of their gossip rose to his feet, wiped the corners of his mouth with a napkin, and made his way up to the rostrum in the middle of the stage.

Titus Gorman was small, slight, his blonde hair wispy and already receding. He wore rimless glasses. His lips were thin and bloodless, his cheekbones prominent. His eyes, a pale blue, were always moving. Gorman interacted with the outside world as much as he felt he had to, which was very little.

The room went quiet as people nudged their neighbours. Someone clapped. Within a few seconds, the applause stretched to every corner of the room.

Titus Gorman stood at the microphone and waited for the clapping to subside. Experience told him it would be a long wait. No one wanted to be the first to stop. He could buy everyone in the room a hundred times over, and they knew it. Their show of respect and enthusiasm was driven by self-interest, and a crude financial calculation.

He smiled and held up his hands for silence.

Titus Gorman symbolised the American Dream for millions of aspiring computer coders. Probably the child of Jewish immigrants from Russia, almost nothing was known about his background, despite a slew of theories. The likeliest explanation for the information vacuum surrounding his background was that, when it came to information, no one was more talented than Titus at manipulating it.

Titus was a coder. Not just any coder, but a legendary figure among anyone who had ever attempted to write programs on any computer platform. His games were addictive and dominated the market in the early 2000s. His breakout hit, DieScum, was a POV shoot-'em-up combining over-the-top cartoon violence with monsters who were witty and—in a revolutionary, and much copied, twist—often sympathetic. The awe in which he was held by fellow coders, hackers, and designers was such that, even when his company became a behemoth, they separated their distrust of the corporate monster from their love of the rebel at the heart of it.

Even the name of the company itself represented Titus giving the global market the middle finger. Glob. It was ugly-sounding, childish. Hard to take seriously. Media reaction in the early months was negative, generating headlines, such as **Titus Gorman admits Glob is bad name, changes to Booger.**

Titus didn't respond to press coverage. He let his product do the talking. No one thought the world needed another search engine and, when it was first released, only dedicated Titus fans tried it. They did it out of loyalty, curiosity, and the hope that they might, one day, be able to tell their kids they were among the first to realise that Glob would take over the world.

These days, that was exactly what they were telling their kids.

It took a week for the unique power of Glob to become clear. The search algorithm itself was a thing of beauty, but no one expected any less. Coders were loudly critical of Titus's sand-boxed programming, but, as he always delivered the best user experience, their protests were half-hearted.

Where Glob broke new ground was in the way it handed power to the consumer. Power over the market. Titus wasn't starting a revolution. He seemed, rather, to accept consumerism. What Glob did was to transform the relationship between buyers and sellers.

The concept was not a new one, but it was the first time it had been attempted on a worldwide scale. The first person to discover how it worked on Glob was a software designer. Everyone knew her now as Patience Zero. Back then, she was Patience Hobbes, a freelancer in San Francisco. Her story was picked up by an online news network, when, within four weeks of its launch, Glob was handling ten million searches a day. When the Patience story went viral that figure rose to over a billion searches a day. Inside a year, Glob was not only the biggest player, it was virtually the only player. Rival search engines either disappeared or became niche-based to survive.

Patience was the first person to form a Globule. Her autobiography tells it this way:

I was looking for a new laptop. I had narrowed my options to three different products and was globbing for prices. We didn't call it globbing back then. Hard to imagine now! When I decided the Tertia 800 was my favourite, a message popped up on my screen: would you like to form a Globule for this search? *I didn't know what that meant, but, hey, this was Titus Gorman, it had to be something cool. I clicked on yes, checked a box promising hourly notifications and closed it. Next thing I know, there's a personal email from Titus in my inbox. I couldn't believe it. I printed it, emailed a copy to another account and took a screenshot. I knew no one would believe me otherwise.*

The email said I was the first user to start a Globule and it might take a little time to work. Titus asked me to give it twenty-four hours. He sent me a gift, too. One hundred Glob shares. I thought it was a nice gesture. Thought they might do ok. I had no idea they'd pay my mortgage, buy me two more houses, and mean I could give up work within five years.

Anyway, I checked after an hour. There was a message on the right of the glob search bar. It said that sixty-four people had joined my Globule. I didn't have a clue what it meant. I went to bed.

Next morning, I had to go pick up my kid from my ex, so I didn't get back to the computer until that evening. When I did, the message had changed. There were twelve hundred people in my Globule, and an icon had appeared - the famous green drip. I still think it's a teardrop, but my kid says it's snot. Hovering over it, I could see the three best prices for the Tertia 800. I thought it was a joke. I hadn't been able to find it anywhere for less than nine-

teen hundred dollars. The best price from my Globule was just over thirteen hundred, and it was from a company I recognised. There was a countdown next to it, which ran out in three hours. If I paid now, the purchase would go through the next day. The money would be held by Glob for that period, and other people could join the Globule during the countdown. Yeah, it seemed too good to be true. But I read the FAQ, and the principle made sense. If one person wants to buy a laptop, they look for the best deal and pay the asking price. If a company wants to buy twenty laptops for their staff, they get a better deal. A big company might order thousands of them. They get a much lower price per unit. Makes sense.

My Globule comprised everyone else in every country on Glob looking for a Tertia 800. Twelve hundred of us. Glob pooled our money, and the algorithm negotiated for us, bringing down the price of each unit. They would be shipped to a warehouse, then Glob would ship them to us.

I clicked on the button and paid my money. If it had been anyone other than Titus Gorman, but... it was *Titus Gorman!*

I made sure I was in front of the computer when the deal went through.

We got our laptops for just under a thousand dollars. Nine hundred under the retail price. I told everyone I knew about it, they told everyone they knew about it, and the global economy never saw what was coming until it was too late.

Patience Zero still gives interviews. Since no one can get to Titus himself, the earliest Glob adopters have become minor celebrities.

Gorman's masterstroke, the touch of genius which made business people across the planet gasp with admiration, frustration, or sheer jealous hatred, was the monetisation of Glob itself. During the twenty-four-hour period that the Globule's cash was held by Glob, it generated interest for the company. In the case of the first Globule, if the only cash in the company account had been that generated by the Globule, it would have made about a hundred bucks in interest. Not very exciting. Today, an average of 2.6 million Globules are running *per day*, with an average value of ninety-four dollars. Conservative estimates put Glob's daily interest on its Globule accounts at two and a half million dollars. Add that to the revenue generated by sponsorglobs, the ads that run next to search results, and Glob's rise to becoming the world's richest company should have been no surprise to anyone.

In reality, though, it *was* a surprise. Even in the tech world, where change is eye-wateringly rapid, no one foresaw the potential of Titus Gorman's search engine.

And Glob's motto - *Never The Same Old Sh!t* wasn't just deliberately provocative. A year after Glob launched, Titus turned the burgeoning tablet market on its head with the Globlet. Made mostly from recycled materials, it was described by Time magazine as "the most counter-intuitive product of a generation." Under the hood, the Globlet didn't try to compete with other tablets. It had two operating systems. The first, lightweight and lightning-fast, was designed for internet browsing, emails, and simple games. The second, which could be booted up separately, ran programs that rivalled mid-range laptops. But the most revolutionary move was the product's lifespan. Everything could be replaced or upgraded. If a new processor came out, you popped the back off your Globlet and swapped out your old one. It took three minutes, cost twenty to thirty bucks, and a toddler could do it. Same deal with the screen, the sound card, the graphics chip. The tech giants of the day said people were happy to replace their tablets, computers, and phones every two to three years. Titus Gorman said the tech giants were wrong, that people would like to own a product which might last a lifetime. And Titus was right.

Now, looking out at a room full of the richest people in the world, Titus smiled.

He glanced at the cameras on the corners of the stage. Then he looked at the security teams standing ready to protect their employers. Lastly, he looked at those men and women who had risen to the top in the Darwinian arena of global capitalism.

"All of you know I only make speeches when I'm about to do something crazy," he said, still smiling. "You're not here for the fine wine and the ambience. You want to know what I'm up to."

Muted applause greeted his opening remarks.

"I'm known for writing code, for coming up with ideas. Ideas that I often express in elegant algorithms. My algorithms have changed the world of commerce. My secret— the secret of my success, if you like—is very simple. I'm going to let you in on it. But you won't like it."

The few chuckles that greeted this remark sounded forced and quickly died away.

"When Glob became the world's most popular search engine, you were all affected. Adversely affected. You had to adapt. Consumers had the power for the first time. Bulk-buying through Globules led to a tightening of your margins. Many major players have disappeared because they did not recognise what was happening. You are still here because you were the fastest to act, the most ruthless. You cut staff, you cut wages. The only thing you didn't cut was, if you'll excuse the pun, your cut.

"None of you saw what I was trying to do. Not a single one. I wasn't trying to become the world's richest man. I was trying to redistribute wealth. I naively hoped that Glob would help raise standards of living, narrow the gap between the richest and the poorest. It didn't happen. We still believe in capitalism, supply and demand, market forces. In theory, that should mean economic growth and higher standards of living. Yeah, sure. The theory sucks."

The silence was thick in the room now.

"Economic growth can only continue if the population continues to grow. Let me qualify that. *Worldwide* economic growth can only continue to grow if the population continues to grow. If you set aside the global aspect, individual countries *can* continue to grow economically, but only at the expense of other countries. The world cannot sustain a constantly growing human population. Only a fool would claim otherwise, although we have a few of those. If the population cannot continue to grow indefinitely, what happens to a global model whose only measure is economic growth?

"I'm not about to give you a lecture on socialism. Or any kind of ism. I'm no student of economics. But I can see when something is wrong.

"People still die from starvation. They die from diseases we could eradicate. We make our charitable donations, become patrons of foundations. Anything rather than take a good look at the facts."

Titus sighed. His audience was murmuring restlessly.

"I'll cut to the chase. You must think I'm the worst kind of hypocrite, with the wealth I'm sitting on. And you'd be right, *if* I wasn't going to do something about it. But I am doing something about it. I've written a piece of code. It's an algorithm for the planet. I've had this idea for most of my life, but I never thought it could be anything more than a dream. A few years ago, that changed."

He paused. Not a natural showman, Titus nevertheless

appreciated the drama of the moment. He knew this speech, and what was about to happen, would be watched by billions when they released the footage in an hour.

He raised his voice.

"I promised you my secret. Here it is. When I say that I want to make the world a better place, I actually mean it. I see a problem. And I can fix it. I call my solution The Utopia Algorithm."

There was a sound like an explosion and everyone flinched, bodyguards running towards their employers, hands reaching for weapons.

In the chaos that followed, only a handful of people saw what happened next, but the cameras captured the moment perfectly. Huge shards of shattered glass—the strongest bullet and bomb-proof glass in the world—fell from the dome above the stage. When they reached a spot ten feet above Titus's head, they stopped falling, hanging in the air. Six very tall, muscular figures in dark suits followed the glass, floating down from the high ceiling like giant dust motes caught in the spotlight.

They landed on the stage, three on each side of Titus. One of them made a gesture, and the glass hanging above him moved back to the rear of the hall, before sinking to the floor.

The audience stared at the stage, many of them held back by their security teams. Over a hundred guns were pointing at the six strangers.

The husband of the world's most successful fashion designer was the first to say it.

"They're him."

Then everyone saw it. The six men, over seven feet tall and built like linebackers, all looked exactly the same. They all looked like Titus Gorman.

20

Daniel stared at the Globule's screen, his hands shaking. He had just watched a three-minute video euphemistically titled *Welcome*. The man who had planned his kidnapping was Titus Gorman.

In the video, Gorman had apologised. He hadn't taken this course of action lightly; he considered taking another human being's liberty to be a heinous crime, something he would have to live with for the rest of his life, *blah blah blah.*

Gorman had expressed regret that he couldn't tell his guests—*call me your* guest *to my face, you arsehole*—why he had been forced to imprison them. He was a man who understood logic, and logic had dictated his actions. Halfheroes represented the greatest risk to the project he was about to launch, so halfheroes had to be taken out of the equation.

Gorman had concluded by explaining that the Globlet in each room linked to an offline database containing over ten million books, plus almost every album ever released and every movie ever made. There were also courses available in many subjects.

Perhaps I'll take up cross-stitch, you shithead.

Daniel was trying to avoid thinking about the last thing Gorman had said before the video had faded to black. Something about not wanting to keep them locked up longer than was necessary.

Daniel was trying not to think about Station.

Three years. That was what Gorman had said. Three years. Naturally, Titus *hoped* it would be shorter, but his guests should prepare themselves for a three-year stay.

Three years.

Daniel's self-control slid away as a panicked rage burst through his mental defences.

For the next few minutes, he had no conception of who he was, where he was, or what he was doing. He lashed out with his fists, he punched and kicked at the walls and the door. He tried to pull the bed away from the floor, only to find it was bolted in place and he lacked the strength to move it. He lumbered from one side of the room to the other, making incomprehensible, guttural noises. He couldn't form a single thought, because his mind was turning in on itself, away from reality, burrowing into a cocoon of pain. Trying to think was like swimming from the bottom of a dark pool, looking for the light from the surface, but never finding it. The pain from his hands as he repeatedly punched the solid door was sharp enough to break through the numbness, albeit temporarily. Daniel welcomed it, saw the pain as a lifeline, kicked up towards the light revealed by the bones breaking in his fingers as he smashed the door over and over again.

Time passed. Seconds, minutes, hours... he didn't know or care. He saw the surface, a bright light; warm, welcoming. He broke through and floated up into a world of light where he could drift in a haze of no-thought. Shapes, half-visible in cobwebs of fog, came closer before receding and vanishing. Sounds came and went, words spoken on an old radio in a faraway room, tuned somewhere between two stations.

Finally, there was darkness and quiet. There was a peacefulness in that darkness, a sense of a question: *why go back?... stay here.* He stayed, lacking the energy to do anything else. He had stopped caring. The darkness was good. He could rest.

Then the thoughts emerged. Slowly, like air bubbles in slow motion. They originated from far below, he sensed their approach, then watched as they passed, rising out of sight. A long gap then another bubble. Daniel could not look away, could not ignore them.

...

... Halfhero. Not human. And not like Abos. Humans are scared of you. But compared to Abos, you are weak...

...

... You will die one day, but Abos will live in a new body. You are a mistake. You should never have been born...

...

... You are no better than your mother. Just like her, you hate yourself, and, eventually, you will destroy yourself...

...

... At least she produced a child. She left something behind, even something as half-formed and dangerous as you...

...

... You will die like your mother died, unloved...

...

A memory surfaced, sharp and clear. The night he'd typed his mother's name into Glob. Finding there was a tiny shred of feeling left, despite his childhood, despite the contempt she'd shown towards him. She was still his mother. Only, she wasn't. Not any more. Daniel had read the article reporting his mother's death. It had happened six years before he escaped from Station. A car had hit her. She had been drunk, of course. He had felt nothing. Their only connection had been biological. But when he had tried to tell Abos, he had found he couldn't say the words. He had swallowed the knowledge, kept it somewhere dark.

...

... Unloved. And alone...

...

... Your children were monsters, and you can never be a proper father. Not now...

...

Something pulled at his attention. He ignored it, focussing on the thoughts torturing him in the darkness. He agreed with them, and he didn't care anymore. There was a kind of peace here in the dark, even if it was a bleak, empty peace.

Whatever it was that wanted his attention was persistent. It wanted him to look away from the rising thoughts. In the end, he capitulated. Maybe then, it would go away. He had no eyes to see, not there in the darkness, but he opened them anyway, a muscle memory giving him a way of interacting with the nothingness.

There was a face. He didn't see it at first. Then he noticed a symmetry in the blackness, lighter patches becoming visible. Abstract at first, slowly gaining definition. The brain, hard-wired to see patterns, detected a familiar shape, a form.

It was George.

Abos had George's face now. Daniel saw it every day. But this wasn't Abos. It was George. Something about the tilt of the face, the hint of amusement never far from her eyes.

He tried to look away but could not. There was no judgement in her expression. Back then, George had known Daniel would go back to Station with Abos and destroy it, because she had seen it. She had seen his success, just as she had seen her own death, the two outcomes inextricable knotted together. She had accepted her part, and she had treated him as if he were a good man. Not a mistake, not a halfhero. Not half-anything.

Her face looked at him.

The thoughts had gone.

He remembered who he was. And where he was. His awareness returned in bursts, like a car engine misfiring before the spark plugs ignite the petrol and air and the engine starts.

His body hurt. He couldn't move his fingers. He was lying down. Something soft beneath him. He was on a bed.

The darkness made itself present again; a caress, a promise of forgetfulness. Just turn towards it and he would own the darkness and the darkness would own him.

Just give up.

Daniel opened his eyes, blinked against the sudden light, tears blurring his vision. He brought his hand up and wiped away the moisture, feeling something around his fingers. He blinked again and looked. His hands were bandaged, the fingers in splints.

Using the heels of his hands, he pushed himself up against the wall behind the bed, his head throbbing as he did so. He flexed his fingers. They were healing, but not as quickly as his injuries normally healed. Fresh bursts of pain made him hiss, sweat breaking out on his forehead. He bit the end of a bandage and unwound both hands. The bruising was extensive, and colourful, but fading.

This must be how normal people heal.

He looked down at his body. White drawstring trousers,

white T-shirt. Fresh clothes, no bloodstains from his self-destructive rampage.

He was still hungry. Not as hungry as he had been, but his stomach was groaning.

How can I be less *hungry? I haven't eaten.*

He brought his left hand up under his T-shirt to his chest. An area of a few centimetres diameter on his chest had been shaved. There was a small plaster there.

"They fed me intravenously."

Daniel realised he had spoken out loud. His voice sounded harsh and dry. He cleared his throat. There was a plastic cup on a shelf cut into the rock wall. He slid off the bed, lightheaded, taking small steps. He filled the cup from the tap and took a long drink. The first few swallows cut like gravel, but his need for fluids won out over the discomfort, and the pain receded as he drained the cup, refilled and did the same again.

"Daniel? Daniel? Is that you? Are you okay?"

Sara's voice.

Daniel knelt by the door, putting his cheek to the floor. He looked to the right. No one was there.

"Daniel? Thank God. I thought I was alone, apart from that prick and his mates. This way."

He shifted his head towards the sound. Lying on the floor in the cell to the left, her face pressed hard up against the metal door, was Sara.

The last time he'd seen her, she had been in the house in Newcastle being attacked by hundreds of ball bearings hitting her body. He had heard bones break.

"Sara! You okay?"

She smiled. It looked weird from that angle.

"Yeah, fine. A little sore, still."

"But...Sara, you were in bad shape."

"Nothing a few days enforced rest in a psycho's prison couldn't sort out."

"What? How long have we been here?"

"Hard to say for sure. No clocks, no windows. The automatic lights dim to half-strength for eight hours in every twenty-four, so I'm going to guess that's eleven through to seven. In which case, five days, although I wasn't really with it when I arrived. Might be six."

Daniel jerked back from the door in shock, then pressed his face up against it again too fast, squishing his nose. Tears and snot ran down his cheeks.

"Ow! Six days? How long was I unconscious for? Did you see them come into my room? What did they look like? Any idea where we are?"

"Woah, there, boy, slow down, will you? When I woke up, it was all quiet in your cell. A few hours after I'd worked out that I didn't have enough strength to get out because of the child-sized meals, that northern twat up the corridor woke up and had a tantrum."

"Fuck you too, pet. I suppose you like being in here."

Daniel recognised TripleDee's voice. He slid his face to the left so he could see back up the corridor. The drug dealer's face stared back at him, then disappeared back into the cell, with a parting, "Oh, for fuck's sake."

Sara laughed.

"I'd assumed TripleDee got his nickname because his name's Davey Dozy Dickhead, but after the little hissy fit he had when he woke up, I think he might be named after his three GCSE grades. Probably cookery, PE and modern dance."

"Fuck OFF." TripleDee had stayed close enough to the door to listen in.

"Daniel, why were you unconscious so much longer than

the rest of us? I thought your cell was empty at first. But a guard went in every few hours. The last time he left, he had medical equipment with him. What happened to you?"

Daniel didn't mention his own panicked response to being imprisoned. He was sure Sara would understand— she knew a little about his years at Station—but he wasn't proud of his loss of control.

"I was disorientated when I first woke up. I fell. My body's not healing as fast as usual, and I'm weak. They patched me up, fed me intravenously."

"Yeah, Gormless has done his homework. He knows feeding us a survival-level diet means we won't be able to use our powers properly."

Daniel smiled at *Gormless*. Sara wouldn't give up anytime soon.

"You okay now, Daniel?"

"Yeah. Yeah, I'm fine. Peckish, though."

"Tell me about it. I could eat three horses. And a goat."

Daniel thought back to the fight in Newcastle. He remembered losing consciousness, a mask being pulled over his nose and mouth. The whole mission had been a trap. IGLU security had been compromised. He wondered what Saffi was doing, what resources might be available to an organisation the UN had no official knowledge of.

"Hey Triple?"

There was no answer, but he knew the man in the next cell was listening.

"Got double-crossed, did you? Delivered us, the other halfheroes, and yourself, to Gorman. Gift-wrapped with a pretty bow on top. You're probably glad you're in there. I wonder what your new friends would do to you if they had the chance?"

"FUCK OFF."

TripleDee was too easy to wind up. Took a lot of the fun out of it.

Daniel pictured the room in Newcastle at the moment Sara had been overwhelmed. She'd been grabbed by someone who'd walked through a solid wall like it was a shower curtain.

"Wait. Wait. Sara?"

"I'm here."

"In Newcastle, the guy who grabbed you. He walked through a wall. Not like I do. I mean, he went *through* it like it wasn't even there. Is he in here?"

He was quiet while he considered the possibilities. Getting a message to the guy was the first problem. Then there was the issue of not having enough strength to use his power. Maybe if everyone near to his cell gave him a third of their food for a day, by sliding the plates under the gaps across to his cell...difficult, but not impossible...

He could hear laughter from TripleDee's cell, bitter and forced. Then Sara's voice again.

"Daniel, I'm sorry."

TripleDee stopped laughing long enough to shout out.

"He hasn't seen it, has he? Yeah, sounds like a great plan, Danny boy, nice one." He laughed again, but there was no amusement in the sound, just an edge of desperation.

"Sara? What's he talking about?"

"Look at your Globlet. I'll be here when you're done."

Daniel got to his knees, paused a moment while the dizziness passed, then rose to his feet.

The Globlet was brand new. He recalled smashing the last one. It flickered into life when he picked it up. There was no port for a charging cable on the case which meant it was the latest generation, with wireless charging. The computer-loving, Kraftwerk-listening child geek in Daniel couldn't help but be impressed.

This time, when he pressed the welcome icon, it was replaced by folders. Alongside **books, movies, education, music, games,** and **myglob,** was **announcements.** The folder icon, a red light atop a nineteen-seventies American cop car, was flashing.

He pressed it. It contained one file, named **escape attempt.**

Daniel pressed it.

21

A bos looked at the screen. It didn't occur to her to ask Shuck how he had learned to pause and rewind live television. By the time she did wonder how he seemed to know so much without having to study anything, the answer was already obvious. But it was days before that happened, and weeks before she discovered the full implications of what she had discovered.

Titus Gorman was addressing a roomful of people in Geneva. Abos had just watched six members of her own species crash through the ceiling and stand alongside the tech billionaire.

Shuck paused the video and turned to look at her.

"They are as we are?"

She nodded her agreement, staring at the impassive faces of these new members of her species. They all looked as if they'd grown up in an alternative universe where Titus Gorman had been an impressive physical specimen as well as a genius. They towered above the original, the man whose blood had given them life. While his eyes required glasses, theirs did not. His slightly bent nose was straight on their strong faces and his slouched posture contrasted with the athletic readiness of the giants around him.

"But they obey him. Like slaves."

Abos nodded again. She knew of one way the unformed minds of her species could be limited, directed to follow a narrow path laid out by others. By ending Station, she thought she had ended that abusive practice. But this new evidence suggested otherwise. She felt distant from the events unfolding in front of her, unsure how to react. Now in her third *consecutive human body, and a parent, her biological provenance*—whatever it turned out to be—was not the only factor at work in her psyche.

Daniel and his siblings were halfheroes. For the first time, she felt a little of the emotional baggage such an epithet might carry. Could she, after all this time, be considered half-human?

Shuck pressed play, and the images on the screen moved. Titus spoke to the audience, demanding all weapons be handed over. One of his twins jumped from the stage, holding a laundry bag.

"I call them Protectors," said Titus as the giant moved to the first table and held out the bag. The chief bodyguard of the Chinese tech company chairman stared up at the dark-suited man who had just crashed through bombproof glass without injury. He hesitated. His employer hissed something. The tension in the room was palpable even when viewed on the small screen in a Cornish farmhouse kitchen.

Shuck pressed pause again. He evidently had no sense of drama.

"No one else is calling them Protectors."

He held up the tablet. There was a stream of comments running across the screen. Only one in twenty concerned porn or cat videos, the rest were reactions to what had happened in Geneva that afternoon.

"You're using social media?" When she had left him that morning, Abos had only hoped he might get to grips with the basics of written vocabulary and grammar.

"Yes."

She read the comment he was pointing at, which had been shared over six million times already.

Can't call them 'Protectors'. Makes them sound like a condom. How about titans?

"That's what they're calling them. Titans."

Abos had started as Powerman, but the world had preferred The Deterrent. She had been Amy for over thirty years. Now she had grown fond of being named after her dormant state as an Amorphous Blob Of Slime. Names were important.

Shuck pressed play again, and the Chinese bodyguard made his decision, lifting his weapon and firing two rapid shots into the towering figure in front of him. One to the heart, one to the head.

The suited man didn't flinch, but a ricochet from the body shot hit a young woman at the table, and she screamed. The bodyguard barely hesitated after the failure of his initial attack. A knife appeared in his hand, and he plunged it into the titan's stomach. At least, he tried to. The blade stopped dead after piercing the crisp white shirt, and the shock waves sent back up the bodyguard's arm made him drop it.

No one doubted the bravery of the man, but most questioned his sanity when he launched into a weaponless martial arts attack, his hands a blur as he punched and chopped at the side, neck, and face of his opponent.

In response, the titan put a huge hand on the chest of his

assailant, balled up a fistful of jacket and shirt, and lifted him off his feet, holding him over his head as if he were a toy.

At the rear of the room was a casual sitting area with sofas and armchairs. The titan drew back his arm and threw the bodyguard towards it. He sailed across a hundred and thirty feet, narrowly missing a chandelier as he passed above the heads of the world's richest business people, before landing in a large armchair. His momentum caused the chair to continue for another ten feet before it hit the rear wall. The bounce after the impact threw the bodyguard forward, and he landed on the parquet floor, groaned once and was still.

Titus Gorman allowed his audience a few moments to recover. Everyone must know now what they were dealing with. Earth may not have seen a superhuman for over three decades, but a superhuman was not something you easily forgot.

"They will not attack, but they will retaliate if they, or I, am threatened. I named them Protectors for a reason. Please, place the rest of your weapons in the bag."

The rest of the security guards did as instructed, placing guns and knives into the laundry bag. Meanwhile, the hotel doctor had been called and was attending the injured girl.

Abos turned to Shuck.

"They have been manipulated. They are half-aware, their minds clouded by drugs and the suggestions of those controlling them."

Shuck looked at her.

"It happened to you." It was a statement rather than a question.

"I cannot let it happen again."

Shuck corrected her.

"We cannot. But we must wait for her." He looked towards the laboratory outside where Susan was growing.

"No. It could be many weeks."

"It won't be. Because we are here. You know this."

Abos looked at him. She knew he was right, but she did not know how she knew.

"Yes," she said. "How long?"

"A week. Perhaps less. We must wait."

Abos was used to the human way of making decisions She and Daniel would discuss before deciding. This was different. No discussion. And yet she felt a sense of consensus. She added it to the list of mysteries surrounding Shuck.

Gorman was speaking again.

"The Protectors were not created to protect me. They were created to protect ordinary people from those who will fight the Utopia Algorithm. And, yes, the superhumans alongside me are brothers of the being we knew as The Deterrent. I want you, and the rest of the world, to remember the power of The Deterrent. You see six such beings in this room today, all with equal power. When we leave here, we will be joined by other Protectors. Do not waste time, or risk lives, trying to prevent the inevitable."

Titus nodded at the five titans still on stage. The sixth titan walked into the middle of the ballroom, holding the bulging laundry bag. He swung it once over his head then, on the next pass, released it, sending it soaring towards the ceiling. As it reached the apex of its flight, the five titans on the stage raised their hands.

The bag ripped open, sending pistols, semi-automatic weapons, knives, machetes and knuckle dusters in all directions. As the weapons flew outwards from the bag, they twisted and spun, pulling themselves apart. Every component part of every gun separated itself from its neighbour, bullets spinning out and away from the chambers that housed them. Knife hilts opened, releasing the blades. Objects designed to hurt, maim, or kill, were broken down to their individual parts, spinning and dancing in the thousand lights of the chandeliers.

The audience watched it all open-mouthed. It was more spectacular than any cabaret performance.

The titans lowered their arms, and the weapons fell towards the watching audience.

The spell was broken, and the second and a half it took for the weapons to fall was full of shouts and screams as the people below covered their heads.

Then silence. A gradual peeking out from behind trembling fingers, a slow, synchronised exhalation.

The weapons hung above them, ten feet from the floor. They slowly revolved, allowing everyone to see the time, effort, and craftsmanship that had gone into the production of these terrible objects.

Then, as if obeying a call, the weapons floated towards the stage. A telescopic baton was first, coming to rest above Titus's head. A knife blade was next, sticking to the baton with the click of metal on metal. Faster and faster the weapons came, one on top of the other, clinging as if magnetised, but with such great force that items were bending as they stuck to each other, compressing towards the centre.

A ball of metal, wood, and plastic formed. The bullets were last. Thousands of them. They had waited, hovering above the tables. When called, they flew from their places as if fired, hitting the ball, deforming on impact and sticking there. Each bullet followed its predecessor after a gap of perhaps a hundred milliseconds. The result was an impossibly fast, regular metallic snare roll.

When every weapon and piece of ammunition was accounted for, a shining sphere spun above the stage like a piece of modern art.

With no telltale build up of energy, the spinning globe shot upwards at such speed it seemed to disappear. Less than a minute later, it burned up in Earth's atmosphere.

Titus smiled at his audience, and at the cameras focussed on his face.

"I'm not here to moralise. The Utopia algorithm came about through the application of logic. The world is a wonderful place if you're not dirt poor. The problem is, most people are. They are unhealthy, their life expectancy is low, and infant mortality is high. If you're poor, you'll spend more of your life ill, some of your kids will die and you won't be around long enough to meet your grandchildren. The rich escape that fate. Life is a lottery. We can do better than that.

"I used to believe humanity's progress, or lack of it, was due to fear and greed. If you have more than the next guy, you fear someone might take it from you. If you don't have as much as the next guy, you get greedy. But that's not quite true. The world runs on fear and need. If you can't get a job that pays enough to feed your family, if your child will die because you can't afford the treatment that a profit-making pharmaceutical company has developed, that's not greed. It's need."

Members of the audience exchanged uneasy glances as they listened. Whatever else they had thought about him, they'd assumed Titus was one of them. No one became the richest person in the world through philanthropy and hand-wringing.

"I'm putting my money where my mouth is. Ted?"

A shocked-looking man in his sixties raised a hand at a table near the stage.

"As of today, I own Ralion-Baxter."

The man cleared his throat and laughed good-naturedly.

"I don't think so, Titus. Now stop trying to scare us with your new toys. You're in danger of making some powerful enemies today."

It was Titus's turn to laugh.

"Oh, you guys are the least of my worries. Enjoy your retirement, Ted. I've been buying your stock for months. Passed the point of no return this morning. I'm taking Ralion-Baxter back into private ownership. Two reasons. Want to hear them?"

Ted's mouth was hanging open. His wife, looking at her mobile phone, whispered something, and he glared at the stage.

"It's the biggest pharmaceutical company in the world. Your research department has patented more life-saving drugs than any other in the last fifty years. Commendable. Except you have to make a profit, so most folk who need your products can't afford them."

"Now listen, Gorman, what the hell gives you the right to—"

"I'm not singling you out, Ted. Everyone here colludes in preserving the fiction we all live by. That this is, somehow, okay. That it's the way of the world. That it can't be changed. But that's all over now. So, like I said, two reasons. First, profit. That's over. Ralion-Baxter will now sell at cost plus enough to pay for wages, infrastructure, and research. No profit."

Ted made a sound like an elephant seal in labour.

"Second, the pay structure of the company will be changed. It will be the first company to do so, but not the last. I'll expect all others to follow suit after the Utopia Algorithm has taken effect. It's a simple structure. The highest paid executive can never be paid more than ten times the lowest paid worker."

Ted made another strange noise and muttered something. Titus acknowledged him with a smile.

"You think the higher-paid employees will leave? Maybe. But I don't think so. Give the algorithm a little time to work, then see what happens."

Titus gestured to the titan still on the main floor to join him on stage. When all six were flanking him, he looked at the camera.

"It will be too risky for me to make public appearances for a while. I'll leave you with a promise and a warning. I promise, from tomorrow, the world will be a fairer place. It's time we evolved. Let's not value people by the amount of money they've accumulated. And a warning for those whose fear leads them to violence: you will be stopped. I have the means and the determination to do it. Don't test me."

He stepped backwards, and the titans moved around him. They stopped when he raised a hand.

"One more thing," he said, then grinned, which made him look like a gawky teenager. "I've always wanted to say that. The algorithm runs tonight. Tomorrow we all wake up to a new world. A fairer world."

He stepped backwards again, and the whole group flew upwards through the shattered dome and into the warm Swiss evening.

Shuck turned the television off.

"No one knows what he means by the Utopia Algorithm. There are lots of discussions online."

Abos was still staring at the blank screen.

"We have to help them. But Daniel is missing."

"Look for him. I will stay here. When Susan wakes, I'll call you. Then we will find the other titans."

"You're calling us titans too?"

"Does the name matter?"

"I don't like it. I know it's based on his name, but it suggests superiority."

Shuck's expression was, as always, unreadable.

"Are we not superior?"

22

At first, the picture on the screen was so familiar Daniel thought it was a live feed of his own cell. The point of view was from above and behind, showing a man dressed in a white T-shirt, sitting at a desk, holding a Globlet. Daniel jumped, looked behind him, then back at the screen. He waved a hand in the air, but the image on the screen didn't change.

He pressed pause and looked at the spot on the wall where the camera must have been concealed. Nothing. The surface of the stone was uneven, discoloured. Either there wasn't a camera there, or the cameras used were as fine as a human hair. But cameras like that were stupidly expensive. Who would...?

Oh. Titus Gorman. World's richest man. That'll be it, then.

He sat down again and pressed play. After half a second, the point of view switched to show the man's face as he looked at the Globlet. A camera in the Globlet itself, then.

The man was about Daniel's age. All halfheroes were born in the same two-year period. There was no family resemblance. Daniel had seen photographs of dozens of halfheroes and met a few face-to-face. He would never have guessed they shared the same father. It was as if Abos's genetic inheritance had little effect on the physical appearance of the children.

The man on the video put the Globlet down, walked up to the door and stopped. He held out a hand, placing his fingertips on the metal.

The next scene showed an empty corridor, identical to the one outside Daniel's cell. As he watched, a hand appeared through the solid door in the centre of the frame. The hand was followed by an arm, then a face and chest as the occupant of the cell walked through solid matter and freed himself.

"Cool," said Daniel, channelling his inner nerd. He'd always liked magicians, and this guy could earn a fortune on stage.

The magician looked both ways along the corridor, then walked out of frame.

A succession of camera shots followed, showing his progress. When he had passed through the door at the end his corridor, he was in a large, circular, room with microwaves, large storage cupboards, and a line of food trolleys. There were lots of identical exits leading out of the room, one of which was a double door. The man stuck his head through three of the solid doors in turn, then left via the double doors. Another series of cameras tracked him in a longer corridor, which led to a lift. He pressed buttons on a keypad, but nothing happened. The camera inside the empty lift shaft showed a head appear, looking up. The camera was too far away to pick up any facial expression, but Daniel saw the man shake his head in frustration before withdrawing.

To the right of the lift was another corridor, which opened into a wide, high tunnel, big enough to accommodate a truck. After walking for about twenty yards, the magician stopped. He looked at something on the ceiling, but the angle of the shot prevented Daniel seeing what it was. Then he stripped off his T-shirt, balled it up and threw it, underarm, in front of him. A series of flashes followed. It took the camera a few seconds to adjust and re-focus. When it did, it showed smoke rising from the tattered remains of the T-shirt.

"No good going that way, then," muttered Daniel.

According to the time stamp at the top right of the video, nothing much happened for the next ten minutes as the magician walked the corridor, looking for an alternative exit. A series of cuts in the footage showed him facing a wall. Daniel watched the man look at the solid rock for thirty-three seconds, his face and body relaxing.

The magician was preparing himself. He must have watched Gorman's welcome video and decided three years in prison wasn't for him. He didn't know how thick the rock walls were, or what lay on the other side, but Daniel guessed the man's ability to pass through solid matter would fail him soon if he didn't get more calories into his body.

The point of view shifted to somewhere outside. Daniel leaned forward, looking for clues as to their location. It was a sheer rock face, the colour of which—as far as he could tell from the footage—was a pale grey similar to that of the walls of his cell. For a couple of seconds, he thought he was looking at a still photograph, then something moved in the upper right corner.

Daniel wished he could zoom in, get a better look at the

movement. It looked like some strange bird was stirring on its nest and preparing to fly.

It wasn't a bird, and it couldn't fly. Daniel was glad he couldn't zoom in now. He wanted to look away as the tiny figure, unmistakably human, arms and legs wheeling in empty space, fell thousands of feet to his death.

There was no sound, but Daniel couldn't stop himself imagining the man's screams.

After the video faded to black, words appeared on the screen:

Escape is impossible. Please accept it. You will be freed when it is safe to do so. I am sorry that Howell had to lose his life to make this clear. Titus.

Daniel looked into the camera he knew was in the Globlet.

"Let *me* make something clear, Gorman. We're not on first name terms, you prick. You're responsible for that man's death, and you will pay the penalty for that."

He turned the Globlet face-down on the desk, despite knowing there were at least two other cameras watching him. Kneeling at the door, he called Sara's name.

"You've seen it." It wasn't a question.

"Yes."

Sara was one of the most intelligent people he had ever met. If anyone could find a way out of this place, it was her.

Sara sighed.

"I know what you're thinking, Daniel."

"And?"

"And I'm working on it. But it doesn't look good."

"We have to get out." Daniel thought of Abos. Would she be looking for him? He knew the answer to that, but he doubted even someone as powerful as Abos could find him here. Wherever here was. Not many clues from the footage he had just watched. The rock face hadn't looked like anywhere he recognised. Geography had never been his strong point.

He half-wished he had told Sara and Gabe about Abos. And about the other beings Abos was searching for. Of all the halfheroes locked up in this place, he was the only one who knew what had happened to The Deterrent, their father. Most of them believed he was dead. He had planned on talking to Abos about it, arranging a meeting with the IGLU team. It was time they trusted someone else. Too late now. And anything he said to Sara would be overheard by TripleDee.

"Any idea where we are?"

It wasn't Sara who answered.

"We could be anywhere in the world, like, but I'm guessing America."

Neither Daniel nor Sara answered.

"All right, I get it." It sounded more like all *reet* in Triple-Dee's Newcastle accent. "You don't trust me. If it weren't for me, you wouldn't be here." *Hee-ar.* "But you are here, and so am I, and, probably, every other halfhero Gorman could find."

Sara responded to that.

"I agree. He said halfheroes were a threat in the first video. I guess he means all of us."

"Sara? This guy just ambushed us, beat the crap out of us, sold us out to Gorman... he's the reason we're here. And what, we're going to forget all that? Talk to him like he's not a complete bastard?"

"That's rich coming from you, pal." TripleDee's voice was mocking. "Just coming to see me for a cup of tea and a chat, were you? Not planning to throw me in prison and throw away the key, then?"

Sara and Daniel were silent.

"Not denying it, then? Yeah, right, so get the fuck off your high horse. We're here now, we want to get out. I'm a practical man. We need to work together."

"In your dreams, mate. You're just a piece of shit drug dealer. You'd stab me in the back as soon as look at me."

"Yeah, as it's you, maybe I would, but you'd do the same. And I'm a businessman, Harbin. Plain and simple."

"Businessman? Selling crack to kids and pimping women?"

"Shut up, you two. Daniel, TripleDee's right. We need to work together."

"Thank you." TripleDee sounded smug.

"TripleDee, Daniel's right. You are a lowlife piece of shit." Daniel laughed.

"But that means nothing now. We all want out. Let's focus on that."

Daniel and TripleDee both grunted their assent.

"Start by answering a question. How did you know about us, back in Newcastle?"

"Robertson. Gorman's man. I didn't know that at the time, mind. He showed us pictures, videos. He said the UN had secretly funded you three to clean up rogue halfheroes and lock them away."

"The way you say it, you make it sound like a bad thing."

"Who appointed you as judge and jury?"

"Don't get sidetracked." Sara was focussed on the immediate problem. "Robertson, or rather, Gorman, knew about IGLU, knew about Daniel, me, and Gabe. We were told that information could never get out. And yet he found us. We have to assume he knows more than we think he *can* know. Our backgrounds. Our powers."

"He knows enough to keep us half-starved." Daniel felt

like the lack of food was affecting his ability to think. He wondered how Sara was staying sharp.

"Right," she said, "practicalities. We're inside a mountain. The access comes from above, hence, the lift shaft we saw in the video."

"So?" TripleDee sounded dismissive.

"So this prison was tunnelled out. You'd need machinery and manpower for a project like this. If we're right about him trying to catch all the halfheroes, how many others are in here?"

Daniel had seen the reports of how many halfheroes had died during the onset of puberty.

"Not so many. I'd be surprised if there were fifty of us."

"I'm guessing there are thirty-three cells," said Sara.

"That's very precise for a guess."

"On the video, there were twelve doors leading off the circular room."

Trust Sara to have counted them.

"The double door led to the lift. He checked two other doors but didn't explore. The likeliest reason for him dismissing them is because he saw corridors just like the one he had just escaped from, identical to ours. Three cells in every corridor. Eleven corridors. Thirty-three cells."

"Smarty-pants."

"You know it. Right. There's the three of us from IGLU. How many were with you in Newcastle, Trip?"

"Trip?"

"I can't keep saying TripleDee. It makes you sound like a busty eighties pornstar."

"If it makes you happy, pet."

"I think we're a fair distance from happy. How many?"

"Eight. Nine including me."

"That's twelve plus the four from Gravesend."

"Gravesend?" said TripleDee. Sara ignored him.

"I'm assuming they're here too. Sixteen of us that we know of."

"Thirteen of which are criminals," said Daniel. "Let's hope that if there are any others, they're not scumbags too."

"I'm just ganna pretend I didn't hear that, okay?"

"Seventeen halfheroes we didn't even know about. Picked up before us. Gorman has been planning this for a long time. We watched Howell walk through a wide corridor on the video. To build this place, they must have bored a tunnel leading down into the mountain."

"And put some nice machine guns in there," said Triple-Dee. "Or did you forget what happened to Howell's Tee-shirt? Get past the guns and there's probably a private army waiting for us."

"Maybe," said Sara, "but I don't think so. Hard to hide an army. Titus Gorman is a computer genius. Look at this place - it's almost completely automated. How many guards does he need? I've seen two guys deliver the food, that's all. I don't think there's an army. If we trigger the alarms, I'll bet the place is rigged to cave in, bury us here forever."

"Well, thanks for your fucking cheery analysis."

"My pleasure. No point wasting time on things we can do nothing about."

"Sara?" Daniel tried not to sound as dejected as he felt. "What is there that we *can* do something about?"

"I'm working on that, Daniel. So far, nothing."

TripleDee pulled his face away from the door.

"Brilliant. I'll just bang me head against the wall in here, then, shall I?"

"Sara?"

She looked at Daniel.

"Nothing? Really?"

"Nothing. You'll be the first to know when that changes There has to be a way."

Daniel wasn't sure she was right. He distracted himself by worrying about Abos. Without him around, she would be even more isolated - and if she'd brought back another of her kind from her Egypt trip, there would be three of them to take care of. What chance did she have of finding him? How could she leave the others?

Ten nights later, when Daniel woke from dreaming someone else's dream, he had no idea that an escape method had just been revealed to him.

23

Midnight is an arbitrary moment chosen to symbolise the end of one day and the beginning of another. It arrives at different times as the Earth continues its elliptical orbit of Sol, in the outer arm of the Milky Way.

Samoa and Kiribati are the first to let off fireworks every January first, followed by New Zealand and Australia. The celebrations continue through parts of Russia, Japan, and Korea, then Indonesia, India, Afghanistan, into Europe via the Mediterranean islands, before crossing the Atlantic to Brazil, South America, North America, Alaska, and Canada.

The Utopia Algorithm began its work at midnight on the twenty-first of May. When banking groups and other financial institutions began reporting problems, it started in Australasia. Other countries, on high alert after Titus Gorman's announcement, reassured the powerful that every precaution had been taken, security was their top priority, everyone's money was safe. Financial cyber-security was a billion-dollar industry, and the foremost suppliers of on and offline systems made reassuring noises to their high-end clients. International finance was an edifice constructed over centuries, a multi-faceted organism where each part relied on another; every bond, share, mutual fund, loan, mortgage, deposit, bill, currency exchange and financial instrument winding inextricably around the next, insinuating electronic tentacles into the market's every available orifice.

The fear was undoubtedly there from the very first second after midnight, but it was concealed by blinkers so old, so established, and so firmly affixed to the financial system, that everyone feeling the bile rise in their throats swallowed it down and shook their heads in denial. The tsunami approached, and they kept raising their gaze to look over it at the sky beyond, pretending it wasn't there. Even as the sky disappeared behind an unstoppable torrent destroying everything in its path, even as they saw the flailing bodies of those who had issued statements encouraging calm, they said, "It's not happening. It can't be happening." Then they, too, were carried away by the giant wave.

CROYDON, UK

DONALD K STURGEON was a man for whom book-keeping was almost as satisfying as his collection of nineteen-fifties West Coast jazz. Since retiring from his managerial position in Croydon Post Office a decade earlier, he had devoted nearly as much time to learning online personal finance software as he had to cataloguing his vinyl.

Eschewing the more conventional alphabetical method,

Donald filed his albums chronologically. Not only did he find it more aesthetically pleasing, it gave him the opportunity to travel in time. He could walk around the purpose-built shelves, feeling the years passing again and again.

He lived alone, had done for seven years, since the day he had come back early from golf to find Martha in the study with his brother, Frank. The two of them were pushed up against the nineteen-fifty-four shelves, Frank's rough hands on her buttocks. Her eyes had been closed. Donald had avoided the mid-fifties section since then.

Tonight, he was in nineteen-fifty-nine with the Dave Brubeck Quartet. The street was dark outside. It was almost midnight. He had a bottle of beer on a coaster. He wasn't much of a drinker, but the sight of a brown bottle, ice cold, condensation trickling down its neck, was the perfect accompaniment to Blue Rondo A La Turk. The opening track of the album followed a metre unusual in jazz. Until you had listened to it as many times as Donald, it sounded odd. You couldn't dance to it. Martha had once said you couldn't do *anything* to music like that, let alone dance. Donald had smelled gin on her breath that night. She had sat on his lap, despite knowing that his spreadsheet of monthly expenditure and investment performance would take another thirty minutes to complete. He was so distracted by her actions, it took him over an hour to make the figures balance. He had slept in the spare room that night.

Just like appreciating Brubeck, understanding personal finance software had been hard work at first, but, now that he had mastered it, he found it immensely satisfying. Predictable. Reliable.

Take Five was just coming to an end. The one track on the album not written by Brubeck, it had been its only hit.

Its popularity confirmed the superficiality of the track, in Donald's view. Paul Desmond, the saxophonist who wrote it, undoubtedly had an easy charm about his playing and was one of the few alto players with impeccable intonation. But Donald felt the lazy phrasing of Desmond's improvisation detracted from the precision of Brubeck's playing. Not that he would skip the track, of course. Every album must be listened to in its entirety.

As he got up to flip to side two, a flicker on the screen caught his attention. He turned back to the computer. The *total* figure was orange, denoting a conflict between his spreadsheet and his bank account. Donald snorted. Suspecting a glitch in the software—which would mean a strongly-worded email to the developers in the morning—he clicked out of the program and logged into his bank direct. Personal—checking—current—balance—refresh.

Donald didn't blink for eight long seconds. Then he hit refresh for a second time, rubbed his eyes and looked again. Finally, he walked into the hall, opened the address book at B, and called the automated banking line, entering his details as instructed. Five sub-menus and forty-seven bars of Vivaldi later, the computerised voice announced a number which tallied with the one on Donald's screen.

Replacing the receiver in shock, he walked back into his study and paused, leaning heavily on nineteen-fifty-one while he regained his composure.

For the first time ever, Donald's spreadsheet was at odds with the amount in his account.

How could this be?

With a shaking hand, Donald picked up the beer and drank deeply.

His bank account was *down*. His calculations weren't

wrong. They couldn't be. Which only left one possible conclusion.

He'd been robbed.

Robbed!

Of seven pounds and fifteen pence.

~

Detroit, USA

Carl stood in front of the ATM, praying. Pappa had always said the worship of money was the root of all evil, but he'd died of a cancer better healthcare insurance would have detected long before he couldn't piss without crying. Since then, especially since he'd had a kid of his own, Carl had been a little more flexible in his attitude to money.

"C'mon, Lord, you know I don't ask you for much. Shit, I don't ask you for nothing, mostly, am I right?"

A more responsive deity might have pointed out that Carl had stopped speaking to Him, let alone asking Him for anything, at the age of eight when he didn't get a bike for Christmas.

"But, listen, Jesus, I ain't asking for myself, you know that. I'm asking for Jessie. She's two years old. She's just a baby. Her legs ain't right. Now, I ain't blaming anyone, don't get me wrong. Pattie says it's a punishment, but I don't believe that. I don't believe in a god that would give a kid a bone problem cause their mom and pa don't go to church."

Carl looked at the words on the screen again as the ATM spat the card back a second time.

"Insufficient? Insufficient? How am I s'posed to turn that

into sufficient, motherfucker? Tell me that, why don't you? Not you, Lord, I was talking to this cocksucker. This machine, I mean, sorry for my language. I get riled, is all. Riled. You know I work all the hours they'll give me. You know Pattie still tends bar when her mom can sit with Jessie. She's all we got, and if we don't get her fixed up, doctor says she'll limp for the rest of her life. If that first quack had set the bone right, we'd be fine, right, but he didn't, so here we are. The man's a fucking bum— excuse me—but you know he is. If Jessie had fallen off that swing in the morning, we'd have caught him hungover. He does his best work then, everyone knows that. But no, it was after school. He'd been hitting the hard stuff since lunch. Could've been worse. At least he put the cast on the broken leg."

Carl looked around the parking lot. It was empty other than some kids sitting on the hood of a car at the far end, drinking, then throwing empty bottles at the recycling point, most of them missing and shattering, accompanied by cheers. He knew they would rob him if they thought he had anything to take. But they knew he didn't. He had forty-six dollars in his checking account. Forty-six dollars. The doctor they had found said she would operate for three thousand dollars cash. That was cheap, she said. She might as well have said three hundred thousand dollars.

"Bitch," muttered Carl. "Sorry, sorry."

He was drunk for the first time in a year. A pint of cheap rum had chased down the beers he had bought in Lacey's. He'd just wanted to feel like a regular guy again. Someone who could go out sometimes, meet his buddies, have a few beers, talk about sport.

"Shit, I'm sorry about the drink, okay, I'm sorry." Papa had put drink narrowly behind money in his list of sinful preoccupations.

"Look, Jesus, here's the thing. I swear, no more drink, no

more cussing, no more..." Carl searched his mind frantically for anything else that might be considered ungodly. There wasn't much. When he finally thought of something, he grasped it enthusiastically.

"Okay, an' I swear I won't think about Denise that way again. Next time she bends over to pick something up, I'll turn away. I will, I'll do it, I promise in your name. Why that woman has to keep dropping things all the time beats me, anyhow."

Carl kissed his ATM card, made the sign of the cross with it, said as much of the Lord's prayer as he could remember, then slid it back into the slot.

"C'mon, Jesus, God, Mary, please. For Jessie. For my baby."

He closed his eyes. When he opened them again, he was looking at a different figure.

"Mother*fucker.*"

Remembering his promise to stop cursing, he slapped his forehead.

"Shit! No, not shit, fuck, I mean, sorry, fuck it, sorry. I got this."

He took a deep breath in and a deep breath out, looked at the screen again, then took out the maximum cash allowed: five hundred dollars. He held the money for a moment and checked the screen again. The figure had changed to account for the five hundred he was now holding. It was still more money than he ever thought he'd have. He smiled so broadly he could taste his tears at the corners of his lips.

"Now that's what I'm talking about. Thank you, Lord. And Amen."

∽

WASHINGTON DC, USA

THE TABLE WASN'T LAID, and the room was dark. After opening the curtains herself, Cynthia checked the clock on the mantelpiece. Two minutes after seven. She sniffed. No coffee brewing.

She walked through the dining room, straight across the marble-floored lobby and into the kitchen. A wave of the hand and the LEDs glowed into life, revealing a huge, gleaming room a boutique hotel would be proud of. Every work surface was clean, every prep area tidy. The saucepans, twenty-six of them, hung in size order from hooks along the far wall. The Italian coffee machine near the door—placed there on her instruction, so she could smell the freshly-brewed coffee when she came downstairs—was plugged in, but not switched on. She had paid a small fortune to have that particular machine shipped from Turin to Washington. Cynthia Ganfrey didn't believe in compromises when it came to coffee. She wasn't a big believer in compromises, full stop.

She frowned. Her favourite brand of cup, which had just the right thickness of china, stood next to the machine. The beans were in the grinder.

"Miriam?"

Her voice bounced off the walls. Cynthia was struck with a sudden certainty: she was alone in the house. She didn't question her intuition, she knew she was correct. Cynthia was not a woman who believed in hunches; she was, rather, a woman who trusted conclusions made by instinct before her rational brain had caught up. Her business rivals, back in the days when she still had some, said she had killer instincts. Such comments were uncannily accurate, although none of her rivals knew it. Her first husband knew it, but wouldn't be telling anyone, as he was buried in the foundations of the building project he'd tried to cut her out of.

She flicked the switch to warm up the coffee machine.

"Miriam?"

She was immediately annoyed with herself for calling out a second time. It was as if she were playing the lead in a melodrama, the rich widow panicking in an empty mansion.

Cynthia wasn't the panicking kind.

If her third husband, had been here, he would have tried to take the lead, start making phone calls. He would have paced up and down speaking too fast and jabbing his finger into the air. She was so glad he was dead. She'd married him for his political influence. God knows he'd offered her little else. The heart attack came after six years of marriage, but it could have come five and a half years earlier as far as Cynthia was concerned.

When asked, she would describe herself as being "currently between husbands." The truth was she would never marry again. She was fifty-eight, still a handsome woman, but marriage offered no advantages now. Sex wasn't an issue. She had regular assignations with younger married men who thought they were using her, poor fools. She didn't crave companionship. Most people were dullards. The few that weren't were often as self-centred and narcissistic as Cynthia. The difference was, she knew it. She embraced it.

She placed her Globlet face-down on the kitchen table. Coffee first, news later. If the world had ended, she would read the details after her first cup, not before.

The light on the coffee machine was green, so she

ground the beans while swirling the cup in hot steam. The aroma was delightful. Cynthia would not countenance using beans roasted more than five days ago. She tamped the ground beans in the basket, and twisted it firmly in place above the warm cup, before pressing the button. Four seconds later, the first drops of crema began to drip from the spouts, turning into an even flow. Twenty-four seconds after that, she picked up the cup and sat at the table.

Only after the last rich, complex, mouthful did she finally turn on the Globlet and read the headlines.

"Well, well."

She clicked on her emails. Miriam's was the forty-third from the top in order of time received. Its subject was **My resignation**.

"Tiresomely predictable, Miriam. And a bad decision to boot."

Cynthia did a little reading, concentrating on the media coverage around Titus Gorman. She already knew more about him than most Americans. Gorman was, according to the Forbes list at least, the world's richest human. Although she considered herself semi-retired, it would hardly have been wise of her not to investigate a man who might be almost as wealthy as she was.

She re-watched an early interview with him. Lately, he had limited his contact with the media.

"No one can spend the kind of money I'm starting to make. In another ten years, I'll have more money than some countries. That's crazy."

"Do you have plans for the money, then?"

"Plans? Yes, you could say that. I have plans."

"Care to let us in on them?"

"No. It would ruin the surprise. It's going to take a few years to line everything up, then everyone will understand."

"Okay, mysterious to the last. Thank you, Titus Gorman."

Mysterious was the right word. Cynthia had dropped nearly a million dollars scratching around for more information about Gorman. That had been eight years ago. There had been little to find. Even his name, apparently lifted from a favourite author's rambling fantasy trilogy, gave no real clues. He was a phantom. In a world that had digitised every piece of information, a self-confessed master hacker could make himself disappear.

Cynthia didn't understand what drove Titus. In the same interview, he claimed to have no interest in money. That was one point on which she and the mystery man agreed, although she doubted he shared her rationale. Cynthia saw money as a way of keeping score. She didn't care that no one else knew what her score was, she only cared that she was winning. And winning big.

She turned on her mobile phone. There were no messages. The handful of people who had her number knew to email. She would speak to people at a time *she* chose. She dialled one of her five wealth managers.

"Rory, how much money is in the account? Yes, I know, don't try to explain unless you have access to information that no one else does. Do you? Then just tell me the amount. Thank you. No, that will be all."

She didn't cry, but she came closer to doing so than ever before. Her body shook with the force of the suppressed sobs. She was very glad Miriam was not there to see it.

Cynthia didn't bother calling her other brokers. The number she had just heard, multiplied by five, came to seventeen thousand, four hundred and sixty dollars. Which was, according to every news organisation she had checked, the exact amount in every person's bank account on the planet.

24

S huck's call, when it came, was a relief.

"She's awake."

"Already?"

Abos didn't know why she responded with surprise. Habit, she supposed. She knew that Rasputin's new body—Susan—was conscious. She had known it as a stirring of fresh consciousness in her own mind, an opening of sorts. Unmistakable. Something similar had happened with Shuck, but, until it the second time, she had not known what it meant.

She was speaking to Shuck from the top of the tallest building in New York. Shuck was probably standing in the yard in Cornwall as the mobile phone signal was strongest there. Abos could picture what he was seeing almost as clearly as the sun that was sinking behind skyscrapers in front of her.

"I'll call you back."

Something had been happening to her for days when she allowed it. A freeing up of areas of her consciousness. Abos would have been hard-pressed to describe it. How do you describe a new smell to someone if there are no grounds for comparison? How do you describe a new taste if it's neither sweet nor sour, rich nor thin, sharp nor bitter? In the simplest terms, she knew she was now able to experience a little of what Shuck, or Susan, were experiencing. She wasn't privy to their every thought. It was more like an extra sense, always present. She knew if they were awake or asleep.

Abos was perched on the top of the spire of One World Trade Center. This reminded her of another thing she hadn't understood in the superhero movies Daniel had shown her.

"Why do they always do that? Find a high place in the city and stand, or squat there?"

"Probably cause it looks great. The cape blowing in the wind. Moody, atmospheric. You know."

She didn't know.

"And what about the way they land? Many times they ruin the surface, crack the concrete because they are not landing properly. If they can fly, they can certainly land without causing an earthquake. It's irresponsible."

"Abos, I'm not sure superhero movies will ever be your thing."

Now she thought she understood. She wanted to be alone, unreachable.

She had failed Daniel.

Abos had spent the previous days following a trail that was never really there. Someone had taken Daniel, the rest of his IGLU team, the Newcastle drug dealer and his companions. Whoever was behind this had the resources to break into the Gravesend prison—a place no one was supposed to even know existed—and to use an unlisted private jet with no flight plan history.

Twenty-six hours earlier, she had been in Tokyo hotel investigating a sighting of a Gulfstream G650 that morning. The lead had been a dead end. An email response from Palindrome hadn't lifted her spirits.

D,

Have you inherited some money, or what? Should I be putting my prices up? These babies aren't cheap if you're thinking about buying one.

There are two-hundred-and-sixty-seven G650s in operation, but we're talking about the usual suspects. Saudi, UAE, China, USA. A couple in Korea, one in the UK. List attached, but it may not be entirely accurate. The very, very rich sometimes make deals where no money changes hands. A hotel complex gets built, and, as part of the deal, a Gulfstream changes hands. It's done on a handshake. What I'm saying is, if you're trying to trace the owner, you might be shit out of luck. Especially if they don't want their identity known. Very few G650s are owned by an individual, anyway. Two-hundred-and four belong to shell companies based in tax havens. I can trace the actual owners if you like. It'll take three to four months at least, even if I drop the other thing. Oh, about that. Getting closer. And it's getting weirder. If I'm right about where Hopkins diverted all that money, you'll never believe it. I'll let you know when I'm sure. I'm such a tease...

PALINDROME DIDN'T KNOW Abos existed, so she had used Daniel's details, email address, and passwords, even going as far as copying his sentence constructions and vocabulary. Palindrome had been George's most prized criminal contact. If Palindrome thought someone other than Daniel was using this email address, that would mean a sudden, and permanent, end to their working relationship.

Abos had gone through the list of companies, but it had left her no closer to finding Daniel. She couldn't think of anything else to try. Daniel would have come up with fresh ideas if their roles were reversed, but she had come up against an insurmountable obstacle: her imagination. She didn't have one. Abos had abilities humans might never match, but she also had limitations. Her mind just didn't work like a human's.

Abos suspected she'd never had an original thought. Her mental processes were efficient and logical. She had experienced empathy, and she had an aversion to violence, but the spark of originality that humans treasured? No.

This new opening of consciousness with Shuck and Susan suggested there were parts of her mind that she was yet to explore. But they would take her further away from her affinity with humanity.

She watched the cars crawling along the streets. The sounds of the city were barely audible at this distance.

Someone had rounded up halfheroes and taken them somewhere. Who? And why? Had it been against their will? Abos lacked the imagination to suggest answers to her own questions. She had come to America because the highest number of Gulfstreams were bought by Americans.

And, in America, she'd run out of ideas.

As the evening air grew cold on top of One World Trade Center, she remembered the night on the Shard in London with Daniel. There was pain in allowing the memory to surface, but it was a pain she welcomed. Her connection with humanity was, as far as she knew, uniquely strong among her species. She was a parent. Shuck and Susan were not.

She wanted, more than anything, to find Daniel.

A loud snap called her back to reality. Abos had been squeezing the iron structure at the top of the tower and a piece of the spire had broken away. She stared at the fractured metal in the half-light. There was nothing she could think of to do for Daniel. But there were others who needed her.

She took out her phone again and called Shuck.

"I'm coming home."

25

He was in a restaurant, and he was speaking French.

This should have been surprising, as he hadn't spoken a complete sentence in the language since failing his GCSE. Yet he was as unconcerned by the improbability of his fluency as he was by his opulent surroundings; the candles, the heavy drapes, the white tablecloths and silver cutlery.

A waiter stood at his elbow. He ordered coffee and two large Armagnacs, specifying the brand. The waiter nodded in approval. He was no tourist. After his mother and step-father had been killed in a car accident, he had moved to Paris with no plan other than getting away from everything and everyone he knew.

That memory was so real, so convincing, that he did not challenge the fact that it had never happened.

Sophie was sitting opposite. Her smile had gone, her dark eyes looking into his. She loved him and he had just told her he was leaving her, leaving Paris.

It had all been a beautiful, glorious lie. A lie spun with the best intentions. A lie begun in grief and completed in love. But a lie nonetheless. He had hidden everything about himself from her, even his name. He was a fiction, a fantasy. And he had let Sophie *live in the story he had written, not thinking about how it might hurt her. He regretted it now, a little. He didn't yet know it was a regret that would continue to grow, one he would carry for the rest of his life.*

Now, in the way she looked at him, the way she paused before sipping the Armagnac, in a hundred unspoken ways, he saw Sophie fall apart.

When she left, she did it without saying goodbye. She finished her drink—she'd always loved a good Armagnac—closed her eyes as if listening to music, stood up, and walked away without a backward glance.

He felt the weight of it settling on him.

The waiter brought a second Armagnac, setting it down quietly before withdrawing. Over the next hour, as the restaurant emptied, no one disturbed him. The waiter addressed him in English as he held open the door.

"Goodbye. And good luck."

"Merci, André."

Back in the apartment he packed a small bag, then tried to sleep. Every time he closed his eyes, he saw Sophie the first night she had stayed. The little moue of pleasure he'd noticed for the first time that night, the half-laughs he had grown to love. He remembered the softness of her lips, the touch of her fingers as she traced a line from his shoulders onto his chest, cupping his soft breasts before—

Wait, cupping what?

Daniel opened his eyes and sat up in bed.

He went to the sink and splashed water onto his face. A little embarrassed, and hunching over so the cameras wouldn't see what he was doing, he brought his hand up to his chest, half-expecting to find breasts. When his fingers traced the solid slab of muscle, a little less defined now from the poor diet, he was almost disappointed.

It wasn't just that the dream had been more real, more vivid than any he had experienced before. That wasn't the reason he was breathing heavily, feeling shaky. It was the complete loss of self that was making him look again in the mirror, checking the face staring back was his own.

The lights were still dim, which meant it wasn't morning yet, whatever 'morning' meant in a windowless cell.

Daniel laid back on the bed and closed his eyes, but sleep wouldn't come. The dream had disturbed him at such a profound level that he was scared to sleep in case he lost his identity again. What if he woke up and couldn't remember who he was? He hadn't just dreamed about being someone else, it was far more powerful than that.

Exercise might help make sleep possible. After seven push-ups, he felt lightheaded, pinpricks of light floating into the edges of his vision. He tried stomach crunches. After four repetitions, his head started to swim again, and his muscles complained. He ignored it and made it to ten, before rolling onto his side, sweating and trembling, his pulse throbbing in the skin around his face and scalp, bile rising in his throat.

"I'll get out of here, Gorman," he whispered into the concrete floor. "I swear it. I'll get out or die trying."

The day passed as all days passed. Food arrived about an hour after the lights came on. Much later, long after any normal person would have eaten lunch, another meal appeared, as insubstantial as the first. That was it as far as sustenance was concerned.

Daniel had hoped he might learn to accept the constant state of hunger, but it hadn't happened. The physical effect of receiving only survival-level nutrition was one thing, but the mental effects were even more debilitating. It was hard to concentrate, to focus on any one thought for more than a few seconds before hunger interrupted any attempt at cogent reasoning.

Sara had made a better job at overcoming the mental effects of a near-starvation diet. She called out to him three or four times a day. He listened, mostly. He tried to contribute to the conversation, but was thick-witted and slow, often unable to follow her reasoning.

"It's not that you're less intelligent than me," she said that morning. Daniel hadn't been paying attention. He'd been trying to convince himself that the second, and final, meal of the day was imminent. His bowels told him he was wrong. He always took a shit about two hours after breakfast, long before he was even halfway through the wait for the next tray of food. As he hadn't yet done so, it was still morning, no matter how vehemently he pretended otherwise.

He realised Sara had said something.

"What?"

"I weigh much less than you. You're the biggest guy I've ever seen. You eat as much as two people - three when you're working. But there's no fat on you. You're a freak of nature."

"Thanks."

"You're welcome. We all are. I eat much more than other women my size because the calories enable me to do what I do. Halfhero powers need fuel. Having that fuel rationed has prevented me using my powers, but I can still think straight. Just about. I'm amazed you can even stand up, let alone put together a coherent sentence."

"Are piss taking the you?"

"You still have a sense of humour. Amazing."

"Yeah." Daniel fought off the lethargy pulling at him. "Amazing." He had started allowing himself a nap in the afternoon, but no more. It was too easy to sleep, and that twilight existence was too reminiscent of the years he had spent drugged at Station.

"Here are my observations so far. We see the same two guards every day, one in the morning, one in the afternoon. We saw no one at all during Howell's attempt to get out. The place is mostly automated. My best guess is eight guards in total."

"Why eight?"

"When one guard is doing meals on wheels down here, there must be another in a control centre watching. If anything goes wrong, he or she can shut the place down. We know there's a shift change before the second meal, so let's assume the control centre guy changes too. Three eight-hour shifts is six guards. Two more to cover time off and sickness. If they work twelve-hour shifts, there are six of them."

TripleDee's voice broke in.

"Or there could just be the two ugly twats that we see every day. It's not a tough job, is it? And have you noticed what they've got in common?"

Sara, unable to see the drug dealer from her cell, raised her eyebrows at Daniel.

"Go on."

"They're both deaf."

"Pardon?"

"I said, they're...oh, very fucking funny, pet. The hours just fly by with you around."

"Why do you think they're deaf?"

"You heard me scream, right?"

Daniel looked across at TripleDee. His beard was coming through, blonde and silver. His eyes were hooded and dark, the lines around them more pronounced than

Daniel remembered. He looked older. Years older. Daniel knew he had fared no better.

"Yeah, we heard you. Could hardly miss it. I'm surprised he fed you at all after that."

"Right, but you didn't see me do it. I timed it perfectly. I'm the first one he passes. It was dead quiet, like. I backed away from the door so he couldn't see I was lying there waiting. The closest he gets is just before he flicks the tray under the door. When I saw him step forward to do it, I stuck my mouth up to the gap and screamed as loudly as I could."

"Yep," said Sara. "I remember. I was glad I was sitting on the crapper."

"He didn't flinch. Nothing. No reaction at all. No earbuds, no headphones. Stone deaf."

There was silence for a moment.

"Well, bloody hell," said Sara. "You are full of surprises, Triple."

"Nah. Not really. You just underestimated me cause I'm a criminal and a Geordie. Wouldn't be the first time."

Another silence before Sara spoke again.

"You're right. I have underestimated you. I'm sorry."

"Sorry?" Daniel almost choked on the word.

"Yes, sorry. Daniel, you're going to have to get past this if we're going to work together. And we have to work together if we want to get out."

"You heard the lady. Get over it, big boy."

Daniel drew breath but didn't speak straight away. Sara was right. He had to put aside the urge to punch the drug-dealing, human-trafficking waster until they had broken out. Then he could punch him very hard.

"Okay," he said, "they're deaf. Smart move by Gorman. You can't bribe or threaten someone who can't hear you."

"Maybe not so smart." Sara always spoke more slowly

when she was thinking things out. "If he can't hear a scream, he can't hear a door being broken open and someone coming up behind him."

"And what about your guard upstairs, watching it all?"

"One problem at a time. As much as I'm enjoying the wonderful library our host has provided, I want out of here. The longer we wait, the weaker we become."

TripleDee spoke. "Ready when you are, pet."

"Daniel," said Sara, "we've got to try something. You're the strongest. What if we give you most of our food for a day or two? Would you be able to break down the door? And ours?"

Daniel rolled on to his back and looked up at the solid metal.

"No problem at all if I'm fit."

TripleDee called over. "You'd better be bloody sure if I'm ganna give you me scran."

Daniel had no idea what that meant.

"Un homme seul est toujours en mauvaise compagnie," he said, a snatch of conversation from his dream coming back to him.

Sara, surprised, translated.

"A man alone is always bad company. Paul Valéry. I didn't know you liked French poetry."

"I don't." Daniel hadn't even known he was quoting someone.

"You never told me you speak French. Que cachez-vous d'autre?"

"Um. I can't speak French, Sara. I just must have heard it somewhere. You never said you could speak French, either."

"Oui. I lived in Paris for a few years."

Daniel experienced a sudden sense of certainty,

although there was no logic behind it. Before he could stop himself, he said it out loud.

"Did you know someone called Sophie? Did you break up with her there?"

The silence that followed his question was so long that he knew he was right. When she answered, her voice was tight.

"How the fuck did you know that?"

26

Financial institutions do not hold all the money in the world. At one end of the scale, there are people who keep their cash under the mattress or in a biscuit tin behind the cookbooks. At the other end, there are those who would rather keep their cash reserves low, instead holding gold, silver, platinum, palladium, or diamonds. Classic cars are another favourite, as are art, wine, racehorses, and first editions of classic novels.

The Utopia Algorithm caused chaos, but there were unexpected winners and losers in the immediate fallout. The richest were hit hardest, but there were no riots on the streets. Privilege is an easy state of mind to get used to, and the vast majority of the wealthy, seeing their money disappear overnight, decided that their best course of action was to complain to the authorities, then sit it out. Riots are anti-establishment in nature. The rich *were* the establishment. Who were they supposed to rage against?

The cash-rich did well. Drug dealers thought Christmas had come early. For the first time in history, pawnbrokers got most of their business through house calls, as the wealthy became regular customers, handing over watches, jewellery, and heirlooms for a fraction of their true value.

The super-rich made calls to their peers, and to politicians who owed them favours. Those that had inherited their wealth felt the beginnings of panic while those who had built their own empires—the initial shock wearing off more quickly—shored up the resources they could still access and prepared themselves to rebuild.

Pensioners were hit hard when their savings disappeared, but an email to the banks from Glob promised a monthly payment equivalent to the average national wage would be paid into the accounts of those over seventy years old.

The president of the United States government received an email from Titus Gorman the day after the algorithm ran. A copy was sent to every other government and all major international news outlets. It was concise.

MR. PRESIDENT,

My name is Titus Gorman. As of yesterday, I control the world's financial systems. Please don't waste too much time trying to undo what I have done. I appreciate that you have to make the effort, but you won't succeed. Here's why. The bots I sent out three years ago were programmed to hide in the world's banking systems and learn. They are intelligent, tireless, and perfectly coded. I should know. I coded them.

By the time I triggered the algorithm, each bot had learned the structural language of the system in which it had been placed. The Utopia Algorithm isn't an algorithm per se. I just thought the name was catchy. I sent a packet of instructions to my bots yesterday, and they implemented them by translating my orders into the unique structural language they have learned in their individual placements.

Can you undo that? No. Your tech experts will explain, once they've understood my achievement, that the only way to stop me would be to build new, sandboxed systems. Eventually, you'll work out a way to connect them again without leaving a backdoor for me to exploit. It'll take years, though, by which time the landscape will have irrevocably changed.

The world is a fairer place today. I've levelled the playing field. And I'm watching you.

I expect you'll be calling me a cyber-terrorist by now. Whatever. It's mostly the rich who are terrified, so I'm sure you'll get that label to stick. I don't care either way. It's almost accurate. Terrorists take hostages and make demands, right? I have hostages, trillions of them. And I'm prepared to release them. You'll never be as rich as you were, but I'll let you pursue your dreams of wealth and power again. Just so long as you meet my demands.

1. All employers must change their pay structure. No individual can earn over ten times the salary of the lowest-paid employee.

2. Education and healthcare are rights, not privileges. No profit allowed. Same pay structure imposed.

*3. The national average salary is now the national **minimum** salary.*

That's it for now. I know the wheels of government turn slowly, and I'm not an unreasonable man. You have until Thanksgiving.

At this point, you're thinking, "or what?" It's a fair question. Yesterday, you met six of my titans (I preferred Protectors, but who am I to resist the opinion of social media?). I have more. It's not an army, but considering that Britain felt The Deterrent was powerful enough to protect a whole country, I'd suggest you think twice before crossing me.

I'm not a violent man, Mr. President. I think our foreign policy sucks. Every time I hear the words "civilian casualties" or "collateral damage" I want to scream. However, I'm not a pacifist either, and the weapons at my disposal are not blunt instruments. Compared to military intervention, drones, or threats of nuclear strikes, the titans are the equivalent of pinhole surgery.

Consider this. If I gave the order, one of my titans could be at the White House within an hour. Your firepower would be useless against him. He has none of my scruples about violence, he just does as he's told. Think on that, Mr. President, think on that.

In the meantime, I will have to take a few lives. I fear you won't work on my demands otherwise.

I'll be back in touch in a few days.

Titus Gorman

WHILE EVERY COUNTRY felt the impact of the Utopia Algorithm, some were more damaged than others. America was doubly wounded. Not only did it hold most of the richest, or previously richest, individuals in the world, but Titus Gorman was one of their own.

A huge manhunt was underway before the end of the first day of the algorithm running. Gorman's face was everywhere, and the unprecedented fifty-million-dollar reward drew plenty of attention. The FBI, CIA, and NSA put aside professional enmity and combined forces, shared every piece of information, dropping everything to, in the words of their Commander-in-Chief, "catch that sorry sonofabitch."

While the nation's covert specialists were hunting, the US military was ordered to make an example of Titus

Gorman's company, send him a message the rest of the world would see. Maybe even lure him out into the open.

Glob's headquarters were just outside San Diego, an anonymous cluster of white-fronted, smoked-glass buildings. The company had moved there five years earlier, but, over the last eighteen months, the staff had thinned out considerably. Programmers had been told to work from home, managers were encouraged to find positions in rival organisations. Anyone coming with a glowing reference from Glob was guaranteed a prestigious job.

Four days after the algorithm ran, watched by the world's media, US army tanks rolled over the gates and closed off all exits, their barrels pointing directly at the Glob buildings. Staff emerged with their hands in the air. They were herded into a field behind the line of tanks and soldiers and held there. As helicopter gunships approached, names, addresses, and occupations of the assorted employees were noted by the officer in charge. Once the gunships were in place, a three-minute warning was issued through a PA system to anyone yet to leave the buildings. No one else emerged.

The helicopters landed and stood ready.

The lieutenant collecting the names from the terrified employees called the nearest one forward.

"Where is everyone else?"

The young Mexican man looked at the hard-faced woman in military uniform, a heavy gun on her hip.

"There is no one else, Ma'am. No one. We are the only ones who work here."

The Lieutenant looked out at forty-eight scared faces, some crying, some white-faced, some praying. She nodded at the soldiers guarding the employees, then reported to the general.

"Sir, there are only forty-eight of them."

"Where are the rest?"

"There aren't any more. And the ones we have, sir, none of them really work for Glob."

"What the hell does that mean?"

"They're all contract staff, sir. Temporary. We have twenty-seven cleaners, nine maintenance engineers, six receptionists, and six telephone operators."

"Shit."

The general turned to a nearby subordinate.

"Send them in."

A squad of military technology experts were escorted into each building. They knew what they were looking for, and it took two hours for them to confirm that it wasn't there.

"No mainframe?" The General rolled his eyes. "Yeah, I figured as much. He knew we'd come here first. But the boss wants a show, and we can't let the TV folk down."

He gave the order, the tanks pulled back, and the gunships moved back into position.

"Waste of time and money," he muttered as four missiles left the helicopters with tails of orange flame and levelled the entire business park. Every news channel showed it on a loop for most of the day.

Titus Gorman emailed again, as promised, an hour after his headquarters was reduced to a pile of smoking rubble.

MR. PRESIDENT,

Remember my analogy about pinhole surgery? What you just did, destroying empty buildings that housed nothing important, was the equivalent of using a massive dose of chemotherapy.

On the wrong patient. You achieved nothing other than making yourself look foolish.

I warned you I was prepared to use violence. I need to convince you, and everyone watching, of your impotence and my strength.

One week from today, therefore, three individuals will die. They will be notified, as will you, on the morning of their deaths. You cannot save them, but I, and the world, expect you to try. They will be dead before midnight a week from today. All of them. I need you to understand this: you cannot protect anyone now. I will post their files online the day after their deaths so that anyone interested can see who they were, and what they have done. None of them will deserve to be mourned. One of them is a politician, another a serving member of the US army. The third is a prominent entertainment lawyer. I will email their names to you at six am on the day of their execution.

Their lives are in your hands. You will fail. Please take this as a warning, and a promise. I can get to anyone, I am not negotiating, and I have given you a generous deadline before which you must meet my initial demands.

Until Thanksgiving, then.

TG

A WEEK LATER, in Washington, in Nevada, and in Los Angeles, two men and one woman received identical emails.

You thought your crimes would go unpunished, but you were wrong. You die today. Make your peace with whoever you think might give a damn.

Titus Gorman

27

T he sun had gone down in Cornwall, and Abos, Shuck, and Susan were testing their limits. With plenty of cloud cover to obscure their flight, they headed for the coast, leaving the land behind and soaring south, before coming to a stop above the Bay of Biscay. Two thousand feet below them, the water surged and roared as storms that had raged across the Atlantic hit the continental shelf and found themselves with nowhere to go.

They looked at each other as they hovered in the deceptive calm above the clouds. Abos spoke to Susan without words.

—*You're sure* —

—*Yes. I'm ready*—

Susan had woken into her new human body just as Abos, and Shuck, had done before her. Shuck's mental development had been blindingly fast compared to the weeks of adaptation Abos had gone through, but Susan had taken it to a new level.

When she opened her eyes for the first time, Susan had climbed out of the bath, walked over to the farmhouse, and fixed herself some soup. Shuck had been picking up supplies at the nearest shop but had been immediately aware she was conscious. When he'd returned, Susan had displayed no disorientation at all. As he'd put the shopping bags on the floor, she had pointed at the hob.

"Soup's still hot. Here's a bowl."

Without a word, Shuck had filled his bowl and sat down opposite her. She'd finished her soup before speaking again.

"I understand why Abos is looking for Daniel. However, she is unlikely to find him. But we can sense other titans, even in their dormant state. We need to find them, wake them. Starting with those who are being used. Call Abos. She is the alpha."

No one has to teach a dog to cock its leg when it takes a piss. As puppies, dogs urinate by stretching their back legs away from the business end and leaning close to the ground. In the first year, the dog will start cocking his leg and marking his territory. As a domesticated animal, he has no parent to teach him this behaviour. He just starts doing it. Something in his brain, linked to sexual maturity and territorial urges, tells him how.

This was the analogy Abos had thought of when she met Susan, who exhibited no signs of disorientation.

Something new was happening, some biological change was unlocking new abilities.

Abos knew her brain was changing. Something had triggered it when Shuck had emerged, and Susan's awakening, thousands of miles away, had accelerated the pace of change.

Whatever she was—whatever her species was—did not conform to the human model of individual consciousness. She was an individual, but she was more than that. How much more, she was yet to find out.

—You remember nothing of your life as Rasputin? St Petersburg? Your death?—

Abos looked at Susan as they communicated without words. The stars glittered above all three of them, reflecting on the motorcycle helmets they held by their sides. A few thousand feet up, a passenger jet began its descent to Bilbao airport, unaware of the unlikely triumvirate occupying the airspace below.

Susan closed her eyes.

Images, sounds, and odours surfaced and disappeared in her mind. Abos experienced them almost as a listener might hear sounds on headphones, each one placed in a different part of the stereo spectrum. Panned hard right, an image of a group of bearded men huddled in a cave, murmuring the same phrase over and over. Just left of centre, a woman, eyes closed, rough fingers on her body, unclasping her underwear. Further left, a child, pale and ill. In the centre, the smell of food and the clench of poison in the guts, a weakened body, bullets causing pain, nearly penetrating the skin, the shock of cold water and no strength left to get to the surface of the river. A man leaning over the bridge as the body shut down.

—I remember little—

Abos was glad. Rasputin had been power-crazed, deluded. What if her species carried the ghosts of previous incarnations in their new bodies, the same way that a glass of water might still taste of the wine it held previously? Fortunately, Susan's new body seemed to have shaken off Rasputin, just as Shuck showed few signs of his life as a mythical dog. Another effect of their combined consciousness, perhaps? Or just a gradual loss of influence due to the passage of time between the death of their last bodies and the birth of their new ones?

—*Good. Are you ready?*—

—*I am*—

—*Shuck?*—

—*Ready*—

There was no preparation, no ritual necessary to achieve the state of awareness they required. They simply had to accept Abos as alpha. If they wanted to merge, to become both individuals and a single organism simultaneously, to expand their awareness and abilities, there had to be a dominant mind.

Abos took overall control, and the three became onemind.

She turned and flew south. Shuck headed north, back towards Cornwall. Susan peeled off to the east and the French coast. They matched their speed, flying far slower than normal. At ten miles, the connection was still present. At twenty-five miles, it was there, but imperfect, like a badly tuned radio station, interrupted by static. Between twenty-five and thirty miles, the three of them slowed down as the signal became intermittent, before disappearing. They were three individuals again, although still connected at a basic level, each still aware of the others.

Checking the coordinates later on their phones, they found that, to maintain onemind, they needed to keep within twenty-two miles of the nearest titan.

—*You cannot think of a better word than titan?*—

—*not yet*—

They ran experiments, tried different combinations. First, Abos and Susan stayed together, and Shuck flew away from them. Then Abos and Shuck waited while Susan flew. The results were the same, their connection breaking up before the twenty-five-mile limit.

Then Abos, as alpha, took control. The others allowed it,

their individuality receding, rather than disappearing. She became three. It was both the strangest, and the most natural-feeling moment she could remember since first opening her eyes in 1978.

Onemind saw the ocean, the stars and the coast of Spain, skimmed low over the waves until the salt spray flecked its body, at the same time as it headed up towards the silence of the stars, their light merging into the head-lamps of ten thousand cars making a chaotic mandala of Bilbao.

Abos understood, within onemind, the responsibility, and dangers, of entering this state of consciousness. the biggest danger was her, the alpha, the dominant mind. That mind, if strong enough, could take over. The forming and un-forming of onemind was down to the alpha. It could be forced on the others.

What was interesting about the sense of this danger was how it had arisen within their shared consciousness. It felt like a warning from history, a distant warning from their species.

Near the water, they called silently and watched as a school of common dolphins, thirty strong, broke the surface. Contact occurred as onemind sent mental commands, which were accepted by the mammals as if originating in their own brains. They swam in a large circle, then a figure-of-eight, finally a large V which turned in any direction onemind wished.

The collective consciousness released its hold, and the dolphins returned to normal behaviour, then cleared a space as creatures from the deep arrived.

Grey skin pushed through the waves, and a water-blow jetted into the night air, high enough to reach the closest onemind body. A fin whale appeared with a slow, muscular movement as its sixty-five-foot body displaced the surrounding water. At onemind's command, it rolled over like a trained dog, before diving.

The last creature had been called from further away and took another ten minutes to appear. The blue whale, at nearly two hundred tonnes and over ninety-five feet long, stayed on the surface for twenty minutes before sliding back into the deep.

Abos un-formed the collective and onemind fell away, one becoming three once again.

They flew back to the farm.

—The blue whale was aware of us—

It wasn't a question.

—It is intelligent—

—unlike human intelligence—

Accessing Abos's memory, they all knew of the decimation of other species over the past few centuries. Blue whales, once believed to have numbered over a quarter of a million, now had a population less than a tenth of that.

The three non-humans turned their attention to their brothers with Titus Gorman, mistreated by humans, their minds imprisoned. Abos knew that by finding, and freeing the others of her kind, they would more easily find Daniel If the onemind could become nine, twelve, or fifteen, it would increase in power and understanding.

—What do we know about Gorman? Where is he likely to be?—

—We know little. He is American, his company is American. We should start there—

—America is a very large country. A good place to hide if you don't want to be found—

—But we must find him—

—Then there is no alternative. We will search, however long it takes—

Abos poured tea. She made toast. The marmalade was homemade, picked up from a stall at the side of the road outside Mrs Peabody's gate, half a mile along the winding road that led to the village.

Coincidentally, Mrs Peabody was, at that moment, putting on a cardigan and preparing to leave her cottage. She had been selling homemade marmalade for a decade, eight or nine jars a week, her customers leaving the money in a tin. The small profit fed her three cats. Her turnover had risen since the farmhouse down the road had been sold to the quiet couple, and she had upped her production correspondingly. She was glad of the extra custom, and, as soon as the latest batch had cooled, decided to give them a complimentary jar.

A few yards before reaching the driveway of the newcomers' house, an unexpected movement caught her eye, and she stopped. Behind the farmhouse, three helmeted figures had risen into the air. They were moving at speed, and, after a quick rub of her eyes, she caught sight of the soles of three pairs of boots before they vanished into a cloud.

"Well," she murmured. "Just no telling what these London types get up to, is there?"

She left the jar on the doorstep with a card. After all, a good customer was a good customer.

High above her, still climbing, Abos checked her compass before she, Shuck, and Susan banked west, heading for America.

28

America had never experienced a day like today. Those who weren't able to sit in front of computers kept their phones and tablets close by, refreshing the screens every few seconds. The media had been informed that three Americans would die, that the government could do nothing to prevent this, and that they should take this as a sign that the old world order was finished.

A website address had been released. A blank, black box on the otherwise featureless webpage contained the words **Live feed will be streamed here. Each titan will wear body cams. Watch this space.**

The revolution would be televised. More accurately, it would be streamed live to devices as large as a home cinema screen and as small as a TimeGlob, the tiny watch-like devices that were Glob's latest success story.

By the time midnight arrived at the end of that long day, no one in the world was sure whether they were safer, or in more danger than they'd ever been before.

CURTIS HART-DAVIS WAS THE FIRST. On receiving an email from Titus Gorman that morning, he opened his safe and removed fifteen thousand dollars in cash plus a gun. He told his wife he was going for a ride.

A delay of an hour between his email arriving and the local authorities being informed he was a target, meant that by the time the local sheriff knocked on the door, Hart-Davis was already forty miles away.

A bemused and concerned Mrs Hart-Davis told the police officers to take a seat. Curtis often rode the Harley on Sundays, and she was sure he would be back soon. When the officers remained standing and asked intrusive questions about her husband's business and their private life, concern became panic.

Hardly hearing the next few questions, she asked some of her own. These were batted aside with practised ease, and, as quickly as they had arrived, the police officers were gone. They left one patrol car behind in case Mr Hart-Davis should return, but the sheriff didn't even try to hide the fact that he was sure he wouldn't.

As the last car turned out of their driveway, and the heavy iron gates rolled closed, she turned to the young officer, and asked him outright what was going on. He'd seen the same look of worry on his own mother's face every time he put on his uniform and left the house.

"Don't you worry, Ma'am. I'm sure it'll all work out fine. Sheriff says the titans are after him, that's all. Ain't they a football team? Ma'am?"

Mrs Hart-Davis couldn't respond, as she'd dropped to the floor like a bag of cement.

At the same moment, in a roadside diner near the state

line, her husband had just made the worst deal of his life. Making deals was what Curtis was good at. Better than good. In a career full of deals that had made history in entertainment law, Curtis had built a reputation as the lawyer to call if you wanted not only to screw the other guy, but also his entire family, and their descendants, in perpetuity.

Trading his eighteen-month-old Harley-Davidson Low Rider S for a nineteen ninety-eight Honda would have stopped his career in its tracks, had any of his clients been there to see it. But, since Titus Gorman had promised him that his career, along with his life, would be over by the end of the day, he didn't give a shit what anyone thought.

Ten miles along the highway, he pulled into a gas station, ducked into the restroom and shaved off his neat white goatee. He hesitated before starting on the plugs he'd paid twenty-thousand bucks for. He sighed, then hacked away at his suspiciously luxurious hair with a pair of nail scissors, before shaving what remained down to his pink scalp.

The face that stared back from the cracked mirror was that of a stranger. Good. He closed his eyes for a moment and thought of Clarice, the fourteen-year-old he'd been grooming. His excitement about her had been building, and he knew she would be ready in a month. Then the game would begin. The meetings, the back of the car, the motel rooms, the photographs and films for his collection. She was already vulnerable, as her father had recently passed. That made her even more desirable. Curtis was planning six months of fun with this one, before the meth he would introduce her to made her too strung-out and wasted to be worth bothering with. Then he'd hand her over to the pimp he used.

Except, now, that would not happen. Curtis knew he'd get caught one day. He'd made contingencies. A new identity in a deposit box, a long bus-ride, easy access to a few million dollars, and he'd be starting a new life within a week.

The million dollars had gone now, thanks to Gorman. All he had was the cash from home, the gun, and half a million in bearer's bonds which might, eventually, be worth something again when the government caught this asshat.

He gave a few seconds' thought to his wife. She'd have the house, the cars, and the knowledge that the side of Curtis's life she'd avoided asking about was far worse than she'd imagined. The woman had always been weak. She might even kill herself, the stupid bitch.

Curtis shook his head, as he guided the Honda west, just an anonymous rider on a Sunday morning. Soon to be truly anonymous. No more Curtis Hart-Davis, Entertainment Lawyer of the year six times in the last decade. That life was gone.

He looked ahead, along the dusty highway. The Honda had none of the romantic associations of the Hog, but it was still a bike, and he was still in America, the land of the free, with the open highway stretching out in front of him.

Things could be worse.

Then, abruptly, they were. Considerably.

The Honda revved into the red, and he relaxed his grip on the throttle. As the engine note returned to normal, he noticed something unusual. The sound of the tyres on the surface of the highway had stopped. He revved the engine again. The rear wheel spun, but there was no traction, no corresponding surge of acceleration, just that same scream of revs.

Curtis looked down.

The surface of the blacktop was about a foot and a half underneath his wheels. The bike was flying.

Even as he noticed what was happening, the front wheel tilted upwards, and he rose further as if climbing an invisible ramp. For a crazy moment, he stood up on the footpads, considering jumping for it, but by that time he was about sixty or seventy feet in the air. As he sank back onto the seat, he could hear the squeal of brakes as vehicles on both sides of the highway below came to a stop. Doors were opening, people were shouting and pointing up at him.

Curtis looked down at the strangers, many of them holding their phones towards him and shading their eyes. No. They weren't pointing at him. There was something above him.

He knew what he would see if he looked up. He resisted the urge to do so. His shoulders sagged.

Curtis had seen a certain expression appear on the faces of his opponents in some of the more high-profile cases he had handled. It was an expression he had never tired of seeing, because it proved he was the best at what he did, and that anyone who thought of taking him on would be well-advised to remember it. It was the look of defeat. Not just defeat. Defeat with no hope of a reprieve.

He didn't need a mirror to know the same expression had now appeared on his freshly-shaved features.

He looked up.

Along the highway, about another ten feet above him, a man floated. Not a man. A titan. Stupid name.

Curtis cracked open the visor of his helmet and shouted at the huge figure staring impassively down at him as they hung in space above the highway.

"Stupid name, it's a stupid name. Fuck you. Fuck you

and fuck Gorman, and fuck you fuckers with your fucking cameras and fuck the President and fuck America."

In a career marked by oratorical successes, this last speech was somewhat of a blemish on his record.

The titan looked down at the assembled crowd, their cars, pickups and trucks blocking the highway.

"Yeah, shithead, you have an audience." Curtis hoped he sounded braver than he felt.

The titan pointed at Curtis, and he was jerked away from the Honda. Then he fell. At the last moment, he shut his eyes. When he felt the blacktop underneath his boots, he took an unbalanced step to one side and opened his eyes again.

He was back on the road. Unhurt. Alive. The whole death-threat angle had been just that. A threat, no more. Gorman wasn't the killing kind. He should have known. Computer geek with a messiah complex. The kid was a pussy.

Curtis had just started to laugh when the Honda landed on his head, crushing the helmet, his skull, and neck, snapping his spinal cord in seventeen places as it drove the top half of his body through his pelvis before forcing his corpse through the blacktop.

The crater was fifteen feet deep and eleven feet wide. Smoke rose from within as the little fuel left in the bike's tank ignited. The resulting fire kept Curtis's corpse smoking until the fire department arrived fourteen minutes later.

A small crowd gathered around the perimeter. It was oddly like a graveside scene, the mourners assembling on each side of the open grave. Only, instead of bibles or orders of service, they were clutching their phones.

By the end of the day, the death of Curtis Hart-Davis was the most viewed YouTube clip of all time.

BEING in the army was boring. Piloting drones across Afghanistan was boring.

Niles hated the camaraderie, and he hated the stupid jargon. Insurgents were *innies*, civilians were *outies*. The children who appeared as small black shadows on the drone's screens were *fun-sized Bin Ladens*. Terrorists in the top ten of the USA target list were *blue ghosts*. That one was a Pacman reference, a game Niles could win while asleep.

The air force had insisted any drone pilots they recruited needed to be actual, real-life, qualified pilots, but the army had taken a more practical approach. They saw technology being developed for remote drone piloting, and made the obvious connection. It looked like a game. The army began quietly recruiting gamers.

Niles Cahill was a gaming legend. Not under his own name. The worldwide gaming fraternity knew him only as KaKill.

The recruiting officers had turned up at his parents' house in a gleaming black car, wearing crisp uniforms and smiling. It had taken Mr and Mrs Cahill ninety-seven minutes to sign the form committing their son to a year at military school. Patriotism was undoubtedly a factor, but the new car that appeared on his parent's drive the day before Niles left for Nevada suggested cruder motives.

Not that he had been sad to go. At seventeen, he was still living in the same room in the same house in the same town, seeing the same idiots at the same stupid high school every day. When he was away from a screen, he felt dull, half alive. He had passed through the school system like a piece of flotsam carried along by a river.

If anyone had known his identity as KaKill, his life

would have become a living hell. His anonymity as one of the best gamers in the country was central to his sense of identity. As KaKill, he could be whoever he wanted to be. No one knew he was a pasty kid in a shitty small town in the Midwest. No one knew a single thing about him.

The army guys, though. They knew. Which confirmed everything Niles had always suspected about his country's government. They spied on people.

When they had asked his parents to leave the room and the older guy had said, "Hello, KaKill," he was convinced his entire existence was about to unravel.

Only it didn't. The army dudes were smarter than that. They explained it all to him, and he could see it made sense. They needed to kill scum on the other side of the world. No point risking the lives of Americans if they didn't have to. The best gamers, the ones who had honed their reflexes over tens of thousands of hours playing made them the perfect candidates to be drone pilots. Niles could be a hero.

All the talk of military school was just a front. They made it clear it was his decision to take part. Or not. They didn't threaten him, didn't say they would expose his identity. They didn't have to. He told them what he wanted, and they agreed.

Which meant, a week later, when he arrived in Nevada, his new home had a high-speed military-grade fibre-optic connection, and his front room was a gamer's wet dream, with all the hardware and software he had demanded.

Each month, his bank account was credited with more money than he'd ever imagined earning. The training was laughably simple compared to some of the strategy and combat games he had mastered.

His first kill had been fun. Kind of. His spotter had directed him to a potential training camp, his superior officer had confirmed it as a target and given him the green light. Niles had positioned the drone, fired, and the sensor operator had guided the missiles, hitting three buildings which flashed brilliant white on the screen. When the smoke had cleared, there were no buildings, no *innies*. No nothing. Level One cleared.

But it got boring, fast. There was no Level Two. After a few months, he asked his commanding officer for some changes. Otherwise, he'd walk. He'd been surprised when he was given what he'd asked for. He found out later that his record was already better than the most experienced air force drone pilots. The army loved beating the air force at its own game. Now Niles had a private space for his shifts. He only had to interact with the rest of them at debriefings.

His other request made everything more interesting for a while. He didn't want his sensor operator piloting the missiles. What was the point of that? He'd fly the drone, then had to let some jerk in the next room flew the missiles. No. Niles wanted all the credit for. And, as he'd promised, his record improved still further.

The boredom had been inevitable. The army dudes weren't stupid. They'd prepared for it. When they saw how bored Niles was in debriefings, they called him in.

That was when they had shown him the leaderboard. It was all off the record. Imagine if the lib-tard media found out drone pilots were competing against each other for the most kills. Niles loved it.

Then, eight weeks earlier, the impossible had happened. He'd been knocked off top spot of the leaderboard. The air force had responded. Wingman#1 was top of the board. What kind of lame user name was Wingman#1?

The problem was, once Wingman had got the top spot, he pulled away. There was nothing Niles, or the army, could do about it. According to his commanding officer, the air force had been given priority coverage of a busy area of Afghanistan. Things might change, in a few months.

A few months was an eternity in the gaming world.

Niles got creative.

At first, he put more hours in. When that wasn't enough, he changed tactics on the strikes. Instead of the pinpoint targeting, he looked for maximum casualties. He used three Hellfire missiles when one would have done the job. His kill rate went up by thirty percent. He was their best pilot; so long as he didn't get too enthusiastic, they would overlook some collateral damage.

Niles worked out that the scoring system didn't award any points for killing the *mini Bin Ladens*. Where the hell did they get off? Little kid terrorists would only grow up to be adult terrorists, right? He got halfway down the corridor to the commander's office before stopping himself. Instinct told him that not everyone might see the problem the way he did.

Even within the unfair limitations, Niles got tantalising close to Wingman's high score. The problem was, he couldn't see any way of overhauling it.

The answer, when it came, was obvious. It would take all his ingenuity, some advanced hacking, and some fancy piloting.

In his cockpit, he used the dead time flying long passes far above the Afghan countryside to patch into the training drones kept on the base. There were six in total, four of which were flight ready.

Niles wasn't stupid. He knew that his superior officers looked down on him. A gamer, however good, was still a gamer. Not a soldier. They thought he knew nothing about his country's enemies.

They had underestimated him. Niles knew *exactly* who his country's enemies were. The drone strikes in Afghanistan, in Iraq, in Yemen. The speeches he'd heard on TV. The stuff he'd read online. Muslims were the enemy. Everyone knew it, but few dared say it out loud.

It had taken Niles all of ten minutes to find the biggest mosques in the United States. Friday prayers was the busiest time. They'd be packed with terrorists then. He had military flight plans ready to upload when the day came. Four drones would go out on training missions. All four fitted with a full complement of Hellfire missiles.

Wingman would never catch him after next Friday. In eight days' time, he would be a real hero. KaKill would be a legend.

The titan showed up five hours into his shift. Niles hadn't seen the email from Titus Gorman, but his superiors had. While he sat in his cockpit, cocooned in his private world, the full might of the US army rolled into action around him. The fact that Niles had insisted on a private working area meant it was easy for the base to be evacuated without his knowledge. By two in the afternoon, he was the only living soul in the long, low building that served as the drone control centre.

The call patched through to his headset was from the boss, General Storrman. Niles knew the guy hated him. He also knew the general needed him. So he showed him no respect at all.

"General Stores! How's it hanging, big man?" As Niles Cahill, he couldn't look other people in the eye, let alone speak to them, but as KaKill, he was fearless, cocky, and didn't give a shit what anyone thought. "Got some new ragheads you want me to obliterate?"

The response, when it came, was as unexpected as it was terrifying.

"Cahill, shut up. You may only have minutes to live. I want you to listen and I want you to listen good. Have you checked your email?"

Niles tapped keys while he spoke, bringing up a separate window on his third screen, filtering emails by time and date.

"Not had time, what with touring Afghanistan, keeping our guys and gals safe out there, blowing up shit and HOLY FUCK."

He was looking at an email from Titus Gorman. A personal email. From Titus Gorman to Nile Cahill. But not the one he dreamed about when Titus invited him over to talk about developing and testing new games for him. No. This one said there was a titan on its way over to kill him. Niles felt tears sting his eyes, hot and shameful. The voice in his ear spoke again.

"Good. Then you know what's coming. You fall under my protection as a member of the US Army, and I don't intend to let Gorman's flying man come over here and murder you."

Niles snivelled. "Thank you, sir."

"Shut up and listen. We have air defence patrolling the area, ground-to-air missiles are ready, and an entire battalion is surrounding the base to protect your worthless ass."

Niles swallowed. The general was still on the line, but he wasn't speaking. The seconds dragged by. Niles felt outrage grow alongside his terror. Why would Gorman target him? Not only was he a geek, he was a hero.

"Cahill. We are allowing you to defend yourself. The training drones are available. You can use one of them. I gave orders for them to be armed and found four of them were already battle-ready. Would you know anything about that?"

"Give me all of them!"

"What?"

Niles was babbling now. "All of them. I can control all four."

"No. No one can control two safely, let alone—"

Niles heard another voice, sounding as if it were on speakerphone, before the sound cut out. The general had muted the line. The voice had sounded a hell of a lot like the president.

"Cahill. You have control of all four. The titan has been sighted. Good luck."

Niles was too busy to pick up the lack of sincerity in the general's tone. He was sending commands to the four drones on the base, and watching all his screens at once as they left the hangar and took to the air. Information from radar and from the pilots circling the base was already coming in.

The titan approached from the south. The patrolling aircraft opened fire, but the target flew erratically, sometimes dropping like a stone, then reversing direction. Its flight path often took it between two aircraft, making it impossible for them to attack without risking hitting each other.

While the aerial battle continued, the massed troops on the ground could only look on.

In quick succession, all twelve of the fighter jets, and the six helicopters backing them up dropped from the sky, one by one. They hit the ground hard enough to shake up their occupants, without causing serious injury. The aircraft themselves, after landing, continued to move. Wings bent or snapped, rotor blades knotted into each other like twisted cable ties.

Three minutes after the first sighting, the titan was alone in the sky as the drones rose to meet it.

Niles relaxed, fear dissolving into excitement as he used his phenomenal gaming skills to their limit, his eyes flicking between all four screens, his fingers a blur of speed across the keyboard. He also used voice commands he had programmed himself, and two Bluetooth foot-pedals he had adapted to allow him to switch between the various cameras mounted on the drones.

There was no more Niles Cahill, there was only Kakill, the most feared gamer on the planet. As he sighted the titan and moved his drones into position as if they were his own limbs, even Kakill disappeared. There was only a succession of moments seen on four screens from twenty cameras. Time had no meaning. Death had no meaning. There was just the game. And winning.

Niles spoke the command he had planned for his mosque attack, sending it to every drone at once.

Sixteen Hellfire missiles detached, four from each drone. The screens were now split into grids. Adrenaline flooded into Niles' brain as he tried to pilot sixteen missiles. He could see the titan. It was moving away, heading west, fast.

The missiles' cameras tracked the titan as Niles guided them, keeping the fleeing figure in sight. He was gaining on it.

The titan pulled the same trick it had with the planes, dropping suddenly. The Hellfire missiles were far more nimble than any plane. Nudging one joystick with his left hand while using keyboard shortcuts to link the other missiles to the movements of the first, Niles flipped the Hellfires at a speed which would have made any human pilot unconscious.

He spotted the target below and followed again, baying for blood. The missiles were definitely gaining. He could make out details now. The dark outfit and helmet worn by the flying man, the ground rushing by in a blur of sand, dusty roads and metal fences. Then concrete, some yellow markings.

He looked beyond the titan at the long, low building it, and the missiles were approaching. It looked familiar.

"Shit."

Niles hit the override and pulled the missiles into a climb.

Nothing happened. He hit the button a second time, then a third.

On-screen, the titan changed course and headed up. A second after it did so, forty ground-to-air missiles chased it into the sky. The Hellfires continued on their ground-level trajectory.

Kakill's final word was broadcast to General Storrman, the assembled officers present in the briefing room, and the President and White House staff listening remotely.

"Mommy."

Milliseconds later, the complex was destroyed by sixteen Hellfire missiles. The ground-to-air attack on the titan culminated in an impressive, and expensive, firework display heard as far away as Albuquerque.

The military prepared a press release announcing the titan's death, but the video footage shot by the superbeing in question, showing the spectacular result of their failed attack, left them looking powerless and frustrated, just as Titus Gorman had promised.

CONGRESSWOMAN TENNESSEE MURDOCH was the third name on Titus Gorman's email. Her chief of staff alerted her to the fact at 6:45am, during their breakfast meeting. All other meetings and public appearances for the day were cancelled, and Murdoch was taken into protective custody.

The president called her personally and assured her that her safety was now his top priority. Murdoch, whose affair with the president had begun before he took office and was still ongoing, believed him.

She spent the day in a bomb-proof shelter. The coffee was bad, the pastries stale, and her temper was short. Shortly before the news of the titans' first victim was announced, the shelter inexplicably lost the satellite link, and the television went blank. Her mood, now, was as black as the screen, particularly as there was no cellphone signal. Murdoch raged at her staff, her security team, and anyone who got close. The hours passed slowly for all present.

Thirty minutes after the death of Niles Cahill in Nevada, the president of the United States received a text on his personal cellphone. After he had read the message, it vanished, and he could find no trace of it.

The president dismissed everyone from the Oval Office and sat, unmoving, with his head in his hands for four minutes. Then he sighed and picked up a phone, asking for a secure line.

The message had read:

Titus Gorman here, Mr. President. I'm not planning on killing Tennessee Murdoch. I'm going to make her an offer. I know about the two of you, but that's small beans. When she emerges, unscathed, at midnight—when, in other words, I've failed—she will receive a text offering my protection in return for everything she knows about the funding, and running, of your presidential campaign. I think she'll take my offer. Don't you? If she makes it through the day, that is.

At 11:42pm, an extremely unusual tragedy unfolded in the Washington bunker. A security specialist's firearm malfunctioned, and Senator Tennessee Murdoch was accidentally shot twice in the head and once in the chest. She died of her wounds before reaching the hospital. The president sent thoughts and prayers to her husband and children at such a difficult time.

29

"If you can dream my dreams, if you can get inside my head while I'm sleeping, maybe you can send me a message. If you can do that, maybe you can do the same with Gabe, or with someone else here."

Sara had been thinking aloud most of the day. TripleDee wasn't convinced Daniel's apparent ability to slip into someone else's dream was useful.

"Just stay the fuck out of my head, freak."

"You're missing the point." Sara was more patient with Triple than Daniel thought he deserved. "A group of halfheroes has never been together in one place like this before. We might unlock new abilities."

It was no surprise to Daniel when Sara's intuition proved to be correct. The following morning, TripleDee admitted to the most vivid dream he'd ever had. He'd woken up drenched in sweat, still half-convinced he was with a team of mercenaries, breaking into a palatial building in an African country. In the dream he was there to plant the suggestion in a prince's brain that he should depose his father.

"Thing is," he admitted to Daniel and Sara, "that's not one of my abilities. I'm just strong, and bulletproof."

"And stupid," added Daniel.

"Daniel, you're not being helpful," said Sara.

"Sorry. Just didn't want him to miss out one of his special abilities."

"Piss off, Harbin, you're no Stephen Hawker."

"King."

"That's where you're wrong. Stephen King's a writer, you thick bastard. Ha!"

Sara interrupted.

"The dream, Triple."

"Yeah, right. In the dream, Ray was there, telling us the route was clear."

"Ray?"

"The little guy Danny boy couldn't hit back at the house. He can see a few seconds into the future. Handy. Thing is, I'd never met him until he came to Newcastle."

Sara admitted she was the only one of the three who wasn't sure she'd dreamed someone else's dream. Her night had been filled with disconnected images, sounds, and smells that changed quickly, overlapping. Nothing clear. But she was sure few of the dream fragments had originated from her own subconscious.

"I have homework for the pair of you," said Sara.

Homework turned out to be straightforward. The three of them agreed to keep silently asking themselves two questions: *am I conscious?* and, *am I dreaming?* In her teens, she had read about the technique in a book on lucid dreaming.

"But what's the bloody point?"

Daniel wondered, not for the first time, if he'd be able to resist the temptation to give the Geordie whinger a big, satisfying slap when they were out.

"The point is to wake up inside your dream. If you can become conscious *within* a dream, you can take control, direct your actions. Instead of being an actor, you become the director. If you are connecting with the other halfheroes, you might be able to do the same when you're awake."

Daniel shifted on the stone floor, looking over at Sara's face in the other cell.

"And if we can connect, what happens then?"

Sara smiled. "I don't know. But I hope it's good."

TWO NIGHTS LATER, Daniel dreamed of George. She had planted ideas in others' minds so subtly that they believed they'd had the idea themselves. Her ability had enabled them to break out of Station. In this dream, she was doing the same, leading him through stone corridors, following the route they'd seen Howell take on his ill-fated escape attempt. As he pushed her wheelchair, Daniel watched her gesture towards cell doors, which disappeared as he looked at them.

Something strange was happening around Daniel's body. Silvery lines, the thickness of a single strand of a money spider's web, flowed alongside him, reaching outwards like deep sea creatures blindly groping for food. He looked down. The strands originated in his solar plexus, his heart and—when he turned to check—his head.

He slowed as he passed the open cells. All was darkness, a smudged blackness which coiled in on itself like something living. Strands similar to those drifting around him floated out of the gloom, lit from within, their sinuous progress purposeful as they sensed, and responded to, his presence. They swam towards his own strands, coiling around them, releasing, then coiling again.

The window was open. It was hot, mid-summer hot. No one could sleep in this heat. The woman with the knife was panting, her eyes wide. She thought I was there to rob her. I just meant her to keep her distance. I didn't know it would happen. She took three paces back, four, five. I could have stopped her. The curtains moved in the breeze, and she fell.

He was back in the corridor. He was Daniel Harbin. The image of the woman falling was a sun-bleached Polaroid, the ghost of someone else's dream.

As he walked, a new point of view became available. He observed his progress from above as if he was being filmed. The vantage point would have been impossible in reality as his vision would have been blocked by solid rock. He looked to one side then the other. There was only darkness at first, then, as his body below continued to push George's wheel-chair down the corridor, he discerned brighter patches in the shadows. He drifted closer. Each patch was made up of three sources of light close together, a slow-motion writhing flow of bright threads.

Some were brighter than others. He directed himself downwards. As he approached, he saw the three light sources were identical to the living strands reaching out from his body.

Daniel remembered to ask the questions.

Am I conscious?

The answer was yes.

Am I dreaming?

Unless reality had taken a thoroughly bizarre turn, that was another yes.

This was a lucid dream. Sara had been right. In which case, he was supposed to make contact within the dream.

Communicate with Gabe or anyone else in the prison. But how, floating through space, surrounded by a phosphorescent spider's web?

He decided to return to his body in the corridor with George. At least there had been familiarity there, a geography that mirrored the real world. Daniel looked for his other body. It had gone. There was no George. No corridors. No prison. Just this dark space.

The darkness wasn't empty. It had boundaries, a thickening of the shadows where he couldn't make any further progress. The space was three dimensional. As he 'looked' around him, using senses he knew couldn't be physical, he detected more and more sources of light coming into being from every direction.

The strands around him were stretching now, searching for others and, as they found them, coiling and knitting together, a dance of light threading its way through the dream space.

Thoughts, images, feelings, memories came through the connections as they formed and dissolved, grasping and releasing, a web of shared dreams with no centre.

If I just stay long enough to make some real money, I can escape for good

It's going to hit me. It's skidding, the back-end is jerking one way, then the other. What do they call it? Jack-knifing. A forty-foot jackknife, a truck hitting my chest, the shop window smashing. The screams. They think I'm dead. I should be dead, but I'm angry. I get up, and the screaming stops for a second. Then it starts again.

He says he loves me, and I know he's lying. Yesterday, I would have believed him. Yesterday, I didn't know he was undercover, didn't know he was police. He smiles, and I grit my teeth. The kitchen drawer opens behind him, and its contents float into the air. A spatula, a potato masher, a rolling pin, a vegetable peeler, a bread knife. I choose the vegetable peeler.

*They chase me into the trees and I run I run as fast as I can but there are four of them and they are spreading out and they know there's nothing but the cliffs after the trees. They don't know I won't stop at the cliffs. I'm done. I'll keep running and I won't be scared or sad or ashamed I'll just be dead and that's fine that's fine that's fine. The trees are behind me now and they've stopped running. There's nowhere to go. My legs are tired my arms are tired my head is tired but when the edge comes and I keep running I'm not tired any more I'm free. I close my eyes and fall. Only I don't I don't fall I fly. I fly and I scream and I laugh and I d*on't look back.

Daniel felt heat on his back, like the sun coming out from behind a cloud while he was lying on a beach.

He turned and saw the brightest light source of all. He felt no fear as he was drawn towards it, saw its strands reaching towards him like a parent reaching for a child. This was a very different dynamic. Before, he had been the one reaching out and making contact. Now, he was no longer dominant. He was opening, receiving. He did so gladly, there was no malice here, but there was purpose, clarity, leadership.

His strands tangled with the brightness which, he now saw, occupied a central position among all the lights. If the web analogy was still good, he was about to meet the spider.

—hi, Daniel—

—Sara?—

—in the flesh. Well, no flesh at all, but you know what I mean—

—what now?—

—I connect with everyone else, and we break out of here—

—when?—

—if I can connect with everyone, or even most of them, then we should go now—

—now?—

—why not, you got a hot date or something?—

—no, but—

—but nothing. Let's go. Last one out buys breakfast—

30

Abos, Shuck and Susan began their search at the Mexican border, flying from the east coast to the west. Since Gorman's newly destroyed headquarters had been based in San Diego, Abos hoped he might not be too far away. Access to a Gulfstream 650 meant he could be anywhere, but America was Gorman's home and it was a big enough country to hide in. Staying within twenty miles of each other to maintain onemind, the three of them swept across the landscape at a speed of one hundred and fifty miles per hour. Any slower, and they would have lost the cover of darkness before reaching San Diego. Any faster, and they risked missing their targets.

As a new day dawned in San Diego, they ate three omelettes each, followed them up with peanut butter-stuffed French toast with banana, shared a stack of twelve pancakes and washed it all down with six litres of orange juice. The waitress collected twenty bucks from the cook when she put the clean plates on the counter. They both watched the strangers walk across the parking lot, sunglasses on, holding their helmets.

"Now just where in the hell are their bikes?"

After checking into the nearest motel, Abos, Shuck and Susan were asleep within minutes.

They allowed themselves eight hours sleep. They could get by with far less, but they had no idea how long the search would take. Fifteen-hundred miles of flying every night, even stuffed with protein and carbs, would take its toll.

They picked another restaurant for their evening feast, attracting a few gawping staff members and customers as they consumed enough food to feed seven or eight hungry people.

When darkness fell, they formed onemind, spread out and flew west. They reached Corpus Christi before dawn, then turned back to find a motel and diner south of San Antonio.

While the others slept, Abos awoke from a dream about Daniel. It was the first time she had ever remembered a dream. She was agitated, disturbed.

Abos stood by the window. The curtains were closed against the daylight, but she could hear the hum of activity as people went about their daily lives.

In her dream, Daniel had been flying alongside her. She was not supporting him, he was staying aloft under his own power. He looked gaunt, unhealthy. She signalled that they should land, and they did so on top of a hill. She spoke to her son, but no words came from her lips. He answered, but the sound was muted. She reached out, and he responded, but when their hands met, their fingers slid away. They tried again and again to reach one another, but no amount of effort made any impression on the invisible barrier between them.

When Daniel looked over her shoulder, she turned and

saw figures approaching. The first to come was a short man who greeted Daniel with a smile before they hugged. Next came a man nearly as big as Daniel, who nodded before standing alongside the first man.

From all sides of the hill, they approached now, men and women, most of them tall, many powerfully built, but all looking haggard and weak. They crowded around Daniel, then turned to Abos. She tried speaking again, but there was only silence. Although the group, thirty or more by now, all looked her way, it was as though none of them saw her. Their eyes sometimes rested on her momentarily before looking elsewhere as if not registering her presence.

A final figure approached. A woman, tall, strikingly beautiful. Abos knew she was Sara. She realised the first man must be Gabe. The others... their size, the look in their eyes... survivors.

They were her children. Her children.

Daniel spoke to Sara, turned her towards Abos, pointed, tried to make Sara see her. Sara looked towards Abos, squinting, frowning, concentrating. She shaded her eyes against the sunlight. Her wrists were so thin, they looked like they belonged to an old woman. The skin was almost translucent, the veins visible.

Her children. When her vision blurred, Abos wiped away the tears. Had she ever cried before? She only remembered one occasion, when she last saw Cressida Lofthouse. Tears were a human response. She was not human.

Her children. Why were they so weak? Why couldn't they see her?

She felt the dream slip away, her body involuntarily rising, floating away from the hilltop.

Abos tried to reverse her ascent, but she had no agency in this dream state. She was an observer. She focussed on

Sara's face, glowing, as every other face darkened around her, then the entire group moved fluidly away from her as if they were one organism.

As she rose from the hill, she twisted in the air and, as the dream ended, she caught sight of white hills. Those hills, perhaps thirty or forty miles away, were lower than the one Daniel and Sara had been standing on. The sun above her was hot, the landscape arid and dry. How could there be snow on the distant hills?

She went back to bed, puzzled. She knew dreams were an area of human consciousness still relatively unmapped. Why, after all these years living as a human, did she have her first vivid dream now? She felt exhaustion wash over her. There had been truth in the dream. Her children, the minority who had lived beyond their teens, were out there somewhere. Had she just seen them?

An hour before darkness fell, Shuck, Susan, and Abos ate again and prepared to make their third sweep of the country, the second from east to west.

Their planned route would take them over White Sands, New Mexico, which, from above, might easily be mistaken for a snowy landscape. Thirty miles further west was a mountainous region. Hidden in that range of hills, was the most high-tech prison ever built. Nearly twelve hours before Abos and his companions reached them, the thirty-two occupants imprisoned there would attempt to break out.

The three of them flew west.

31

Sara's guess about the number of guards was inaccurate. She had failed to factor in Titus Gorman's confidence in his automated systems. Four guards ran the entire prison. Three eight-hour shifts, one guard covering each, the fourth on a four-day break.

Which meant only one guard to deal with. Plus some sophisticated alarm and security systems.

TripleDee had been right about the deafness, but wrong about Gorman's recruiting criteria. He didn't employ deaf guards. He had found suitable candidates and offered them three-year contracts, which paid enough to mean they would never have to work again. There was just one catch. Titus had researched each candidate so well that no one refused to undergo the operation, despite the fact that the procedure was irreversible.

That morning, the guard was Frank Decroix, a former marine with two ex-wives and six estranged children. A recovering alcoholic, this particular Tuesday marked four years, three months, and two days since Frank's last drink.

The offer from Titus Gorman meant he could pay off the debts from a couple of bad business decisions, make sure his kids would never starve, and buy himself a nice condo in New Orleans. He loved New Orleans, but hated blues and jazz with a passion, so the deafness was almost a bonus.

He loaded the rationed food into the hub's microwaves, then walked each of the twelve corridors in turn, using the stick provided to flick the trays under the doors. No faces glared out from the gaps anymore. Not since they'd found they wouldn't get any food if they did. The first few days, they screamed at him. He'd seen the spit fly from their lips, the veins standing out in their necks as they mouthed threats he couldn't hear. Not that he blamed them. Solitary confinement was no fun. And he'd once had a cat he fed better than his prisoners.

Still, for this money, he was content to not give a shit.

When he'd flicked the last meal under the thirty-second door, he reloaded the microwaves. When their displays reached zero, he stacked the trolley and opened the door to the first corridor for the second time that morning. The clean plates and trays had been pushed out for him to collect. That was another habit they had learned. If you don't return your plate, tray and cutlery, you go hungry. He picked them up one by one, replacing them with a fresh meal, which he flicked into each cell.

He spent the next twenty minutes repeating the same actions in the other corridors before loading the microwaves for a third time. The part of his brain that might have questioned just what in the hell he was doing had fallen silent. He felt a pleasant, low-level buzz as he walked his route again and fed the prisoners for the third time in less than an hour. It was like being drunk. No, not exactly. It was like the best moment on the way to getting drunk, when you feel the alcohol taking effect, the booze-fired optimism kicking in. That magic time, which might last an hour but, more likely was over in ten minutes as the cheap whisky ushered it angrily away. Frank Decroix felt it that morning. Warm, happy, convinced that come what may, things would turn out for the best because, deep down, everyone was a good guy.

After his sixth trip, he ran out of crockery. He'd stacked the industrial dishwasher, but it would be another hour before it was done. Frank stared at it, bemused, then up at the open cupboards where two more portions each were waiting in their individual packets. He guessed they could eat straight out of the packet. Why not? Then—and this idea was such a good one, he laughed out loud when he thought of it—he could open the prisoners' doors, and they could help him wash the dishes. Afterwards, they could all go topside and order more food.

It was 11 am when he approached the first door. He stood outside it, waiting. He didn't know what he was waiting for until it happened. The lights went off. Then the emergency lights flickered into life as the backup generator kicked in. A few seconds later and the emergency lights went out as the second generator shut down. He felt a moment of panic as he became blind as well as deaf. Then he clicked the flashlight on and shone it at the door.

Frank hurried back to the hub and the laptop. Emergency protocol in the event of a power failure meant he had to be ready to respond. The laptop was running on its battery, connected to White Sands via a cellphone-based relay system, which Robertson—Frank's boss—had explained, but Frank hadn't understood. The main thing was, he had to memorise codes and type them in when prompted.

The screen was flashing. Frank typed in an eight-digit number. He had to answer three security questions. The third, which asked the name of his first wife, was the one he was supposed to answer incorrectly. That way, if he had been compromised, and either someone else was entering the information, or he was doing so under duress, he could alert Robertson without giving himself away. He answered the first two questions correctly, then entered *Elizabeth* as the third. His first wife's name had been Trixie, but he'd always liked Elizabeth.

The screen cleared, then Robertson's message appeared.

What happened?

Power outage, sir.

Backup generator?

Frank didn't hesitate.

Working perfectly, sir.

Good. Sit tight. I'll have a maintenance team come in with Kremmer at two.

Kremmer was the guard for the afternoon shift. Frank checked the time. It was seven forty-five.

All cells secure?

Yes, sir.

Good. Robertson out.

Frank shone the flashlight into the corridor.

The cell doors were masterpieces of engineering. They were uncomplicated, and they were mechanical. Titus Gorman may have made his fortune with software and electronics, but when it came to keeping a solid barrier between him and thirty-two angry superpowered enemies, he had gone old school. The doors could only be opened from the outside, by turning a handle three hundred and sixty degrees. The gears engaged and three solid bars slid out of the stone wall and back into their recesses in the door.

Frank spun the handle. The door swung open.

A beautiful woman was sitting on the bed. He didn't need to be able to lip-read to understand what she said, her voice—man, he *loved* British accents, but how the hell did he know she was British?—was clear. Like she was speaking inside his head.

"Hi, Frank. You know what to do?"

"Yes Ma'am, I sure do."

"Call me Sara. Let's go get them. Did you bring the torches?"

He had to think about that one.

"Uh, you mean the flashlights?"

The woman nodded. Brits spoke funny.

"I sure did. Ten of 'em. They're in the hub."

She took his arm. She was unsure, a little unsteady. But when Frank opened the first door, she straightened up and smiled.

Frank expected her to hug the guy inside. Or shake hands since they were Brits. He'd watched the video feed, seen their faces pushed up against their cell doors while they talked for hours. They obviously knew each other.

But the big guy—and he was huge—walked out like he was dreaming, and followed them. The next guy, nearly as big, did the same. In the next corridor, and the next, this was repeated. Most of them—women and men—were big. Not fat, but tall and broad. Some were shorter, skinnier, but they were the exceptions. They were all silent.

None of the prisoners were mad when they saw him, no one attacked him. It seemed a little strange, sure, but it was as if they barely noticed Frank at all. Or Sara, or each other.

By the time he had walked back through the hub, picked

up the flashlights, and headed into the wider tunnel past the elevator, Frank was at the head of a ragged line of zombie-like figures, unspeaking, shuffling behind him.

He handed flashlights back down the group, keeping his own. It was still dark.

Occasionally, an individual figure would break away from the group, becoming more active. Whenever this happened, Sara would ask Frank to wait—man, hearing that lovely voice made him feel a little bit regretful about the whole deafness angle—and she would close her eyes. That meant he could look right at her without being caught. She really was beautiful. Somehow, he knew she was a good person too. Kind, funny, great to be around. And he knew she liked him. Didn't know how he knew it, but he knew.

When the stray prisoner had gotten back in line, Frank looked away again, before Sara opened her eyes and caught him staring.

About halfway up the gently ascending corridor, he saw the ceiling-mounted machine guns which hung in their cradles as they passed below. He remembered his briefings. They were supposed to fire at anything bigger than a rat that moved down here. But with the backup power gone, they were just ugly, expensive ornaments.

When, twenty minutes later, the group reached the huge steel double doors that stood between them and freedom, Frank stopped, unsure of what to do. He stood back as two huge guys took one side each and, putting their shoulders against the steel, bent their knees and pushed.

The doors made a grating sound as they shifted a few inches, then stopped.

"Wait."

The four men looked at Sara. She closed her eyes, as did everyone in the group behind her. Frank turned back to the men at the doors. Their eyes were also closed. They bent to their task, and, with no drama, the doors moved. A long shaft of bright sunlight widened as the landscape beyond came into view.

The group shuffled forward, squinting.

They were out.

~

IT WAS like waking from a vivid dream, but it had none of the stuttering, lurching twitches that Daniel associated with the transition between deep sleep and alertness.

Perhaps, he thought, it was more like being a method actor. They dressed, spoke and thought like the characters they played, on and offstage. When the job finished, the actors went back to being themselves. Maybe that was closer to this experience, emerging from a state of consciousness unique, as far as he knew, in human experience.

He had stepped away from individuality, shed his unique personality and been partially subsumed by the web of light around Sara. The boundaries separating him from the others didn't so much disappear as reveal their illusory nature. There had been something seductive about the experience. No longer Daniel, but Daniel/Sara, then Daniel/Sara/TripleDee, then more than that, personalities he didn't recognise. Then, still more expansive, no names, but a deeper bonding, and a shared purpose.

Sara was the guiding consciousness, and, for the linking of minds to work, each halfhero had to submit to her. It was easier for some than others. Daniel and Gabe had been the first. TripleDee had followed, and those who knew him were next. Subjectively, it seemed a laborious process, glacially slow. And yet it must have been done in one night, because by the time Frank Decroix arrived for his shift at six am, the webmind, as Daniel thought of it, was coherent enough to reach out and control him.

Less than three hours later, they were out.

But where the hell was *out*?

Daniel looked away from the blinking, confused group of halfheroes and took in the landscape. They were standing on an artificial plateau carved into the top of a mountain. Or a very high hill. He never could remember the difference between one and the other.

He shook his head, trying to clear it, and looked again, studying the land for clues. Gorman was American, the guard was called Frank, and he'd caught fragmented thoughts of New Orleans as they followed him out of the interior. Assuming this was America, he thought Arizona was a fair bet for their location.

Yellowed stone had been exposed where Gorman had cut into the mountainside to make his bespoke prison. Sand-like dust swirled at Daniel's feet, and the only vegetation he could see were coniferous trees, clinging defiantly to rocky outcrops. There were no buildings in sight, no towns in the valley below. As he turned, putting the sun in front of him, he stopped in surprise, shading his eyes.

"Is that snow?" He was looking at a large, white area in the middle distance. The sight was surreal, as if someone had lifted a ski resort and dropped it in a desert.

No one answered, and he realised he had spoken too quietly, his voice unused to projecting further than the gap between two cell doors. He licked his dry lips, relishing the gritty breeze on his face and the already burning sun on his neck.

"Is that snow?"

Sara, taking in the view with a slow smile on her face, answered him.

"According to our guide here, that's a national park. It's white because the minerals making up the sand are mostly calcium sulphate and gypsum."

Daniel raised an eyebrow.

"Frank read a book about it," she said. "Most of the land is open to the public, but fifty square miles are fenced off and inaccessible. The locals think it's some kind of research lab, and since the owner has made some generous donations to local communities, no one asks too many questions."

"Titus Gorman," said TripleDee.

Sara nodded.

"Yep. It's about a twenty-mile hike, so take on plenty of fluids from the restroom up here."

Daniel looked round the group, many of whom had either had a run-in with him, Sara, and Gabe, or knew they were on the IGLU list for the same treatment. They had a common enemy now, but the cooperation between them wouldn't last. The webmind they had formed, whatever it was, had been fragile. Sara had needed to stop the group many times to repair damage done by someone detaching from the shared mind, fighting to regain their individuality.

Someone spoke.

"Let's go kill this guy."

Sara shook her head. "No killing. We're taking him in."

There was enough residue left from her dominance to suppress any real dissension. A woman shouted, "at least let us hurt him a little."

"No argument from me," said Daniel, thinking of how close he'd come to losing his mind in his stone cell.

Gabe was looking across at the bizarre white dunes in the distance.

"Where the hell is that, anyway?"

Sara smiled that small, grim smile of hers Daniel had seen before every mission.

"That, people, is the imaginatively named White Sands. Welcome to New Mexico."

32

Daniel, Gabe, and Sara formed the vanguard of the group hiking across the dry, rocky, and sandy terrain between the prison and White Sands. Daniel felt the dull ache in his left foot that always accompanied a long walk. His missing toes needed scratching. He needed to think about something else.

He thought about Abos. Daniel didn't expect her to react like a human parent to his absence, but he knew she would look for him. But how could she come after him when she had another Abos growing in the lab? Maybe more than one by now - she had been planning trips to Russia and Egypt. She might have three blobs of slime growing new bodies in the farm's outbuilding. She could hardly leave them to look for Daniel. He would have called her, but the first thing Sara had done when they'd got out was to crush the guard's mobile phone.

"I'm sure we all have someone we have to call, but it'll have to wait."

She'd pointed to a mast near the bent doors leading out of the mountain's interior.

"It can't be hard for a technological genius to monitor calls. No. Business first. Then call whoever you like."

After the first hour's walking, to Daniel's surprise and annoyance, TripleDee joined them.

"Well, they're all spoiling for a fight, like, but I don't think there's a snowball's chance in hell you'll ever pull that Jedi mind trick on them again. Half of 'em reckon we should kill you now. I mean, not only are you with IGLU, you're a witch."

"What about the other half?" Sara was smiling.

"They want to wait until Gorman's dead before killing you."

"That's sweet of them," said Sara.

The first three miles were downhill. The next ten miles crossed flat, almost featureless, desert. Then, as the sand transitioned from a dirty brown to a pure white, the terrain changed, and they climbed again, heading up the side of a pale mountain in a heat haze. Three miles short of their destination—its high fence clearly visible—Sara stopped the group. She turned to a terrified Frank Decroix, who had taken each step towards Gorman's headquarters thinking it might be his last. Even if the psychos who'd taken over his mind didn't kill him, he was sure Robertson would shoot him when he figured who'd led them to his front door.

"Okay, Frank, you're free to go. It's about fifteen miles to that gas station you pointed out."

Frank leaned forward. His lip-reading should be better by now, but he'd never practised much. She'd definitely said his name, and, he thought, something about Idaho and damnation, which was weird. It had been easier when she could speak to him inside his head. Freaky, but easier. When Sara mimed walking away with her fingers, he got it. Frank took a few steps, then looked over his shoulder, hardly daring to believe they would let him go. Most faces were turned his way, and it was plain the majority didn't agree with Sara about letting him go. He broke into a jog, taking a quick look back every few paces. No one followed. He figured once he got to the gas station, he would steal a car, drive across the border and disappear forever.

Gabe hadn't said much since they'd got out. Now he rolled his neck, stretched his arms overhead and cracked his knuckles.

"Here's how I see it, boss. We're in the middle of a desert. We are about to turn up, unannounced, at the headquarters of the richest guy in the world, who rounded up every halfhero we knew about, and a few we didn't. He got us out of the country and into a prison we shouldn't have been able to break out of. Not without that spooky mental shit you pulled, anyway. Right?"

"Good summary." Sara was still smiling. Daniel hoped it was because she had a brilliant plan ready, but he suspected she was still on a high from controlling the webmind.

"I'm not just a pretty face," said Gabe. He waited for Daniel to comment.

"Saving my energy," said Daniel. "I guess you think Gorman won't be unprotected. And he's surprised us once."

Gabe reached up and patted Daniel's broad back.

"Our pet gorilla is on the money, Sara. You sure just breaking down Gorman's door is gonna work?"

In answer, Sara nodded towards something behind him in the sky. Squinting in the bright sunlight, Gabe turned in time to see a man drop from the sky and land ten yards away.

"Well?" said Sara.

"Two exits. The main one in front of us, and another to the south-east. One SUV outside. There may be more vehicles in the garages. No aircraft, but there's an airstrip about fifteen miles further west. Two hangars, and the runway's in fair condition. The road between there and here looks like it gets used. That's his way in and out, guaranteed."

"Thanks. No helicopter or helipad?"

"No. There's plenty of space for one to land, though."

"Good. Looks likely that he drives up from the airstrip, then. TripleDee?"

He looked at her, surprised.

"Yeah?" A few of the halfheroes he'd fought alongside in Newcastle looked up sharply, waiting to see if he would take orders from Sara.

She was aware of the potential problem.

"What do you think we should do?"

He paused. He knew she could take charge, but that would increase the risk of them losing cohesion as a fighting unit. If that happened, they might end up turning on each other before the job was done.

"A few of us could wreck the second exit, make it impossible for him to get out that way, right? That's what I would do. Then one group can storm the front door while the other covers the south."

She waited. TripleDee nodded, almost imperceptibly.

"Tell you what, pet. I'll take some volunteers, go round the side. In thirty minutes, we'll hit that entrance while you hit the front. We meet in the middle and take him."

"I agree," said Sara.

Daniel was impressed by Sara's leadership. Not that it would make the slightest difference once Titus was in custody as he was ninety-nine-point-nine percent sure the others would kill Gorman then turn on them.

"Great," said Triple. "Come on, let's go and get the little Globshite." He waited for a response to his witticism. When none was forthcoming, he picked out nine halfheroes, and they jogged away.

Daniel put a hand on Sara's arm.

"Something doesn't feel right about this. I mean, he's got security fences, a few cameras, but even normal humans could get through them. What else has he got?"

Sara waved away his concern.

"You worry too much. Remember, he doesn't know we're coming, and he thinks he's locked up every halfhero. Look around you."

Daniel looked at the group, many of whom looked steadily back, the promise of future retribution clear in their expressions.

"Hmm."

"Daniel, we have strength like yours, some of us can fly short distances, others can bend metal with their minds. How can he defend himself against that?"

The question was meant rhetorically, but it was categorically answered twenty-seven minutes later.

HALF AN HOUR after TripleDee had set off, Sara led the rest of the group to the front gate. Six cameras covered the approach. Anyone coming by road would be seen half a mile away.

Of the twenty-two halfheroes jogging towards the gate, two could fly. They waited until the last second before taking to the sky. Even after the feast at the prison, they were still suffering from three weeks of malnutrition. Best to save their abilities until they were absolutely necessary and use them for as short a time as possible.

The flyers, one male, one female, were quick to report.

"There's nothing to see," shouted the woman, scanning the road inside the gates for defences. "You're clear."

The cameras crumpled, their lenses shattering as they were crushed. Sara had divided the group according to their abilities, and the telekinetics, who could manipulate matter, were at the front. With the cameras out of commission, they turned their attention to the gates. The steel held for a few seconds as the second line of halfheroes, with enhanced strength, moved up and added brute strength to telekinesis. Then, with a sharp crack, something broke inside the locking mechanism. The gates jolted backwards.

As they jogged the exposed quarter of a mile from the gates to the low, white building beyond, a series of bangs and crashes from the west confirmed TripleDee's group had done their job.

Titus Gorman's hideaway was a masterpiece of minimalist design. Perched on the side of a mountain, its white, concrete walls blended with the sand surrounding it. From the air, it was almost invisible. Seen from the ground, it was unimpressive. One storey, windowless at the front like a warehouse, the interior was all the more stunning because it was so unexpected.

Coming in through an unlocked front door, shrugging in surprise as she did so, Sara motioned Daniel, Gabe, and the rest to join her. When they did, they all stood in silence for a moment, awed by the sight.

The low building seen from outside was not the ground floor of the building. It was the top floor. The halfheroes stood on a marble surface that stretched out about thirty yards either side, and maybe twenty yards in front. It ended at a wood and chrome bannister, beyond which, after a gap of another fifty yards, was the biggest window Daniel had ever seen. The space in between was filled with sculptures.

Ranging in size from a few feet to towering, thin figures twenty feet high or more, they were abstract, modern pieces in metal or stone. Daniel knew nothing about art, but Sara's eyes widened in disbelief.

As they walked into the huge room, no one said a word. There was something cathedral-like about the ambience. At the bannister, they looked out at the view, the same view they'd seen behind Titus Gorman's desk on the Globlet in their cells.

Stairs from the mezzanine on which they were standing created wood and metal Xs down to the bottom level, three floors below. But it wasn't just depth. Doors led off into the mountain itself.

"A super-villain with a lair inside a mountain?" whispered Daniel to Sara. "You couldn't make this stuff up."

"Super-villain?"

TripleDee and his crew joined them at the railing.

"Speccy twat, more like. Now, where is the little wanker?"

Gorman's office was easy to spot two flights down, with its brushed-steel desk and abstract artwork. No one was sitting in the massive chair. The office, and other rooms—a gaming area, a gym, a communications centre with dozens of screens and maps—seemed to hang in front of the massive windows. They were reached by staircases peeling away from the main stairs. Daniel tried to work out how the structure worked, with these platforms that appeared to float in space. The architect may have earned his fat cheque after all.

It was Gabe who said what everyone was thinking.

"Something ain't right."

A door opened somewhere out of sight below, and footsteps echoed around the space. Daniel felt himself tense, adrenaline flooding his system. Everyone around him shifted into readiness, breaths becoming more shallow, feet moving into fighting stances.

A figure walked into the area at the bottom of the staircases, three floors down. A man wearing dark overalls. A face tilted up towards them. No glasses, but it was Titus Gorman.

"Alone?" said Daniel.

Behind them, the front door opened. They looked away from Gorman and swung their attention towards the newcomer.

It was Titus Gorman. Again. He was followed by four other figures. They were all Titus Gorman.

TripleDee broke the silence.

"There's something off about them. Something wrong."

Gabe shot him a look. "Apart from the fact that there are, what, six of him, you mean?"

"Yeah. Look at them."

They all looked back at the Gormans, who were standing in a line either side of the door. It was Sara who noticed it first.

"Oh, shit. The size of them."

Then Daniel saw it. The door had been high enough that even he hadn't needed to duck to get in, but the figures who had followed them had done just that. They were at least seven feet tall.

As he looked, one figure in the group of halfheroes turned back to face the window. Daniel recognised Ray, the man who could see a few seconds into the future. He turned and saw the Gorman from the ground floor rise to their level. He had golden eyes.

"Oh, fuck," said Daniel. "Fuckity, fuckity, fuck."

33

There were thirty-two of them, the biggest number of halfheroes ever gathered in one place. There must be a handful more that Gorman hadn't rounded up or didn't consider a threat. Daniel knew of at least one - Saffi's friend, the woman who gave the IGLU a pre-cognitive advantage on their missions. Other than her, and perhaps a few others that had escaped attention, this building in White Sands, New Mexico currently contained The Deterrent's known children.

Daniel looked at the faces of his half-brothers and sisters as they watched the golden-eyed figure floating in front of them. Behind, five identical beings now walked between the sculptures towards them. There was little fear in the halheroes' expressions. He saw anticipation. This was what they did best. Growing up in a world that doubted their existence, treated with suspicion or hostility by those who knew about their powers, they had become self-reliant, strong, and lonely. Daniel didn't see a group, he saw a collection of individuals, spoiling for a fight.

He looked at Sara and Gabe. They were friends, weren't

they? A team? And yet, he had shared nothing other than his time with them. Their banter was lively, but superficial. He only knew Sara had lived in France because he had dreamed it. He knew virtually nothing about Gabe. And what had he told them about himself? Nothing important. The survival of their parent, for instance. That would have been a good starting point.

He had been a fool. A blind, lonely fool.

And now it was too late.

Sara was shaking him, her hand on his arm. Her face was blurred by his tears.

"Daniel. What is it?"

"I'm sorry, Sara, I'm so sorry. Run. It's your only chance. Run."

TripleDee had overheard.

"You're kidding, right? There are thirty-two of us and—unless my maths is completely fucked—only six big nerds. I like those odds."

"Jesus, Triple, they're not halfheroes."

Daniel remembered his fight with Abos in Station, when an adrenaline-laced hallucinogenic compound released into his bloodstream had sent him into a psychotic rage. He had hurt Abos, but only because she was trying to save him. She had wrapped a steel door around his body. At any moment, had she wanted to, she could have crushed him like an insect.

"What the fuck are they, then?"

"Abo- Deterrent. The Deterrent."

"What? The what?"

Sara had heard something in his voice.

"Daniel, what do you mean? What haven't you told us?"

Then the screaming started.

The titans walking towards them had raised their hands.

The closest halfheroes collapsed, one by one. They fell as if someone had thrown a switch in their brains, turning off every bodily function. Their screams were cut short as windpipes snapped and ribs folded as if an invisible fist had grabbed them, squeezing lungs and pulping hearts.

Six of the group fell this way, dying in agony before anyone could react. When they did react, it was with a mixture of practised aggression seasoned with unfamiliar panic and terror.

Those who could fly did so. Daniel saw a woman rise, then abruptly swerve to the side at unimaginable speed as if swatted out of the air. She hit the exposed brickwork hard, her body bursting like overripe fruit.

The titans encountered their first resistance then. Half a dozen of the sculptures tipped and scraped along the marble floor before the halfheroes mentally threw them towards their attackers. It bought them a few seconds' respite from the onslaught. The sculptures stopped as if hitting an invisible wall. They hung there, bizarre, vaguely humanoid shapes turning in mid-air, before the titans gestured, and the statues hurtled towards the halfheroes.

Everyone scattered. Three weren't fast enough, and the statues hit them at a bone-breaking speed before pushing them through the snapping bannister, past the floating titan and down to their deaths below.

Daniel turned away from the slaughter, looking for an exit. If he could find a way out, he might save a few. Sara and Gabe, at least. He scanned the vast window, but it opened onto a sheer drop. There were doors downstairs to the left, leading into the mountain. There might be other exits underneath the mezzanine.

He looked at the titan floating opposite, about three yards from the railing. His face was blank. Impossible to read. Daniel had a sudden flash of the famous photograph of Abos when she was The Deterrent, carrying a car bomb away from the centre of London along the Thames. Since getting to know Abos, the iconic picture had been marred for him by the knowledge that its subject was drugged and brainwashed at the time. Looking at it again, he had seen the blankness in The Deterrent's eyes. The steely determination and strength millions of people assumed was behind that expression—that heroic gaze into the far distance—was nothing of the sort. It was an absence of self-determination, a drug-addled half-awareness of reality. He saw that same expression now in the eyes of the giant Titus Gorman clone.

"Oh, God." History was repeating itself. He had to get away, tell Abos. She wasn't the only one who had found other members of her species.

He had to act. But how? What could he do? Only a few seconds had passed while Daniel was thinking, but during that time, he had heard, with perfect clarity, sounds he knew would haunt his dreams until his dying day. Snapping bones, punctured flesh, the slap of soft skin meeting solid walls, the splash of blood on marble, the screams of the injured and the blood-wet coughs of the dying.

"Daniel!"

Sara, watching the same bloody scene, had seen a way through, while each of the five titans behind were busy killing. He turned and saw it too. TripleDee turned from the rail. Gabe was there, too, nodding. If they were fast, if they moved—

"Now!" Sara hissed the word and broke into a run. As if watching a video frame by frame, Daniel saw TripleDee and Gabe turn to face the door. Daniel began his own turn, bracing his foot against a supporting post and tensing his muscles, ready to join the others in a sprint for freedom.

Then, as frame followed frame with the same inevitability of pre-recorded film footage, he saw it. The hovering figure beyond the railing turned its head, and those golden eyes, those inhuman eyes, locked onto Sara, tracking her movements. The seven-foot body tilted in preparation, a predator fixed on its prey, a falcon about to bring death to its unwitting victim.

Sara didn't see the threat. The gap she had spotted would close in seconds, as the nightmare versions of Titus Gorman ripped, crushed or tore apart their targets before looking for the next halfhero to kill.

She ran. Gabe and TripleDee followed.

None of them saw Daniel turn back.

The golden eyes widened a little just before Daniel ploughed into the flying figure, but it was slow to react to the unexpected turn of events. Daniel had taken three steps and thrown himself over the wooden railing, hands raised above his head as he jumped into space. Every thought was gone now. The horror around him had vanished as had everything other than the simple course of action he was committed to. Run, jump, kill.

Daniel brought down his fists with every ounce of strength he still possessed. He swung at a slight angle, aiming at the side of the giant's head. Gravity assisted him as his body began its fall. He was above his enemy, and his descent added to the force of the blow that caught the left cheekbone and snapped the head to the side. The brutal impact would have broken a human neck, but this was no human. Where Daniel got lucky was the fact that even a super being cannot avoid the laws of physics. The super-brain inside the super-skull followed the progress of the cranium a fraction of a second later and smacked into the bone, deforming, bouncing off and hitting the other side.

Again, this would have been fatal in a human. The flying figure experienced a gap in consciousness which lasted nearly a second and a half.

Long enough for him to lose the ability to fly. Long enough to fall.

Daniel and the titan plummeted to the marble floor three stories below. Keeping the giant between himself and the floor would, Daniel hoped, lessen the extent of his own injuries. He closed his eyes.

Above him, Sara, Gabe and TripleDee were more than halfway across the room. The human response to extreme danger had long been reduced to fight or flight. Higher brain functions were not required when life or death decisions were made, the reptilian, ancient part taking over. The three sprinting halfheroes were in a Zen-like state of simplicity. Living in the moment, it seemed, was a doddle when the moment involved running away from super-powered killers intent on ripping you into small pieces.

And so it was that, when Gabe slipped on freshly spilled blood, and, on scrambling to his feet, found himself staring up into implacable golden eyes, neither Sara nor TripleDee noticed. There was just the door, ever closer, and the possibility of not dying. Nothing else. Not even the sickening crack as Gabe's neck was broken.

Three floors below, another pair of golden eyes reopened and, four feet before hitting the unforgiving concrete, the titan whose chest Daniel was kneeling on regained his power of flight. There wasn't enough time to prevent the impact, but it slowed itself sufficiently to avoid any serious injury.

Daniel rolled to one side, groaning, as the titan rolled the other way and curled its knees up towards its chest, gasping.

He had hit it with everything he had, and it had fallen three floors onto concrete with Daniel on top. The result of which was, it was a bit winded. Winded. Daniel looked for a way out. Underneath the mezzanine was a laboratory of sorts. Huge metal tables, monitoring equipment. Stainless steel tubs big enough to contain two friendly humans. Or one Abos. It made the outbuilding in Cornwall look cheap, but Daniel knew it had been built for the same purpose.

There was a door at the far end. Maybe it was a way out. If he could just—

A massive hand grabbed Daniel's neck and lifted him off his feet. He looked into the eyes of the being about to kill him. There was no expression at all in the face of the titan. No hatred, no anger. Nothing.

Daniel hoped he had bought Sara and the others enough time to get away

There was a crash from upstairs and a shout. The huge face turned. He threw Daniel backwards through the window and flew away without looking back.

Daniel tucked his head forward before hitting the glass so that his shoulders took the impact. He had always known his brain was capable of throwing up inappropriate reactions in stressful situations, but, as the glass shattered and the warm desert air flowed over his skin in the moments he presumed would be his last, he outdid himself.

"Must be a bugger to keep clean," he thought as his progress outwards ceased, shards of glass reflecting a thousand suns, before he dropped down the cliff face beyond.

Sara threw herself through the door and kept running. There was an SUV parked outside the garage to her right. In one motion, she opened the door, slid onto the seat and put her hand where she hoped to find the ignition key.

It was there. Who would steal Titus Gorman's car?

She started it, the engine coughing into life as TripleDee opened the other door and got in.

"Gabe? Daniel?"

He glanced back at the open doorway and shook his head. With a sob, she threw the shift into Drive and pushed the accelerator to the floor. The car's wheels spun on the white sand before they gripped, sending it lurching towards the open gates.

Daniel didn't scream. He fell in near silence. The only sound was the air bending itself around his plummeting body. He relaxed. It wasn't surrender, it was one last instinctive decision by his brain. The impact, when it came, would be less devastating on a relaxed body than on tensed muscles.

There was no fear.

Time had no meaning.

Pain had no meaning. Not yet.

His hip shattered as it caught an outcropping of rock first and sent him spinning. His descent slowed, and he fell end over end.

The tree that saved his life broke five of his ribs, his jaw, the radius and ulna shafts and all four fingers and thumb in his left hand, before cracking his pelvis, snapping his right femur into three uneven pieces and tearing every ligament it could find around his right foot.

Daniel flipped face down before the final drop to the floor. The speed of his descent had been almost completely scrubbed off by then, but there was just enough left to enable a small stone on the pure white sand to puncture his left eye.

By then, mercifully, he was unconscious.

Back in Gorman's headquarters, an old man walked through the door leading from the interior of the mountain, and climbed the steps to the platform that served as Titus's office. He settled himself into the leather chair, hanging a silver-topped cane on its arm. He placed his hands in his lap and looked up at the mezzanine.

Blood dripped from the top floor, pooling on the concrete beneath. The old man swivelled in the chair and looked at the hole in the glass. The sounds of fighting were over now, the only sound that of the air rattling the jagged edges of the broken window.

"Titan," he called.

The closest giant floated over the railing and landed in front of the desk.

"Sir?"

The old man jerked a thumb towards the glass. "That's gonna need fixing. Survivors?"

"Two, sir. They stole a car. We can catch them before they reach the highway."

The old man shook his head. "Let them go. Gorman wanted them locked up because he thought they might stop you. I guess we just found out he was worrying unnecessarily, didn't we? No, if they're the last two halfheroes alive, let them tell their story. Makes Gorman look even worse."

He tapped his long, thin fingers together.

"Clean up the mezzanine. Gather all the bodies and incinerate them."

The titan nodded and turned to go.

"Oh," said the old man. "Almost forgot. There are two more bodies back in the chamber. Don't burn them. Put them in the freezer. They should look their best when I present them to the President. It's time to go public, boys."

The titan walked away, down the steps and through the same door the old man had entered by. He followed the corridor past the sleeping quarters and the medical room and walked through the enormous archway that led into a natural cavern inside the mountain. Strange equipment that looked like it had grown out of the rock dominated the centre of the cavern. The titan looked at the nearest slab, one of four that projected from the central rocks like the spokes of a wheel. He had been awakened there, but he had no memory of that time. Smaller figures slept there now, but it was the sleep of death.

The titan picked up Robertson and tucked him unceremoniously under one arm. He paused at the second body, looking at the unbreathing features of the human whose blood had given him life.

He scooped up Titus Gorman, walked back to the medical room, and placed both corpses in the freezer.

34

W hen Daniel's consciousness returned, bits of it were missing. This was a problem because, although he knew something—in fact, a great number of things—was seriously wrong, he didn't know what those things were. He didn't know how he had got here, or even where here was. He couldn't remember his name.

The blackouts lasted longer than the periods of wakefulness. It was so unlike anything he had ever experienced, he found himself fascinated by what was happening. Until now, he had experienced life from a central point, a place of cohesion and selfhood, continuity and potential. In the present moment, the self engaged with the outside world. But the sliver of time constituting the present moment was so tiny. The remembered past and the imagined future were so much bigger, a vast city around a speck of dust. And the past and future could be arranged into a rational, understandable order. The reimagined past became the story of a life. The imagined future was entirely malleable and, on the many occasions it replaced plans with chaos, a little patience was all that was needed. As soon as the chaotic future slid through the present, it became the writable past. The story continued.

A woman fell from a cliff. She looked up at him as she fell.

Now, as near to death as he had ever been, his story was unreadable. The fictional narrative that was Daniel Harbin had been torn up into tiny pieces and thrown into the air, words, sentences, and paragraphs falling randomly, some caught by the wind, others landing beside his broken body.

His mother pouted, watching him from a double bed on the white sand beside him. The word *mother* had no meaning. She wore a negligee, one black strap hanging, exposing most of her right breast. She was young, her eyes as yet undulled by a diet predominantly consisting of vodka.

"He made me feel special. Chosen." She wasn't talking to Daniel. Her eyes looked towards someone who wasn't there. "That's all anyone wants, isn't it? Not even to feel special, really. Just to be *seen*. By somebody. Anybody."

Dark. Complete blackness. Eyes open, nothing to see. Then a thin vertical yellow line hanging in the nothingness.

"You awake?"

The line widening, light from outside spilling into a simple room. A bed, a desk.

Station.

A memory. Daniel tried to cling to the word. Station. He didn't know who, or what he was, but this was a strong image, a momentary sense of being someone, somewhere, sometime.

A warm, soft form crawling into bed next to him, reaching for buttons. Hands on skin. Urgent, passionate. A night-time gift that could never be spoken of in daylight. Someone wanted him. He responded. Again and again, he responded.

A woman fell from a cliff.

"I." The word came from Daniel's cracked lips, sand and blood mingling on his thick, furred tongue. One splintered tooth had made a deep cut in his lower lip. Four more of his teeth marked waypoints on his journey down the cliff. The tree had kept two of them, one so deeply embedded in its trunk that it would remain there until the tree withered and died.

"I."

The word was all he could say, but it held no meaning. It was a sound his throat, mouth, and lips wanted to shape. It was agony, but he said it again, an open sound followed by a constrictive movement at the back of his broken jaw.

A woman fell.

"I."

When the golden eyes looked into his, he gave no response. Did golden eyes meant comfort or threat? He couldn't remember.

He watched the woman fall.

"He is close to death."

The golden eyes looked away. There were two figures standing behind.

The words meant nothing, but the voice fired up a sequence buried in a backroom at the end of a cluster of synapses, a tiny response flaring into life when everything else was shutting down.

His lips found new shapes.

"Help me."

A gust of wind caught the tiny pieces of his story and

scattered them, like sparks rising from a fire, burned carbon flaring and vanishing into the emptiness.

THE FIRST TWELVE hours at ULH Hospital, Albuquerque, were critical for Daniel. The two weeks that followed were filled with procedures, the surgeons working their way through the long list hanging on the end of his bed.

Highly trained, expensive medical professionals did what they were paid for. Broken bones were set, wounds cleaned and sewn up. Lost blood and fluids were replaced. A punctured lung was drained and re-inflated. An artificial coma was induced to allow the body to tackle the major repair work. And, when they saw how fast this particular body healed, the hospital's many specialists found daily excuses to visit the new patient. Other hospitals might have leaked the story, but ultra high-end facilities like the one in Albuquerque relied as much on their reputation for discretion as they did on the skill of their staff.

The patient occupied the suite on the top floor. CEOs, senators, investment bankers and criminal bosses had all been treated there. They arrived and departed by helicopter. Their own John Doe must have arrived the same way, but the helipad log was blank.

The senior registrar had signed the patient in, placing private possessions in a drawer next to the bed, including a collection of British credit cards.

Since every bank account on the planet had been wiped out and the money redistributed, platinum credit cards didn't quite hold the same cachet. But they denoted the likelihood that—when everything returned to normal, as the President had promised it would—the injured man would have no problem paying. What the registrar didn't know was that all of Daniel's money had been moved out of cash and into gold days before the Utopia Algorithm had launched. George Kuku's brokers had followed her instructions, emailed to them the same week that she had died. The value of gold had risen significantly as soon as the banks had been compromised.

There was another reason for the senior registrar's cooperation. She had been the only one to meet the individual who delivered the patient. There had been no helicopter. The tall woman's instructions concerning the level of care she expected for the injured man had been clear and explicit. On the roof, after handing over the patient, the golden-eyed woman had given her an email address to write to immediately. Then she'd flown away. Without the aid of a helicopter. The registrar had seen the footage from Geneva. She'd seen the lawyer on the motorbike get killed. And the drone base in Nevada blown sky high. She wasn't going to refuse anyone who had golden eyes and could fly.

When Daniel regained consciousness, it wasn't Abos sitting in the visitor's chair, asleep.

He had time to consider the inaccuracy of his first lucid thought in over a week a fraction of a second after he'd thought it.

I can open my eyes.

No. Even as he tentatively confirmed the knowledge with the fingers of his right hand on the oddly flat dressing on his face, he knew the truth.

I can open my eye.

He touched the dressing again. He knew the eye had gone. His field of vision was curtailed. It would take some getting used to.

His lips were dry.

First things first. He reached under the covers with his left hand and felt around. There were so many tubes, dressings and what felt like hard plastic attached to his torso and limbs, that it reminded him of the time he'd put his hand in the back of the television as a child. The memory faded as he found his genitals. They were much as he remembered them. Nothing missing. He prodded, lifted, cupped.

There was a cough.

He looked at the woman in the chair. She was awake. And she was smiling.

"Don't panic, Daniel. The doctors tell me that was the only part of your body you didn't break."

He was all out of snappy responses today. He tried for a smile instead. It hurt his face.

"Are you thirsty?"

He nodded, subtly sliding his hand away from his testicles.

She picked up a glass from the table, filling it from a cooler in the corner before holding it to his lips. He swallowed. It was the most delicious thing he'd ever tasted.

She refilled it after he'd finished, and he drained a second cup.

"More?"

He nodded again, and she handed him the glass this time. His left arm was less damaged than his right, and he was able to grip it without much discomfort. He looked at her properly.

The woman sitting opposite was in her early forties. She had dark hair. Lustrous hair. Daniel had never used the word *lustrous* in a sentence. He wasn't sure he knew what it meant. Whatever internal dictionary provided him with appropriate words for every occasion had selected this one for this moment, and he liked it.

"Pardon me?"

The woman looked amused.

"I didn't say anything."

She leaned forward. "That's strange. I could have sworn you said lustrous."

Daniel laughed to cover his embarrassment. The laugh turned into a gasp of pain as his chest shifted, moving still-healing bones further than they were used to. His arm jerked, and he threw the water all over his face.

The woman grabbed a towel and patted his face, before sitting down on the edge of the bed. She was still smiling.

"I get clumsy," he said. "I mean, I'm clumsy anyway, but apparently it's much worse when I'm close to a beautiful woman. Wait. Did I say that out loud, too?"

She laughed. There was something familiar about that laugh. It was a husky laugh, low and, well...

"Dirty laugh. Really dirty laugh. You're very sexy. Oh God, I'm saying everything I'm thinking now."

He twisted his head. A bag of clear liquid hung next to him.

"You're pumped full of drugs, Daniel. You're not out of the woods yet. The doctors thought you'd be unconscious for another ten days at least. You heal fast. I knew that already, but seeing it up close is something else."

Daniel must have drifted back to sleep for a moment. When he opened his eyes again, she was standing by the door. She looked back.

"I'll tell the doctor you're awake. It's good to finally meet you, Daniel. I only wish it wasn't like this."

Struggling to stay awake, Daniel observed his brain piecing together what it would normally have done within seconds.

"Saffi?"

The dark eyes filled with tears. He fell backwards into a deep, warm, dark hole. His mouth was moving as everything went dark. He hoped he wasn't saying anything embarrassing.

"I knew you'd have a great arse."

35

Nine days earlier

Abos slowed her approach as she got close to White Sands. She was within ten miles of the location, but she could feel nothing, no sense of the others. No, that wasn't true. She could feel her species pulling at her consciousness as keenly as a magnet attracts iron filings. But the specific connection she had established with Shuck and Susan in the Bay of Biscay was missing.

The onemind had gone.

She approached the glass side of the building, a faint glow betraying its presence.

The titans knew she was coming. If she was aware of them, they were aware of her. But there was no sharpness to the signal she picked up from them - it lacked all definition. Her brothers, waiting for her in the building below, were being kept in a half-aware state. Station had done the same to her with drugs and crude, but effective, brainwashing techniques. She imagined psychopharmacological and psychological techniques had come a long way since the early eighties.

Abos came to a stop three hundred yards short of the cliff where she had found her son's twisted body. She had carried him to the city she had seen when they had flown in that afternoon. His heart rate had been low, his breathing shallow. She did not know if he would live or die.

After so much time searching, finding the others of her species and Daniel in the same place had been a shock.

That afternoon, Shuck, Susan, and she had detected the titans' presence at the same moment. Unmistakable. Without exchanging a word, they had begun their descent towards the incongruously white landscape.

As they got closer, Shuck had noticed it first.

—*a building*—

—*yes. I will try to communicate*—

There had been no response, other than a door opening at the front of the building. Five titans stepped out, looking up at them.

—*they may intend to harm us*—

—*I have considered the possibility. We are awake, and we are onemind. We can defeat them if we must*—

—*if they return to the dormant state*—

—*then we can bring them back*—

—*and they will be free*—

—*yes*—

—*wait*—

Abos had felt it then but, for a moment, did not understand. Despite the improbability, it had become clearer, sharper, and—

—*Daniel. Daniel*—

The three of them had broken off their approach and followed the cliff face down to the injured man

—I have to get him to a hospital. He is close to death—

The decision was made in the time it took Daniel to take one, wet, gurgling breath. There had been no debate about whether Abos should go or stay.

Susan and Shuck had watched wordlessly as Abos took to the air, Daniel alongside her, his body carefully held in the position in which he'd been found, by the simple expediency of bringing a chunk of the desert floor along with him. When Abos had left with her son, they turned back to confront the titans.

Three hours later, Abos floated in front of the huge window, its surface now marred by the jagged hole marking Daniel's exit point. Abos knew Susan and Shuck were gone. Her awareness had shrunk, the onemind lost. They might be dead. She had no reason to believe her kind was hard to destroy in their dormant, slime-like state.

She doubted they had been killed, though. Her kind were few, it seemed, and hard to locate. It would be wasteful to destroy two possible slaves, when all it took was fresh blood to bring them back and enslave them in turn.

Then she knew what she had to do. The risk was great, but there was no other option. She could not know if she would succeed or fail, but, if there was a chance of the former, she had to try.

THE OLD MAN sat at the desk and waited. All six titans waited with him. They knew the third newcomer was outside in the darkness. Behind them, two of the stainless steel containers held new occupants.

He folded his hands on his lap, feeling calmer than he had all day. The escape of the halfheroes had worried him, but their confrontation with the titans had solved a potential problem. Until today, he couldn't be sure that the children of The Deterrent wouldn't be able to upset his plans. He would rather have killed, rather than imprisoned, them, but he had still needed Gorman back then, so had held his counsel.

The arrival of the three new titans had disturbed his equilibrium. There had never been a hint that someone else was looking for other members of the species. Yet here they were. In his own back yard. After breaking the bodies of two of them, his titans told him the third had escaped.

That was one problem with psychological programming. You had to be clear in your instructions. Gorman had been unexpectedly helpful for this part of the plan. A background in coding meant he knew how to be clear, logical, and thorough when coming up with a sequential set of commands. Unfortunately, programming a thinking being, rather than a computer, was as much of an art as a science. When confronted with unanticipated problems or complex decisions, the titans fell back to basics. When the third intruder had flown away, they had defended their master against the two remaining threats, rather than split up and give chase. Not a terrible decision. Just not very nuanced.

His watery eyes blinked. Why had the third titan returned? And where had it come from? He might get some answers before destroying it and reprogramming its new body. Calling them titans was pissing him off. He would think of something better.

When Abos flew through the hole in the window, the old man jumped despite himself, his heart palpitating. He looked up at the intruder as the titans rose to meet it.

"A woman? Whatever next?"

He had to admit she was a wonderful specimen, despite

the fact that, underneath that dark skin, behind those glowing eyes and killer cheekbones, was an unappetising blob of slime.

"Let's have a look at her."

The titans went to grab her arms, but she floated down on her own, landing lightly in front of the desk. Two titans protected the old man. The other four formed a square around their visitor.

"Fascinating," said the old man, placing both hands on his cane and getting to his feet. He peered up at the tall figure. Unaware he was doing it, he smoothed what was left of his hair across his liver-spotted scalp and smiled, displaying a set of suspiciously white teeth. She may have been a walking soup, but she was undeniably attractive.

"Well, you have my attention, my dear. No doubt you have a message."

The woman didn't move. She stared at him evenly. The old man thought he had become accustomed to those eyes, but this was different. He felt hot, the skin crawling on the back of his neck.

"Speak up. Someone sent you. A rival. Perhaps he wants to make a deal? Well, we'll see about that. Come on, who sent you?"

In answer, the disconcerting figure took a step closer, looking at his face. He stumbled backwards and might have fallen if it were not for the steadying arm of the nearest titan. Anger and attraction fought for dominance as he leaned on his cane. He was still a sexual man. Not emasculated like the current, limp-dicked millennials. His impulses had diminished with age, but they were still present. Perhaps it was time to indulge again. His titans could restrain her... but no. She was too disturbing. Why the hell was she staring at him that way?

Then she spoke.

"Roger? Roger Sullivan?"

He forgot to breathe, shook off the titan's arm and sat down heavily, before reaching into his jacket pocket and tipping some pills from a bottle into his shaking hand. He swallowed them and looked again into those golden eyes. It was impossible, but who else could it be? Who else knew who he was? No one living, other than Mike.

"Abos?" he croaked. "Is that you?"

36

R oger Sullivan's life, professionally and personally, had been a disappointment ever since his dismissal from Station in nineteen eighty-one following the disappearance of The Deterrent.

He had saved some money during his time in Britain, but much of it went on his new identity. Some might have called it cowardice, but Roger knew leaving his wife and son across the Atlantic and changing his name was essential if he were to survive. Six months after his return to the States, he read that McKean had drowned in Scotland. Station was tying up loose ends. Hopkins was terrifying, and—assuming he was still in charge—was making sure those who knew the origins of Britain's superhero would never go public. Signing the Official Secrets Act wasn't enough of a guarantee for a psycho like Hopkins. Roger watched for news of the other scientists involved in the project, but only Lofthouse's death, seven years earlier, had been reported. It didn't stop Roger presuming the others had been silenced by their government.

He took a job teaching chemistry at a public school near

Boston. He hated every minute. His real field of expertise was metallurgy, but he dared not pursue it lest he be traced by Station. He taught dull-witted adolescents about the periodic table, formulas, and bonding for twenty-two years, until retirement.

His only pleasure in life came from his many sexual encounters. As a young man, he had assumed the thrill of seduction, the pure, ancient, imperative to want to screw every attractive woman he met, would pass. When this failed to happen, he fought against his baser instincts for a while, then, when they showed no sign of abating, embraced them instead.

Professionally, his talents had been wasted. The respect due from his fellow scientists for his work with The Deterrent would never be forthcoming. Worse, he had been driven into hiding, forced to live a life never truly his own. If thousands of shallow, but exciting, sexual encounters were the only compensation, then so be it.

He delayed retirement as long as he could. The school he was working for decided for him. He had shaved a few years off his real age when constructing his fake identity, so he was actually in his seventies when the principal called him in for a little chat. The end of his teaching career was marked by the presentation of a chemistry book he loathed, and the prospect of ten to twenty years of failing health followed by an anonymous death.

Retirement was even worse than teaching. At least there had been a few blouses to look down while students bent their heads over a test paper, a few skirts to look up from between his fingers. Now, on a fixed income, in a cramped apartment, in a small town, there was no escape from the stench of failure.

He travelled, but any cultural enrichment he hoped to experience was spoiled by the drain on his limited finances.

Occasionally, he would look up a colleague from the old days online. Most now enjoyed the kind of sunny retirement available to those with the money to afford it. The resentment curdled his guts. He was always delighted when he found an ex-associate in the obituary column.

When he saw news of a gas explosion near Liverpool Street in London, he experienced a few minutes of exultation. Station was gone. Hopkins dead, surely. And unless the obsessive attitude to secrecy had changed, all records of his work there would be lost. He was free. Exultation gave way to depression. He was an old man now, out of touch with the scientific community. The time for making a name for himself was long gone. He closed the blinds, put some porn on the television and got drunk.

Next morning, he considered suicide for two minutes, before concluding he wasn't the type. He would screw his way out of depression.

He took to visiting coffee shops in Boston at around nine in the morning. He had observed mothers going for coffee after the school run. They were often susceptible to the intelligent conversation and solicitous manner of an older man.

A few months into this new sexual venture, a rare unproductive morning in a coffee shop heralded the most important moment of his life.

He had been finishing his third latte. The only woman who met his requirements had looked him up and down before dismissing his advances with a scornful laugh. Burning with humiliation, Roger ordered another coffee and took his time drinking it, proving to the woman that he was unmoved by her lack of interest.

He had reached for the book he kept in his briefcase and realised it was in the car. Now he had a latte to drink, the obnoxious woman was in his eye-line, and he had nothing to read. Intolerable. He picked up a newspaper from the next table. It was a lowbrow tabloid called the Worldly Enquirer. Things were going from bad to worse. Deciding to brazen it out, Roger opened the appalling rag so that the masthead faced the woman. Yes, he was reading the Worldly Enquirer. What of it?

Then he saw the picture on page five and forgot the woman, the coffee, and the past three and a half decades as David Levenstern, chemistry teacher.

It was a pencil drawing. Artistically, it had no merit whatever. But what it depicted shook Roger so profoundly that he had to put the Enquirer flat on the table, not trusting his fingers to grip the paper.

He forced himself to read the accompanying story methodically, line by line.

The headline was like many others he had seen when passing the magazine racks. Aliens, mutants, and the sexual deviancy of opticians and celebrities were the paper's stock-in-trade. On one memorable occasion, they had combined all their interests: MUTATED MEMBER OF CONGRESS CAUGHT IN MOTEL HAVING S&M SESSION WITH GREY ALIEN. The story Roger was reading now was small fry in comparison, which was why it had made the inside pages.

I FOUND ALIEN MOTHERSHIP IN NEW MEXICO. Humdrum stuff for the Enquirer. The subject of the article, Dwayne Carlsson, went on a bender after finding his wife screwing the mailman. Driving his pickup into nearby White Sands, he wrapped it around the only tree within a three-mile radius, halfway up a mountain road. With night closing in and temperatures plummeting, Mr Carlsson elected to take his litre of cheap liquor for a stroll in the wilderness.

Carlsson found a crack in the mountainside wide enough to squeeze through. Having done so, he fell, knocking himself unconscious. On waking, he used his cellphone's flashlight to illuminate his surroundings. At that point, he panicked, dropping his phone and scrambling up towards the only faint source of light. Once outside, he set out for his vehicle after studying his location so he could find his way back.

Six hours later, a truck driver found him on the edge of the highway and took him to the nearest town. He had walked nine miles in the wrong direction. The police weren't interested in his story. Neither was the local newspaper. Only the Worldly Enquirer had taken him seriously, even going so far as suggesting that his wife might be a mutant.

The whole story was puerile, laughable crap. The illustration based on Carlsson's description was anything but. It showed a cavernous space, at the centre of which was a pillar of rock which looked smooth, like a carved column. Jutting out from the column were four cylindrical objects. There was a more detailed sketch on the opposite page. The cylinders were, according to the caption, over six feet long and around four feet wide. They tapered at either end and were transparent. Inside, as Carlsson described it, was 'a bunch of jello.'

Roger folded the newspaper with trembling fingers and tucked it under his arm. He walked out without even glancing at the frigid woman. He had forgotten she was there.

Three days later, he arrived in El Paso airport and rented

a car. He explored the only ten square miles of White Sands that matched Carlsson's account, based on the article and hours of research online. Roger didn't come empty-handed; he carried a specialist piece of equipment in the trunk of his rental SUV. It had cost him six thousand dollars he couldn't afford. The portable ground penetrating radar system looked like a lawnmower. Roger knew he'd only be able to use it at night. It would take some explaining if he were seen; a man nearer eighty than seventy pushing a lawn-mower around White Sands in the early hours of the morn-ing. He decided he'd feign academic eccentricity and hope for the best.

Roger needn't have worried. He struck gold on the first night. Rolling the machine laboriously over a hillside, it emitted a low *bing,* and a green light flashed on the control panel.

It wasn't long before sunrise, so Roger buried the old iPhone he had brought for that purpose and went back to his hotel.

That day, he woke at least twice an hour. He got up at lunchtime, ate a desultory meal, and sat in the window seat of a diner, watching the sun move more slowly than seemed possible across the New Mexico sky.

Finally, night came. A bag of lighting, a battery and camera equipment accompanied his climb. Roger followed his *find my iPhone* feature. It brought him within five hundred yards of his goal, and he spotted the pile of rocks he'd arranged on the previous night.

He took twenty minutes to find the fissure Carlsson had described, and another ten to descend the slope his prede-cessor had slipped down. On reaching the bottom, he stepped on something that cracked loudly. He picked it up.

Carlsson's phone. He arranged his lights, plugged them into the battery and turned them on.

He faced the centre of the chamber, camera in hand. There, underneath the strange alabaster surface of White Sands, New Mexico, and for the first time since the woman in the Boston coffee shop, Roger Sullivan got a boner.

37

After that night in White Sands, New Mexico, Roger Sullivan was a changed man. Renewed, invigorated. He felt like he was in his twenties again. He went home and made plans.

There were some savings in the bank, and a pension. He applied, and was accepted, for five credit cards.

His photographs and video footage showed four cylinders in the White Sands cave. They were all identical to the one found in London in nineteen-sixty-nine. The slime inside them, unless Abos was unique, could grow into superhumans. Now that Abos was gone, it would be the scientific coup of the millennium. And Roger Sullivan would be the man who made it happen. He could go public if he played this right.

He went to London. It took all his courage, and he grew an ugly white and grey beard before leaving. Logically, he knew he was being paranoid, but fear has little to do with logic.

He was looking for Mike Ainsleigh, and Mike Ainsleigh proved easy to find.

Enough time had passed since the Deterrent project for Roger to admit that Mike had been under-used by the scientific team. He was a gifted scientist with a precise mind and a rare ability to explore multiple hypotheses before suggesting one or two perspicacious solutions. Roger knew everyone on the team had often found an excuse to come in early, or stay late, and run a few ideas past Mike. Since Ainsleigh was shy to the extent of avoiding unnecessary human contact, it was easy enough to claim his ideas as one's own at team meetings. They had treated him as a glorified janitor, but he had more insight into the nature of Abos than the rest of them put together.

Before leaving for the UK, Roger had searched online for Ainsleigh. He only had one lead, but it was a good one. He was on a roleplaying forum, along with a photo of a Dungeons & Dragons group in Bethnal Green. Mike's early obsession with The Beatles had given way to a passion for the game, an American import which never quite took off as dramatically in Britain. Already a Tolkien nut, Mike had found his spiritual home in the roll of a ten-sided die.

They met in the Woodbine, a hot, malodorous café whose signature dish appeared to be something called an egg and mushroom bap. Roger ordered a latte which, to his surprise, was excellent.

Mike didn't recognise him, but Roger knew Ainsleigh at once. The long hair, tied back in a ponytail, was grey now, the glasses rimless, but he still looked like an awkward kid.

When Roger confessed he wasn't there to sell his rare collection of Tolkien first editions, Mike dropped his chip butty. Roger slid the White Sands photograph onto the table between them. Mike took a quick look, turned away, then back again, scratched his nose, had a murmured conversation with himself, stammered a question.

"Wh- wh- who are you?"

"It's me, Mike. Roger Sullivan."

"R-Roger?"

"In the flesh."

Mike looked at the proffered hand. His social graces hadn't improved.

"Are they real?" He pointed a dirty fingernail at the cylinders in the photograph.

"They are, yeah."

"Can I see them?"

Roger smiled.

"Yep, Mike. You sure can."

MIKE AINSLEIGH HAD FORGOTTEN nothing of what had happened during his decades at Station. And when he said nothing, he meant it. He could describe experiments from thirty years previously, down to the time, date, and the names of those present. He knew which drugs had been given to Abos, and how often, to increase the superbeing's susceptibility to suggestion. Mike had even helped record the instructions played to Abos while he slept.

Best of all, as far as Roger was concerned, was that Mike felt no guilt about his involvement with the drugging and psychological programming of an intelligent being. It was as if he had no moral compass at all. Well, that wasn't quite true. He hated to see anyone inflict physical pain, even on an animal. But he didn't see a disconnect between his acceptance of Station's treatment of Abos and his instinct to protect others from harm. It was a huge ethical blind spot, and Roger was keen to exploit it. Mike was at his happiest being told what to do, and when Roger demanded he drop everything and come to America, he agreed. His only concern was leaving his Dungeons & Dragons group, but when Roger reminded him that the game had been invented in the States, he brightened considerably.

The next part of Roger's plan was the most important, if he were to retain control of his discovery. Roger knew he couldn't go to the authorities, in any form, for fear of being ignored or, even worse, taken seriously. If they listened to his story and investigated the cavern, he would be cut out. He might stay centre stage for a while if he admitted his history with The Deterrent, but his government would be suspicious of a man who had helped another nation gain a superhero. No. He could be an American hero himself if he stuck to his plan.

What he needed was money. A lot of money. A shit ton of money.

And he knew where to get it.

Titus Gorman was the richest man on Earth. Glob's founder was never seen at a White House dinner, rarely spoke at high-octane business gatherings. This was partly due to his semi-reclusive lifestyle, but that wasn't the whole picture. The main reason was ideological. No one trusted him. He was the cuckoo's egg invading the capitalist nest, and the few early interviews with him before he made his fortune revealed a fierce critic of the American way of life. He found the American Dream an appealing idea in theory, but claimed it was a catastrophic failure in practise.

The earliest interview Roger found had a photograph of a young, intense Gorman in a room full of circuit boards and cannibalised computers. The piece in question— printed in The Man, a radical Californian art magazine— had been quoted many times after Gorman had achieved his incredible success.

One section in particular diminished his chances of ever being asked to address industry conferences.

GORMAN: *Well, the system is broken. It's plain to see, although no one wants to talk about it. America is supposed to be the land of opportunity, a fresh start away from the suffocating class system and feudal network of old Europe. But what have we done? Recreated the same inequities over here. Worse than that, we've made everything about money. The dream is that everyone, whoever they are, whatever their background, can achieve greatness. People tell their kids, work hard, and you might be president. But it's horseshit, and we know it. I'm not saying individuals don't escape poor backgrounds and become successful. It happens, for sure. But they are exceptions. Take two kids born on the same day, one in the worst neighbourhood in Detroit, with an absent father and a drug-addicted mother, the other to a rich family in New York, with Ivy League parents. Land of opportunity? For one of them, sure. The other one, statistically, will be lucky to reach thirty without a spell in prison. We've let it get away from us as a nation, and now everyone acts like it's too late to change.*

The Man: *Isn't it?*

Gorman: *No. It would take guts. A politician will never have the balls.*

The Man: *To do what?*

Gorman: *Start over. Level the playing field. Stop people inheriting wealth. If we wanted to, we could make sure every baby born in this country started life with the same amount in their bank account as everyone else. It's a simple enough algorithm to code into the banking system. That kid in New York would have the same as the kid in Detroit.*

. . .

HE HAD BEEN FORCED to apologise for that comment. Some American banks took it as a threat. He had laughed it off, saying he had no intention of hacking the US banking system that week. There had been rumours since that Gorman was a revolutionary, a communist, a socialist, a fascist, a lunatic, a deluded visionary. He stopped giving interviews, only facing the media when he had an announcement to make.

Ultimately, his eccentric views were tolerated, because, as rich as he was, he was a private individual with no way of implementing any whacky ideas.

Unless... unless he was backed up by four superbeings who could protect him from any threat of retaliation.

Roger emailed Titus Gorman, claiming he had developed a metal compound that was not only lighter and cheaper than the components Glob currently used, but contained a new twist on built-in obsolescence. The material would biodegrade automatically after ten years and could be composted. The email, and the few details attached, were mostly nonsense, but Roger's background meant he could keep the idea plausible. He was banking on the fact that Gorman famously gave time to innovators and developers with fresh ideas.

It worked. Roger was given a ten-minute slot with the man himself.

Roger rehearsed that ten-minute pitch for weeks, worked on it harder than anything since he had left Station. He had photographs of the cylinders, and he had laptop footage from the cave. Most importantly, he had an old photograph of the Station team from 1970. When he slid that across the table to Gorman and watched the super-nerd hesitate before turning to his screen and running some searches, he knew he had him.

He was forced to sweat it out for three days after the meeting, but Gorman called. He sent his private jet to Boston to pick him up. When Roger boarded, Titus himself met him at the top of the stairs.

"Okay, Roger, you have my attention. Show me your superheroes."

ROGER HAD ASSUMED it would take over a year to assemble the equipment to excavate the site, remove the cylinders, and set up a lab. He had failed to factor in the trillionaire effect. Titus Gorman put everything else aside and threw money at the project. Instead of moving the cylinders, he built the lab around them, then built his own headquarters around the lab.

Work continued on the headquarters while Roger and Mike locked the door to the lab and got to work. Four vials of Titus Gorman's blood and two weeks later, they were playing psychological programming files to four seven-foot giants as they slept the sleep of the heavily sedated. The following month saw them gradually allowed longer periods of consciousness every day until they were ready.

The day after Titus had seen his new employees for the first time, he called Roger to his new 'office,' a floating platform in the open-plan minimalist monstrosity he had built on the side of the mountain.

"They're perfect," he said. "But something occurred to me when you described the history of The Deterrent."

"Really?" Roger was irritated by Gorman's casual acceptance of the superbeings he had created for him. If he had genuinely made them solely for Gorman's purposes, he would have been angry, but he had bigger fish to fry, so said nothing.

"Sit down, Roger."

Roger sat down. And listened as Titus told him about the prison he'd built at the same time as his headquarters. He had researched The Deterrent; including every fact, story, or rumour about the children attributed to the British superhero. He'd concluded that halfheroes were the only threat to his plan and acted accordingly.

Roger was impressed by how far Gorman would go to protect his stupid commie scheme, but smiled inwardly at what the tech genius had missed. The greatest threat to his plans was sitting opposite him.

What Gorman said next really did surprise him.

"The Deterrent was found in Britain, the four examples you have uncovered were in America. There must be others. I've been looking for them."

"You've been looking?" Roger felt like an idiot for not considering the possibility.

"I doubt the Protectors—" (Roger hated the name, but he knew he wouldn't have to suffer it for much longer) "—turned up only in the last half-century. I built an algorithmic search tool based on physical height, strength, unusual eye colour, superhuman abilities, plus a few other parameters.

Of course you did, thought Roger.

"I found a few possible matches in myth and legend, but two historical candidates were stronger still."

"You think there are other cylinders."

Gorman's smile was patronising.

"I don't think, Roger, I know. Not cylinders, though. The dormant slime within. Robertson found the first one in the east of England. It had been a queen in Roman Britain -

Boudicca, or Boadicea, depending on which accounts you read. Defeated the Ninth Legion and destroyed the Roman's capital. A tribe of early Britons defeating a Roman army? I don't think so. The second was in Egypt. A cat god. Too many unrelated sources with near-identical descriptions of a giant feline displaying incredible intelligence and godlike powers."

Roger didn't say anything because he was fighting a minor panic attack and giving himself an internal talking to.

It's all right, it doesn't affect the plan. I'll have two more Aboses to program and play with, that's all.

Roger's panic attack was joined by a bad case of acid reflux. Gorman was too sharp, too intelligent. The sooner he could kill him, the better.

He calmed down, congratulated his boss, and prepared to indoctrinate an extra two candidates.

38

Eight months later, when the plan had reached the point of no return, with Gorman's neck snapped by one of his own titans, and Roger about to break the biggest news story in history, the impossible happened.

Roger waited for the medication to take effect and calm his heart palpitations. While he did so, he looked afresh at the tall, golden-eyed woman opposite.

"The world thought you were dead. *I* thought you were dead. Where have you been?"

Abos looked back at him, saying nothing.

Those golden eyes were different to the other titans. Unnervingly so. Very unlike Roger remembered them back in the eighties. The intelligence behind them was so powerful it was like looking into the sun. Roger dropped his gaze, another prickling of the skin under his shirt collar giving him an urge to loosen it. He fought that urge. The Deterrent had been superior to his human masters physically, but the brainwashing regime had kept him dull-witted. The same as with the titans now surrounding Roger.

But Abos must have been clear-minded for the best part of four decades. What if his, or—rather–her species was more intelligent than humanity? What then?

"You're a woman," said Roger, unaware he was echoing Daniel Harbin's words when first meeting Abos. Then, after considering the consequences of this change of gender, Roger laughed. He couldn't stop himself.

"Oh, no, this is too good. All that time, Station... Hopkins... they never thought... they were all looking for a guy. Oh, that's great, that's so funny... "

Abos waited him out. When he could speak again, he asked the obvious question.

"What do you want?"

"First, my friends. They were here earlier today. I know they have been killed. Are you giving them new bodies?"

Briefly considering lying, Roger decided against it, partly because he remembered Abos's uncanny ability to read body-language, but mostly because there was no real advantage in hiding the truth.

"Yes. They should be back with us in ten days."

Abos shook her head. "Sooner. The process is much faster after the first time."

She looked at the titans one by one.

"It was you, not Titus Gorman. You are using my brothers just as I was used. You know this is wrong."

Roger shook his head. That naivety was still there, then. He could see The Deterrent in this woman now.

"I don't expect you to understand. Gorman was responsible for a cyber-attack on a global level. He is an enemy of our country, and the world. He brainwashed the titans. I got control of them and stopped him doing any more damage."

He waited. That was a big, fat lie. Abos didn't go for it.

"You insult me," she said. "I know you are lying. And if Titus Gorman truly controlled my brothers, you would be powerless to stop him. No. You have always been in control."

That was the part of Roger's plan that had given him the most pleasure. It was also a secret he would take to the grave. The titans were programmed to obey any of Gorman's commands unless they might harm Roger. Right until the moment Roger said the words that transferred their allegiance back to their true master. When he'd said, "Game over, Titus," the geek had chuckled for a moment until every titan walked away from him and stood at Roger's side. Even the most brilliant mind has weaknesses, and, once Gorman had been convinced Roger also cared about redistributing wealth, he had trusted him implicitly. He'd still had that look of hurt incredulity on his face after a titan had broken his scrawny neck.

"Yes," admitted Roger. "You're right."

He sighed. The cost of what he was about to do was clear to him. Killing this body and bringing back Abos as a titan would mean snuffing out that intelligence. It was a high price to pay.

But Roger had resigned himself to this a long time ago. He was on the verge of becoming not only the most envied scientist on the planet, but a true American hero. He had to think of the bigger picture.

"Kill her."

⌇

ABOS FLEW OUT of the building the same way she had come in, pursued by four of the six titans. She drew them away from the mountain and up into the thin desert air.

She had been surprised to see Roger Sullivan at first, then it had made sense. Very few people who knew what had happened to The Deterrent were still alive. Those who knew about the brainwashing techniques were fewer still.

She had felt a brief surge of rage at what he had done, but it passed through her and was gone like a flame flickering into life before being blown out. What followed was pity. This was a man near the end of life, and these were the choices he had made. He was a pathetic figure.

The conversation she'd had with Roger Sullivan was only part of what had happened during the past twenty minutes. Most of her attention had been focussed on the other titans.

Her awareness of the other members of her species was very different to what she experienced with Shuck and Susan. During her years as a teacher, she had often used lego with the children, enjoying helping them find new and creative ways to connect the brightly coloured blocks. Sometimes, the box of lego would contain pieces made by a different company. There was no way of making them fit together, however hard the children tried. This was a similar experience, but far more painful and frustrating. Abos *knew* her mind should fit with the others, but the connection was wrong, the shape was awkward, every approach she tried failed.

As she flew upwards, she hoped that fixing the titans' minds on a common goal—even if it was killing her—might bring them together and make it possible for her to find a way in.

It didn't work. Nothing worked. Their minds weren't closed, exactly, they were just twisted out of their natural shape. She couldn't undo the damage.

As the air grew cold at the altitude she'd reached, Abos

stopped, turned head over toe like a stalled aircraft, and fell. From this height, White Sands looked like a cloud which had drifted to the ground to die.

The other titans watched her fall. They followed as she picked up speed. Abos could make out details now, see the telltale regular lines of the building below, white on white.

The appeal behind the human concept of gambling had, so far, eluded Abos, but she knew what she was about to do was the equivalent of sitting at the roulette table and putting everything she owned on red.

She could see the moonlight reflecting on the broken window now. She adjusted the angle of her descent a little.

If she died, she knew Roger would bring her back. Or, rather, she believed Roger would bring her back. Oh, all right, she acknowledged to herself as the wind screamed past her plummeting body, she *hoped* Roger would bring her back.

If he did, she thought her unparalleled experience of multiple human existences would enable her to fight the drugs and psychological conditioning to which she would be subjected.

If Roger didn't bring her back, she would die. If he brought her back and she couldn't fight the conditioning, she would be a slave. Perhaps the roulette analogy was unfair. More accurately, Abos was putting all her money on a single number. The odds weren't good.

The impact would shatter this body. The internal trauma would crush its internal organs. As she was travelling head-first, bits of the brain would splatter every wall in Titus Gorman's headquarters. If Roger Sullivan was still sitting at that desk, he would be covered in pieces of brain matter, blood, and flesh.

She checked, just before hitting the glass. Roger *was* still sitting there.

Good.

39

The hospital registrar had been nervous when she'd delivered Abos's message. Daniel was used to making people feel nervous—he was built like a professional wrestler, after all—but at that stage, he'd needed someone to wet his lips with ice twice an hour, and it would be another ten days with the catheter before he'd even be able to piss into a bottle. Her nerves were nothing to do with him.

"Your friend - the one who brought you here. She asked me to give you a message."

Daniel hoped, with every ounce of his being, that the registrar wasn't about to say, "She said she was going back to White Sands."

"She said she was going back to White Sands," said the registrar.

Bollocks.

It was fifteen days after his arrival. In the morning, the chief surgeon of the hospital had assured him that, with his self-healing abilities, he might be discharged within six to eight weeks. Once he was out, he should rest in bed with daily check-ups for another six weeks. Following that time, he might try a short walk every other day, for no more than ten minutes. All things considered, if Daniel followed the program that had been prepared, it was possible he would be back to full fitness inside a year.

Daniel decided he was walking out of the hospital by the end of the week.

His decision wasn't solely because he was bloody-minded, and didn't intend to let any sodding doctor, however many sodding letters she had after her sodding name, give him a sodding timetable for his sodding recovery. It was more than that. It was the past six days since he'd regained consciousness, with Saffi. It was the two visitors she'd brought with her yesterday, and it was the video they'd shown him this morning.

Saffi was, well... Saffi was... Daniel had never had a girl-friend, never had a sexual relationship with anyone he could pick out in a line-up the following day. In Station, he'd been visited by several women in the darkness of his room —some more than once—but none had ever acknowledged what had passed between them. He'd caught the eye of a few possible suspects during mealtimes but had always been blanked.

So this thing with Saffi was an enigma. He wasn't even sure if it *was* a thing. She was there every day. She helped him take his first few steps. After watching the physiothera-pist work, she repeated the exercises in between sessions, moving Daniel's legs and arms through a range of motions. Saffi talked about her life when Daniel was too tired to speak, telling him about her privileged childhood as the daughter of a diplomat in the Middle East.

She had led a sheltered existence right up to the point a car bomb planted by supporters of the extremist Wahhabi sect took her religiously moderate, tolerant, wise and loving father from her. Her mother had died within a year, leaving Saffi—an only child—halfway through a university course. She abandoned her literature and film studies degree and went back to the United Arab Emirates to put her mother's affairs in order.

It was while she was home that she found out her best friend from childhood was now a paraplegic. Nayla had always been ill, suffering from a wasting condition that baffled even the expensive specialists. Now, Nayla told Saffi the truth about herself. Her father, she said, was not her father. Her mother had been pregnant when they married.

Nayla's real father was The Deterrent. The abilities she'd inherited from her non-human parent had, in her case, been more of a curse than a blessing. Since her late teens, her body had progressively weakened.

"Nayla is the reason I'm here," Saffi told Daniel. "Last time I saw her, she said she'd had a vision of me in a hospital room with someone I—, er, someone badly injured. She knew it was America. She told me to pack and wait for an email. I came as soon as I received it. I have a question for you."

Daniel had a feeling he knew what the question would be. The time for keeping that secret was past.

"You were unconscious when they brought you in. The registrar said she'd been given my email address. You didn't give it to her. Who did?"

He opened his mouth to speak when there was a knock on the door. The handle turned and rattled. Muffled voices could be heard outside.

"You're supposed to use the security card. Hold it against the panel. No, the other way round. No, now you've got it upside down. Look, move out of the way and let me—"

At that point, the door flew off its hinges, skidded halfway across the room, pirouetted on one corner, and fell to the floor with a crash.

Daniel pushed himself up on the pillows, wincing with the effort. Saffi leaped out of the chair and stood next to him. She was holding his hand.

"Alreet, you soft southern ponce? You look like shite."

Daniel gawped at TripleDee. Then he broke into a smile as a figure emerged from behind Triple's bulk and ran to the bed, was about to throw herself into his arms, then stopped as she took in the bandages, drips and tubes.

"Sara!"

Daniel shrugged.

"Sod it, it might hurt, but it'll be worth it. Give me a hug."

She leaned over tentatively. Daniel wrapped his plaster cast right arm around her neck and drew her in.

"Ow. God, it's good to see you. Argh, my ribs, how did you get away? My bastarding shoulder. Nah, don't kiss me that side, I can't see you."

Daniel started crying just before Sara did. The sobs were painful, lighting up his broken ribs with every heaving breath, but neither of them cared. They wept for Gabe, and for every brother and sister, every halfhero they never got to know, and now, never would.

When they disengaged, Sara hugged Saffi while TripleDee stepped forward.

"I, er, well, I'm sorry how it all turned out, man. No one could have known about those *things* waiting for us. No one could have known."

Daniel narrowed his eyes. "What, I'm supposed to trust you now, am I? You one of us? Turned your back on the pimping, the drugs, and the murdering?"

Triple stood his ground.

"Well, yeah, actually. And I hardly did any murdering. Not of anyone who might be missed, anyhow."

"Oh, well, that's all right then."

Sara moved forward again.

"He helped me escape, Daniel. He's helped ever since. And when we broke out of the prison when we were... connected... I could see he regretted his bad choices. I could see a better man."

Daniel's expression didn't change, but he knew he would never forget the webmind. It had only lasted a few hours, but when they were all linked, no one could hide. It had changed him. He had seen the good and the bad clearly enough to know the gulf between them was not so great. People he labelled as evil were not so easily categorised when you shared their mind. It should have come as no surprise that human personalities were so nuanced, but Daniel felt more than a little shame at his black and white attitude.

He looked at TripleDee, then lifted his less damaged left arm from the sheets. The big man shook his hand gently.

"Probation," said Daniel. "That's what this is. Thank you for helping Sara. I'm willing to give you a chance, but it'll take more than a few days good behaviour to make me trust you. I might never trust you."

Sara caught his eye. He looked back at Triple.

"But I'll try."

"I canna ask for more than that. Thank you. And thank you for what you did back there. I think you, well, you did, you - you saved my life. Both of our lives."

He pulled a battered paper bag out of a pocket.

"I brought you some grapes," he said, pulling out two grapes on the end of what had, until recently, been a big bunch. "Got hungry in the lift. Sorry."

Daniel knew Sara would have called Saffi as soon as they found a phone. But that must have been two weeks ago.

"What took you so long?"

Sara raised her eyebrows in mock-indignation. "Well, that's charming. We've been hanging around forever trying to get in. Your doctor told Saffi not to mention us to you until you were out of the woods, then they said we could visit today."

Saffi coughed. "Next week. They said you could visit next week."

"Oops. Must have got my dates wrong. I'm so scatty sometimes."

Daniel laughed at the thought of Sara as scatty. He looked at the three of them standing around his bed. IGLU was finished. Apart from Saffi's friend Nayla, every known halfhero still alive was here in this room.

"You'd better all sit down," he said. "There's something I need to tell you."

Because of his weakened condition, the telling of that story took the rest of that day and half of the next. Daniel had to stop and sleep every couple of hours, and his physiotherapist and medical checks couldn't be postponed.

Daniel's time at Station was already well known to Saffi, and he had told Sara a little about it, but he had told no one about Abos. As far as the world knew, The Deterrent had died in the storms of nineteen-eighty-one. When his story reached the point at which he got to George's flat in Putney and met his father for the first time, only to discover his father was now his mother, the hospital room fell silent.

He told them how Station had been destroyed, how he had nearly killed Abos. He told them about George, and about the blood she had provided to give Abos a new body.

Finally, he told them about Shuck, and the other members of her species Abos was hoping to find.

When he had finished, Sara spoke.

"Those creatures we met at White Sands - they are the same species as The Deterr—as Abos—then."

Daniel nodded. "Yes. And they must have been brainwashed, like Station did to Abos. What the hell is Gorman playing at?"

Sara, TripleDee, and Saffi exchanged a quick look.

"What?" said Daniel. "What have I missed?"

Saffi came and perched on the bed next to him.

"Titus Gorman is dead, Daniel."

"Saves us a job, I guess." He looked around the three faces. No one looked happy about Gorman's demise. "What?"

Sara reached into her bag and pulled out a laptop.

"What you've just told us about brainwashing makes perfect sense, Daniel. But it couldn't have been Gorman who was doing it. I didn't want to show you this today, but I think I need to."

"Show me what?"

Sara put the laptop on the wheeled tray that pushed into position over his bed at mealtimes. She and TripleDee stood by the picture window that looked out over Albuquerque and the red-hued desert beyond.

Saffi took Daniel's hand again. Maybe he wasn't kidding himself. Maybe she didn't pity him. She was old enough to know what she wanted, and she was making it clear she wanted him. Unless his inexperience meant he was reading her all wrong. The tiny bit of pressure from her soft, dry fingers on his skin was all he could think about. It was as if nothing else existed. He thought he could never pay attention to anything else while she was touching him. A bomb could go off, and he'd still be sitting there with the same goofy half-smile on his face.

Then he glanced at the laptop and forgot Saffi was even there.

"Holy shitbuckets."

~

THE PRESIDENT of the United States was sitting at the Oval Office desk, TV makeup taking some of the usual shine off his face, hair sprayed in place. Nothing unusual about that. What *was* unusual was the entourage. Besides the usual aides and advisers, three huge figures, ducking to get into the room, were taking their positions, one on each side of the President, the third a few paces behind. All three wore airforce-style helmets and flying suits, the American flag displayed on their breast pockets.

"My fellow Americans," was the familiar opening statement. A few minutes of waffle about national security, the threat of terrorism, the misguided leadership of many other countries, and the inspired greatness of his own talents in that regard. Daniel couldn't take his eyes off the immobile figures who had accompanied him into the Oval Office. The dark goggles covered much of their features.

The President got to the point.

"Many of you will have heard the news about the death of the traitor Titus Gorman. He tried to crush our dreams, and the dreams of all who believe hard work deserve to be rewarded. His attack on the economic system of the free world has failed, as all who care about freedom knew it would."

Saffi had told him about Gorman's Utopia Algorithm, which economists were predicting would take a generation to overturn. Daniel still didn't know if he hated or loved the idea.

The President stood up, rounded the desk and gestured to someone out of shot.

"The citizens of America owe this man a debt too great to repay. Despite his age, and failing health, the man I am about to introduce—one of our greatest scientists, a truly great, great scientist—not only defied Gorman, he undid the great damage he was doing and turned his evil work against him. In a desperate battle, he defeated the most heinous criminal our nation has ever known and destroyed the creatures called titans. He killed all of them. A great guy. A great, great guy. And he has brought the technology used to create those monsters to us so that our nation can use it to protect our high, and great, ideals. My fellow Americans, this man did what few others could have done. I could have done it, for sure, but the fact is that he did a great, great thing. Roger, step up here. Roger Sullivan."

Daniel stared at the screen.

"Roger Sullivan? Roger Sullivan?"

Repeating the name didn't make it any more believable, but when an old man with a silver cane shuffled across the rug to shake the President's hand, Daniel accepted it. It made sense. Who else would know what had happened at Station? Almost all of them were dead. A shame this octogenarian sex pest wasn't one of them.

On screen, the President was pinning something to Sullivan's jacket.

The caption read: **Scientist Roger Sullivan receives the Presidential Medal Of Freedom With Distinction.**

The two figures flanking the desk took their helmets off and, for a moment, Daniel thought he would puke. They were younger, more handsome versions of the president himself. Of course they were.

Then the final helmeted figure moved to stand next to Sullivan, put his hands up to the helmet and waited. The President glanced around for a few seconds, then found the autocue again.

"Our country is about to enter a new, unprecedented era of peace and prosperity. The man standing next to Roger Sullivan has returned from nearly forty years of wandering the globe to help make this happen. And he has chosen the United States Of America as his new home. My fellow citizens, may I introduce the leader of a new generation of superpowered peacekeepers."

Even before the helmet came off, Daniel knew.

"The Deterrent."

He looked exactly like he did in the photos and the films from the eighties. Roger had used his own blood to bring back Abos.

Daniel actually did puke then, everywhere.

40

Ten days later

They held a memorial service for their fallen brothers and sisters. They drove until the lights of the city had faded, taking the highway east, then turning southeast into the mountains that lay between Albuquerque and White Sands.

The night was full of stars. They drove in silence, Sara at the wheel of the rental pickup, Daniel beside her, TripleDee sprawled across the back seat. Saffi had been called back home. Her friend Nayla was in intensive care after a seizure. Saffi had promised to come back as soon as Nayla was out of danger.

When they had stopped climbing, and the narrow road was snaking its way through the mountains, eight thousand feet above sea level, Sara touched Daniel's arm, and he woke up. He was still weak and drifted to sleep a few times a day. His body was healing rapidly, and his strength was returning. His right arm was in a sling, and, although he could walk again, it was with a slow, stiff-legged gait that, he knew, had all the elegance of a deformed duck.

"How about here?" said Sara, bringing the pickup to a halt on the shoulder and pointing up at a small plateau. The silver light of the moon lent the scene an almost mystical grandeur.

"Perfect," said Daniel. Then, after a few seconds, "Triple?"

"Yeah. It's good."

There were no graves to dig, no bodies to bury. Gorman's headquarters was now a military zone. Local television had been showing little else. As no statement had been released about what had been found there, reporters were either describing the vehicles going in and out of the facility or speculating about what was inside. At no stage was any mention made of any bodies. Daniel, Sara, and TripleDee had to accept that they would likely never find out what had happened to the corpses of the halfheroes.

Sara stopped walking. TripleDee and Daniel joined her on the plateau. The Geordie drug dealer had slowed his pace to allow Daniel to keep up. Daniel didn't thank him.

Sara spoke.

"We don't know the names of many of those who died. We know little about them, their backgrounds, their childhoods, what use they made of their powers. But we all connected back there in Gorman's prison. During that time, we knew each other, I believe, in a deeper way than any human being has ever experienced."

Sara reached into her bag and brought out a miniature spade—the kind a child might take to a beach—and a small book. She held the book up so they could see it. It was a concise American English dictionary.

"This is all I have left of Gabe. He gave me this so I could learn to speak English the way he thought it should be spoken."

Daniel half-laughed, half-cried. Sara continued.

"I worked with him for nearly a year before Daniel joined us. We both felt Daniel completed the team, although he would never have admitted it."

Daniel nodded, not speaking.

"I'm sorry, Gabe," she said, looking at the dictionary. "I don't think I'll ever speak the language properly."

They buried the dictionary there in the mountains under the star-speckled sky. There were no more words. They stood in silence for a few minutes, the children of The Deterrent. Long after they were gone, the mountains would remain, and on certain nights, the moonlight would once again paint the same scene silver and blue. Life, in its infinite forms, continued.

They drove back to the hotel without exchanging another word. There was a sense of release, the human need to mark important events satisfied. Whether the improvised ritual had done anything other than try to make sense of the senseless, they neither knew nor cared. It had worked. They could move on.

DANIEL, Sara and TripleDee watched the President's next press conference in the hotel bar. They were only a block away from some drinking spots with live music and other, less salubrious forms of entertainment, so they had the place to themselves.

TripleDee put three bottles on the table and sat down.

"Gnat's piss, but at least it's cold gnat's piss."

Daniel took a mouthful, barely tasting it. He had been in the bar all afternoon.

He had been thinking about Cressida Lofthouse. How she'd been the key to unlocking Abos's mind back in nineteen-eighty-one. Despite being brainwashed, Abos had never forgotten her, visiting her twice. Her influence had been so strong, she had reached through the haze of drugs and connect with the being she knew. Was it love that drew The Deterrent to return to her? Was it love that prompted her to tell him the truth? Did it even matter? Would Daniel be able to reach Abos in the same way, given the opportunity? If Cress could do it, there was a chance. Abos was Daniel's parent, and the bond between them had deepened and strengthened during the year and a half they had spent together.

Abos needed to remember who she was. Who *he* was. Whatever.

And only Daniel could make that happen.

Over the past week, America had reversed its recent fortunes in dramatic style. Its seat at the head of the top table in world governance had looked untenable for a while after the Utopia Algorithm took effect. The US banking system had been affected more than most, with the super-rich hit the hardest. Economists had predicted a devastating re-assessment of America's economic might, barring a miracle. The miracle had occurred, but the world was still smarting from the social, and economic, fallout. The rich may have made the most noise about their losses, but the poor had enjoyed a brief respite from worrying about how the rent might be paid, or the children fed, and they weren't quite ready to go back to how things were. Titus would have his legacy, although it was too early to say what it might be.

The immediate legacy was plain enough: America had

The Deterrent and, now that Shuck and Susan had joined the existing group, an unstoppable team of ten titans under the President's command. North Korea and Iran had found their nuclear capabilities forcibly curtailed, their military resources crippled as the superbeings buried bases under thousands of tons of rubble.

China and Russia were left alone, the American President speaking warmly of the friendship between them. Both countries explored new ways of cementing their relationship with the United States. The balance of power had shifted and, while every other world leader was looking over their shoulder for titans, it looked unlikely to shift back.

Daniel drank his beer and wondered how he would get to Abos. He was no closer to a solution than he had been when he first saw the face of The Deterrent on Sara's laptop, back in his hospital room.

The press conference was beginning. The world would be watching.

Daniel muted the sound and put the subtitles on. He couldn't bear to hear the voice of the man who, when presented with the knowledge that a new, intelligent species, had been discovered, chose to bury that information and continue brainwashing Abos and his kin. He could hardly bring himself to look at the screen, but he knew he must.

After the usual introductory remarks, the President of the United States announced it was time America celebrated the beginning of its new golden age. There was a montage of footage showing the titans—all of whom, apart from The Deterrent—were still younger, taller versions of the President himself. They performed various acts of heroism, demonstrating their powers. There was no need to threaten unfriendly nations when a few minutes of film said everything necessary.

When the montage ended, the President spoke to camera. Daniel turned up the sound.

"Next month, our nation celebrates Thanksgiving. This year, there is more than ever to be thankful for. Instead of our usual parade in New York City, we will hold a bigger, better, parade the day after Thanksgiving. It'll be the best parade ever, a great, great parade. We will officially welcome The Deterrent and the titans, now American citizens, to our great country. Let us celebrate our many blessings. Let us look to the future with a new sense of hope and confidence. And, my fellow Americans, let's party."

The press conference over, Daniel muted the television.

"I have to get close to Abos," he said. "I can reach him if we're face to face. We have to try. I'm not going home without her. Him."

"I know," said Sara. "I've been thinking about nothing else. I've looked at every piece of information about the titans I could uncover, I watched every news story over and over. The titans are kept in a secret location, and when I say secret, I mean I can't find a single clue."

On screen, the news anchor was speaking over a graphic showing the planned route of the parade through New York.

TripleDee drained his beer. "So Daniel needs to have a chat with the hardest to get to being on the planet, right? How do we make that happen? There must be a way? Sara?"

"If there is, I haven't thought of it. I have no idea."

They sat glumly, the empty bottles on the table between them. Then a voice spoke from the doorway, and they all turned.

"I have an idea."

41

S affi looked older. Tired. Worse than that; exhausted, wrung out. Daniel stood up. He put a hand up to the eye patch he had worn for the past few days. Despite his impressive healing, the hole where his eye used to be was doing nothing for his looks. He wondered how she would react. He was already half-convinced that the relationship he had imagined developing between them was just that: imagined.

She watched him limp across the room. He stopped a few feet away, and she looked at his face, taking in the black patch.

"Arrrr," she said. "Jim lad."

They smiled at each other, he tentatively, Saffi sadly. Then she dropped her bag and stumbled towards him.

He held her. She put her head on his chest and wrapped her arms as far as she could around his bulk. She didn't speak, and, after a short time, he realised she was crying. He stroked her hair

"How's Nayla?"

She pulled away then but didn't wipe her eyes. Her

usually immaculate hair looked half-combed, her mascara was running, and she looked ten years older. Daniel thought he'd never seen anything so beautiful.

"She's dead."

THEY TURNED the television off and TripleDee brought another round of drinks over. The usual expressions of condolence were offered and accepted. They had all experienced so much death Daniel was surprised to find their sensitivity to it had not been dulled. Perhaps the human capacity to mourn was as limitless as the human capacity to love. Not, Daniel mused, that he had experienced much of the latter. There was no self-pity in this admission.

They gave Saffi time to gather her thoughts.

"IGLU is finished," she said. "I was expecting it, but... well. We're on our own."

No one was surprised. How could IGLU function, with the halfhero population decimated, and Nayla gone?

"I was nearly too late," said Saffi. She was looking at the table. "For Nayla, I mean. I went straight there from the airport and she died half an hour later. She was waiting..."

Her voice trailed off, and she sipped her bitter lemon, still looking down. No one spoke.

"She was waiting for me. Waiting to die. She was in such pain, but she hung on, she fought against it until she could see me. And when she did, when I held her hand and said her name, she didn't talk about her life. No regrets, no bitterness about her illness. She had nothing negative to say. She spoke about her final vision. When she had finished, she said she loved me. I listened to her breathing slow down. Then it stopped."

The hotel bar was silent. Even the bartender had picked up on the atmosphere and taken ten minutes.

"When I walked out of the hospital, I saw them - her parents. I was getting into a taxi. They didn't see me. I wanted to go to them. I wanted to grieve with them. Since my parents died, they've always been so good to me. But I got into the taxi to the airport because that's what Nayla had said to do. She described this scene - here in this bar. It was the first part of her vision."

She stopped again. He looked at the others, each acknowledging, in their own way, the death of another halfhero.

Saffi finished her drink and looked up.

"Nayla knew who Abos was. I don't know how long she'd known, and I didn't have the chance to ask. She told me she had seen Daniel and Abos. She said the vision was hazy, unclear. It means it might not happen the way she saw it. It's possible, it's one outcome, but there are no guarantees. Everything has to fall into place for it to occur, but she couldn't tell me how. There was one clear image, and she said everything depended on it. I will describe it as she described it. I hope it means something to you because it doesn't to me."

She took a few deep breaths. Daniel reached out for her hand, and she gripped his fingers. She closed her eyes, remembering.

"She is looking at Daniel. Daniel standing on top of a glass building in a city. High up. It's night time. Daniel isn't moving. It's as if she's looking at a photograph rather than a real scene. But she feels a definite sense of scale, and if it is a photograph, then it's an enormous photograph, because she has to look up to see the top. After the image fades, she sees Abos, The Deterrent, from Daniel's point of view.

Daniel is holding out his hand, Abos is about to take it. That's it."

The silence that followed this description was partly due to no one quite believing the vision was so short. And rather less helpful than they'd hoped for.

"Um." TripleDee was the first to speak. "Is that it, like?"

A little more blunt than Sara or Daniel might have been.

"There was one other thing, but it makes no sense," said Saffi.

"And the rest did?"

"Shut up, Trip," said Sara.

"Sorry."

Saffi shook her head. "She hummed a tune. Well, part of a tune."

"Part of a tune?" TripleDee's eyes were wide. Sara shot him a warning glance.

"Go ahead, Saffi."

Saffi hummed four notes. They stared at her. She repeated them. Three descending notes, then one higher. A regular rhythm. She did it a third time.

"Anything?"

TripleDee shook his head.

"I don't recognise it," said Sara. "Daniel?"

"One more time?" He squeezed Saffi's hand. She turned to him and hummed the four notes again.

It was his turn to close his eyes, as he hummed the four notes back, trying to empty his crowded mind of every expectation and pressure on this moment.

"Nothing. I don't know what it means."

There seemed little to say after that. They talked through the vision as far as they could. Daniel named the building as the Shard in London as the most likely candidate. But he couldn't see the relevance. Abos was in America. What did a London landmark have to do with anything?

Saffi's grief was so raw, that TripleDee stopped himself saying aloud what all of them were thinking: "Well, that's us fucked, then."

DANIEL STAYED in the shower a long time, letting painfully hot water cascade over his skin. His body was still covered in bruises, but they were yellow now, or light green, and fading fast.

He stepped out of the shower and rubbed the mirror with his towel. His face emerged out of the steam, one eye looking back at him. The socket where its twin should have been was empty, pink and scarred. He glanced down at his left foot, the missing toes a permanent reminder of his encounter with the hybrids in Station half a lifetime ago.

"Lose any more body parts and you won't even qualify as a halfhero," he said to his reflection.

The knock at the door was so quiet he thought he'd imagined it. He opened the bathroom door, his skin breaking into goosebumps as the air-conditioning touched it.

The knock came again. He wrapped the towel around his waist and crossed the room to open the door. It was Saffi.

He stood aside and let her in.

Daniel felt his mouth dry as he tried to say something that didn't sound trite, stupid, or both.

Saffi didn't give him the opportunity. She reached up, placed a hand on the back of his neck, and pulled his head towards her. They kissed for a long time. Whenever the kiss was about to end, one of them would hungrily resume, as if they never wanted to stop.

Daniel had never been kissed this way, had never kissed anyone this way. Nothing in the world was so awful that it couldn't be subsumed by the power of this white-hot passion, no evil was powerful enough to withstand the wonder of moments like these. Two souls, in two bodies, abandoning everything to the other, giving and giving, never taking because taking had been transformed into more giving.

Daniel's mind quieted in acknowledgement of the pure moment of infinite desire that had flared into existence between them.

Well, either that or he couldn't think straight because of a massive erection.

Saffi reached down and pulled the towel away before pushing him back onto the bed as she undid her blouse.

The two-and-a-half minutes that followed were the best of Daniel's life. The ninety-seven minutes after that were even better.

DANIEL WOKE SUDDENLY, with no memory of dreaming, no trace of the usual drowsiness that accompanied the transition from sleep to wakefulness. He sat up and stared into the darkness of his hotel room, his heart racing.

He hummed four notes, three descending, one ascending. He added three repeated notes to the end of the phrase, then hummed the whole thing three times. The fourth time he varied it, then began a new phrase.

Saffi sat up beside him.

"Daniel?"

He turned towards her. His eye was adjusting to the darkness now, and he could make out the shape of her face.

"I've got it," he said. "I know what the tune is. I know why she saw a picture. I know what we have to do. I know how we can try to save Abos."

She was quiet in the darkness, but he knew she was smiling.

"Should we tell the others now?" he said. "Or in the morning?" As she spoke, Saffi took Daniel's hand and placed it on the underside of her left breast. Daniel swallowed.

"The morning's fine. No point disturbing them. Let's tell them in the morning."

42

Four weeks later

It was the day after Thanksgiving. Black Friday. Traditionally, the stores in Manhattan would be crammed with bargain hunters, determined to spend hundreds, thousands, even tens of thousands of dollars, then brag about how much money they had saved in the sales

Not today, though. Not this Black Friday. The administration had tried to rename it Deterrent Day. When that was ignored, they pushed hard for Freedom Friday. No one outside Washington paid any attention. Black Friday it had always been, and Black Friday it would remain.

There was one major difference though. The stores were, for the main part, closed. Food and drink establishments were open - they were expecting their best day of the year. Souvenir stores and street stalls were hawking disposable tat. There were titan T-shirts and caps, Deterrent tea towels, boxer shorts, and thongs. Toy titans, battery-operated, which marched up and down, fists pumping. Optician's window displays were full of gold contact lenses.

With the traditional Macy's parade cancelled to make way for this one-off celebration, New York City was determined to show the world it knew how to party.

At five am, secret service agents followed street sweepers along the parade route. A few early arrivals had already claimed their spots, determined to get a good view. The President had elected not to attend, stating, "Freedom Friday is about the superheroes who are protecting our nation. It's not about me, your President. I will be there to greet our new heroes at the end of the parade." The media commentators weren't buying it, gleefully pointing out that, in a parade full of beautiful super beings who could fly, no one would look at the President.

The route had been chosen to enable the maximum number of people a view of the titans. It stuck closely to that of the Macy parade, starting on Central Park West, but, after turning onto 34th Street, it headed north again on 8th Avenue, finishing in Times Square.

Neighbouring streets had been checked in the days leading up to the event, but no one expected any trouble. Not against titans.

Other streets were making the most of being off-route, knowing they were guaranteed a quieter day. The stretch of 7th Avenue between 34th and 42nd Street was already busy with billboard erectors, pasting new advertisement hoardings. At street level, they were putting together a huge PA system for a party that night. Construction work continued on most city sites, contractors working overtime to get ahead of schedule, while those along the route had suspended work for the day.

By eight-forty-five, every float was in place, the cheerleaders were warming up, the giant inflatable titan figures, filled with gas in Central Park the previous night, tied to the trucks pulling them. They were accompanied by a giant inflatable turkey. Marching bands, majorettes, dance troupes, acrobats, jugglers, street magicians, and fire-breathers prepared themselves for the start of the parade.

On a flatbed truck decorated—against his better judgement—as a Hollywood version of a scientist's laboratory, Roger Sullivan turned to Mike Ainsleigh and asked the same question for the fourth time in twenty minutes.

"Is my tie straight, Mike?"

Mike looked again.

"Yes, Roger. It's straight." He looked around him. "Th-there will be a lot of people. I don't know. M- maybe I should leave."

Roger patted him on the arm.

"Mike, it's your day as much as mine. Without your help, we would never have saved the titans from Titus Gorman. You're a hero too. In your own way."

Mike was unappeased.

"But, but, Roger, how have we saved them?"

Roger waved his arm, indicating the parade.

"A few months ago, they were public enemy number one. Now they are the toast of New York, American heroes. The protectors of freedom. You helped make that happen."

Mike shook his head.

"But, but, but..."

"But, but what, Mike? Lighten up a little. Neither of us are spring chickens. Did you ever think you'd live to see a day like this?"

"But, but they are still being drugged, Roger. You're using the same—"

He broke off as Roger grabbed his arm and stared at him, his face reddening with anger.

"Now listen here, Ainsleigh. I've explained this to you. It's about the greater good. And you cannot, I repeat can*not* talk about this. It's a matter of national security. You mention anything, to anyone, ever, about any of the methods we use and you'll spend the rest of your miserable existence in a cell. Do you understand? Do you?"

"Well, yes, Roger, yes, I do, but, but, well, it isn't right, is it?"

Roger leaned in close.

"Now you listen, you stupid motherfucker. One more word about any of this, and I'll have you taken away and shot. I can make it happen anytime I like. So shut. The. Fuck. Up. Got it?"

Mike nodded, and Roger released his sleeve. If he hadn't been so reliant on him, he might have gone through with his threat. Mike was making discoveries in the lab, examining tissue harvested from the titans, his brilliant mind engaged with the joy of pure research. He was exploring worlds Roger couldn't even begin to understand. But, like a kid pulling at Santa's beard because he thought he looked suspiciously familiar, Mike kept coming back to the question of ethics. It annoyed the fuck out of Roger.

Ainsleigh was trembling. Mike hated any kind of physical contact, and confrontations could upset him for hours.

"Look, Mike, I'm sorry. I'm nervous, is all. It's a big day. Try to enjoy yourself."

Mike nodded automatically and walked over to the table where dry ice was rising from a large beaker. He tried picking it up, but it was glued in place.

"It's Hollywood, Mike. Like a movie set. You and I are mad scientists."

Looking at Mike's decades-out-of-fashion glasses and long, lank, grey hair, Roger considered the role wouldn't be much of a stretch for him.

Then someone screamed something, there was a huge roar from tens of thousands of voices, and he looked north in time to see a V-formation descending from hundreds of feet above.

The Deterrent led the others, his iconic outfit from the eighties updated but still recognisable. His helmet was painted with the American flag, as were those of the titans who swept down behind him, taking up position above the massive inflatable versions of themselves.

Roger reached into his pocket for his walkie-talkie. He had tried an earpiece but found it too uncomfortable. All the titans were wearing one, naturally.

"Deterrent?"

"Yes, Professor Sullivan."

He wasn't a professor, but an honorary doctorate had arrived after his medal of distinction and, since he considered his services to science dwarfed anyone since Einstein, he was happy to use the title.

"Radio check, please."

He listened to every other titan check-in.

"Sir?"

A secret service agent was leaning over the side of the flatbed.

"It's nine. We're ready to start the parade. Whenever you give the word, sir."

Roger smiled. For a second, he had a flash of memory from his time at Station; McKean, that uptight prick, punching him on the nose. What he wouldn't give to have that self-righteous Scot see him now. It was almost a shame he was dead. He straightened his tie one last time.

"You may proceed, son."

THE PARADE WAS, as expected, a huge success, attracting the biggest live television audience in history. The titans made a show of it, swooping down to street level and walking for half a block, shaking hands and giving high fives, before rising into the air again, performing loop the loops and barrel rolls for the cheering crowds.

The Deterrent was the star of the show. The other titans were popular, but social media had been buzzing for weeks with criticism of the president's decision to have the titans look like giant, incredibly fit versions of himself. No information had been forthcoming from the White House regarding why, or how, this had happened, but speculation was rife about genetic engineering, secret labs, and alien technology.

The Deterrent was a different story, and the media had fastened their teeth onto it like a rabid dog with lockjaw. A thirty-seven-year absence during which only the most extreme conspiracy theorists had believed he was alive, followed by a dramatic reappearance, a change of political allegiance and no explanation. It was the biggest mystery, the biggest news story, in the world.

Everyone there wanted to see The Deterrent for themselves; a piece of folklore made flesh, a superpowered and apparently ageless being who wore the flag of their country. Tens of thousands of selfie-sticks were held aloft by fans determined to get their face in the same image as The Deterrent. This led to tangled sticks, some arguments, a handful of impromptu fencing matches, and one trip to hospital by a young man whose selfie stick was subsequently removed from his rectum.

The crowds cheered, the camera flashes provided a constant light show, children dressed as miniature titans waved at the real thing. Men and women leaned barebreasted out of upper windows. Every media network covered every square inch of the route.

Ten minutes in, Roger Sullivan sat in a leather armchair on his laboratory-themed float, while Mike Ainsleigh squatted with his back against the cab up front and played a text-based adventure game on his phone. Roger popped a few pills into his mouth. No one was looking at his float. No one cared who he was. He regretted agreeing to take part. His place in history was already assured. There was no need for him to be part of this side-show. Oh well, lesson learned.

As the parade turned west onto 34th Street, The Deterrent at its head, Sara watched from a fifth-floor window on the intersection with 7th Avenue. She sent a text: *count to a hundred, then do it.*

On top of a building on 34th Street, forty yards on from the intersection where Sara waited, TripleDee received her text, slid a ceiling tile aside and lowered himself into the empty restroom below. Once in, he replaced the tile and checked his appearance in the mirror. Black suit, white shirt, black tie. Dark glasses and an earpiece. He couldn't have looked more like a Secret Service agent if he had been wearing a badge reading *Secret Service Agent.* He stretched and rolled his neck, eliciting a brief cannonade of clicks, cracks, and pops.

TripleDee scowled at himself.

"Scary bastard," he told his reflection, before blowing a raspberry and raising his middle finger in a mock salute. "Reporting for duty."

On the roof of the 34th Street building, a crowd of revellers had gathered around a crane. It towered above the office workers, who were cheering as they caught sight of the front of the parade.

TripleDee burst out of the door to the roof bellowing so loudly that half a dozen people dropped their drinks.

"MAKE YOUR WAY TO THE GROUND FLOOR IN AN ORDERLY FASHION IMMEDIATELY. THIS IS NOT A DRILL."

Triple had no idea if anyone had ever had a drill involving a shouty bloke from the north of England ordering people around, but he was relying on the outfit, his size, and crowd psychology when confronted by an extremely loud authority figure to see him through.

Everyone froze and looked at him. TripleDee did some more shouting.

"I SAID MAKE YOUR WAY TO THE GROUND FLOOR IMMEDIATELY. **IMMEDIATELY.** THIS IS NOT A DRILL. MOVE. NOW."

People headed towards the door, but too slowly. Perhaps he had overdone the 'orderly fashion' bit. He decided to, as the Americans would no doubt put it, *incentivize* them. He pointed and shouted even louder.

"THAT CRANE IS PACKED WITH EXPLOSIVES. THE TIMER COULD TRIGGER ANY SECOND. WHEN IT DOES, THE TOP THREE FLOORS OF THIS BUILDING AND THE ONE NEXT TO IT WILL BE VAPORISED, ALONG WITH ALL OF US. SO IF YOU COULD JUST HURRY ALONG..."

Triple stood aside as sixty people tried to get through a single doorway. They managed it remarkably quickly.

Once the roof was clear, he shrugged off his jacket and ran to the crane. He'd already put in some groundwork the previous night, loosening the huge bolts which secured the construction equipment to the roof. Now he worked fast, finishing the job and tossing each huge bolt aside.

Once he was done, he remembered he hadn't counted to a hundred.

"Er... eighty-one, eighty-two, eighty-three."

Sara, meanwhile, was watching the parade get closer and closer. She had finished her own count twenty seconds earlier.

"Come one, come on, come on," she muttered, her breath coming in short, nervous gasps, her throat tight. She trusted TripleDee now, but this was the first time she'd had to rely on the newly reformed drug dealer who'd spent the rest of his adult life building a criminal empire.

"Oh, shit, shit, shit, shit, what if he's buggered off?"

She paced the small room. The name-plate on the door had said *Vice President*, but Sara had seen bigger toilets.

"Come on, come on, come on..."

In a rare moment of perfect synchronicity, TripleDee was saying the same words at precisely the same moment, before launching into a deluge of swearing as every muscle in his body screamed. He had his back against the side of the crane, his legs bent beneath him, and he was pushing with every bit of strength he possessed.

"Come on, come on, come on, come on you shitty piece of shit, you shitty piece of crane, you craney piece of shit, you shit crane, come on, fucking move move move, you absolute bastard twat crane. COME ON, YOU ARSE-LICKING COCK SHITTING PISSFLAP OF A TWATTING FART GOBBLER."

Whether he had found one last reserve of strength, or whether the words pissflap of a *twatting fart gobbler* were, in fact, imbued with mystical properties able to alter the molecular structure of metal, Triple neither knew nor cared. The result was the same. As the veins on his neck stood out so far they looked like they'd had enough of being trapped under his skin and wanted to see what it was like on the outside for a change, the crane shifted an inch. Triple felt it move and whooped, digging his heels hard into the roof. Another inch, then three or four, then a couple of feet.

Triple fell backwards as the crane reached the point of no return and toppled away from the building. There were screams from below as the crowd looked up and saw what was happening. The people on the roof opposite had spotted the danger and were running away from the piece of construction equipment tipping towards them.

The crane crashed into the building opposite and came to rest, wedged against a billboard.

Sara let out a whoop of her own before bringing binoculars up to her face and focussing on the lead truck in the parade convoy. The driver was looking at the panic ahead, his eyes wide, but it was the older woman next to him that Sara watched. She was on point for the Secret Service, and it was her job to decide whether the chaos ahead meant the parade should be abandoned. Sara could see the woman thinking, her eyebrows coming down in a frown. She was reaching for her walkie-talkie.

Now.

Sara reached out with her mind and sent a strong, targeted nudge at the agent in the truck.

Accident ahead on 34th. Send the chopper to investigate. Parade re-routed. We'll take 7th Avenue instead of 8th.

Below her in the truck, the agent hesitated. She had been about to abort the parade, and the alternative that had suddenly occurred to her had made her pause, her finger on the send button of the walkie-talkie.

Sara sent a second mental nudge so strong that she had to sit on the floor after doing it. She concentrated on breathing while her vision, which had narrowed to a dark tunnel with flickering points of light, cleared.

It might have been ten seconds before she stood up and looked out of the window, but they were the longest ten seconds of her life.

"Yes! YES."

The lead vehicle had turned and was heading up 7th Avenue.

She made a call. Not to TripleDee this time. To a DJ who called himself dubbytranz. He was about to make the easiest ten thousand dollars he'd ever make in his life.

The number rang and rang. No one answered. It cut into a voicemail message.

"What up? dubbytranz coming at ya, so—"

Sara ended the call and listed all the painful and physically improbably things she would do to dubbytwat if he didn't pick up next time.

She dialled again. It rang three times.

"Yo! Crazy rich lady, what's happening? Was just taking a leak."

Sara spoke calmly, enunciating each word as she imagined nailing the DJ's incorrectly worn baseball cap to his shaved skull.

"Do. It. Now."

"Got ya. Nice doin' bidness. Look, for an older lady, you are fine. If you ever want to, ya know..."

"Now."

"Okay, chill, we'll talk about it later. Got it."

She held the phone to her chest, waiting. Listening. Something was happening to her perception of time. She was trapped in an endless loop of a second and a half where nothing happened, and nothing would ever happen.

She didn't know she was doing it, but Sara was talking again, although her lips were barely parting enough to make the sounds.

"Come on, come on, come on, come on, come on..."

43

The Deterrent, high above the crowds, observed the crane fall a block ahead. He watched the parade come to a halt before the lead truck turned right. He followed, swooping low as instructed at the pre-parade briefing, to thrill the fans lining the streets.

Seventh Avenue wasn't as tightly packed with people since it was never intended to be part of the parade route, but it was still busy, and hundreds of faces tilted upwards as he flew above, waving.

A mother held her baby over her head. Only a few months old, the infant was dressed in a flying suit and helmet like the one The Deterrent wore. He gave them the thumbs up, and the woman shrieked with joy.

It was while he was returning to his position alongside the inflatables that the music started.

Further back in the line of vehicles, still twenty yards away from turning into 7th Avenue, Roger Sullivan looked up as a sound cut through the already painfully loud roar of the crowd.

"What the hell is that?"

Mike Ainsleigh looked up from his phone and nodded his head along with the music. Then he broke into a rare smile and sang along.

"Dee da da dum, dada dee da da dum, dada dee da da dum, dada dee da da dum in ca-rs, dur dum, dedum."

His head was bobbing now, and his grin was broad.

Roger looked at him incredulously.

"What are you doing?"

"Cars!" shouted Ainsleigh, the music getting louder as they turned the corner.

Roger stared at him.

"Gary Numan!" shouted Ainsleigh, as if that would clear everything up. "Cars, by Gary Numan. Brilliant song. You know! Dee da da dum, dada dee da da dum, dada dee da da dum, dada dee da da dum in ca-rs, dur dum, dedum."

Mike Ainsleigh was having a seizure. Either that or he was dancing. Roger Sullivan lacked the expertise to ascertain which of the two it was. Then he looked at the street they were turning into, saw The Deterrent, and froze.

THE DETERRENT WAS FLOATING about twenty-five yards along 7th Avenue, his helmeted head turning from right to left. He was looking at the huge advertisement hoardings put up that morning.

Roger Sullivan was looking too, as were some of the thousands of people following the diverted vehicles.

The billboards, which must have cost hundreds of thousands of dollars, seemed to serve no commercial purpose. There was no brand name, no product placement.

The first poster featured four letters, white on black, and meaningless to almost everyone who saw it: Abos.

The second poster showed a kitchen. If it was intended to advertise a kitchen designer, it had failed. The kitchen was old, tired, and untidy. There was a big farmhouse table, with a laptop on it. An old-fashioned stove. A big, deep sink full of unwashed pans. The floorboards were unswept. There were muddy footprints everywhere. On the back of the door were two jackets and two motorcycle helmets. The view from the window took in rolling, green fields.

The third poster showed the interior of a shed with a rough stone floor and unpainted walls. There were low, wooden beams. A radio hung from one. Two big tables and two bathtubs dominated the space. A huge fridge stood in one corner. Water pipes from the baths weren't connected to anything. The purpose of the room was unclear. The photograph itself was blurred, as was the one of the farmhouse. They looked as if they had been enlarged from a format not supposed to be viewed on billboards a hundred feet across.

The fourth, and final, photograph looked, at least, as if it might be promoting something. A movie, perhaps?

It showed a city, at night, seen from the top of a high building. City lights, a river, and a bridge. Not just any bridge. Even the least-travelled adult standing on 7th Avenue knew which city they were looking at. It was London, the most famous bascule bridge in the world straddling the Thames far below: Tower Bridge.

The strangest part of the billboard image was the man in the foreground. He was a big guy dressed in motorbike leathers. But, if this was a movie poster, why was the star facing away from the camera, an anonymous silhouette against a million tiny lights?

Abos took it all in as the soundtrack blared out of the massive PA system, and tens of thousands of people were treated to the iconic electronic hit that had, in the autumn of

1979, made its way onto a compilation tape given to Mandy Harbin, in Essex, Great Britain. Nine years afterwards, her young son had found it in a drawer, put it on the stereo, and a love affair had begun. Daniel had moved on to Kraftwerk, Vangelis, Tangerine Dream, then the Prodigy, Air, Chemical Brothers, The Orb, Moby, but he always came back to his first love. There was something about the simplicity, the raw new synth sounds, and the almost harsh vocal that still hooked him, decades after that first hearing.

And now Abos, soaked in sound, staring at the billboard showing his son's silhouette at the top of the Shard, felt something crack open and loosen in his mind. His sense of identity shifted abruptly. The shock made him drop fifty feet, hitting the street hard enough to crack the surface.

People screamed, and the lead truck came to a shuddering stop a few yards short of his immobile body. The Secret Service agent in charge threw open the door and ran to the prone superhero. She stood and stared down at the giant. This scenario wasn't covered at the briefing. She spoke into the walkie-talkie.

"Medic. Man down, er, titan down. The Deterrent, he's hurt, he's not moving. Wait, he's... wait."

She took the walkie-talkie away from her mouth as Abos got to his feet.

"Sir? Sir? Are you okay? Do you need medical attention? Sir?"

Abos took a step away, looking up. She followed his gaze and looked at the billboard with the silhouetted figure and the view of London. As her eyes flicked back to The Deterrent, he moved so fast it was almost as if he vanished. She followed the blur of speed upwards as the superhero disappeared into the clouds.

"Shit. SHIT."

She reached for her walkie-talkie again.

Sara was watching from a second office in the corner building as Abos flew.

"Yes!" She hit a button on her phone.

"Saffi, it's working. Do it now."

Twenty seconds later, on the far side of the Hudson, a row of half-constructed warehouses exploded.

Saffi watched in satisfaction as flames consumed a stretch of the site covering a city block. Black smoke belched into the sky as she heard the first sirens.

She walked for ten minutes before hailing a cab. She called Sara from the back seat.

"Well, by my calculation, we spent half a million dollars, including your advertising campaign and impromptu concert. Are the titans on their way?"

"Not yet. They're hovering up there. Waiting orders, I guess. Stay on the line."

Saffi held her breath without knowing she was doing it, then let it out in a rush when Sara spoke again.

"Yes, they're heading towards the fire. We've done it. At least, I hope we have. It's up to Daniel now."

ROGER LAY on his back in the middle of the fake laboratory, blinking. He couldn't get up. God, he hated being old.

Ainsleigh offered him a hand, and he got to his feet, his joints cracking. His heart was racing, so he took an extra pill. He looked at Mike.

"What the hell - did you push me over?"

Mike shook his head.

"Someone pushed me and I fell. Into you. Sorry."

Roger looked around for the walkie-talkie. He needed to

order the titans to pursue The Deterrent. Something had gone terribly wrong. That much was obvious. Nothing was more important than getting him back and reinforcing his conditioning.

The agent in charge had called on the walkie-talkie, asked him for orders before he'd fallen. There had been an explosion across town. She wanted to send the titans over there to help. Roger had been about give the order to go after The Deterrent, when Ainsleigh had... he looked around. Where the hell had he gone?

Ainsleigh's head popped into view at the side of the truck. He was holding something in his hand. He placed it on the floor of the truck. It was what was left of the walkie-talkie, a crumpled mess of plastic, metal and wires.

"I, er, that is, I er, think that, well, someone may have stood on it, Professor Sullivan," said Mike. Roger looked at him sharply. Mike never showed any initiative. Had it been an accident? Had he really been pushed? No. No. Impossible. Not Mike Ainsleigh.

Roger tried to get down from the truck, shout orders to the nearest agent, but his breath was short, and his heart was fluttering, despite the extra pill. He cursed his infirmity as he gave in to physical weakness and sat down, waiting for the feeling of faintness to pass.

He was dimly aware of activity in the sky above him, accompanied by more gasps and cheers, as the titans flew towards the scene of the explosion.

He felt a hand patting his shoulder like someone comforting a small child.

"Oh, well, never mind. You don't look well at all. I'll tell you what, I'll get you a bottle of water. You sit tight, I'll be back in a minute."

Roger clenched his fists as Mike Ainsleigh walked away, suspicion flitting into his mind once more.

No. Surely not.

He grunted in shock and pain as his shoulder developed a severe case of pins and needles. Which spread down his left side.

No, not this. Not now.

He moved his head to one side. Ainsleigh was talking to a Secret Service agent. The agent was turning - good, he would see that he needed urgent medical attention. Mike put a hand on the man's arm and bring his attention away from Roger.

But Ainsleigh was looking over at him. He could see what was happening. Roger grunted again as he fell sideways. Why wasn't Ainsleigh doing something? Why?

Why?

44

London. 4:30 pm

It had already been dark for half an hour, and it was cold on top of the Shard. Cold, and windy. Daniel stamped his feet as hard as he dared on the narrow metal walkway, trying to bring back some feeling in the seven toes he still possessed.

Daniel looked at his wrist, then remembered he'd thrown his watch into the Thames after checking it for the three hundredth time. He flexed his fingers, trying to keep some feeling in them. He should have worn two pairs of gloves.

His eyepatch was in his pocket. For this to work, he needed Abos to see him looking as close to his old self as possible.

His mobile phone was turned off. He knew Saffi and Sara would text, or call, either to tell him Abos was on her way—*his* way, Daniel reminded himself—or to break the news that no one was coming. Whichever it was, he didn't want to speak to anyone.

He would stay here until dawn if he needed to. If the sun came up and he was still alone, he'd go home. After that, he didn't know. He couldn't think that far ahead. Nayla had clung onto life long enough to pass on the message which had convinced him this plan might work. If it failed, what then? How would Saffi feel, knowing her best friend's dying words had led to nothing, helped no one? Would she still want him?

Daniel steered his thoughts away from Saffi. It was still early days, and the passion and commitment on both sides had surprised both of them. He was experiencing a superstitious reluctance to imagine their future together as if doing so might be the catalyst that obliterated any chance of it happening. Stupid, maybe, but there it was.

When he turned away from the river and saw Abos hovering to the north, about twenty feet away, the adrenaline hit him hard, his fists clenching and his body tensing. It wasn't *his* Abos, and the sight of the British poster boy from the nineteen-eighties was a shock, even though he'd known what to expect.

Abos had removed his helmet, holding it in one hand. He was looking at his son, his face and body as expressive as if made of stone.

Daniel looked back, knowing his feelings were easy to read for the figure floating above London. He didn't hide anything. He was elated, excited, and scared. There was guilt and shame at the way Abos had sacrificed her freedom for him, hope that they might now find a way forward together. And love, of course. Love for the creature that had given him life, and love for the person Abos had become. Was still becoming.

When Abos spoke, the voice was a shock. That same voice from the news clips. The same but different. Weathered, richer, the tone and cadence shaped by the million shocks of joy or sadness life thrown into the path of every life.

"Who is the halfhero, Daniel?"

He didn't look away from the intense golden eyes, although it was hard not to.

Abos gestured towards him.

"You have always given all of yourself, Daniel. You accepted that which many of your brothers and sisters could not. You are a crossbreed, an outsider, but you have not used your origins as an excuse to make lazy moral choices."

A light rain began to fall, the wind blowing stinging droplets into the side of Daniel's face.

"I am not human, although I wear this body," said Abos. "And I am not a hero. Why did they call you *halfheroes*? The human half of you is the source of your heroism. There is little of that in me. The world called me a hero when I was a slave."

"You destroyed Station."

"Destruction. Death. I prevailed against the hybrids because I was the stronger. I lived. They died."

"You saved my life."

Abos was silent for a long time.

"What parent wouldn't save their child?"

"I need you, Abos. We need you. Sara and TripleDee - your children."

"There were other survivors?"

"Only the three of us, as far as we know."

"So much death. If I had known them as I know you... a human parent would have sought them out, tried to form relationships. I am lost, Daniel."

Daniel didn't interrupt the silence.

"And I failed my other family," said Abos. "The titans. I

thought I could fight the drugs, the brainwashing. I thought I could form onemind and free them, but I was wrong. I couldn't fight it. When onemind formed, it was weak, it was wrong. Like hearing voices in the fog and not knowing where they're coming from. I failed."

"You tried, Abos. What you did, it was... you might never have come back."

Daniel remembered George. Without her, he would have given up, died in his room in Station. She had shown him, with humour and love, that he still had a choice. He could never have made it this far on his own.

"You're talking as if you're alone, but you're not. That's how it works."

"How what works?"

"The whole thing. Life, I don't know. I'm crap at this sort of thing, it doesn't come out properly. I know what I want to say, but I'll get it wrong. Oh, sod it. Look, on my own, I'm a fuckup. Guaranteed. But with George, with you, with Saffi, with Sara—all right, even with TripleDee—I'm nearly who I'm supposed to be. I'm not stuck inside myself. I'm part of a whole."

"A hole? Like a rabbit hole?"

"No, not like a rabbit hole. A whole," —Daniel made a circle with his hands— "you know, like a... hang on a minute."

Abos was smiling. Daniel squinted at him.

"Was that a joke? Did you crack a joke? You? I mean, it was a shit joke, but still... really?"

Abos flew forward and joined Daniel on the platform.

"Look," said Daniel, "what I'm trying to say is, you're not half of anything, Abos. Nor am I, nor are the others. Halfheroes is a stupid name. I don't know what I am, I don't know what you are, but I'm not sure that's important. You've missed the point. I told you I'd cock up if I tried to put it in words. I'm just no good at—"

Abos threw his arms around Daniel and, after a stunned half-second, Daniel hugged him back.

"You said it perfectly, Daniel."

They stayed that way for a few minutes. Then Daniel looked at Abos.

"We okay now?" he said.

"We are."

"Coming home?"

"Yes. Please. Home. But I have little strength left."

"Don't worry," said Daniel, picking up his motorbike helmet, "I'll give you a backie."

Abos hesitated as they reached the door leading off the roof. He was shaking his head.

"What is it?" said Daniel.

"Cars? Gary Numan? I don't even like that song."

"I know. But I *love* it."

Their voices trailed away into the night.

"And what is a backie? Is it like a biccy? I am hungry."

"No, you get on the back of the bike. For a lift."

"Oh. So you are having a frontie?"

"No, it doesn't... never mind."

45

A bos had tried alcohol on one occasion while being interviewed by a journalist from the NME. After two pints of beer he'd fallen asleep. That was nearly four decades ago, and he'd avoided it since.

Until the day he and Daniel returned to the Cornwall farmhouse.

That day was, possibly, the strangest of Saffi's, Sara's, and TripleDee's lives so far. Sara and Triple met their parent for the first time, knowing he had been a woman for most of his life and had only recently become male again. His new body was identical to the one that had made him world famous, and it took everyone a while to stop staring. The conversation was awkward at first, but they relaxed as the day wore on.

Sara and Abos discussed onemind for a long time. Sara's experience of what she, Daniel, and TripleDee had called webmind was similar, but clear differences emerged. Her control of the halfhero group mind had taken an effort of will, and a constant willingness by all participants to remain passive and allow her to use their pooled power. With Abos,

Shuck, and Susan, the link had been automatic, and was there, albeit in a low-powered form, even when they were not consciously using it. When they linked fully, no effort was required by anyone. It was as natural a process as breathing. The dominant mind took ultimate control, but the other minds could still keep a certain amount of autonomy. Abos, as the dominant mind, could control the amount of autonomy available to the others while they were onemind.

Sara wondered aloud why she had been dominant when the halfheroes had linked, but the others didn't let her speculate for long.

"You're the cleverest. By a long way," said Daniel.

Saffi shrugged. "He's right. You're smart, Sara. Beyond smart, actually."

"Not only are you a smart-arse, you're bloody gorgeous, like. On behalf of all men, I'm insulted by your gayness."

Sara patted TripleDee's leg.

"I want you to know, Trip—and I mean this from the heart—"

"Yes?"

"You're a sexist nob. It's not nineteen-seventy-five. You know that, don't you?"

"Right. Thanks for that, pet. I was only kidding about you being gorgeous. Your... neck is too long. Yeah, now I think about it, you're like a sort of sexy giraffe. *Ugly* giraffe. I meant to say ugly."

Saffi and Daniel didn't join the discussions as much as the others. They were both increasingly aware that they were still alive and still together. This knowledge led to them heading upstairs after lunch and not re-emerging until the sun was disappearing behind the swell of the fields opposite.

TripleDee eyed them as they walked into the kitchen.

"You finally finished that DIY job, then?"

Daniel and Saffi looked at him blankly.

"Well, you sounded like you were having trouble for a while. Took you ages to bang the nails in. Ten out of ten for effort though."

Daniel blushed like a teenager, but Saffi was less easily riled.

"Oh, Triple," she said, "we're sorry. That was a little insensitive of us. I'm sure you'll get some. One day. Eventually. Maybe."

Triple laughed sardonically. He'd decided he was never going back to Newcastle. Better that everyone thought he was dead. Including Tammy, his on-off girlfriend for five years. She could do better than the man he'd been, and he didn't think she'd ever believe he could change. Not that he could blame her. Last time he'd promised to clean up his act, she'd found him in bed with a crack pipe and two skanky prossies. Nah, she could keep the cash in his safe and start over.

"Some what?" asked Abos. Daniel was never sure if Abos was as guileless as everyone assumed.

"Never mind," said Sara, taking a two-litre bottle of vodka out of the freezer. "Abos, we have a little tradition on our planet."

"I'm not an alien," said Abos.

"Whatever. You've been through the shittiest, shite time imaginable. We all have. But we're alive, we're together, and we have vodka. Let's get wankered. Daniel, you with us? Daniel?"

Daniel shut the laptop screen. It was the first time since they'd got back that he'd opened it.

"What?"

"Us. Booze. Get shitfaced. Now."
"Oh. Oh, God, yes."

THE NEXT DAY was lost to epic hangovers.

Saffi, who didn't drink, followed the news online. America's reaction to losing The Deterrent was, at first, denial. He wasn't missing, he was on a secret mission. Constant repetition by every media outlet of the footage before the superhero had vanished eroded any confidence in that version of events. The look on the face of The Deterrent as he stared at the billboards, the way he came to a sudden stop when he heard the synth riff from Cars blaring out from the PA. The sudden fall to the street. No. No one was buying the 'secret mission' garbage.

Another piece of footage shown almost as regularly showed the other titans at the exact moment The Deterrent left New York. They all stopped as one, their heads turned towards the direction he'd taken. They seemed unsure of what to do until—again as one—they headed across the Hudson to tackle the warehouse fire.

The next official statement was closer to the truth and absolved the United States of any responsibility for what might happen next. A sweating press secretary read it aloud and refused to take questions.

"This individual has already shown his mental instability when he abandoned the United Kingdom and disappeared. Professor Roger Sullivan has given this administration a detailed report regarding the possible psychological problems of The Deterrent. We are doing everything we can to find him and get him the help he requires. If a member of the public has any information as to his whereabouts, they should not approach him, but call the number on the screen. We have posted a five-million-dollar reward for any information that leads to his, er, discovery. The other titans are completely unaffected by the weakness of The Deterrent."

By the evening, and after a pint of coffee, Sara was able to stand unaided, and her breath was no longer capable of killing houseplants at ten paces. Saffi showed her the footage and filled her in on the extent of the manhunt.

"It's just a matter of time. They'll find him. And he's still connected to them somehow. Right, Abos?"

"Yes. The link is there. It is weak, but I cannot break it. They are still in America now, but they will hunt me. And they will try to find any others of my kind. America, Britain, any country who thinks they can control us. They will not stop until my entire species is enslaved.

"You need to change appearance again."

Abos agreed. He had no desire to look like Roger Sullivan any longer than was necessary. As they had no ready access to blood, they drew straws. Saffi got the short straw. Although she was willing, Daniel was unsure how she, or he, would cope with the constant presence of a younger, taller, physically perfect version of her.

"What choice do we have?" said Saffi.

The reboot, as TripleDee insisted on calling it, was scheduled for that night. Saffi's blood was in the fridge, a bath in the outhouse had been cleaned, the floor swept, and a delivery of fresh fruit, vegetables, nuts, and pulses was emptied into the tub.

At seven that evening, they gathered in the outbuilding. Daniel looked around.

"Where's Sara?"

TripleDee answered. "Haven't seen her for a couple of hours, but she knows we're starting at seven."

Daniel turned to Abos.

"How do you make it happen? I mean, I know it starts when your body dies - like at White Sands, or at Station, but you never told me how you did it when you stopped being The Deterrent first time around."

"I stop breathing."

"You do what?" TripleDee was looking at Abos in disbelief.

"I stop breathing. The body needs oxygen to survive. It shuts down. It dies. I return to my original form."

"You just... like... stop breathing?"

"Yes. I am ready now."

Daniel and TripleDee emptied bag after bag of food into the bath. Saffi folded the clothes Abos removed and put them on the table. When the bath was half full, the naked superbeing climbed into the bath and stopped breathing.

No one spoke. For a while, they all held their own breath.

After a while, they couldn't take it anymore and took a few heaving gasps. Abos showed no signs of discomfort, but his skin had a sheen of sweat, and his lips and the tips of his fingers were turning blue.

The door of the outbuilding flew open with a crash.

"Stop! Stop it now. Don't do it, Abos."

They all turned to look at Sara. Abos took a long breath.

"What is it, Sara?"

"Come back to the house."

Sara paced the kitchen floor while TripleDee made tea. Abos was the calmest among them as they sat around the table, despite having been close to death in the lab. He wore one of Daniel's dressing gowns and ate toast.

Sara was asking him questions.

"Abos, you formed onemind with the titans, right?"

"Of a sort, yes. It was weak and confused, but it was there. It still is."

"And you are the dominant mind?"

"Yes. But I cannot influence them. The drugs prevent it."

"I know. Okay, fine. The way I see it, we have a choice. We can run, like we were planning. Hide, and when they come for us, find somewhere new. Keep moving. Or..."

"Or?" Saffi leaned forward.

"Or we fight back. We hit them first. They won't be expecting it."

"That's right, they won't," said TripleDee. "Because only a fucking idiot would do it. You are talking about ten super-shits, sorry Abos, and the entire military might of the United States of America, right?"

"Right. But I have a plan."

She told them, then sat back and let them think about it. There were questions, but she had already asked them of herself and found answers she could live with.

After three hours, and four cups of tea, Daniel held up his hands for quiet.

"We could talk about this for weeks, but I don't think we'd get any further. If anyone could come up with a plan that might work, might save a whole species, it would be Sara. Now, I think her plan is incredibly risky and unlikely to succeed."

He waited. They all looked at him.

"But I also think there's a chance it could work. And it's the only chance we'll have. Before they get their shit together, I mean. We'll only get one shot."

He looked at Saffi. She was smiling at him.

"So I'm in."

He sat down.

"Me too," said Saffi.

"Thank you," said Abos. "Thank you."

They all looked at TripleDee. His expression was grim.

"We're all gonna die if we do this, you know that, right?"

No one answered. He sighed.

"So, yeah. Fuck it. Let's do it."

THAT NIGHT, Daniel put the laptop in the bottom drawer of his wardrobe, while Saffi was in the bathroom. In a few weeks time, if Sara's plan turned out to be not quite insane enough to get them all killed, he and Saffi could talk about the future.

He could bring up the contents of Palindrome's email then. Not before.

Palindrome had proved to be worth every penny, but Daniel half-wished he had never paid her to unravel Hopkin's last secret.

He should have left it alone.

Daniel looked at the other side of his bed, the side Saffi slept on. He could see the indentation on the pillow where her head had been resting, one long, black hair catching the light from the bathroom. He had never been in love, had never known he needed to be in love. Now that he was, he understood what all the love songs were banging on about. Not that he was about to change his musical allegiances. *Cars* was still the best pop song ever, obviously. But he was beginning to understand why so many people liked The First Time Ever I Saw Your Face, which he'd previously considered to be just a little bit shit.

Saffi came out of the bathroom and, once again, took his breath away.

He took her in his arms and almost forgot the last three lines of Palindrome's email.

Almost.

Hopkins was paying the director of a fertility clinic to use the same, single, donor for physically fit couples looking for IVF treatment. It was your sperm, Daniel. You are the father of one hundred and eight children.

THE END

AUTHOR'S NOTE

It's two years and two days since I uploaded the manuscript of The World Walker to Kindle Direct Publishing. It would be fair to say I was in one of my *transitional* periods back then. I wasn't sure what I wanted to do with my life. I've never been sure. I don't think I even understand the concept.

Here are some ways I've earned money: clothes shop assistant (went for lunch on day one, didn't go back), piano/keyboard player and singer (most of my life), trainee journalist, scheduling clerk, transport clerk, puppet wrangler, stockbroker and financial adviser, vending machine business owner, piano teacher, corporate communication writer, composer, arranger, musical director, stand-up comedian, choir leader... author. I bet I've missed some out, too.

I've been accused of lacking stickability. Fair comment. But the interesting thing about that long list of failures, almost-dids, and wish-I-hadn'ts is the way they've all proved to be worth it. I've made friends, met people I would never otherwise have met, come across different points of view which have challenged me, travelled extensively, learned the ancient art of bouncing back. Nothing was wasted. I know a little about a lot, and that has helped my writing. Now, I won't do that thing of looking back at my life and saying IT ALL MAKES SENSE, IT WAS MEANT TO HAPPEN, because that would take all the fun out of it. But, I'll admit this much: if you want to write novels for a living, it doesn't hurt to have some life experience.

Now I sit in front of this screen six mornings a week and make stuff up, out of my head. This, let me tell you, is the perfect job for someone with no stickability. If I get bored at work, I know I've gone off track with the story. Time to go for a walk and think it out. The book you've just read (thank you for doing that) is a case in point. There was a moment halfway through when I got bogged down. For a few days, I wandered around looking as if I couldn't remember where I'd left the car keys. Or the car. Then, in the shower (it's almost always in the shower. I should put a desk in there), I saw where I was going wrong, and where the story was heading. I could see a New York Street, with enormous hoardings plastered with photographs that would only make sense to Abos. I could hear the Gary Numan song. I was back on track, and it was the best job in the world again.

A few notes on the Halfheroes series. This book became much easier to write once I knew it was part two of a trilogy. I know that sounds strange, not knowing how many books it takes to write a story, but that's the way I work. So far. From the moment I came up with Abos, I knew his back-story, the story of her species. I didn't want to shoehorn it into Book One, as I liked the mystery around The Deterrent. This time around, with the appearance of more Aboses, (Abae?) and the existence of a linked consciousness, we find out a little more. But the truth about the titans (they do have a proper name, it's in the next book) is the subject of the final novel.

We'll find out about their past, and how that will affect the future for everyone.

With Daniel, Saffi, Sara, TripleDee, and Abos, we have a team at the end of Halfheroes - pushed as far as they can be pushed. Ready to fight back.

I only realised after I'd finished how neatly the beginning fits with the end. A vasectomy near the beginning, then end with a hundred and eight children. The subconscious is a wondrous beastie, isn't it?

I get a fair few emails asking about writing. How I got started, what my process is, etc. There are lots of great books on the subject, but if you're interested in my thoughts, I've blogged about it on my website: www.ianwsainsbury.com. If you want exclusive free bits of writing and notification of new books etc, plus the juicy deleted scenes from Children Of The Deterrent, click Bonus Chapters

I'm also on Facebook:

https://www.facebook.com/IanWSainsbury

I have a title, a beginning, ending and some major developments for the final book... but I won't spoil anything for you. I'm excited about getting started.

Thank you for reading. If you enjoyed the book, please leave a review on Amazon - it makes a huge difference to independent writers. I read them all. Maybe I shouldn't, but I do. Link here: Halfheroes

And don't forget, if you don't know what to do with your life, you're in good company.

Ian Sainsbury
Norwich, 24th April 2018

ALSO BY IAN W. SAINSBURY

Thriller

Bedlam Boy 1

Bedlam Boy 2

Bedlam Boy 3

Psychological Thriller

The Picture On The Fridge (Winner of the 2019 Kindle Storyteller
Award)

Science Fiction

The World Walker (The World Walker 1)

The Unmaking Engine (The World Walker 2)

The Seventeenth Year (The World Walker 3)

The Unnamed Way (The World Walker 4)

Children Of The Deterrent (Halfhero 1)

Halfheroes (Halfhero 2)

The Last Of The First (Halfhero 3)

Fantasy

The Blurred Lands

Printed in Great Britain
by Amazon